T0165701

The Perfume of
the Lady in Black

The Perfume of the Lady in Black

Gaston Leroux

MINT EDITIONS

The Perfume of the Lady in Black was first published in 1909.

This edition published by Mint Editions 2021.

ISBN 9781513282947 | E-ISBN 9781513287966

Published by Mint Editions®

 MINT
EDITIONS
minteditionbooks.com

Publishing Director: Jennifer Newens
Design & Production: Eachel Lopez Metzger
Project Manager: Micaela Clark
Typesetting: Westchester Publishing Services

Contents

I

Which Begins Where Most Romances End

The marriage of Mr. Robert Darzac and Miss Mathilde Stangerson took place in Paris, at the Church of St. Nicolas du Chardonnet, on April 6, 1895, everything connected with the occasion being conducted in the quietest fashion possible. A little more than two years had rolled by since the events which I have recorded in a previous volume—events so sensational that it is not speaking too strongly to say that an even longer lapse of time would not have sufficed to blot out the memory of the famous "Mystery of the Yellow Room."

There was no doubt in the minds of those concerned that, if the arrangements for the wedding had not been made almost secretly, the little church would have been thronged and surrounded by a curious crowd, eager to gaze upon the principal personages of the drama which had aroused an interest almost world wide and the circumstances of which were still present in the minds of the sensation-loving public. But in this isolated little corner of the city, in this almost unknown parish, it was easy enough to maintain the upmost privacy. Only a few friends of M. Darzac and the Professor Stangerson, on whose discretion they felt assured that they might rely, had been invited. I had the honour to be one of the number.

I reached the church early, and naturally, my first thought was to look for Joseph Rouletabille there. I had been somewhat surprise at not seeing him, but, having no doubt that he would arrive shortly, and, I entered the pew and already occupied by M. Henri-Robert and M. Andre Hesse, who, in the quiet shades of the little chapel, exchanged the undertones reminiscences of the strange affair at Versailles, which the approaching ceremony brought to their memories. I listened without paying much attention to what they were saying, glancing from time to time carelessly around me.

A dreary place enough is the Church of St. Nicolas du Chardonnet. With its cracked walls, the lizards running from every corner and dirt—not the beautiful dust of ages, but the common, ill-smelling, germ-laden dust of today—everywhere, this church, so dark and forbidding on the outside, is equally dismal within. The sky, which seems rather to be withdrawn from the above the edifice, sheds a miserly light which seems to find the greatest difficulty in penetrating through the dusty panes of unstained glass. Have you read Renan's "Memories of Childhood and Youth?" Push the door of St. Nicolas du Chardonnet and you will understand how the author of the "Life of Jesus" longed to die, when as a lad he was a pupil in the little seminary of the Abbe Duplanloup, close by, and could only leave the school to come to pray in this church. And it is in this funeral darkness, in a scene which seemed to have been painted only for mourning and for all rites consecrated to sorrow, that the marriage of Robert Darzac and Mathilde Stangerson was to be solemnised. I could not cast aside the feeling of foreboding that came over me in these dreary surroundings.

Beside me, M. Henri-Robert and M. André Hesse continued to chat, and my wandering attention was arrested by a remark made by the former:

"I never felt quite easy about Robert and Mathilde," he said—"not even after the happy termination of the affair at Versailles—until I know that the information of the death of Frederic Larsan had been officially confirmed. That man was a pitiless enemy."

It will be remembered, perhaps, by the readers of "The Mystery of the Yellow Room" that a few months after the acquittal of the Professor in Sorbonne, there occurred the terrible catastrophe of La Dordogne, a transatlantic steamers, running between Havre and New York. In the broiling heat of a summer night, upon the coast of the New Worl, La Dordogne had caught fire from an overheated boiler. Before help could reach her, the steamer was utterly destroyed. Scarcely thirty passengers were able to leap into the life boats, and these were picked up the next day by a merchant vessel, which conveyed them to the nearest port. For days thereafter, the ocean cast up on the beach hundreds of corpses. And among these, they found Larsan.

The papers which were found carefully hidden in the clothing worn by the dead man, proved beyond a doubt his identity. Mathilde Stangerson was at last delivered from this monster of a husband to whom, through the facility of the American laws, she had given her hand in secret, in the unthinking ardour of girlish romance. This wretch, whose real name, according to court records, was Ballmeyer, and who had married her under the name of Jean Rouseel, could no longer rise like a dark shadow between Mathilde and the man whom she had loved so long and so well, without daring to become his bride. In "The Mystery of the Yellow Room," I have related all the details of this remarkable affair, one of the strangest which has ever been known in the annals of the Court of Assizes, and which, without doubt, would have had a most tragic denouncement, had it not been for the extraordinary party played by a boy reporter, scarcely eighteen years old, Joseph Rouletabille, who was the only one to discover that Frederic Larsan, the celebrated Secret Service agent, was none other than Ballmeyer himself. The accidental— one might almost say "providential"—death of this villain, had seemed to assure a happy termination to the extraordinary story, and it must be confessed that it was undoubtedly one of the chief factors in the rapid recovery of Mathilde Stangerson, whose reason had been almost overturned by the mysterious horrors at the Glandier.

"You see, my dear friend," said M. Henri-Robert to M. André Hesse, whose eyes were roving restlessly about the church, "you see, in this world, one can always find the bright side. See how beautifully everything has turned out—even the troubles of Mlle. Stangerson. But why are you constantly looking around you? What are you looking for? Do you expect anyone?"

"Yes," replied M. Hesse. "I am waiting for Frédéric Larsan!"

M. Henri-Robert laughed—a decorous little laugh, in deference to the sanctity of the surroundings. But I felt no inclination to join in his mirth. I was an hundred leagues from foreseeing the terrible experience which was even then approaching us; but when I recall that moment and seek to blot out of my mind all that has happened since—all those events which I intend to relate in the course of this narrative, letting the circumstances come before the reader as they came before us during their development—I recollect once more the curious unrest which thrilled me at the mention of Larsan's name.

"What's the matter, Sainclair?" whispered M. Henri-Robert, who had noticed Something odd in my expression. "You know that Hesse was only joking."

"I don't know anything about it," I answered. And I looked attentively around me, as M. Andre Hesse had done. And, indeed, we had believe Larsan dead so often when he was known as Ballmeyer, that it seemed quite possible that he might be once more brought to life in the guise of Larsan.

"Here comes Rouletabille, remarked M. Henri-Robert. "I'll wager that he isn't worried about anything."

"But how pale he is!" exclaimed M. Andre Hesse in an undertone.

The young reporter joined us and pressed our hands in an absent-minded manner.

"Good morning, Sainclair. Good morning, gentlemen. I am not late, I hope?"

It seemed to me that his voice trembled. He left our pew immediately and withdrew to a dark corner, where I beheld him kneel down like a child. He hid his face, which was indeed very pale, in his hands, and prayed. I had never guessed that Rouletabille was of a religious turn of mind, and his fervent devotion astonished me. When he raised his head, his eyes were filled with tears. He did not even try to hide them. He paid no attention to anything or anyone around him. He was lost completely in his prayers, and, one might imagine, his grief.

But what could be the occasion of his sorrow? Was he not happy at the prospect of the union so ardently desired by everyone? Had not the good fortune of Mathilde Stangerson and Robert Darzac been in a great measure brought about by his efforts? After all, it was perhaps from joy, that the lad had wept. He rose from his knees, and was hidden behind a pillar. I made no endeavour to join him, for I could see that he was anxious to be alone.

And the next moment, Mathilde Stangerson made her entrance into the church upon the arm of her father, Robert Darzac walking behind them. Ah, the drama of the Glandier had been a sorrowful one for these three! But, strange as it may seem, Mathilde Strangerson appeared only the more beautiful, for all that she had passed through. True, she was no longer the beautiful statue, the living marble, the ancient goddess, the cold Pagan divinity, who, at the official functions at which her father's position had forced her to appear, had excited a flutter of admiration whenever she was seen. It seen, on the contrary, that fate, in making her expiate for so many long years and imprudence committed in early youth, had cast her into the depths of madness and despair, only to tear away the mask of stone, which hid from sight the tender, delicate spirit. And it was this spirit which shone forth on her wedding day, in the sweetest and most charming smile, playing on her curved lips, hiding in her eyes, filled with pensive happiness, and leavings its impress on her forehead, polished like ivory, where one might read the love of all that was beautiful and all that was good.

As to her gown, I must acknowledge that I remember nothing at all about it, and am unable even to say of what colour it was. But what I do remember, is the strange expression which came over her visage when she looked through the rows of faces in the pews without seeming to discover the one she sought. In a moment she had regained her composure, and was mistress of herself once more. She had seen Rouletabille behind his pillar. She smiled at him and my companions and I smiled in our turn.

"She has the eyes of a mad woman!"

I turned around quickly to see who had uttered the heartless words. It was a poor fellow whom Robert Darzac, out of the kindness of his heart, had made his assistant in the laboratory at the Sorbonne. The man was named Brignolles, and was a distant cousin of the bridegroom. We knew of no other relative of M. Darzac, whose family came originally from the Midi. Long ago he had lost both father and mother; he had neither brother nor sister, and seemed to have broken off all intercourse with his native province, from which he had brought an eager desire for success, an exceptional ability to work, a strong intellect and natural need for affection, which had satisfied itself in his relations with Professor Stangerson and his daughter. He had also as a legacy from Provence, his native place, a soft voice and slight accent, which had often brought a smile to the lips of his pupils at the Sorbonne, who, nevertheless, loved it as they might have loved a strain of music, which made the necessary dryness of their studies a little less arid.

One beautiful morning, in the preceeding spring, and consequently a year after the occurrences in the yellow room, Robert Darzac had presented Brignolles to his pupils. The new assistant had come direct from Aix, where he had been a tutor in the natural sciences, and where he had committed some fault of discipline which had caused his dismissal. But he had remembered that he was related to M. Darzac, the famous chemist, had taken the train to Paris, and had told such a piteous tale to the fiancé of Mlle. Stangerson that the Darzac, out of pity, had found the means to associate his cousin with him in his work. At this time, the health of Robert Darzac had been far from flourishing. He was suffering from the reaction following the strong emotions which had nearly weighed him down at the Glandier and at the Court of Assizes; but one might have thought that the recovery, now assured, of Mathilde, and the prospect of their marriage would have had a happy influence both upon the mental and physical condition of the professor. We, however, remarked on the contrary, that from the day that Brignolles came to him—Brignolles, whose friendship should have been a precious solace, the weakness of M. Darzac seemed to increase. However, we are obliged to acknowledge that Brignolles was not to blame for that, for two unfortunate and unforeseen accidents had occurred in the course of some experiments, which would have seemed, on the face of them, not at all dangerous. The first resulted from the unexpected explosion of a Gessler tube, which might have severely injured M. Darzac, but which only injured Brignolles, whose hands were badly scarred. The second, which might have been extremely grave, happened through the explosion of a tiny lamp against which M. Darzac was leaning. Happily, he was not hurt, but his eyebrows were scorched, and for some time after his sight was slightly impaired, and he was unable to stand much sunlight.

Since the Glandier mysteries, I had been in such a state of mind that I often found myself attaching importance to the most simple happenings. At the time of the second accident I was present, having come to seek M. Darzac at the Sorbonne. I myself led our friend to a druggist and then to a doctor, and I (rather dryly, I own) begged Brignolles, when he wished to accompany us, to remain at his post. On the way, M. Darzac asked me why I had wounded the poor fellow's feelings. I had told him that I did not care for Brignolles's society, for the abstract reason that I did not care for his manners, and for that concrete reason, on this special occasion, that I believed him to be responsible for the accident. M. Darzac demanded why I thought so, and I did not know how to answer, and he began to laugh—a laugh that was quickly silence, however, when the doctor told him that he might easily have been made entirely blind, and that he might consider himself very lucky in having gotten off so well.

My suspicions of Brignolles were, doubtless, ridiculous, and no more accidents happened. All the same, I was so strongly prejudiced against the ridiculous, and the accidents never happened again. All of the same, I was so strongly prejudiced against the young man that, at the bottom of my heart, I blamed him for the slow improvement in M. Darzac's physical condition. At the beginning of winter, Darzac had such a bad cough that I entreated him to ask for leave of absence and to take a trip to the Midi—a prayer in which all his friends joined. The physicians advised San Remo. He went thither, and a week later he wrote us that he felt much better—that it seemed to him as though a heavy weight had been lifted from his breast. "I can breathe here," he wrote. "When I left Paris, I seemed to be stifling."

This letter from M. Darzac gave me much food for thought, and I no longer hesitated to take Rouletabille into my confidence.

He agreed with me that it was a most peculiar coincidence that M. Darzac was so ill when Brignolles was with him and so much better when he and his young assistant were separated. The impression that this was actually fact was so strong in my mind that I would on no account have permitted myself to lose sight of Brignolles. No, indeed. I verily believe that if he had attempted to leave Paris, I should have followed him. But he made no such attempt. On the contrary, he haunted the footsteps of M. Stangerson. Under the pretext of asking news of M. Darzac, he presented himself at the house of the Professor almost every day. Once he made an effort to see Mlle. Stangerson, but I had painted his portrait to M. Darzac's fiancée in such unflattering terms, that I had succeeding in dusting her with him completely—a fact on which I congratulated myself in my innermost soul.

M. Darzac remained four months in San Remo and returned home at the end of that time almost completely restored to health. His eyes, however, were still weak, and he was under the necessity of taking the greatest care of them. Rouletabille and myself had resolved to keep a close watch on Brignolles, but we were satisfied that everything would be right when we were informed that the long-deferred marriage was to occur almost immediately and that M. Darzac would take his wife away on a long honeymoon trip far from Paris—from Brignolles.

Upon his return from San Remo, M. Darzac had asked me:

"Well, how are you getting on with poor Brignolles? Have you decided that you were wrong with him?"

"Indeed, I have not," was my response.

And Darzac turned away, laughing at me, and uttering one of the Provencal jests which he affected when circumstances allowed him to be gay, and which found on his lips a new freshness since his visit to the Midi had accustomed him again to the accents of his childhood.

We knew that he was happy. But we had formed no real idea of how happy he was—for between the time of his return and the wedding day we had had few chances to see him—until we beheld him walking up the aisle of the church, his face fairly transformed. His slight erect figure bore itself as proudly as though he were an Emperor. Happiness had made him another being.

"Anyone could guess that he was a bridegroom!" tittered Brignolles.

I left the neighbourhood of the man who was so repulsive to me, and stepped behind poor M. Stangerson, who stood through the entire ceremony with his arms crossed on his breast, seeing nothing and hearing nothing. I was obliged to touch him on the shoulder when all was over to arouse him from his dream.

As they passed into sacristy, M. Andre Hesse heaved a deep sigh.

"I can breathe again," he murmured.

"Why couldn't you breathe before, my friend?" asked M. Henri-Robert.

And M. Andre Hesse confessed that he had feared up to the last moment that the dead man would reappear.

"I can't help it," was the only response he would make when his friend rallied him. "I cannot bring myself to the idea that Frederic Larsan will stay dead for good."

And now we all—a dozen or so persons—were gathered in the sacristy. The witness signed the register, and the rest of us congratulated the newly wedded pair. The sacristy was yet more dismal than the church, and I might have thought that it was on account of the darkness that I could not perceive Joseph Rouletabille, if the room had not been so small. But, assuredly, he was not there. Mathilde had already asked for him twice, and M. Darzac requested me to go and look for him. I did so, but returned to the vestry without him. He had disappeared from the church.

"How strange it is!" examined M. Darzac. "I can't understand it. Are you sure that you looked everywhere? He may be in some corner dreaming."

"I looked everywhere, and I called his name," I told him.

But M. Darzac was still not satisfied. He wanted to look through the church for himself. His search was better rewarded than mine, for learned from a beggar, who was sitting in the porch with a tambourine, that Rouletabille has left the church a few minutes before and had been driven away in a hack. When the bridegroom brought this news to his wife, she appeared to be both pained and anxious. She called me to her side and said:

"My dear M. Sainclair, you know that we are to take the train in two hours. Will you hunt up our little friend and bring him to me, and tell him that his strange behaviour is grieving me very much?"

"Count upon me," I said.

And I began a wild goose chase after Rouletabille. But I appeared at the station without him. Neither at his home, nor at the office of his paper, nor at the Café du Barreau, where the necessities of his work often called him at this hour of the day, could I lay my hand on him. None of his comrades could tell me where I might chance to find him. I leave you to think how unwillingly I turned my steps in the direction of the railroad station. M. Darzac was greatly disturbed, but as he had to look after the comfort of his fellow travellers (for Professor Stangerson, who was on his way to Mentone, was to accompany his daughter and her husband to Dijon, changing cars there, while the Darzacs continued their trips to Culoz and Mt. Cenis,) he asked me to break the bad news to his bride. I performed the commission, adding that Rouletabille would, without doubt, present himself before the train started. At these words, Mathilde began to cry softly, and shook her head:

"No—no!" she whispered. "It is all over. He will never come again."

And she stepped into the railway carriage.

It was at this point that the insufferable Brignolles, seeing the emotion of the newly-made bride, whispered again to M. Andre Hesse, "Look! Look! Hasn't she the eyes of a maniac? Ah, Robert has done wrong. It would have been better for him to wait." M. Hesse gave him a disdainful glance, and bade him to be silent.

I can still see Brignolles as he spoke those words, and can recall as vividly as though it were yesterday the feeling of horror with which he inspired me. There was no longer any doubt in my mind that he was an evil and a jealous man, and that he would never forgive his relative for having placed him in a position which might be considered subordinate. He had a yellow face and long features that looked as if they had been drawn down from forehead to chin. Everything about him seemed to diffuse bitterness and everything about him was long. He had a long figure, long arms, long legs and a long head. However, to this general rule of length, there were exceptions—the feet and the hands. He had extremities small and almost beautiful.

After having been so rudely silence for his malicious words by the young lawyer, Brignolles immediately took offense and left the statin, after having paid his respects to the bride and bridegroom. At least, I believe that he left the station, for I did not see him again.

There were three minutes yet before the departure of the train. We still hoped that Rouletabille would appear, and we looked across the quay, thinking once or twice that we saw the form of our young friend approaching, among the hurrying throng of travellers. How could it be that he would not advance, as we were so used to seeing him, in his quick, boyish fashion, rushing through the crows, paying no heed to the cries and protestations that his method of pushing his way usually evoked while he seemed to be hurrying faster than any one else? What could he be doing that detained him?

Already the doors were closed. The bell on the engine began to sound its first slow strokes, and the calls of hack driver began to arise: "Carriage, Monsieur? Carriage?" And then the quick last word which gave the signal for the departure. But no Rouletabille. We were all so grieved, and moreover, so surprised, that we remained on the platform, looking at Mme. Darzac, without thinking to wish her a pleasant journey. Professor Stangerson's daughter cast a long glance upon the quay, and, at the moment that the speed of the train began to accelerate, certain now that she was not to see her "little friend" again, she threw me an envelope from the car window.

"For him," she said.

An almost as though moved by an irresistible impulse, her face wearing an expression of something that resembled terror, she added in a tone so strange that I could not help recalling the horrible speeches of Brignolles:

"Au revoir, my friends—or adieu."

II

In Which There is Question of the Changing Rumours of Joseph Rouletabille

In returning alone from the station I could not help feeling some surprise at the singular sensation of sad ness which oppressed me, and of the cause of which I had not the least idea. Since the affair at Versailles, with the details of which my existence had become so strangely intermingled, I had enjoyed the closest in timacy with Professor Stangerson, his daughter, and Robert Darzac. I ought to have been completely happy on the day of this wedding, which seemed in every way so satisfactory. I wondered whether the unexplained absence of the young reporter did not account in some measure for my strange depression. Rouletabille had been treated by the Stangersons and by M. Darzac as their deliverer. And especially since Mathilde had left the sanitarium, in which, for several months, her shat tered nervous system had needed and received the most assiduous care—since the daughter of the famous professor had been able to understand the eextraordinary part which the boy had played in the drama that, with out his help, would inevitably have ended in the bitterest grief for all those whom she loved—since she had read by the light of her restored reason the short-hand reports of the trial, at which Rouletabille appeared at the last moment like some hero of a miracleshe had surrounded the youngster with an affection little less than maternal. She interested herself in everything which concerned him; she begged for his confidence: she wanted to know more about him than I knew, and, perhaps, more even than he knew himself. She had shown an unobtrusive but strong curiosity in regard to the mystery of his birth, of which all of us were ignorant, and on which the young man had kept silence with a sort of savage pride. Although he fully realised the tender friendship which the poor soul felt for him, Rouletabille maintained his reserve and in his dealings with her affected a formal politeness which astonished me, coming from the boy whom I had known so exuberant, so whole-hearted, so strong in his likes and dislikes. More than once I had mentioned the matter to him, and he had answered me in an evasive manner, laying great stress, however, upon his sentiments of devotion for "a lady whom he esteemed beyond anyone in the world, and for whom he would have been ready to sacrifice his all, if fate or fortune had given him anything to sacrifice for anyone." He would take strange whims at such times. For instance, after having made, in my presence, a promise to take a holiday and remain all day with the Stangersons, who had rented for the summer (for they did not wish to live at the Glandier again) a pretty little place at Chennevieres, on the borders of the Marne, and after having shown an almost childish joy at the prospect, he suddenly and without any reason refused to accompany me. And I was obliged to set out alone, leaving him in his little room, in the corner of the Boulevard St. Michel and the Rue Monsieur-le-Prince. I wished as I departed that he might experience as much pain as I knew that he would cause Mlle. Stangerson. One Sunday, she, vexed at the lad's behavior, made up her mind to go with me to his den in the Latin Quarter, and surprise him.

When we reached his lodgings, Rouletabille, who had answered our knock with an energetic "Come in," sat working at a little table. He arose as we entered, and turned so pale that we believed that he was about to fall in a faint.

"Good heavens!" cried Mlle. Stangerson, hastening toward him. But he was quicker than she, and before she reached the table on which he leaned, he had thrown a cover over the papers which were spread over the surface, hiding them entirely.

Mathilde had, of course, noticed the action. She paused in amazement.

"We are disturbing you," she said.

"Oh, not at all," replied Rouletabille. "I have finished my work. I will show it to you sometime. It is a masterpiece—a piece in five acts, for which I am not able to find the denouement."

And he smiled. Soon he was again entirely master of himself, and made us a hundred droll speeches, thanking us for having come to cheer him in his solitude. He insisted on inviting us to dinner, and we three ate our evening meal in a Latin Quarter restaurant—Foyot's. It was a happy evening. Rouletabille telephoned for Robert Darzac, who joined us at dessert. At this time M. Darzac was not ill, and the amazing Brignolles had not yet made his appearance in Paris. We played like children. That summer night was so beautiful in the solitude of the Luxembourg!

Before bidding adieu to Mlle. Stangerson, Roulet abille begged her pardon for the strange humor which he evinced at times, and accused himself of being at bottom a very disagreeable person. Mathilde kissed him and Robert Darzac put his arm affectionately around the lad's shoulders. And Rouletabille was so moved that he never uttered a word while I walked with him to his door; but at the moment of our parting, he pressed my hand more tenderly than he had ever done before. Poor little fellow! Ah, if I had known How I re proach myself in the light of the present for having judged him with too little patience!

Thus, sad at heart, assailed by premonitions which I tried in vain to drive away, I returned from the railway station at Lyons, pondering over the numerous fanta sies, the strange caprices of Rouletabille during the last two years. But nothing that entered my mind could have warned me of what had happened, or still less have explained it to me. Where was Rouletabille? I went to his rooms in the Boulevard St. Michel, telling myself that if I did not find him there, I could, at least, leave Mme. Darzac's letter. What was my astonish ment when I entered the building to see my own servant carrying my bag. I asked him to tell me what he was doing and why, and he replied that he did not know—that I must ask M. Rouletabille.

The boy had been, as it turned out, while I had been seeking him everywhere (except, naturally, in my own house), in my apartments in the Rue de Rivoli. He had ordered my servant to take him to my rooms, and had made the man fill a valise with everything necessary for a trip of three or four days. Then he had directed the man to bring the bag in about an hour to the hotel in the "Boul' Mich."

I made one bound up the stairs to my friend's bed chamber, where I found him packing in a tiny hand satchel an assortment of toilet articles, a change of linen and a night shirt. Until this task was ended, I could obtain no satisfaction from Rouletabille, for in regard to the little affairs of everyday life, he was extremely particular, and, despite the modesty of his means, succeeded in living very well, having a horror of everything which could be called bohemian. He finally deigned to announce to me that "we were going to take our Easter vacation," and that, since I had nothing to do, and the *Epoch* had granted him a three days' holiday, we couldn't do better than to go and take a short rest at the seaside. I made no reply, so angry was I at this high-handed method, and all the more because I had not the least desire to contemplate the beauties of the ocean upon one of the abominable days of early spring, which for two or three weeks every year makes us regret the winter. But my silence did not disturb Rouletabille in the least, and taking my valise in one hand, his satchel in the other, he hustled me down the stairs and pushed me into a hack which awaited us before the door of the hotel. Half an hour later, we found ourselves in a first-class carriage of the Northern Railway, which was carrying us toward Trepot by way of Amiens. As we entered the station, he said:

"Why don't you give me the letter that you have for me?"

I gased at him in amazement. He had guessed that Mme. Darzac would be greatly grieved at not seeing him before her departure, and would write to him. He had been positively malicious. I answered:

"Because you don't deserve it."

And I gave him a good scolding, to which he inter posed no defense. He did not even try to excuse himself, and that made me angrier than ever. Finally, I handed him the letter. He took it, looked at it and in haled its fragrance. As I sat looking at him curiously, he frowned, trying, as I could see, to repress some strong feeling. But he could no longer hide it from me when he turned toward the window, his forehead against the glass, and became absorbed in a deep study of the landscape. His face betrayed the fact that he was suffering profoundly.

"Well?" I said. "Aren't you going to read the letter?"

"No," he replied. "Not here. When we are yonder."

We arrived at Trepot in the blackest night that I remember, after six hours of an interminable trip and in wretched weather. The wind from the sea chilled us to the bone and swept over the deserted quay with weird sounds of lamentation. We met only a watch man, wrapped in his cloak and hood, who paced the banks of the canal. Not a cab, of course. A few gas jets, trembling in their glass globes, reflected their light in the mud puddles formed by the falling rain. We heard in the distance the clicking noise of the little wooden shoes of some Trepot woman who was out late. That we did not fall into a huge watering trough was due to the fact that we were warned by the hoofs of a stray horse, which passed that way to drink. I walked behind Rouletabille, who made his way with difficulty in this damp obscurity. However, he appeared to know the place, for we finally arrived at the door of a queer little inn, which remained open during the early spring for the fishermen. Rouletabille demanded supper and a fire, for we were half starved and half frozen.

"Ah, now, my friend," I said, when we were settled after a fashion. "Will you condescend to explain to me what we have come to look for in this place, aside from rheumatism and pneumonia?"

But Rouletabille, at this moment, coughed and turned toward the fire to warm his hands again.

"Oh, yes," he answered. "I am going to tell you. We have come to look for the perfume of the Lady in Black."

This phrase gave me so much to think about that I scarcely slept at all that night. Besides, the wind howled continuously, sending its wails over the water, then swallowing itself up in the little streets of the town as if it were entering corridors. I heard someone mov ing about in the room next to mine, which was occupied by my friend: I arose and tried his door. In spite of the cold and the wind, he had opened the window, and I could see him distinctly waving kisses toward the shad ows. He was embracing the night.

I closed the door again and went quietly back to bed. Early in the morning I was awakened by a changed Rouletabille. His face was distorted with grief as he handed me a telegram which had come to him at the Bourg, having been forwarded from Paris, in accordance with the orders that he had left.

Here is the dispatch:

"Come immediately without losing a minute. We have given up our trip to the Orient, and will join M. Stangerson at Mentone, at the home of the Rances at Rochers Rouges. Let this message remain a secret between us. It is not necessary to frighten anyone. You may pretend that you are on your vacation, or make any other excuse that you like, but come. Telegraph me general delivery, Mentone. Quickly, quickly, I am waiting for you.

Yours in despair
Darzac

III

THE PERFUME

W ell!" I cried, leaping out of bed. "It doesn't surprise me!"
"You never believed that *he* was dead?" demanded Rouletabille,
in a tone filled with an emotion that I could not explain to myself, for
it seemed greater even than was warranted by the situation, admitting
that the terms of M. Darzac's telegram were to be taken literally.

"I never felt quite sure of it," I answered. "It was too useful for him to
pass for dead to permit him to hesitate at the sacrifice of a few papers,
however important those were which were found upon the victim of the
Dordogne disaster. But what is the matter with you, my boy? You look
as though you were going to faint. Are you ill?"

Rouletabille had let himself sink into a chair. It was in a voice
which trembled like that of an old man that he confided to me that,
even while the marriage ceremony of our friends was going on, he
had become possessed with a strong conviction that Larsan was not
dead. But after the ceremony was at an end, he had felt more secure.
It seemed to him that Larsan would never have permitted Mathilde
Stangerson to speak the vows that gave her to Robert Darzac if he
were really alive. Larsan would only have had to show his face to stop
the marriage; and, however dangerous to himself such an act might
have been, he would not, the young reporter believed, have hesitated
to deliver himself up to the danger, knowing as he did the strong
religious convictions of Professor Stangerson's daughter, and knowing,
too, that she would never have consented to enter into an alliance with
another man while her first husband was alive, even had she been freed
from the latter by human laws. In vain had everyone who loved her at
tempted to persuade her that her first marriage was void, according to
French statute. She persisted in declaring that the words pronounced
by the priest had made her the wife of the miserable wretch who had
victimised her, and that she must remain his wife so long as they both
should live.

Wiping the perspiration from his forehead, Rouletabille remarked:—
"Sainclair, can you ever forget Larsan's eyes? Do you remember, 'The
Presbytery has not lost its charm or the garden its brightness?'"

I pressed the boy's hand; it was burning hot. I tried to calm him, but he paid no attention to anything I said.

"And it was after the wedding—just a few hours after the wedding, that he chose to appear!" he cried. "There isn't anything else to think, is there, Sainclair? You took M. Darzac's wire just as I did? It could mean nothing else except that that man has come back?"

"I should think not—but M. Darzac may be mistaken."

"Oh, M. Darzac is not a child to be frightened at bogies. But we must hope—we must hope, mustn't we, Sainclair, that he is mistaken? Oh, it isn't possible that such a fearful thing can be true. Oh, Sainclair, it would be too terrible!"

I had never seen Rouletabille so deeply agitated, even at the time of the most terrible events at the Glandier. He arose from his chair and walked up and down the room, casting aside any object which came in his way and repeating over and over: "No, no! It's too terrible—too terrible!"

I told him that it was not sensible to put himself in such a state merely upon the receipt of a telegram which might mean nothing at all, or might be the result of some delusion. And there, too, I added, that it was not at this time, when we needed all our strength and fortitude, that we ought to give way to imaginary fears which were particularly inexcusable in a lad of his practical temperament.

"Inexcusable! I am glad you think so, Sainclair."

"But, my dear boy, you frighten me. What is there you know that you have not told me?"

"I am going to tell you. The situation is horrible. Why didn't that villain die?"

"And, after all, how do you know that he is not dead?"

"Look here, Sainclair—Don't talk—Be quiet, please—You see, if he is alive, I wish to God that I were dead!"

"You are crazy. It is if he is alive that you have all the more reason to live to defend that poor woman."

"Ah, that is true! That is true! Thanks, old fellow! You have said the only thing that makes me want to live. To defend her! I will not think of myself any longer—never again."

And Rouletabille smiled—a smile which almost frightened me. I threw my arm around him and begged him to tell me why he was so terrified, why he spoke of his own death and why he smiled so strangely.

Rouletabille laid his hand on my shoulder, and I went on:

"Tell your friend what it is, Rouletabille. Speak out. Relieve your mind. Tell me the secret that is killing you. I would tell you anything."

Rouletabille looked down and steadily into my eyes.

Then he said:

"You shall know all, Sainclair. You shall know as much as I do, and when you do, you will be as unhappy as I am, for you are kind and you are fond of me."

Then he straightened back his shoulders as though he had already cast off a burden and pointed in the direction of the railway.

"We shall leave here in an hour," he said. "There is no direct train from Eu to Paris in the winter: we shall not reach Paris until 7 o'clock. But that will give us plenty of time to pack our trunks and take the train that leaves the Lyons station at nine o'clock for Marscilles and Mentone."

He did not ask my opinion on the course which he had laid out. He was taking me to Mentone, just as he had brought me to Trepot. He was well aware that in the present crisis I could refuse him nothing. Besides, he was in such a state of mental strain that even if he had wished it, I should scarcely have left him. And it was not hard for me to accompany him, for we were just beginning our long vacations, and my affairs were so arranged that I felt entirely at liberty.

"Then we are going to Eu?" I inquired.

"Yes: we will take the train from there. It will scarcely take half an hour to drive over."

"We shall have spent only a little time in this part of the country," I remarked. "Enough, I hope—enough for me to find what I am looking for."

I thought of the perfume of the Lady in Black, but I kept silence. Had he not said that he was going to tell me everything? He led me out to the jetty. The wind was still blowing a gale, and we were almost taken off our feet. Rouletabille stood for an instant as if lost in thought, closing his eyes as if in a dream.

"It was here," he said, "that I last saw her."

He looked down at the stone bench beside which we were standing.

"We were sitting there. She held me to her heart. I was a very little fellow, even for nine years old. She told me to stay there—on this bench—and then she went away, and I never saw her again. It was night—a soft summer evening—the evening of the distribution of prizes. She had not assisted at the distribution, but I knew that she would come that night—that night full of stars and so clear that I hoped every moment that I would be able to distinguish her face. But she covered it with her veil and breathed a heavy sigh. And then she went away. And I have never seen her since."

"And you, my friend?"

"I?"

"Yes, what happened to you? Did you sit on the bench for very long?"

"I would have—but the coachman came to look for me and I went in."

"Where?"

"Into the school."

"Is there a boarding school at Trepot?"

"No, but there is one at Eu—I went to the school at Eu."

He motioned me to follow him.

"We will go there," he said. "I can't talk here. There is too much of a storm."

In another half hour we were at Eu. At the foot of the Rue des Marroniers our carriage rolled over the pavements of the big, cold, empty place, as the coachman announced his arrival by cracking his whip, filling the dead town with the noise of the snapping leather.

Soon we heard the sound of a bell—that of the school, Rouletabille told me—and then everything was quiet again. We alighted and the horse and carriage stood motionless upon the street. The driver had gone into a saloon. We entered the cool shades of a high Gothic church which faced upon the square. Rouletabille cast a glance at the castle—a red brick structure, crowned with an immense Louis XIII roof—a mournful facade which seemed to weep over the glory of departed princes. The young reporter gased sorrowfully at the square battlements of the City Hall, which extended toward us the hostile lance of its soiled and weather-beaten flag: at the Cafe de Paris; at the silent houses; at the shops and the library. Was it there that the boy had bought those first new books for which the Lady in Black had paid?

"Nothing has changed."

An old dog, colourless and shaggy, upon the library steps, stretched himself lazily on his frozen paws.

"Cham! Cham!" called Rouletabille. "Oh, I remember him well. It is Cham—it is my old Cham."

And he called him again, "Cham! Cham!"

The dog got upon his feet, turned toward us, listening to the voice that called him. He took a few steps, wagged his tail, and stretched himself out in the sun again.

"He doesn't remember me," said Rouletabille sadly.

He drew me into a little street which had a steep down grade, and was paved with sharp pebbles. As we went down the hill he took my hand and I could feel the fever in his. We stopped again in front of a tiny temple of the Jesuit style, which raised in front of us its porch, ornamented with semicircles of stone, the "reversed consoles" which are the characteristic features of an architecture which contributed nothing to the glory of the Seventeenth Century. After having pushed open a little low door, Rouletabille bade me enter, and we found ourselves inside a beautiful mortuary chapel, upon the stone floor of which were kneeling, beside their empty tombs, magnificent marble statues of Catherine of Cleves and Guise le Balafre.

"The college chapel," whispered Rouletabille.

There was no person in the chapel. We crossed the room hastily. On the left wall, Rouletabille tapped very gently a kind of drum, which gave out a queer, muffled sound.

"We are in luck!" he said. "Everything is going well. We are inside the college and the concierge has not seen me. He would surely have remembered me."

"What harm would that have done?"

Just at that moment a man with bare head and a bunch of keys at his side passed through the room and Rouletabille drew me into the shadow.

"It is Pere Simon. Ah, how old he has grown He is almost bald. Listen: this is the hour when he goes to superintend the study hour of the younger boys. Everyone is in the classroom at this time. Oh, we are very lucky! There is only Mere Simon in the lodge—that is, if she is not dead. At any rate, she can't see us from here. But wait—here is Pere Simon back again!"

Why was Rouletabille so anxious to hide himself? Decidedly, I knew very little of the lad whom I believed that I knew so well. Every hour that I had spent with him of late had brought me some new surprise. While we were waiting for Pere Simon to leave us a clear field once more, Rouletabille and I managed to slip out of the chapel without being seen, and hid ourselves in the corner of a tiny garden, laid out in the middle of a stone court, behind the shrubbery of which we could, leaning over, contemplate at our leisure the grounds and buildings of the school. Rouletabille hung on to my arm as though he were afraid of falling. "Good Heavens!" he murmured, in a voice broken with emotion. "How things are changed! They have torn down the old study where I found the knife and the leather hangings where the money was hidden have, doubtless, been destroyed. But the chapel walls are just the same. Look, Sainclair: lean over the hedge. That door that opens in the rear of the chapel is the door of the infant class room. But never, never did I leave that class room so gladly, even in my happiest play hours, as when Pere Simon came to fetch me to the parlour where the Lady in Black was waiting for me. Ah—suppose that they have destroyed the parlour!"

And he cast a quick look toward the building behind him.

"No—no: it is all right—beside the mortuary. There is the same door at the right through which she came. We shall go there as soon as Pere Simon is out of the way."

And he set his teeth.

"I believe that I am going crazy!" he said with a short laugh. "But I can't help my feelings. They are stronger than I. To think that I am going to see the parlour—where she waited for me! I had been living only in the hope of seeing her, and after she had gone, although I had promised to be good and sensible, I fell into such a despondent state that after each of her visits, they feared for my health. They were only able to save me from utter prostration by telling me that if I fell ill they would not let me see her any more. So from one visit to another, I had her memory and her perfume to comfort me. Never having seen her dear face distinctly, and being so weak that I was ready to swoon with joy every time she pressed me to her heart, I lived less with her image than with the heavenly odour. Often on the days after she had come and gone, I would escape from my comrades during the recreation hours and steal to the parlour, and when I found it empty, I would draw deep breaths of the air which she had breathed and remain there like a little devotee, and leave with a heart filled with the sense of her presence. The perfume which she always used and which was indissolubly associated in my mind with her, was the most delicate, the most subtle, and the sweetest odour I have ever known, and I never breathed it again in all the years which followed until the day I spoke of it to you, Sainclair. You remember—the day we first went to the Glandier?"

"You mean the day that you met Mathilde Stanger son?"

"That is what I mean," responded the lad in a trembling voice.

(Ah, if I had known at that moment that Professor Stangerson's daughter, as the result of her first marriage in America, had had a child, a son, who would have been, if he had lived, the same age as Rouletabille, perhaps I would have at last comprehended his emotion and grief, and the strange reluctance which he showed to pronounce the name of Mathilde Stangerson there at the school, to which, in the past, had come so often the Lady in Black!)

There was a long silence, which I finally broke.

"And you have never known why the Lady in Black did not return?"

"Oh!" cried Rouletabille. "I am sure that she did return. It was I who was not here."

"Who took you away?"

"No one: I ran away."

"Why? To look for her?"

"No—no! To flee from her—to flee from her, I tell you, Sainclair. But she came back—I know that she came back."

"She may have been broken hearted at not finding you."

Rouletabille raised his arms toward the sky and shook his head.

"I don't know—how can I know? Ah, what an unhappy wretch I am! But, hush, Sainclair! Here comes Pere Simon! Now, he's gone again. Quick—to the parlour!"

We were there in three seconds. It was a common place room enough, rather large, with cheap white curtains in front of the shadeless windows. It was furnished with six leather chairs placed against the wall, a mantel mirror, and a clock. The whole appearance of the place was sombre.

As we entered the room, Rouletabille uncovered his head with an appearance of respect and reverence which one rarely assumes except in a sacred place. His face became flushed, he advanced with short steps, rolling his travelling cap in his hands as if he were embarrassed. He turned to me and said in low tones—far lower than he used in the chapel:

"Oh, Sainclair, this is it—the parlour. Feel how my hands burn. My face is flushed, is it not? I was always flushed when I came here, knowing that I should find her. I used to run. I felt smothered—I do now. I was not able to wait. Oh, my heart beats just as it used when I was a little lad! I would come to the door—right here—and then I would pause, bashful and shame faced. But I would see her dark shadow in the corner: she would take me in her arms and hold me there in silence, and before we knew it, we were both weeping, as we clung together. How dear those meetings were. She was my mother, Sainclair. Oh, she never told me so: on the contrary, she used to say that my mother was dead, and that she had been her friend. But she told me to call her Mamma—and when she wept as I kissed her, I knew that she really was my mother. See—she always sat there in the dark corner, and she came always at nightfall, when the parlour had not yet been lit up for the evening. And every time she came, she would place on the window sill a big, white package, tied with pink cord. It was a fruit cake. I have loved fruit cake ever since, Sainclair!"

The poor lad could no longer contain himself. He rested his arms on the mantel and wept like a little child. When he was able to control himself a little, he raised his head and looked at me with a sad smile. And then he sank into a chair as though he were tired out. I had not had the heart to say one word to him during his reminiscences. I knew well that he was not talking with me, but with his memories.

I saw him draw from his breast the letter which he had placed there in the train, and tear it open with trembling fingers. He read it slowly. Suddenly his hand fell, and he uttered a groan. His flushed face grew pallid—so pallid that it seemed as though every drop of blood had left his heart. I stepped toward him, but he waved me away and closed his eyes. He looked almost as though he were sleeping. I walked across the room, moving as softly as one does in the chamber of death. I looked up at the wall, where hung a heavy wooden crucifix. How long did I stand gazing on the cross? I have no idea. Nor do I know what we said to someone belonging to the house, who came into the parlour. I was pondering with all my strength of concentration on the strange and mysterious destiny of my friend—on this mysterious woman who might or might not have been his mother. Rouletabille had been so young in those school days. He longed so for a mother, that he might have imagined that he had found one in his visitor. Rouletabille—what other name did we know him by? Joseph Josephin. It was without doubt under that name that he had pursued his early studies here. Joseph Josephin, the queer appellation of which the editor of the *Epoch* had said to him, "It is no name at all!" And now, what was he about to do here? Seek the trace of a perfume? Revive a memory—an illusion? I turned as I heard him stir. He was standing erect and seemed quite calm. His features had taken on the serenity which comes from assurance of victory.

"We must go now, Sainclair. Come, my friend."

And he left the parlour without even looking back. I followed him.

In the deserted street, which we regained without meeting anyone, I stopped him by asking anxiously:

"Well—did you find the perfume of the Lady in Black?"

He must have seen that all my heart was in the question and that I was filled with an ardent desire that this visit to the scenes of his childhood might have brought a little peace to his soul.

"Yes," he said, very gravely. "Yes, Sainclair, I found it."

And he handed me the letter from Professor Stangerson's daughter.

I looked at him, doubting the evidence of my own senses—not understanding, because I knew nothing. Then he took my two hands and looked into my eyes.

"I am going to confide a secret to you, Sainclair—the secret of my life, and perhaps some day the secret of my death. Let what will come, it must die with you and me. Mathilde Stangerson had a child—a son. He is dead—is dead to everyone except to the two of us who stand here."

I recoiled, struck with horror under such a revelation. Rouletabille the son of Mathilde Stangerson! And then suddenly I received a still more violent shock. In that case, Rouletabille must be the son of Larsan.

Oh, I understood now, all the wretchedness of the boy. I understood why he had said this morning: "Why did he not die? If he is living, I wish to God that I were dead!"

Rouletabille must have read my thoughts in my eyes, and he simply made a gesture which seemed to say, "And now you understand, Sainclair." Then he finished his sentence aloud. The word which he spoke was "Silence!"

When we reached Paris we separated, to meet again at the train. There, Rouletabille handed me a new dispatch, which had come from Valence, and which was signed by Professor Stangerson. It said, "M. Darzac tells me that you have a few days' leave. We should all be very glad if you could come and spend them with us. We will wait for you at Arthur Rance's place, Rochers Rouges—he will be delighted to present you to his wife. My daughter will be pleased to see you. She joins me in kindest greetings."

Just as the train was starting, a concierge from Rouletabille's hotel came rushing up and handed us a third dispatch. This one was sent from Mentone, and signed by Mathilde. It contained two words: "Rescue us."

IV

En Route

N ow I knew all. As we continued on our journey, Rouletabille related to me the remarkable and adventurous story of his childhood, and I knew, also, why he dreaded nothing so much as that Mme. Darzac should penetrate the mystery which separated them. I dared say nothing more—give my friend no advice. Ah, the poor unfortunate lad! When he read the words "Rescue us," he carried the dispatch to his lips, and then, pressing my hand, he said: "If I arrive too late, I can avenge her, at least." I have never heard anything more filled with resolution than the cold determination of his tone. From time to time a quick movement betrayed the passion of his soul, but for the most part he was calm—terribly calm. What resolution had he taken in the silence of the parlour, when he sat motionless and with closed eyes in the shadow of the corner where he had used to see the Lady in Black?

While we journeyed toward Lyons, and Rouletabille lay dreaming, stretched out fully dressed in his berth, I will tell you how and why the child that he had been ran away from school at Eu, and what had happened to him.

Rouletabille had fled from the school like a thief. There was no need to seek for another expression, because he had been accused of stealing. This was how it happened.

At the age of nine, he had already an extraordinarily precocious intelligence, and could arrive easily at the solution of the most perplexing problems. By logical deductions of an almost amazing kind, he astonished his professor of mathematics by his philosophical method of work. He had never been able to learn his multiplication tables, and always counted upon his fingers. He would usually get the answers to the problems himself, leaving the working out to be done by his fellow pupils, as one will leave an irksome task to a servant. But first, he would show them exactly how the example ought to be done. Although as yet ignorant of the rudiments of algebra, he had invented for his own personal use a system of algebra carried on with queer signs, looking like hieroglyphics, by the aid of which he marked all the steps of his mathematical reasoning, and thus he was able to write down the general formulae so that he alone could interpret them. His professor used proudly to compare him to Pascal, discovering for himself without knowledge of geometry, the first propositions of Euclid. He applied his admirable faculties of reasoning to his daily life, as well as to his studies, using the rules both materially and morally. For example, an act had been committed in the school—I have forgotten whether it was of cheating or talebearing—by one of ten persons whom he knew, and he picked out the right one with a divination which seemed almost supernatural, simply by using the powers of reasoning and deduction, which he had practiced to such an extent. So much for the moral aspect of his strange gift, and as for the material, nothing seemed more simple to him than to find any lost or hidden object—or even a stolen one. It was in the detection of thefts especially that he displayed a wonderful resourcefulness, as if nature, in her wondrous fitting together of the parts that make an equal whole, after having created the father a thief of the worst kind, had caused the son to be born the evil genius of thieves.

THIS STRANGE APTITUDE, AFTER HAVING won for the boy a sort of fame in the school, on account of his detection of several attempts at pilfering, was destined one day to be fatal to him. He found in this abnormal fashion a small sum of money which had been stolen from the superintendent, who refused to believe that the discovery was due only to the lad's intelligence and clearness of insight. This hypothesis, indeed, appeared impossible to almost everyone who knew of the matter, and, thanks to an unfortunate coincidence of time and place, the affair finished up by having Rouletabille himself accused of being the thief. They tried to make him acknowledge his fault; he defended himself with such indignation and anger that it drew upon him a severe punishment. The principal held an investigation and a trial, at which Joseph Josephin was accused by some of his youthful comrades in that spirit of falsehood which children sometimes possess. Some of them complained of having had books, pencils, and tablets stolen at different times, and declared that they believed that Joseph had taken them. The fact that the boy seemed to have no relatives, and that no one knew where he came from, made him particularly likely, in that little world, to be suspected of crime. When the boys spoke of him, it was as "that thief." The contempt in which he was held preyed upon him, for he was not a strong child at best, and he was plunged in despair. He almost prayed to die. The principal, who was really the most kind hearted of men, was persuaded that he had a vicious little creature to deal with, because he was unable to produce an impression on the child, and make him comprehend the horror of what he had done. Finally, he told the lad that if he did not confess his guilt, it had been decided not to keep him in the school any longer, and that a letter would be written to the lady who interested herself in him—Mme. Darbel was the name which she had given—to tell her to come after him.

The child made no reply and allowed himself to be taken to his little room, where he had been kept a prisoner. Upon the morrow he had disappeared. He had run away. He had felt that the principal, to whose care he had been entrusted during the earliest years of his childhood (for in all his little life he could remember no other home than the school), and who had always been so kind to him, was no longer his friend, since he believed him guilty of theft. And he could see no reason why the Lady in Black would not believe it, too—that he was a thief. To appear as a thief in the sight of the Lady in Black He would far rather have died.

And he made his escape from the place by climbing over the wall of the garden at night. He rushed to the canal, sobbing, and, with a prayer, uttered as much to the Lady in Black as to God Himself, threw himself in the water. Happily, in his despair, the poor child had forgotten that he knew how to swim.

If I have reported this passage in the life of Rouletabille at some length, it is because it seems to me that it is all important to the thorough comprehension of his future. At that time, of course, he was ignorant that he was the son of Larsan. Rouletabille, even as a child of nine years, could not without agony harbour the idea that the Lady in Black might believe him to be a thief, and thus, when the time came that he imagined—an imagination too well founded, alas!—that he was bound by ties of blood to Larsan, what infinite misery he experienced His mother, in hearing of the crime of which he had been accused, must have felt that the criminal instincts of the father were coming to light in the son, and, perhaps—thought more cruel than death itself—she may have rejoiced in believing him dead.

For everyone believed him dead. They found his footsteps leading to the canal, and they fished out his cap. How had he lived after leaving the school? In a most singular fashion. After swimming to dry land and making up his mind to fly the country, the lad, while they were searching for him everywhere in the canal and out of it, devised a most original plan for travelling to a distance without being disturbed. He had not read that most interesting tale, *The Stolen Letter*. His own invention served him. He reasoned the thing out, as he always did.

He knew—for he had often heard them told by the heroes themselves—many stories of little rascals who had run away from their parents in search of adventures, hiding themselves by day in the fields and the wood, and travelling by night—only to find themselves speedily captured by the gendarmes, or forced to return home because they had no money and no food, and dared not ask for anything to eat along the road which they followed, and which was too well guarded to admit of their escape if they applied for aid. Our little Rouletabille slept at night like everyone else, and travelled in broad daylight, without hiding himself. But, after having dried his garments (the warm weather was coming on, and he did not suffer from cold), he tore them to tatters. He made rags of them, which barely covered him, and begged in the open streets, dirty and unkempt, holding out his hands and declaring to passers-by that if he did not bring home any money his parents would beat him. And everyone took him for some gypsy child, hordes of which constantly roamed through the locality. Soon came the time of wild strawberries. He gathered the fruit and sold it in little baskets of leaves And he assured me, in telling the story, that if it had not been for the terrible thought that the Lady in Black must believe that he was a thief, that time would have been the happiest of his life. His astuteness and natural courage stood him well in stead through these wanderings, which lasted for several months. Where was he going? To Marseilles. This was his plan:

He had seen in his illustrated geography views of the Midi, and he had never looked at those pictures without breathing a sigh and wishing that he might some day visit that enchanted country. Through his gypsy-like manner of living, he had made the acquaintance of a little caravan load of Romanies, who were following the same route as himself, and who were journeying to Ste. Marie's of the Sea to render homage to a new king of their tribe. The lad had an opportunity to render them some small service, and finding him a pleasant, well-mannered little fellow, these people, not being in the habit of asking everyone whom they met for his history, desired to know nothing more about him. They believed that, on account of ill treatment, the child had run away from some troop of wandering mountebanks, and they invited him to travel with them. Thus he arrived in the Midi.

In the neighbourhood of Arles, he separated himself from his travelling companions, and at last came to Marseilles. There was his paradise! Eternal summer—and the port.

The port was the favourite resort of all the gamins of the locality, and this fact was the greatest safeguard for Rouletabille. He roamed over the docks as he chose, and served himself according to the measure of his needs, which were not great. For example, he made of himself an "orange fisher." It was at the time that he exercised this lucrative calling that, one beautiful morning upon the quay, he made the acquaintance of M. Gaston Leroux, a journalist from Paris, and this acquaintance was destined to have such an influence upon the future of Rouletabille that I do not consider it out of place to transcribe here in full the article in which the editor of *Le Matin* recorded that first memorable interview.

THE LITTLE ORANGE FISHER.

As the sun, piercing through the cloudless heavens, struck with its ardent rays the golden robe of Notre-Dame-de-la-Garde, I descended toward the quay. The scene which met my eyes was one which was worth going far to see. Townfolk, sailors and workmen were moving about, the former idly looking on, while the others tugged at the pulleys and drew up the cables of their vessels. The great merchant vessels glided like huge beasts of burden between the tower of St. Jean and the fort of St. Nicholas, caressing the sparkling waters of the Old Port in their onward motion. Side by side, shoulder to shoulder, the smaller barks seemed to hold out their arms to each other. To throw aside their veils of mist and to dance upon the water. Beside them, tired with the long journey, worn out from ploughing for so many days and nights over unknown seas, the heavy laden East Indiamen rested peacefully, lifting their great, motionless sails in rags toward the skies.

My eyes, sweeping swiftly over the scene through the forest of masts and sails paused at the tower which commemorated the fact that it was twenty-five centuries since the children of Ancient Phoenicia first cast anchor upon this happy shore, and that they had come by the water ways of Ionia. Then my attention returned to the border of the quay, and I perceived the little orange fisher.

He was standing erect, clad in the rags of a man's coat which hung down almost to his feet, bareheaded and barefooted, with blonde curly locks and black eyes, and I should think that he was about nine years old. A string passed around his shoulder supported a big sailcloth sack. His left hand rested on his waist and his right hand held a stick three times as tall as himself, which was surmounted by a little wooden hook. The child stood motionless and lost in thought. When I asked him what he was doing there, he told me that he was an orange fisher.

He seemed very proud of being an orange fisher and did not ask me for a penny, as the little vagabonds of the neighbourhood are accustomed to demand toll of every bystander. I spoke to him again, but this time he made no answer, for he was too intent on watching the water. On one side of us was the beautiful steamer Fides, in from Castellmare and on the other a three masted schooner from Genoa. Further off were two ships loaded with fruits which had just arrived from Baleares that morning, and I saw that they were spilling a part of their cargo. Oranges were bobbing up and down upon the water and the light current sent them in our direction. My "fisher" leaped into a little canoe, came quickly to the vessel, and, armed with his stick and hook, waited. Then he began his gathering. The hook on his stick brought him one orange, then a second, a third and a fourth. They disappeared in the sack. The boy gathered a fifth, jumped upon the quay and tore open the golden fruit. He plunged his little teeth in the pulp and devoured it in an instant.

"You have a good appetite," I told him.

"Monsieur," he replied, flushing slightly as he spoke, "I don't care for any food but fruit."

"That is a very good diet," I replied as gravely as he had spoken. "But what do you do when there are no oranges?"

"I pick up coal."

And his little hand, diving into the sack, brought out an enormous piece of coal.

The orange juice had rolled down his chin to his coat. The coat had a pocket. The little fellow took a clean handkerchief from this pocket and carefully wiped both chin and coat. Then he proudly put the handkerchief back.

"What is your father's work?" I asked.

"He is poor."

"Yes, but what does he do?"

The orange fisher shrugged his shoulders.

"He doesn't do anything, he is poor."

My inquiries into his family affairs did not seem to please him. He turned away from the quay and I followed him. We came in a moment to the "shelter," a little square of sea which holds the small pleasure yachts—the neat little boats all polished wood and brass, the neat little sailors in their irreproachable toilettes. My ragamuffin looked at them with the eye of a connoisseur and seemed to find a keen enjoyment in the spectacle. A new yacht had just been launched and her immaculate sail looked like a white veil against the blue sky.

"Isn't it pretty?" exclaimed my little companion.

The next moment he fell over a board covered with fresh tar and when he picked himself up, he looked with dismay at the stain on his coat which seemed to be his proudest possession. What a disaster! He looked as if he could have burst into tears. But quick as thought he drew out his handkerchief and rubbed and rubbed the spot, then he looked at me piteously and said:

"Monsieur, are there any other stains? Did I get anything on my back?"

I assured him that he had not, and with an expression of satisfaction, he put the handkerchief back in his pocket once more.

A few steps further on, upon the walk which stretches in front of the red and yellow, and blue houses, the windows of which are brave with wares of many kinds, we found an oyster stand. Upon the little tables were displayed piles of oysters in their shells, and flasks of vinegar.

When we passed by the oyster stand, as the fish appeared fresh and appetizing, I said to the orange fisher.

"If you cared for anything to eat except fruit, I might ask you to have some oysters with me."

His black eyes glistened and we sat down together to eat our oysters. The merchant opened them for us while we waited. He started to bring us vinegar, but my companion stopped him with an imperious gesture. He opened his bag carefully and triumphantly produced a lemon. The lemon, having been in close contact with the bit of coal, might have passed for black itself. But my guest took out his handkerchief and wiped it off. Then he cut the fruit and offered me half, but I like oysters without other flavour, so I declined with thanks.

After our luncheon we went back to the quay. The orange fisher asked me for a cigarette and lighted it with a match which he had in another pocket of his coat.

Then, the cigarette between his lips, puffing rings toward the sky like a man, the little creature threw himself down on the ground and with his eyes fixed upon the statue of Notre-Dame-de-la-Garde, took the very pose of the boy who is the most beautiful ornament of the Brussels tower. He did not lose a line of the attitude, and seemed very proud of the fact and apparently desired to play the part exactly.

Upon the following day Joseph Josephin met M. Gaston Leroux once more upon the quay, and the man handed him a newspaper which he carried in his hand. The boy read the article pointed out to him, and the journalist gave him a bright new 100-sous piece. Rouletabille made no difficulties about accepting it, and seemed to even find the gift a natural one. "I take your money," he said to Gaston Leroux, "because we are collaborators." With his hundred sous he bought himself a fine new bootblack's box and installed himself in business opposite the Bregaillon. For two years he polished the boots of those who came to eat the traditional bouillabaisse at this hostelry. When he was not at work, he would sit on his box and read. With the feeling of ownership which his box and his business had brought him, ambition had entered his mind. He had received too good an education and had been too well instructed in rudimentary things not to understand that if he did not himself finish what others had begun for him, he would be deprived of the best chance which he had of making for himself a place in the world.

His customers grew interested in the little bootblack, who always had on his box some work of history or mathematics, and a harness maker became so attached to him that he took him into his shop.

Soon Rouletabille was promoted to the dignity of working in leather, and was able to save. At the age of sixteen years, having a little money in his pocket, he took the train for Paris. What did he intend to do there? To look for the Lady in Black.

Not one day had passed without his having thought of the mysterious visitor to the parlour of the boarding school, and, although no one had ever told him that she lived in Paris, he was persuaded that no other city in the world was worthy to contain a lady who wore so sweet a perfume. And then his little schoolmates, who had been able to see her form when she glided out of the parlour, had often said: "See the Parisienne is here again today!" It would have been difficult to exactly define the ideas in Rouletabille's head, and perhaps he himself scarcely knew what they were. His longing was merely to see the Lady in Black—to watch her reverently—at a distance, as a devotee watches the image of a saint. Would he dare to speak to her? The importance of the accusation of theft which had been brought against him had only grown greater in Rouletabille's imagination as time had gone by, and he believed that it would always be a barrier between himself and the Lady in Black, which he had not the right to try to throw down. Perhaps even—but, come what might, he longed to see her. That was the only thing of which he was sure.

As soon as he reached the capital, he looked up M. Gaston Leroux, and recalled himself to the latter's memory, telling him that, although he felt no particular liking for the life, which he considered rather a lazy one for a man who liked to be up and doing, he had decided to become a journalist. And he fairly demanded that his old acquaintance should at once give him a trial as a reporter.

Leroux tried to turn the youth from his project. At last, tired of his persistent requests, the editor said:

"Well, my lad, since you have nothing special to do just now, go and find the left foot of the body in the Rue Oberkampf."

And with these words, M. Leroux turned away, leaving poor Rouletabille standing there with half a dozen young reporters tittering around him. But the boy was not daunted in the least. He searched through the files of the paper and found out that the *Epoch* was offering a large reward to the person who would bring to its office the foot which was missing from the mutilated body of a woman, which had been found in the Rue Oberkampf.

The rest we know. In "The Mystery of the Yellow Room," I have told how Rouletabille succeeded on this occasion, and in what manner there revealed itself to him his own singular calling—that of always beginning to reason a matter out from the point where others had finished.

I have told, too, by what chance he was led one evening to the Elysee, where he inhaled as he passed by the perfume of the Lady in Black. He realised then that it was Mlle. Stangerson who had been his visitor at the school, and for whom he had been seeking so long. What more need I add: Why speak of the sensations which his knowledge as to the wearer of the perfume aroused in the heart of Rouletabille during the events at the Glandier, and, above all, after his trip to America? They may be easily guessed. How simple a thing now to understand his hesitations and his whims! The proofs brought by him from Cincinnati in regard to the child of the woman who had been Jean Roussel's wife had been sufficiently explicit to awaken in his mind a suspicion that he himself might be that child, but not enough so to render him certain of the fact. However, his instinct drew him so strongly to the professor's daughter that he could scarcely resist his longing to throw himself into her arms and press her to his heart and cry out to her: "You are my mother! you are my mother!"

And he fled from her presence just as he had fled from the vestry on the day of her wedding, in order that there should not escape from him any sign of the secret tenderness that had burned in his breast through so many long years. For horrible thoughts dwelt in his mind. Suppose he were to make himself known to her, and she were to repulse him—cast him off—turn from him in horror—from him, the little thief of the boarding school—the son of Roussel—Ballmeyer—the heir of the crimes of Larsan! Suppose she were to order him to get out of her sight, never to come near her again, nor to breathe the same air which brought back to him, whenever he came near her, the perfume of the Lady in Black Ah, how he had fought, on account of these frightful visions, to restrain himself from yielding to the almost overwhelming impulse to ask each time that he came near her, "Is it you? Are you the Lady in Black?" As to her, she had seemed fond of him from the first, but, doubtless, that was because of the Glan dier affair. If she were really the Lady in Black, she must believe that the child whom he had been was dead. And if it were not she—if by some fatality which set at naught both his instincts and his powers of reasoning, it were not she Could he, through any imprudence, risk having her discover that he had fled from the school at Eu under ban as a thief? No, no—not that! She had often said to him:

"Where were you brought up, my boy? What school did you attend when you were a child?" And he had replied: "I was in school at Bordeaux."

He might as well have answered, "At Pekin."

However, this torture could not last always, he told himself. If it were she, he would know how to say things to her that must open her heart. Anything would be better than to be sure that she was not the Lady in Black, but some stranger who had never held him to her heart. But he must be certain—certain beyond any doubt, and he knew how to place himself in the presence of his memories of the Lady in Black, just as a dog is sure of finding its master. The simile which presented itself quite naturally to his imagination was simply that of "following the scent." And this led us, under the circumstances which I have narrated, to Trepot and to Eu. However, it is by no means certain that decisive results would have been gained from this expedition—at least in the eyes of a third person, like myself—had it not been for the influence of the odour—if the letter from Mathilde, which I had handed to Rouletabille in the train, had not suddenly, with its faint, sweet perfume, brought to us directly the evidence which we were seeking. I have never read this letter. It is a document so sacred in the eyes of my friend, that other eyes will never behold it, but I know that the gentle reproaches which it contained for the boy's rudeness and lack of confidence in the writer, had been so tender that Rouletabille could no longer deceive himself, even if the daughter of Professor Stanger son had not concluded the note with a final sentence, through which throbbed the heart of a despairing mother, and which said that "the interest which she felt in him arose less from the services he had rendered her, than because of the memories which she had of a little boy, the son of a friend, whom she had loved very dearly, and who had killed himself 'like a little man with a broken heart' at the age of nine years, and whom Rouletabille greatly resembled."

V

PANIC

Dijon—Macon—Lyons—certainly the boy could not be sleeping all this time. I called him softly and he did not reply, but I would have wagered my hand that he was not sleeping. What was he planning? How quiet he was! What could it be that had given him such a strange calmness? I seemed to see him again as he had been in the parlour, suddenly standing erect as he said: "Let us go on!" in that voice so composed and tranquil and resolute. Go on to whom? Toward what was he resolved to go? Toward Her, evidently, who was in danger, and who could be rescued only by him—toward her who was his mother and who did not know it.

"It is a secret which must remain between you and me! That child is dead to the whole world, except to us two!"

That was his decision, taken almost in a single moment, never to reveal himself to her. And the poor child had come to seek the certainty that she was indeed the Lady in Black, only to have the right to speak to her! In the very moment that the assurance which he sought was his, he had determined to forget it; he condemned himself to endless silence. Poor little hero soul, which had understood that the Lady in Black, who had such dire need of his help, would have shrunk from a safety bought by the warfare of a son against his father! Where might not such warfare lead? To what bloody conflict? Everything must be expected, no matter how terrible, and Rouletabille must have his hands free to fight to the death for the Lady in Black.

The boy was so quiet that I could not even hear him breathing. I leaned over him; his eyes were open.

"Do you know what I have been thinking of?" he said. "Of the dispatch that came to us from Bourg and was signed 'Darzac,' and the other dispatch which came from Valence and was signed 'Stangerson.'"

"And the more I think of them, the stranger they seem to me. At Bourg, M. and Mme. Darzac were not with M. Stangerson, who left them at Dijon. Besides, the dispatch says: 'We are going to rejoin M. Stangerson.' But the Stangerson dispatch proves that M. Stangerson, who had continued on his journey toward Marseilles, is again with the

Darzacs. The Darzacs might have rejoined M. Stargerson on the way to Marseilles; but if that were so, the Professor must have stopped on the road. Why was this? He did not expect to do so. At the train, he said: 'Tomorrow at ten o'clock, I shall be at Mentone.' Look at the hour that the dispatch was sent from Valence, and then we'll look in the time table and find out the hour at which M. Stangerson would have passed through Valence if he had not stopped upon the journey."

We consulted the time table. M. Stangerson should have passed through Valence at 12:44 o'clock in the morning, and the dispatch was sent at 12:47 o'clock. It had, therefore, been sent by M. Stangerson while he was continuing on the trip which he had planned. At that moment he must have been with M. and Mme. Darzac. Still poring over the time table, we endeavoured to solve the mystery of this re-encounter. M. Stangerson had left the Darzacs at Dijon, where the whole party had arrived at twenty-seven minutes after six o'clock in the evening. The Professor had then taken the train which leaves Dijon at eight minutes past seven, and had arrived at Lyons at four minutes after ten and at Valence at forty-seven minutes after midnight. During the same time the Darzacs, leaving Dijon at seven o'clock, continued on their way to Modane, and, by way of Saint-Amour, reached Bourg at three minutes past nine in the evening, on the train which was scheduled to leave at eight minutes past nine. M. Darzac's dispatch was sent from Bourg, and had left the telegraph office at the station at 9:28. The Darzacs, therefore, must have left their train at Bourg, and remained there. Or, it might have happened that the train was late. In any case, we must seek the reason for M. Darzac's telegram somewhere between Dijon and Bourg, after the departure of M. Stangerson. One might even go further, and say 'between Louhans and Bourg,' for the train stops at Louhans, and if anything had happened before he reached there, at eight o'clock, it is altogether likely that M. Darzac would have sent his message from that station.

Finally, seeking the correspondence between Bourg and Lyons, we reasoned that M. Darzac must have sent his wire from Bourg one minute before leaving for Lyons by the 9:29 train. But this train reached Lyons at 10:23 o'clock, while M. Stangerson's train reached Lyons at 10:24. After changing their plans and leaving the train at Bourg, M. and Mme. Darzac must have rejoined M. Stangerson at Lyons, which they reached one minute before him. Now, what had upset their plans? We could only think of the most terrible hypotheses, every one of which, alas! had as its basis the reappearance of Larsan. The fact which gave the greatest colour to this idea was the desire expressed by each of our friends, *not to frighten anyone*. M. Darzac in his message, Mme. Darzac in hers, had not endeavoured to conceal the gravity of the situation. As to M. Stangerson, we asked ourselves whether he had been made aware of the new developments, whatever they might be.

Having thus approximately settled the question of time and distance, Rouletabille invited me to profit by the luxurious accommodations which the International Sleeping Car company places at the disposal of those who wish to sleep while on a journey, and he himself set me the example by making as careful a night toilet as he would have done in his own room at his hotel. A quarter of an hour later he was snoring, but I believed the snores to be feigned. At any rate, I could not sleep.

At Avignon Rouletabille jumped up from his cot, hastily donned his trousers and coat, and rushed out to the refreshment rooms to get a cup of chocolate. I was not hungry. From Avignon to Marseilles, in our anxiety and suspense, neither of us desired to talk, and the journey was continued almost in silence, but at the sight of the city in which he had led such a chequered existence, Rouletabille, doubtless to keep from showing the emotion which he felt, and to lighten the heaviness of both our hearts as we drew near our journey's end, began to tell funny stories, in the narration of which, however, he did not seem to find the least amusement. I scarcely heard what he was saying. And at last we reached Toulon.

What a trip! And it might have been so beautiful!

Ordinarily, it is always with an almost boyish enthusiasm that I come within sight of this marvellous country, with its azure shores, like a bit of dreamland or a corner of paradise after the horrible departure from Paris in the snow and rain and darkness and dampness and dirt. With what joy that night, had things been otherwise, would I have set my foot upon the quay, sure of finding the glorious friend who would be waiting for me in the morning at the end of those two iron rails—the wonderful southern sun!

When we left Toulon, our impatience became extreme. And at Cannes, we were scarcely surprised at all to see M. Darzac upon the platform of the station, anxiously looking for us. He could scarcely have received the dispatch which Rouletabille had sent him from Dijon, announcing the hour at which we would reach Mentone. Having arrived there with Mme. Darzac and M. Stangerson the day before, at ten o'clock in the morning, he must have left Mentone almost at once, and have come to meet us at Cannes, for we could understand from his dispatch that he had something to say to us in confidence. His face looked worn and sad. Somehow, it frightened us only to look at him.

"Trouble?" questioned Rouletabille, briefly.

"No, not yet," was the reply.

"God be praised" exclaimed Rouletabille, having a deep sigh. "We have come in time!"

M. Darzac said simply:

"I thank you for coming."

And he pressed both our hands in silence, following us into our compartment, in which we locked ourselves, taking care to draw the curtains and so isolate ourselves completely. When we were comfortably settled, and the train had begun to move on, our friend spoke again. His voice trembled so that he could scarcely utter the words.

"Well," he said: "he is not dead."

"We suspected it!" interrupted Rouletabille. "But are you sure?"

"I have seen him as surely as I have seen you."

"And has Mme. Darzac seen him?"

"Alas, yes! But it is necessary that we should use every means to make her believe that it was an illusion. I could not bear it if she were to lose her mind again, poor, innocent, wretched girl! Ah, my friends, what a fatality pursues us! What has this man come back to do to us? What does he want now?"

I looked at Rouletabille. His face was even more full of grief than that of M. Darzac. The blow which he feared had fallen. He leaned back against the cushions as though he were going to faint. There was a brief pause, and then M. Darzac spoke again:

"Listen This man must disappear—he must be gotten rid of! We must go to him and ask what it is that he wants. If it is money, he may take all that I have. If he will not go, I shall kill him. It is very simple—after all, I think that would be the simplest way. Don't you think so, too?"

We could not answer. It was too pitiful. Rouletabille, overcoming his own feelings by a visible effort, engaged M. Darzac in conversation, endeavouring to calm him, and asking him to tell us what had happened since his departure from Paris.

And he told us that the event which had changed the face of his existence had taken place at Bourg, just as we had thought. Two compartments of the sleeping car had been reserved by M. Darzac, and these compartments were joined by a little dressing room. In one had been placed the travelling bag with the toilet articles of Mme. Darzac, and in the other the smaller packages. It was in the latter compartment that the Darzacs and Professor Stangerson had travelled from Paris to Dijon, where the three had left the train, and had dined at the buffet. They had arrived at 6:27 o'clock, exactly on time, and M. Stangerson had left Dijon at eight minutes after seven, and the Darzacs at just seven o'clock.

The Professor had bidden adieu to his daughter and his son-in-law upon the platform of the station after dinner. M. and Mme. Darzac had returned to their compartment—the one in which the small parcels had been deposited—and remained at the window, chatting with the Professor until the train started. As it steamed out of the station, the newly wedded pair looked back and waved their hands to M. Stangerson, who was still standing upon the platform, throwing kisses at them from the distance.

From Dijon to Bourg neither M. nor Mme. Darzac had occasion to enter the adjacent compartment, where Mme. Darzac's night bag had been placed. The door of this compartment, opening upon the vestibule, had been closed at Paris, as soon as the baggage had been brought there. But the door had not been locked, either upon the outside with a key by the porter, nor on the inside with the bolt by the Darzacs. The curtain of the glass door had been drawn over the pane from the inside by M. Darzac in such a way that no one could look into the compartment from the corridor. But the curtain between the two compartments had not been drawn. All of these circumstances were brought out by the questions asked by Rouletabille of M. Darzac, and, although I could not understand his reasons for going into such minute detail, I give the facts in order to make the condition under which the journey of the Darzacs to Bourg and of M. Stangerson to Dijon was accomplished.

When they reached Bourg our travellers learned that, on account of an accident on the line at Culoz, the train would be delayed for an hour and a half. M. and Mme. Darzac alighted and took a stroll on the platform. M. Darzac, while talking with his wife, mentioned the fact that he had forgotten to write some important letters before leaving Paris. Both entered the buffet, and M. Darzac asked for writing materials. Mathilde sat beside him for a few moments and then remarked that she would take a little walk through the station while he finished his letters.

"Very well," replied M. Darzac. "As soon as I have finished, I will join you."

From that point, I will quote M. Darzac's own words:

"I had finished writing," he said. "And I arose to go and look for Mathilde, when I saw her approaching the buffet, pallid and trembling. As soon as she perceived me, she uttered a shriek and threw herself into my arms. 'Oh, my God!' she cried. 'Oh, my God!' It seemed impossible for her to utter any other words. She was shaking from head to foot. I tried to calm her. I assured her that she had nothing to fear when I was with her, and I strove as gently and patiently as I could to draw from her the cause of her sudden terror. I made her sit down, for her limbs seemed too weak to support her, and I begged her to take some restorative, but she told me that she could not even swallow a drop of water. Her teeth chattered as though she had an ague. At length she was able to speak, and she told me, interrupting herself at almost every other word, and looking about her as though she expected to encounter something which she dreaded, that she had started to walk about the station, as she had said she intended to do, but that she had not dared to go far, lest I should finish my writing and look for her. Then she went through the station and out upon the platform. She decided to come back to the buffet, when she noticed through the lighted windows of the cars, the sleeping car porters, who were making up the bed in a berth near our own. She remembered immediately that her night travelling bag, in which she had put her jewels, was standing unlocked, and she decided to go and lock it up without delay, not because she suspected the honesty of the employees, but through a natural instinct of prudence on a journey. She entered the car, walked down the corridor and came to the glass door of the compartment which had been reserved for her, and which neither of us had entered since leaving Paris. She opened the door and instantly uttered a cry of horror. No one heard her, for there was no one in that part of the car, and a train which passed at that moment drowned the sound of her voice with the clamour of the locomotive. What had happened to alarm her? The most terrible, ghastly, monstrous thing that the imagination could devise.

"Within the compartment, the little door opening upon the dressing cabinet was half drawn toward the interior of the section, cutting off diagonally the view of whoever might enter. This little door was ornamented by a mirror. There, in the glass, Mathilde beheld the face of Larsan! She flung herself backward, shrieking for help, and fled so precipitately that, in leaping down from the platform of the car, she fell on her knees in the train shed. Regaining her feet with difficulty, she dragged herself toward the buffet, which she reached in the condition which I have described.

"When she had told me these things, my first care was to try to convince her that she was labouring under some hideous delusion—partly because I prayed that this might be the case, and that the horrible thing which she believed had not happened, but mainly because I felt that it was my duty, if I wished to prevent Mathilde from going mad, to make her think that she must have been mistaken. Wasn't Larsan dead and buried?

As I soothed her thus, I really believed what I said, and I continued to reassure her until there remained no doubt in my mind, at least, that what she had seen was merely a phantom, conjured up by fear and imagination. Naturally, I wished to make an investigation for myself, and I offered to accompany Mathilde at once to the compartment, in order to prove to her that she had been the victim of an hallucination. She was bitterly opposed to the idea, crying out that neither she nor I must ever enter the compartment again, and, not only that, but she refused to continue our journey that night. She said all these things in little halting phrases—she could hardly breathe—and it caused me the most intense pain to look at her and listen to her. The more I told her that such an apparition was an impossibility, the more she insisted that it was a reality. I tried to remind her of how seldom she had seen Larsan while the events at the Glandier were going on—which was true—and to persuade her that she could not be certain that it was his face which she had beheld, and not that of some one who might resemble him. She replied that she remembered Larsan's face perfectly—that it had appeared before her twice under such circumstances as would impress it indelibly upon her memory, even if she were to live for a century—once during the strange scene in the gallery, and again at the moment when they came into her sick room to place me under arrest. And then, now that she knew who Larsan was, it was not only the features of the Secret Service agent that she had recognised, but the dreaded countenance of the man who had not ceased pursuing her for so many years.

"She cried out that she could swear on her life and on mine that she had seen Ballmeyer—that Ballmeyer was alive—alive in the glass, with the smooth face of Larsan and his high, bald forehead. She clung to me, crouching upon the ground like a helpless wild animal, as though she feared a separation yet more terrible than the others. She drew me from the buffet where, fortunately, we had been entirely alone, out upon the platform, and then, suddenly she released my arm, and hiding her face in her hands, rushed into the superintendent's office. The man was as alarmed as myself when he saw the poor soul, and I could only repeat under my breath to myself, 'She is going mad again! She will lose her reason!'

"I explained to the superintendent that my wife had been frightened at something she fancied that she had seen while alone in our compartment, and I begged him to keep her in his office while I went myself to discover what it was that she had seen.

"And then, my friends," continued Robert Darzac, his voice beginning to tremble, "I left the superintendent's office, but I had no sooner gotten out of the room than I went back and slammed the door behind me. My face must have looked strange enough, to judge from the expression of the superintendent's face when I reappeared. But there was reason for it. *I, too, had seen Larsan.* My wife had had no illusion. *Larsan was there*—in the station—upon the platform outside that door!"

Robert Darzac paused for an instant, as though the remembrance overcame him. He passed his hand over his forehead, heaved a sigh and resumed: "He was there, in front of the superintendent's door, standing under a gas jet. Evidently, he expected us and was waiting for us. For, extraordinarily enough, he made no effort to hide himself. On the contrary, anyone would have declared that he had stationed himself there for the express purpose of being seen. The gesture which had made me close the door upon this apparition was purely instinctive. When I opened it again, intending to walk straight up to the miserable wretch, he had disappeared.

"The superintendent must have thought that he had fallen in with two lunatics. Mathilde was staring at me, her great eyes wide open, speechless, as though she were a somnambulist. In a moment, however, she came back to herself sufficiently to ask me whether it were far from Bourg to Lyons, and what was the next train which would take us there. At the same time, she begged me to give orders about our baggage, and asked me to accede to her desire to rejoin her father as soon as possible. I could see no other means of calming her, and, far from making any objection to the new project, I immediately entered into her plans. Besides, now that I had seen Larsan with my own eyes—yes, with my own eyes—I knew well that the long honeymoon trip which we had planned must be given up, and, my dear boy," went on M. Darzac, turning to Rouletabille, "I became possessed with the idea that we were running the risk of some mysterious and fantastic danger, from which you alone could rescue us, if it were not already too late. Mathilde was grateful to me for the readiness with which I fell in with her wish to join her father, and she thanked me fervently, when I told her that in a few minutes we would be on board the 9:29 train, which reaches Lyons at about ten o'clock, and when we consulted the time table, we discovered that we would overtake M. Stangerson himself at that point. Mathilde showed as much gratitude toward me as though I were personally responsible for this lucky chance. She had regained her composure to a certain extent when the nine o'clock train arrived in the station, but at the moment that we boarded the train, as we rapidly crossed the platform and passed beneath the gas jet where I had seen Larsan, I felt her arm trembling in my own. I looked around, but could not see any sign of our enemy. I asked her whether she had seen anything, and she made no reply. Her agitation seemed to increase, however, and she begged me not to take her into a private car, but to enter a car the berths of which were already two-thirds filled with passengers. Under pretext of making some inquiries about the baggage, I left her for an instant, and went to the telegraph office, where I sent the telegram to you. I said nothing to Mathilde of this dispatch, because I continued to assure her that her eyes must have deceived her, and because on no account did I wish her to believe that I placed any faith in such a resurrection. When my wife opened her travelling bag, she found that no one had touched her jewels.

"The few words which we exchanged concerning the secret were in relation to the necessity for concealing it from M. Stangerson, to whom it might have dealt a mortal blow. I will pass over his amazement when he beheld us upon the platform of the station at Lyons. Mathilde explained to him that on account of a serious accident, which had closed the line at Culoz, we had decided, since a change of plans had to be made, that we would join him, and to spend a few days with him at the home of Arthur Rance and his young wife, as we had before been entreated to do by this faithful friend of ours."

At this time, it might be well for me to interrupt M. Darzac's narrative to recall to the memory of the reader of "The Mystery of the Yellow Room" the fact that M. Arthur William Rance had for many years cherished a hopeless devotion for Mlle. Stangerson, but had at last overcome it, and married a beautiful American girl, who knew nothing of the mysterious adventures of the Professor's daughter.

After the affair at the Glandier, and while Mlle. Stangerson was still a patient in a private asylum near Paris, where the treatment restored her to health and reason, we heard one fine day that M. Arthur William Rance was about to wed the niece of an old professor of geology at the Academy of Science in Philadelphia.

Those who had known of his luckless passion for Mathilde, and had gauged its depths by the excess with which it was displayed (for it had seemed at one time to rob the man of sense and reason and turn him into a maniac)—such persons, I say, believed that Rance was marrying in desperation, and prophesied little happiness for the union. Stories were told that the match—which was a good one for Arthur Rance, for Miss Edith Prescott was rich—had been brought about in a rather singular fashion. But these are stories which I may tell at some future time. You will learn then by what chain of circumstances the Rances had been led to locate at Rochers Rouges in the old castle, on the peninsula of Hercules, of which they had become the owners the preceding autumn.

But at present I must give place to M. Darzac, who continued his story, as follows:

"When we had given these explanations to M. Stangerson, my wife and I saw that he seemed to understand very little of what we had said, and that, instead of being glad to have us with him again, he appeared very mournful. Mathilde tried in vain to seem happy. Her father saw that something had happened since we had left him which we were concealing from him. Mathilde began to talk of the ceremony of the morning, and in that way the conversation came around to you, my young friend"—and again M. Darzac addressed himself to Rouletabille—"and I took the occasion to say to M. Stangerson that since your vacation was just beginning at the time that we were all going to Mentone, you might be pleased with an invitation that would give you the chance of spending your holiday in our society. There was, I said, plenty of room at Rochers Rouges, and I was certain that M. Arthur Rance and his bride would extend to you a cordial welcome. While I was speaking, Mathilde looked gratefully at me and pressed my hand tenderly with an effusion which showed me what gladness she was experiencing at the proposition. Thus it happened that when we reached Valence, I had M. Stangerson write the dispatch which you must have received. All night long we did not sleep. While her father rested in his compartments next to ours, Mathilde opened my travelling bag and took out my revolver. She requested me to put it in my overcoat pocket, saying: 'If *he* should attack us, you must defend yourself.' Ah, what a night we passed! We kept silence, each attempting to deceive the other into the belief that we were resting, our eyes closed, with the light burning full force, for we did not dare to sit in the darkness. The doors of our compartment were locked and bolted, but yet, every moment, we dreaded to see *his* face appear. When we heard a step in the corridor, our hearts beat wildly. We seemed to recognize it. And Mathilde had put a cover over the mirror, for fear of glancing toward it and seeing the reflection of that face again. 'Had he followed us?' 'Could we have been mistaken?' 'Would we escape from him?' 'Had he gone on to Culoz on the train which we had left?' 'Could we hope for any such good fortune?' For my own part, I did not believe that we could. And she—she! Ah, how my heart bled for her, wrapped in a silence like that of death, sitting there in her corner. I knew how she was weighed down by despair and agony—how far more unhappy she was even than myself, because of the misery which it seemed to be her lot to bring upon those whom she loved most dearly. I longed to console her, to comfort her, but I found no words. And when once I attempted to speak, she made a gesture so full of misery and desolation that I realised that I would be far kinder if I kept silence. Then, like her, I closed my eyes."

This was M. Darzac's story, although I have shortened it in a certain degree. We felt, Rouletabille and myself, that the narrative was so important that we both resolved on arriving at Mentone, that we would write it down from memory as faithfully as possible. We did as we agreed, and where our versions did not agree, or halted a little, we submitted them to M. Darzac, who made a few unimportant changes, after which the story read just as I have given it here.

The rest of the journey taken by the Darzacs and M. Stangerson presented no incident worthy of note. At the station of Mentone Garavan, they found M. Arthur Rance, who was astonished at beholding the bride and bridegroom; but when he was told that they intended to spend a few days with him, and to accept the invitation which M. Darzac, under various pretexts, had always declined, he was delighted, and declared that his wife would be as glad as himself. He was pleased, too, to learn that Rouletabille might soon join the party. M. Arthur Rance had not, even after his marriage to Miss Edith Prescott, been able to overcome the extreme reserve with which M. Darzac had always treated him. When, during his last trip to San Remo, the young Professor of the Sorbonne had been urged in passing to make a visit at the Château Hercules, he had made his excuses in the most ceremonious manner. But when he met Rance in the station at Mentone Garavan, M. Darzac greeted him most cordially, and complimented him upon his appearance, saying that the air of the country seemed to agree with him perfectly.

We have seen how the apparition of Larsan in the station at Bourg had overthrown all the plans of M. and Mme. Darzac, and had completely overwhelmed them both with grief and consternation, and had made them turn to the Rances' home as to a refuge, casting them, figuratively speaking, into the arms of these people who were not especially congenial to them, but whom they believed to be honest, loyal and willing to protect them. We know that M. Stangerson, to whom nothing had been told of what had occurred, was beginning to suspect something, and we know that all three of the party had called Rouletabille to their aid. It was a veritable panic. And, so far as M. Darzac was concerned, the terror which he felt was increased by news brought to us by M. Arthur Rance when he met us at Nice. But before this there had occurred a little incident which I cannot pass by in silence. As soon as we reached the Nice station, I had jumped from the train and hurried into the telegraph office to ask whether there was any message for me. A dispatch was handed to me, and, without opening it, I went back to M. Darzac and Rouletabille.

"Read this!" I said to the young reporter.

Rouletabille opened the envelope and read:

"Brignolles has not been away from Paris since April 6th. This is an absolute certainty."

Rouletabille looked at me for a moment and then said:

"Well, what does this amount to, now that you have it? What did you suspect, anyway?"

"It was at Dijon," I rejoined, vexed at the attitude of the lad toward the affair, "that the idea came to me that Brignolles might be in some way concerned in the misfortunes that seem to be crowding upon us, and of which warning was given by the telegrams that you received. I wired one of my friends to make inquiries for me in regard to the movements of the fellow during the last few days. I was anxious to learn whether he had left Paris."

"Well," said Rouletabille. "You have your inquiries answered. Are you willing to admit now that Brignolles is not and has never been Larsan in disguise?"

"I never thought of any such thing as that!" I exclaimed with some vexation, for I suspected that Rouletabille was laughing at me.

The truth was that the idea, absurd as it was, had actually entered my mind.

"Will you never stop thinking ill of poor Brignolles?" asked M. Darzac, with a sad smile at me. "He is quiet and shy, I grant you, but he is a good lad, just the same."

"That's where we differ," I retorted.

And I retired to my own corner of the railway carriage. In general my personal intuitions in regard to things were poor enough guides compared to the wonderful insight of Rouletabille, but in this case, we were to receive proof, only a few days later, that even if the personality of Brignolles were not another of Larsan's disguises, the laboratory assistant was nevertheless a miserable wretch. And this time both M. Darzac and Rouletabille begged my pardon and paid their respects to my despised intuitions. But there is no use of anticipating. If I mention this incident here, it is for the purpose of showing to how great an extent I was haunted by the image of Larsan, hiding under some new form, and lurking unknown among us. Dear Heaven! Larsan had so often proved his talent—I may even say his genius—in this respect, that I felt that he was quite capable of defying us now, and of mingling with us while we thought that he was a stranger—or, perhaps, even a friend.

I was soon to change my ideas, however, and to believe that this time Ballmeyer had altered his usual tactics, and the unexpected arrival of M. Arthur Rance was to go far in leading me to this opinion. Instead of hiding himself, the bandit was showing himself openly—at least, to some of us—with an audacity that staggered belief. After all, what had he to fear in this part of the country? He was well aware that neither M. Darzac nor his wife would be likely to denounce him, nor, consequently, would their friends do so. His bold revelation of his presence seemed to have but one end in view—that of ruining the happiness of the couple who had believed that his death had opened the way for their marriage. But an objection arose to that conjecture. Why should he have chosen such a means of vengeance? Would it not have been a better plan to let himself be seen before the marriage had taken place? He would certainly have prevented it by so doing. Yes, but in that case, he would have found it necessary to appear in his own person in Paris. But when had any thought of danger or risk been able to deter Larsan from an undertaking upon which he had determined? Who dared affirm that he knew of one such case?

But now let me tell you of the news brought by Arthur Rance when he joined the three of us on the train at Nice. Rance, of course, knew nothing of what had happened at Bourg, nothing of the appearing of Larsan to Mme. Darzac on the train and to her husband in the station, but he brought alarming tidings. If we had retained the slightest hope that we had lost Larsan on the road to Culoz, Rance's words obliterated it, for he, too, had seen the man whom we so feared, face to face. And he had come to warn us, before we reached his home, so that we might decide upon some plan of action.

"When we were about to return home after having taken you to the station," said Rance to Darzac.; "after the train had pulled out, your wife, M. Stangerson and myself thought that we would leave the carriage for a little while and take a stroll on the promenade walk. M. Stangerson gave his arm to his daughter. I was at the right of M. Stangerson, who, therefore, was walking between the two of us. Suddenly, as we paused for a moment near a sort of public garden to let a tramcar pass, I brushed against a man who said to me, 'I beg your pardon, sir.' The sound of the voice made me tremble and I knew as well beforehand as I did when I raised my head that it was Larsan. The voice was the voice I had heard at the Court of Assizes. He cast a long, calm look upon the three of us. I do not know how I was able to restrain the exclamation which rose to my lips,—how I kept from crying aloud his miserable name! Happily M. Stangerson and Mme. Darzac had not seen him and I hurried them rapidly away. I made them walk around the garden and listen to the music in the park and then we returned to where the carriage was waiting. Upon the sidewalk in front of the station, there was Larsan again! I do not know—I cannot understand how M. Stangerson and Mme. Darzac could have helped but see him—"

"Are you sure that they did not see him?" interrupted Robert Darzac.

"Absolutely sure. I feigned a sudden attack of illness. We got into the carriage and ordered the coachman to drive as fast as he could. The man was still standing on the sidewalk, staring after us with his cold, cruel eyes when we drove away."

"And are you certain that my wife did not see him?" repeated Darzac, who was growing more and more agitated.

"Certain, I assure you."

"But, Good God, M. Darzac!" interposed Rouletabille. "How long do you think you can deceive your wife as to the fact that Larsan has reappeared and that she actually saw him? If you imagine that you can keep her in ignorance for very long, you are greatly mistaken."

"But," replied Darzac, "while we were ending our journey, the idea that she had been the victim of a delusion seemed to grow in her mind and by the time we reached Garavan, she seemed to be quite calm."

"At the time you reached Garavan," said Rouletabille, quietly, "your wife sent me the telegram I am going to ask you to read."

And the reporter held out to M. Darzac the paper which bore the two words, "Save us."

M. Darzac read it with the blood seeming to die away from his face as we looked at him.

"She will go mad again," was all that he said.

That was what he dreaded—all of us—and, strangely enough, when we arrived at the station of Mentone Garavan and found M. Stangerson and Mme. Darzac (who were awaiting us in spite of the promise which the Professor had made to Arthur Rance not to leave Rochers Rouges nor allow his daughter to do so until we came, for reasons which their host said he would tell them later, not being able to invent them on the spur of the moment) it was with a phrase which seemed the echo of our terror that Mme. Darzac greeted Rouletabille. As soon as she perceived the young man, she rushed toward him and it seemed to us that she was making a great effort not to throw her arms around him. I saw that her spirit was clinging to him as a shipwrecked sailor grips at the hand which is stretched out to save him from drowning. And I heard the words that she whispered to him:

"I know that I am going mad!"

As to Rouletabille, I may have seen his face as pale before, but I had never seen it look like that of a man stricken with his death blow.

VI

THE FORT OF HERCULES

When he alights at the Garavan station, whatever may be the season of the year in which he visits that enchanted country, the traveller might almost fancy himself in the Garden of Hesperides whose golden apples excited the desire of the conqueror of the Nemean lion. I might not perhaps, however, have recalled to mind the son of Jupiter and Alcmene merely because of the numerous lemon and orange trees which in the balmy air let their ripened fruit hang heavily on their boughs if everything about the scene had not spoken of his mythological glories and his fabled promenade upon these fair shores. You remember how the Phoenicians in transporting their penates to the shadow of the rocks which were one day to become the abode of the Grimaldi, gave to the little port in which they anchored and to other natural features all along the shore—a mountain, a cape, and an islet—the name of Hercules whom they looked upon as their god—the name which they have always retained. But I like to fancy that the Phoenicians found the name here already, and indeed, if the divinities, fatigued by the white dust of the roads of Hellas, went to seek for a marvellous spot, warm and perfumed, to rest after their strenuous adventures, they could not have found a more beautiful scene. The gods, to my mind, were the first tourists of the Riviera. The Garden of the Hesperides was nowhere else and Hercules had made the place ready for his Olympian comrades by destroying the evil dragon with an hundred heads who wanted to keep the azure shore for himself, all alone. And I am not at all certain that the bones of the ancient elephant discovered a few years ago in the neighbourhood of Rochers Rouges were not those of the dragon himself!

When, after alighting from the train, we came in silence to the bank of the sea, our eyes were immediately struck by a dazzling silhouette of a castle standing upon the peninsula of Hercules, which the works accomplished on the frontier have, alas, nearly destroyed. The oblique rays of the sun which were falling upon the walls and the old Square Tower made the reflection of the tower glisten in the waters like a breastplate. The tower seemed to stand guard like an old sentinel, over the Bay of Garavan which lay before us like a blue lake of fire. And as we advanced nearer, the tower gleaming in the water seemed to grow longer. The sky behind us leaned toward the crest of the mountains; the promontories to the west were already wrapped in clouds at the approach of night and by the time we crossed the threshold of the actual structure the castle in the water was only a menacing hade.

Upon the lower steps of the stairway which led up to one of the towers, we beheld a slender, charming figure. It was Arthur Rance's wife, who had been the beautiful and brilliant Edith Prescott. Certainly the Bride of Lammermoor was not more pale on the day when the black-eyed stranger from Ravenswood first crossed her path, O Edith! Ah, when one wishes to present a romantic figure in a mediaeval frame, the figure of a princess, lost in dreams, plaintive and melancholy, one should not have such eyes, my lady! And your hair was as black as the raven's wing. Such colouring is not of the kind which one is used to attribute to the angels. Are you an angel, Edith? Is this gentle, plaintive little manner natural or acquired? Is the sweet expression that your face wears today an entirely truthful one? Pardon that I ask you all these questions, Edith; but when I beheld you for the first time, after having been entranced by the delicate harmony of your white figure, standing motionless upon the stone stair, I followed the quick, lowering glance of your dark eyes in the direction of the daughter of Professor Stangerson, and it had a cruel look which accorded ill with the sweet tones of your voice and the bright smile on your lips.

The voice of the young wife was her greatest charm although the grace of her entire being was perfect. At the introductions which were, of course, performed by her husband, she greeted us in the simplest and sweetest fashion imaginable—the fashion of the ideal hostess. Rouletabille and myself made an effort to tell her that we had intended to look for a stopping place in the village instead of trespassing upon her hospitality. She made a delicious little grimace, lifted her shoulders with a gesture that was almost childish, said that our rooms were all ready for us and changed the subject.

"Come, come! You haven't seen the château. You must see it—all of you. Oh, I will show you "la Louve" another time. It is the only gloomy corner in the place. It is horrible—so cold and dismal. It makes me shiver. But, do you know I love to shiver! Oh, M. Rouletabille, you'll tell me stories that will make me shiver someday, won't you?"

And chattering thus, she glided in front of us in her white gown. She walked like an actress. She made a singularly pretty picture in this garden of the Orient, between the threatening old tower and the carved stone flowers of the ruined chapel. The vast court which we were crossing was so completely covered on every side with grass, shrubs and foliage plants, with cactus and aloes, mountain laurel, wild roses and marguerites that one might have sworn that an eternal spring had found its habitation in this enclosure, formerly the drilling ground of the château when the soldiers assembled in time of war. This court, through the help of the winds of heaven and the neglect of man had naturally become a garden, a beautiful wild garden in which one saw that the chatelaine had interfered as little as possible and which she had in no way attempted to restore to the beaten track. Behind all this verdure and this wealth of bloom one could see the most exquisite sight which could be imagined in dead architecture. Figure to yourself the perfect arches of gothic brought up to the doors of the old Roman chapel; the pillars twined with climbing plants, rose geranium and vervain uniting their sweet perfume and raising to the azure heavens their broken arch, which nothing seems to support. There is no longer a roof on the chapel. And there are no more walls. There remains of it only the bit of lace work in stone, which a miracle of equilibrium keeps suspended in the air.

And at our left is the immense tower of the Twelfth Century, which, Mme. Edith tells us, the natives call "la Louve" and which nothing—neither time, nor man, nor peace, nor war, nor cannon, nor tempest has ever been able to destroy. It is just as it appeared in 1107, when the Saracens, who sowed devastation in their wake, were able to make no headway in their attacks upon the château of Hercules,—just as it was seen by Salageri and his corsairs of Genoa, when, after they had seised the fort and the Square Tower and even the castle itself, it resisted attack and its defenders held it until the arrival of the troops of the Princes of Provence, who delivered them. It was there that Mme. Edith had chosen to have her own rooms.

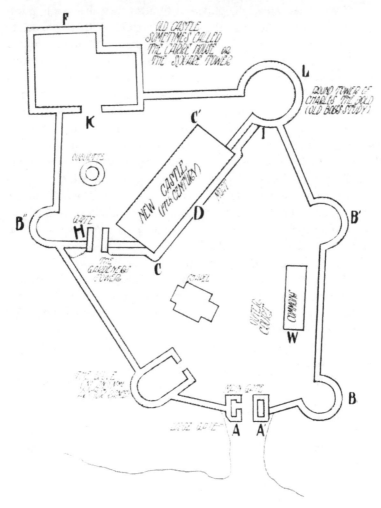

The Plan of the Fort of Hercules

But while she spoke to us in her sweet, clear voice, I stopped looking at the objects around us to look at the people. Arthur Rance was gazing at Mme. Darzac, when my eyes fell upon them, and Rouletabille seemed to be lost in thought, and far, far away from us all. M. Darzac and M. Stangerson were talking in low tones. The same thought was filling the minds of each one of these people—both those who kept silence and those who, if they spoke, were careful to say nothing which could give a clue to the thoughts. We reached the postern. "This is what we call the Gardener's Tower," said Edith, childishly. "From this gate one may see all the fort, and all the castle, both north and south. See!"

And she stretched her arms wide to emphasize her words.

"Every stone has its history. I'll tell them to you some day, if you are good."

"How gay Edith is!" murmured her husband. I thought to myself that she was the only one who was gay in the party.

We had passed through the postern and found ourselves in another court. Opposite us was the old donjon. Its appearance was more than impressive. It was high and square, and it was on account of its shape that it was known as the Square Tower. And, as this tower occupies the most important corner of the fortification, it was also known as the Corner Tower. It was the most extraordinary and the most important part of this agglomeration of defensive works. The walls were heavier and higher than those anywhere else, and half way up they were still sealed with the Roman cement with which Caesar's own columns had welded together the stones.

"That tower yonder, in the opposite corner," went on Edith, "is the Tower of Charles the Bold, so called because he was the Duke who furnished the plans when it became necessary to transform the defences of the château, so as to make them resist the attacks of the artillery. Don't you think I am very learned? Old Bob has made this tower his study. It is too bad, for we might have a magnificent dining hall there. But I have never been able to refuse old Bob anything he wanted. Old Bob," she added, with a charming smile, "is my uncle—that is the name he taught me to call him by when I was a little thing. He is not here just now. He went to Paris on the five o'clock train, but he will be back tomorrow. He is going to compare some of the anatomical specimens which he found at Rochers Rouges with those in the Museum of Natural History in Paris. Ah—here is an oubliette!"

And she showed us in the centre part of the second court a small shaft, which she called, romantically, an oubliette, and above which a eucalyptus tree, with its white blossoms and its leafless limbs, leaned like a woman over a fountain.

Since we had entered the second court, we understood better—or at least I did, for Rouletabille, every moment more deeply lost in his own thoughts, seemed neither to see nor to hear—the topographical plan of the Fort of Hercules. As this plan is of the greatest importance in the proper understanding of the incredible events which were to occur so soon after our arrival at Rochers Rouges, I shall place at once before the eyes of the reader the general scheme of the buildings as it was traced later by Rouletabille and myself.

The castle had been built in 1140 by the Seigneurs of Mortola. In order to isolate it completely from the land, they had not hesitated to make an island of the peninsula by cutting away the narrow isthmus which connected it with the mainland. Upon the mainland itself, they had built a barricade in the form of a semicircular fortification, designed to protect the approaches to the drawbridge and the two entrance towers. Not a trace of this fortification was left. And the isthmus, in the course of the centuries, had again resumed its old form, the drawbridge had been thrown down and the trenches had filled up. The walls of the Château of Hercules followed the outline of the peninsula, which was that of an irregular hexagon. The walls were built upon the rocks, and the latter, in some places, extended over the waters in such a manner that a little ship might have taken shelter beneath them, fearing no enemy, while it was protected by this natural ceiling. This design of building was marvellously well adapted for defence, and gave the inmates of the fortress little reason to fear an attack, no matter from what quarter it might come.

The fort was entered by way of the north gate, which guarded the two towers, A and A', connected by a passageway. These towers which had suffered greatly during the last sieges of the Genoese, had been repaired to some slight extent some time afterward, and had, shortly before we came to Rochers Rouges, been made habitable by Mrs. Rance, who used them as servants' quarters. The front of the tower A served as the keeper's lodge. A little door opened in the side of the tower upon the passageway, and enabled anyone looking out to observe all those who came or went. A heavy double door of oak, with bands of iron, was no longer in use, its twin portals having stood for uncounted years open against the inner walls of the two towers, on account of the difficulty which had been experienced in managing them; and the entrance to the castle was only closed by a little gate, which anyone might open at will. This entrance was the only one by which it was possible to get into the château. As I have said, in passing through this gate, one found himself in the first court, closed in on all sides by the walls and the towers. These walls were by no means as high as when they were built. The old high courtyards which connected the towers had been rased to the ground and replaced by a sort of circular boulevard, from which one mounted toward the first court by means of a little terrace. The boulevards were still crowned by a parapet. For the changes which I have described took place in the Fifteenth Century, at the time when every lord of the manor was obliged to consider the possibility of being obliged to meet an attack of artillery. As to the towers B, B' and B", which had for a considerable time longer preserved their uniformity and their first height, and the pointed roofs of which had been replaced by a platform designed to support the artillery, they had later been rased to the height of the boulevard parapets, and their shape seemed almost like that of a half moon. These alterations had taken place in the Seventeenth Century, at the time of the construction of a modern castle, still known as the New Castle, although it had been in ruins for years when we first saw it. The New Castle on the plan is at C C'.

Upon the flat platform roofs of these old towers—roofs which were surrounded by a parapet—palm trees had been planted, which had thriven ill, swept as they were by the sea winds and burned by the sun. When one leaned over the circular parapet which surrounded the whole domain, it seemed to him as though the château were still as completely closed in as it was in the days when the courtyards reached to the second stories of the old towers. "La Louve," as I have said, had not been changed at all, but still reared its dark hulk against the blue waters of the Mediterranean, a strange, weird figure, looking thousands of years old. I have spoken also of the ruins of the chapel. The ancient commons (shown on the map by W), near the parapet between B and B', had been transformed into the stables and the kitchens.

I am describing now all the anterior portion of the Château of Hercules. One could only penetrate into the second enclosure through the postern (indicated by H), which Mrs. Arthur Rance called "the tower of the gardener," and which was actually only a pavilion, formerly defended by the tower B", and by another tower situated at C, and which had entirely disappeared at the time of the erection of the New Castle (shown at C C'). A moat and a wall started from B" to abut on I at the Tower of Charles the Bold, advancing at C in the form of a spur to the midst of the first court, and entirely isolating the court, which they completely closed in. The moat still exists, wide and deep, but the walls had been torn down all the length of the New Castle and replaced by the walls of the castle itself. A central door at D, now condemned, opened upon a bridge, which had been thrown over the moat, and which formerly permitted direct communication with the outer court.

But this bridge had been torn down or was swallowed up in the waters, and as the windows of the castle, rising high above the moat, were still guarded by their heavy iron bars, one might readily believe that the inner court still remained as impenetrable as when it was entirely shut in by its enclosing walls at the time when the New Castle did not exist.

The pavement of the inner court—the Court of Charles the Bold, as the old guide books of the country call it still—was a little higher than that of the outer court. The rocks formed there a very high seat, a natural pedestal of that colossal black column, the Old Castle, standing square and erect, as though it had been carved from a single block of stone, stretching its awesome shadow over the blue waters. One could only penetrate into the Old Castle (designated by F) by a little door, K. The old inhabitants of the country never spoke of it except as the Square Tower, to distinguish it from the Round Tower, or the Tower of Charles the Bold, as they sometimes called the latter. A parapet similar to the one which closed in the outer court was built between the towers B", F and L, closing the inner court as firmly as the outer.

We have seen that the Round Tower had been in years past torn down to half its former height, as it had been built by the Mortola, according to plans drawn by Charles the Bold himself, to whom the Seigneur had been of some service in the Helvetian war. This tower had a number of tiny chambers above, and an immense octagon chamber below. One descended into this chamber by a steep and narrow stairway. The ceiling of the octagon room was supported by four great cylindrical pillars, and from its walls opened three enormous embrasures for three enormous cannons. It was of this room that Mme. Edith had wished to make a dining room, for it was in an admirable state of preservation, on account of the thickness of the walls, and the light could still penetrate through the great windows, which had been enlarged and made square, although they, too, were still guarded by barriers of iron. This tower (shown on the map at L) was the spot chosen by Mme. Edith's uncle for a workshop, and the abiding place of his collection. Its roof was a beautiful little garden, to which the mistress of the domain had had transported fertile soil and wonderful plants and flowers. I have marked upon the map in array all the portions of the buildings which Mme. Edith had restored, improved and put in shape for habitation.

Of the château of the Seventeenth Century, known as the New Castle, they had only repaired two bed chambers on the first floor and a little sitting room for guests. It was to these that Rouletabille and myself were assigned, while M. and Mme. Robert Darzac were lodged in the Square Tower, of which I shall have to give a more special description.

Two rooms, the windows of which opened upon the balcony, were reserved in this Square Tower for "Old Bob," who slept there. M. Stangerson was upon the first floor of "la Louve," in the rear of the suite occupied by the Rances.

Mme. Edith herself showed us to our rooms. She made us cross over the sunken ceilings of ruined apartments, over broken railings and tumble-down walls; but here and there some mouldy hangings, a broken statue or a ragged bit of tapestry, bore witness to the ancient splendors of the New Castle, born of the fantasies of some Mortola of the wonderful Seventeenth Century. But when we reached them, our little rooms recalled to us nothing of that magnificent past. They had been swept and garnished with a care that was almost touching. Clean and hygienic, without carpets, hangings or upholstered chairs, furnished in the simplest of modern styles, they pleased us very much. As I have already said, the two sleeping rooms were separated by a little parlour.

As I tied my cravat, after dressing for dinner, I called Rouletabille to ask him if he were ready. There was no answer. I went into his room and discovered with surprise that he had already gone out. I went to the window of his room, which opened like my own upon the court of Charles the Bold. The court was empty, inhabited only by a large eucalyptus, the fragrance of which mounted to my nostrils. Above the parapet of the boulevard I saw the vast stretch of the silent waters. The blue of the sea had grown dark at the fall of evening, and the shades of night were visible on the horizon of the Italian shore, reaching already to the pointe d'Ospedaletti. Not a sound, not a breath on the land or in the heavens! I have never yet noticed such a silence and such a complete repose of nature except at the moment which precedes the most violent storms and the unchaining of the elements. But now I felt that we had nothing of the sort to fear. The whole appearance of the night was of the calmest, most serene beauty—

But what was that dark shadow? From whence had come that spectre which glided over the waters? Standing erect at the prow of a little boat which a fisherman was rowing, keeping rhythmic time with the two oars, I recognised the form of Larsan. Why should I try to deceive myself by saying even for one moment that I was wrong? He was only too easily to be recognised. And if those who beheld him should have had the slightest doubt as to his identity, he seemed to desire to set it entirely at rest by this open display of himself, utterly without disguise, as entirely convincing as though he had shouted aloud, "It is I!"

Oh, yes! it was he! It was "the great Fred," as we used to call him when we looked upon him only as the wonderfully resourceful and brilliant Secret Service agent. The boat, silent, with its motionless statue at the prow, rowed completely around the peninsula. It passed beneath the windows of the Square Tower and then directed its course to the shores of the Pointe de Garibaldi. And the man still stood erect, his arms folded, his face turned toward the tower, a diabolical apparition on the threshold of the night, which slowly crept up behind him, enveloped him in its shades and carried him away.

When he had vanished, I lowered my eyes and beheld two figures in the court of Charles the Bold. They were at the corner of the railing near the little door of the Square Tower. One of these forms—the taller—was supporting the other and speaking in tones of entreaty. The smaller attempted to break away—one would have said that it wished to throw itself into the sea. And I heard the voice of Mme. Darzac say:

"Be careful. It is a gage of defiance which he has thrown down. You shall not leave me this evening."

And then came Rouletabille's voice answering:

"He must land upon the bank! Let me hurry to the bank."

"What will you do there?" moaned Mathilde.

"Whatever may be necessary."

And then Mathilde spoke again, and her voice was terrible to hear.

"I forbid you to touch that man!"

And I heard no more.

I descended to the court, where I found Rouletabille alone, seated upon the edge of the oubliette. I spoke to him, but he did not answer. I felt no surprise, for this had often happened of late. I went on into the outer court, and I saw M. Darzac coming toward me, evidently in the greatest excitement. Before I came up to him, he called out:

"Did you see him?"

"Yes, I saw him," I replied.

"And she—my wife—do you know whether she saw him?"

"She saw him, too. She was with Rouletabille when he passed. What bravado the creature showed!"

Robert Darzac was trembling like an aspen leaf from the shock which he had just experienced. He told me that as soon as he had caught sight of the boat and its passenger, he had rushed like a madman to the shore, but that before he had reached the Pointe de Garibaldi the bark had disappeared as if by enchantment. But even before he finished speaking, Darzac left me and hurried away to seek Mathilde, dreading the thought of the state of mind in which he felt that he would find her. But he returned almost immediately, gloomy and grieved. The door of his wife's apartment was locked, and she had said to him that she wished to be alone for awhile.

"And Rouletabille?" I asked.

"I have not seen him."

We remained together upon the rampart gazing at the night which had carried Larsan away. Robert Darzac was infinitely sorrowful. In order to change the direction of his thoughts, I asked him a few questions regarding the Rance household. Here is in substance the information which I succeeded in extracting from him little by little:

After the trial at Versailles, Arthur Rance had returned to Philadelphia, and there, one evening, at a family dinner party, he had found himself seated beside a charming young girl, who had interested him at once by a display of interest in literature and art, the like of which he had not often seen in his beautiful countrywomen. She was not in the least like the quick, independent and audacious type of young women who are often found in America, nor was she of the "Fluffy Ruffles" variety, so much in favour at present. Somewhat haughty in mien, yet gentle and melancholy, she at once recalled to the young man the heroines of Walter Scott, who he soon learned was her favourite author. From the first, she attracted him strongly. How could this delicate little creature so quickly have impressed Arthur Rance, who had been madly in love with the majestic Mathilde? Of such are the mysteries of the heart. Now, fortunately or unfortunately, as you prefer, Arthur Rance had upon that evening so far forgotten himself as to drink considerably more wine than was good for him. He never realised what his offense had been, but he knew that he must have committed some frightful blunder or breach of politeness, when Miss Edith in a low voice and with heightened colour, requested him not to address her again. Upon the morrow, Arthur Rance went to call on the young lady and entreated her pardon, swearing that he would never permit wine to pass his lips again.

Arthur Rance had already known for some time Miss Prescott's uncle, the fine old man who still bore among his friends the nickname of "Old Bob," which had been given him in his college days, and who was as celebrated for his adventures as an explorer as for his discoveries as a geologist. He seemed as gentle as a sheep, but he had hunted many a tiger through the pampas of South America. He had spent half his life south of the Rio Negro among the Patagonians, in seeking for the man of the tertiary period—or, at least, for his fossils, not as the anthropological relic or some other pithecanthropus, approaching in a greater or less extent the race of monkeys, but as the real living man, stronger, more powerful, than those who inhabit this planet in our own day—the man, to speak clearly, who must have been contemporaneous with the immense mammoths and mastodons, which appeared upon the globe before the quarternary epoch. He generally returned from these expeditions with closely filled notebooks and a respectable collection of tibias and femurs, which may or may not have belonged to the aboriginal man, and also with a rich display of skins of wild beasts, which showed that the spectacled old savant knew how to use more modern arms than the stone ax and bow and arrow. As soon as he was back in Philadelphia, he would dispose of his treasures either in his private cabinets or in those of the Museum, and, opening his notebooks, would resume his lectures, amusing himself as he talked by making the splinters from the long pencils, which he was always sharpening but had never been seen to use, fly almost into the eyes of the students on the front benches. All these details were given me later by Arthur Rance himself. He had been one of "Old Bob's" pupils, but had not seen him in many years until he made the acquaintance of Miss Edith. If I have seemed to dwell too minutely on such apparently unimportant things, I have done so because, by quite a natural train of events, we were to make "Old Bob's" acquaintance at Rochers Rouges.

Miss Edith, upon the occasion when Arthur Rance had been presented to her and had forgotten himself on account of overindulgence in wine, had seemed somewhat more melancholy than she usually was, because she had received disquieting news of her uncle. The latter for four years back had been absent on a trip to Patagonia. In his last letter, he had told his niece that he was ill, and that he feared that he should not live to see her again. One might be tempted to wonder why so tender-hearted a niece, under such circumstances, had not refrained from attending a dinner, no matter how quiet, but Miss Edith, during her uncle's many absences from home, had so frequently received such communications from him and had afterward seen him return in such perfect health that she could scarcely be blamed for not having remained at home to mourn that evening. Three months later, however, laying received another letter, she suddenly resolved to go all alone to South America and join her uncle. During those three months important events had transpired. Miss Edith had been touched by the remorse of Arthur Rance, and when Miss Prescott departed for Patagonia, no one was astonished to find that "Old Bob's" old pupil was going to accompany her. If the engagement was not officially announced, it was because the pair preferred to wait for the consent of the geologist. Miss Edith and Arthur Rance were met at St. Louis by the young woman's uncle. He was in excellent health and in a charming humour. Rance, who had not seen him in years, declared to him that he had grown younger—the easiest of compliments to pay and the pleasantest to receive. When his niece informed him of her engagement to this fine young fellow, the uncle manifested the greatest delight. The three returned to Philadelphia, where the wedding took place. Miss Edith had never been in France, and Arthur determined that their honeymoon should be spent there. And it was thus that they found, as will be told a little later, a scientific reason for locating in the neighbourhood of Mentone, not exactly in France, but an hundred meters from the frontier, in Italy, at Rochers Rouges.

The gong had sounded for dinner, and Arthur Rance was coming to look for us, so we repaired to "la Louve," in the lower hall of which we were to dine. When we were all assembled (save "Old Bob," who, as has been mentioned, was absent), Mme. Edith asked whether any of us had noticed a little boat which had made the circle of the fortress, and in which a man was standing erect. The man's strange attitude had struck her, she said. No one replied, and she added:

"Oh, I know who it is, for I know the fisherman who rowed the boat. He is a great friend of Old Bob."

"Ah, then you know the fisherman, madame?" asked Rouletabille.

"He comes to the castle sometimes to sell fish. The people around the village have given him an odd name, which I don't know how to say in their impossible patois, but I can translate it. They call him, 'the hangman of the sea.' A pretty name, isn't it?"

VII

Which Tells of Some Precautions Taken By Joseph Rouletabille to Defend the Fort of Hercules Against the Attack of an Enemy

Rouletabille had not even the politeness to inquire into the explanation of this amazing sobriquet. He appeared to be plunged in the deepest meditation. A strange dinner! a strange castle! strange guests! All the graces and coquetries of Mme. Edith had no effect in awakening us to any semblance of life. There were two newly married pairs, four lovers, who ought to have been radiant with the joy of life, and to have made the hours pass gayly and happily. But the repast was one of the most gloomy at which I have ever been present. The spectre of Larsan hovered about our festivities, and it seemed almost as though the man whom we knew to be so near was actually among us.

It is as well to say here that Professor Stangerson, since he had learned the cruel, the miserable truth, had not for one moment been able to free himself from the thought of it. I do not think that I am saying too much in declaring that the first victim of the affair at the Glandier, and the most unfortunate of all, was this good old man. He had lost everything—his faith in science, his love of work, and—more bitter than all the rest—his belief in his daughter. His faith in her had been his religion. She had been such an object of joy and pride. He had thought of her for so many years as a vestal virgin, seeking, with him, the unknown in the world of higher things. He had been so marvellously dazzled with the thought of her angelic purity, and had believed that her reason for having remained unmarried was that she was unwilling to resign herself to any life which would withdraw her from science and her father, to both of which she had dedicated her existence. And while he was thinking of her almost with reverence, he discovered that the reason that his daughter refused to marry was because she was already the wife of Ballmeyer. The day in which Mathilde had decided to confess everything to her father, and to tell him the story of the past, which must clear up the present with a tragic light to the eyes of the professor, already warned by the mysteries of the Glandier—the day when, falling at his feet and embracing his knees, she had told him the story of her youth, Professor Stangerson had raised the form of his beloved child from the ground and had pressed her to his heart; he had placed a kiss of pardon on her brow: he had mingled his tears with the sobs of her whose fault had been so bitterly expiated, and he had sworn to her that she had never been more precious than since he had known how she had suffered. And by these words, she was a little comforted. But he, when she left his presence, was another man—a man alone, all alone—. Professor Stangerson had lost his daughter and his goddess.

He had experienced only indifference in regard to her marriage to Robert Darzac, although the latter had been the best beloved of his pupils. In vain Mathilde, with the warmest tenderness, had endeavoured to rekindle the old feeling in the heart of her father. She knew well that he had changed toward her, that his glance never dwelt upon her in the old fond way, and that his weary eyes were looking back into the past at an image which he had only dreamed was her own. And she knew, too, that when those eyes rested upon her—upon her, Mathilde Darzac—it was to see at her side, not the honoured figure of a good man and tender husband, but the shadow, eternally living, eternally infamous, of the other—the man who had stolen his daughter. The Professor could work no longer. The great secret of the dissolution of matter which he had promised to reveal to mankind, had returned to the unknown from which, for a moment, the scientist had drawn it, and men will go on, repeating for centuries to come the imbecile phrase, "From nothing, nothing."

The evening meal was rendered still more doleful by the setting in which it was served—the sombre hall, lighted by a gothic lamp, with old candelabra of wrought iron, and the walls of the fortress adorned with oriental tapestries, against which were ranged the old suits of armour dating back to the first Saracen invasion and the sieges of Dagobert.

I looked at the members of the party, and it seemed to me that I was able to see reason enough for the general sadness. M. and Mme. Darzac were seated beside each other. The mistress of the house had evidently not desired to separate a bridal pair, whose union only dated back to yesterday. Of the two, I must say that the more unhappy looking was, beyond a doubt, our friend, Robert. He never spoke one word. Mme. Darzac joined to some extent in the conversation, exchanging now and then a few commonplaces with Arthur Rance. Is it necessary for me to add that at this time, after the scene between Rouletabille and Mathilde, which I had witnessed from my window, I expected to see her in a most wretched state—almost overcome by the vision of Larsan, which had surged up in front of her eyes? But no: on the contrary, I discovered a remarkable difference between the terrified aspect with which she had approached us at the station, for instance, and the easy, composed manner which was here, at present. One would have said that she had been relieved by the sight of the apparition, and when I expressed my opinion to Rouletabille later in the evening, I discovered that he shared it, and he explained the reason for Mathilde's change of manner in the simplest possible fashion. The unhappy woman had dreaded nothing so much as the thought that she was going mad, and the certainty that she had not been the victim of a mental delusion, cruel as that certainty was, had served to make her a little more calm. She preferred to fight even against the living Larsan than against a phantom. In the first interview which she had had with Rouletabille in the Square Tower, while I was dressing for dinner, she had, my young friend told me, been completely possessed by the dread that insanity was coming upon her. Rouletabille, in telling me of this interview, acknowledged to me that he had taken altogether different means to calm Mathilde from those which Robert Darzac had employed—that is, he made no effort to conceal from her that her eyes had seen clearly and had seen Frederic Larsan. When she was told that Robert Darzac had only denied the truth to her because he feared for its effect upon her, and that he had been the first to telegraph to Rouletabille to come to their aid, she heaved a sigh so long and so deep that it was almost a sob. She took Rouletabille's hands in her own and covered them with kisses, just as a mother kisses the hands of her little child. Evidently she was instinctively drawn toward the youth by all the mysterious forces of maternal affection, in spite of the fact that she had every reason to believe that her child had died years before. It was just at this point that the two had first noticed through the window of the tower the form of Frederic Larsan, standing erect in the boat. At first, both had remained, stupefied, motionless and mute at the sight. Then a cry of rage escaped from the agonised heart of Rouletabille, and he longed to pursue the man and reckon with him, face to face. I have told how Mathilde held him back, clinging to him upon the parapet. In her mind, apparently, horrible as was this resurrection of Larsan, it was less horrible than the continual and supernatural resurrection of a Larsan who had no existence save in her own diseased brain. She no longer saw Larsan everywhere around her. She saw him in the flesh, as he was.

At one moment trembling with nervousness, the next gentle and composed, now patient and in another instant impatient, Mathilde, even while conversing with Arthur Rance, showed for her husband the most charming and sweetest solicitude imaginable. She was attentive to him at every moment, serving him herself, and smiling gently at him as she did so, watching him carefully, to be sure that he was not overtired and that the light did not strike too near his eyes. Robert thanked her for her cares, but seemed none the less frightfully unhappy. And his demeanour compelled me to recollect the fact that the resuscitation of Larsan would undoubtedly recall to Mme. Darzac that before she was Mme. Darzac, she had been Mme. Jean Roussel Ballmeyer Larsan before God and herself, and even, so far as the transatlantic laws are concerned, before men as well.

If the design of Larsan in showing himself had been to deal a frightful blow to a happiness which had yet scarcely begun, he had completely succeeded. And, perhaps, as the historian of all parts of this strange affair, I ought to mention the fact that Mathilde had given Robert Darzac at once to understand that she did not regard herself as his wife, since the man to whom she had pledged herself in her early girlhood was still living. I have said that Mathilde Stangerson had been brought up in a very religious manner, not by her father, who cared little for such things, but by her female relatives, especially her old aunt in Cincinnati. The scientific studies which she had pursued with her father had in no wise impaired her faith, while the latter had taken care never to speak against religion to his daughter. She had preserved it, even in the deepest researches into the professor's theory of the creation. She said to him that no matter how plausibly he might prove that everything came from nothingness, that is to say, from the atmosphere, and returned to nothingness in the end, it remained to prove that that nothing, originating from nothing, had not been created by God. And, as she was a good Catholic, she believed that the Vicar of Christ on earth was the Pope. I might have perhaps passed over these religious beliefs of Mathilde in silence, if they had not had so strong an influence on the resolution which she had taken in regard to her second husband, when she discovered that her first husband was still alive. It had seemed to her that Larsan's death had been proven beyond the slightest doubt, and she had gone to her new husband as a widow with the approval of her confessor. And now she learned that in the sight of Heaven, she was not a widow, but a bigamist But, at all events, the catastrophe might not be irremediable, and she herself proposed to poor M. Darzac that the case should be propounded to the ecclesiastical courts of Rome for a settlement as quickly as possible. Thus it was that M. and Mme. Robert Darzac, forty-eight hours after their marriage in the Church of St. Nicolas du Chardonnet, were separated by a gulf over which one could not and the other would not pass. The reader will comprehend from this brief explanation the mournful demeanour of Robert and the gentle sweetness displayed toward him by Mathilde.

Without being entirely conversant with all these details on the evening of which I write, I nevertheless suspected most of them. Leaving the Darzacs, my eyes wandered to the neighbour of Mme. Darzac, M. Arthur William Rance, and my thoughts were taking a new turn, when they were suddenly arrested by the butler's coming to say that Bernier, the concierge, requested to speak to M. Rouletabille. My friend arose, excused himself, and left the room.

"What!" I cried. "The Berniers are no longer at the Glandier?"

Readers of "The Mystery of the Yellow Room" will recall that these Berniers—the man and his wife—were the concierges of M. Stangerson at Ste. Genevieve-des Bois. I have told in that work how Rouletabille had had them set at liberty when they were accused of complicity in the attempt made at the pavilion de la Chenaie. Their gratitude to the young reporter on this account had been of the greatest, and Rouletabille had been ever since the object of their devotion. M. Stangerson replied to my exclamation by informing me that all the servants had left the Glandier at the time that he himself had abandoned it. As the Rances had need of concierges for the Fort of Hercules, the Professor had been glad to send them his faithful domestics, of whom he had never had reason to complain except for one slight infraction of the game laws, which had turned out most unfortunately for them. Now they were lodged in one of the towers of the postern, where they kept the gate, and from which they admitted those who entered and dismissed those who wished to go out of the fort.

Rouletabille had not appeared in the least astonished when the butler announced that Bernier wished to say a word to him, and from that fact, I drew the conclusion that he must be already aware of his presence at Rochers Rouges. So I discovered, without being very greatly surprised at it, that Rouletabille had made excellent use of the few minutes during which I believed him to be in his room, and which I had given up to my toilet and to chatting with M. Darzac.

The unexpected exit of Rouletabille sent a chill to my heart and seemed to spread a general sensation of alarm throughout the company. Every one of us who was in the secret asked himself whether this summons had not something to do with some important event connected with the return of Larsan. Mme. Darzac was very restless. And because Mathilde showed herself to be disturbed and nervous, I fancied that M. Arthur Rance thought that it behooved him to display some little anxiety. And it may be as well to say at this point that M. Arthur Rance and his wife were not aware of the whole of the unfortunate story of Professor Stangerson's daughter. It had seemed useless to inform them of the fact of Mathilde's secret marriage to Jean Roussel, afterward known as Larsan. That was something which concerned only the family. But they were fully aware—Arthur Rance from having been mixed up in the Glandier business, and his wife from what he had told her—of the way in which the Secret Service agent had pursued the young woman who was now Mme. Darzac. The crimes of Larsan were explained in the eyes of Arthur Rance by a mad passion for Mathilde, and this was by no means surprising to the young American who had been for so long in love with her himself, and who perceived in all of Larsan's acts merely the indications of an insane and hopeless love. As to Mme. Edith, I soon found out why the events which had transpired at the Glandier had not seemed so simple to her when they were related to her as they had to her husband. For her to share his opinions on the subject, it would have been necessary for her to have seen Mathilde with eyes as enthusiastic as those of Arthur Rance, and, on the contrary, her thoughts (which I had good opportunities to read without her suspecting it) ran about in this way: "But what on earth is there about this woman which could inspire such an insane passion, lasting for years and years in the heart of any man! Here is a woman for whose sake a detective officer becomes a murderer; for whom a temperate man becomes a drunkard, and for whom an innocent man permits himself to be pronounced guilty of a felony. What is there about her more than there is about myself who owe my husband to the fact that she refused him before he ever saw me? What is the charm about her? She isn't even young. And yet even now my husband forgets all about me while he is looking at her." That is what I read in Edith's eyes as she watched her husband gazing at Mathilde. Ah, those black eyes of the gentle, languid Mme. Edith!

I am congratulating myself upon the explanations which I have made to the reader. It is as well that he should know the sentiments which dwelt in the heart of each one concerned at the moment when all were about to have their own parts to play in the strange and awful drama which was already drawing near in the shadow which enveloped the Fort of Hercules. As yet, I have said nothing of Old Bob nor of Prince Galitch, but, never fear, their turn will come! I have taken as a rule in the narration of this affair to paint things and people as nearly as possible as they appeared to me in the development of events. Thus the reader will pass through all the phases of the tragedy as we ourselves passed through them—anguish and peace, mysteries and their unravelling, misunderstanding and comprehension. If the light breaks upon the mind of the reader before the hour when it broke upon mine, so much the better. As he will be conversant with the same circumstances, neither more nor less, which came under our observation, he will prove to himself if he solves the mystery before it is revealed to him, that he possesses a brain worthy to rank with that of Rouletabille.

W e finished our repast without our young friend having reappeared, and we arose from the table without having mentioned to each other any of the thoughts which troubled us. Mathilde immediately asked me where I thought Rouletabille had gone. As she left the dining room, and I walked with her as far as the entrance to the fort; M. Darzac and Mme. Edith followed us. M. Stangerson had bidden us good-night. Arthur Rance, who had disappeared for a moment, joined us while we were at the passageway. The night was clear and the moon shone brightly. Someone had lighted the lanterns in the archway, however, in spite of the fact that their rays were not needed for seeing. As we passed beneath the arch, we heard Rouletabille speaking, as though he were encouraging those whom he addressed.

"Come on! One more effort!" he cried, and the voice which answered him was husky and panting, like that of a sailor who was working with his fellows to bring his bark into port. Finally, a great tumult filled our ears. It was the two portals of the immense iron doors, which were being closed for the first time in more than an hundred years.

Mme. Edith looked astonished at the act of her guest, and asked what had happened to the gate, which had always served in place of the doors since she had been mistress of the place. But Arthur Rance caught her arm, and she seemed to understand that he was impressing upon her that she must keep silence. But that did not keep her from exclaiming in a not-too-well pleased tone:

"Really! Anyone would think that we expected to undergo a siege!"

But Rouletabille beckoned our group into the garden and announced to us in a jesting tone that if any of us had any desire to make a trip to the village, we must give it up for that evening, for the order had gone forth and no one could leave the château or enter it. Pere Jacques, he added, still pretending to jest, was charged with the carrying out of the command, and everyone knew that it was impossible to bribe the faithful old servitor. It was then that I learned for the first time that Pere Jacques, whom I had known so well at the Glandier, had accompanied Professor Stangerson on his visit and was acting as his valet. That night he was sleeping in a tiny closet in "la Louve," near his master's bed room, but Rouletabille had changed that, and it was Pere Jacques who took the place of the concierges in the tower marked A.

"But where are the Berniers?" cried Mme. Edith.

"They are installed in the Square Tower, in the room on the left, near the entrance; they are to act as caretakers of the Square Tower," replied Rouletabille.

"But the Square Tower doesn't need any caretakers!" exclaimed Edith, whose vexation was plainly visible.

"That, Madame," returned the young reporter, "is what we cannot be sure of."

He made no further explanations, but he took M. Arthur Rance to one side and informed him that he ought to tell his wife about the reappearance of Larsan. If there was to be the slightest chance of hiding the truth from M. Stangerson, it could scarcely be accomplished without the aid and intelligence of Mme. Edith. And, then, too, it would be as well, henceforward, for all of those in the Fort of Hercules to be prepared for everything, *and surprised at nothing*!

The next act of Rouletabille was to make us walk across the court and place ourselves at the postern of the gardener. I have said that this postern (H) commanded the entrance to the inner court; but at that point the moat had been filled up a long time ago. Rouletabille, to our amazement, declared that the next day he intended to have the moat dug out and to replace the drawbridge. For the present, he busied himself with ordering the postern to be closed more securely by the servants of the château by means of a sort of fortification built from the boards and bricks which had been used in the repairs of the château, and which had not yet been taken away by the workmen. Thus the château was barricaded and Rouletabille laughed softly to himself, for Mme. Edith, having been apprised by her husband of the facts of the case, made no further objection, but contented herself with smiling a little contemptuously at the timidity of her guests, who were transforming the old stronghold into an absolutely impenetrable spot, because they were afraid of just one man—one man, all alone. But Mme. Edith did not know what manner of man this was. She had not lived through the mysteries of the yellow room.

As to the others—Arthur Rance among them—they found it perfectly natural and reasonable that Rouletabille should fortify the place against that which was unknown and mysterious and invisible, and which plotted in the night they knew not what against the Fort of Hercules.

At the newly fortified postern, Rouletabille had stationed no one, for he reserved that place that night for himself. From there he could obtain a complete view of both the inner and outer courts. It was a strategic point which commanded a view of the whole château. One could reach the apartment of the Darzacs only after passing by Pere Jacques in A; by Rouletabille at H, and by the Berniers, who guarded the Square Tower at the door marked K. The young man had decided that it would be better for those on guard not to retire that night. As we passed by the "oubliette" in the Court of Charles the Bold, I saw by the light of the moon that someone had displaced the circular board which covered it. I saw also on the margin a flask attached to a cord. Rouletabille explained to me that he had wished to know if this old oubliette (which was really nothing but a well) corresponded with the sea, and that he had found that the water was clear and sweet—a proof that it had nothing to do with the Mediterranean.

The young man walked for a few steps with Mme. Darzac, who immediately took leave of us and entered the Square Tower. M. Darzac and Arthur Rance, at the request of Rouletabille, remained with us. Some words of excuse addressed to Mme. Edith made her understand that she was being politely asked to retire, and she bade us good-night with a nonchalant grace, flinging the words, "Good-night, M. le Captain," at Rouletabille over her shoulder as she passed him.

When we were alone, we men, Rouletabille beckoned us toward the postern into the little room of the gardener, a dark, low-ceiled apartment, where we were surprised to find how easily we could see anything that passed near by without being seen ourselves. There, Arthur Rance, Robert Darzac, Rouletabille and myself, without even lighting a lamp, held our first council of war. In truth, I know not what other name to give to this reunion of frightened men, hidden behind the stones of this old fortress.

"We may make our plans here in tranquillity," began Rouletabille. "No one can hear us, and we shall not be surprised by anyone. If any person should attempt to pass the first gate which Jacques is guarding without the old man's seeing him, we shall be immediately warned by the sentinel whom I have stationed in the very middle of the court, hidden in the ruins of the chapel. I have placed your gardener, Mattoni, at that point, M. Rance. I believe from what I have been told that you can depend upon the man. Is not that your opinion?"

I listened to Rouletabille with admiration. Mme. Edith was right. He had indeed constituted himself a captain, and he had not left one impregnable spot without defence, and had neglected nothing in his cogitations. I felt certain that he would never surrender, no matter on what terms, and that he would prefer death to capitulation, either for himself or for any of the rest of us. What a brave little commander he was And, indeed, it seemed to me that he displayed more bravery in undertaking the defence of the Fort of Hercules against Larsan than the Lords of Mortola had shown in holding the castle against a thousand of the enemy. For they had fought merely against shot and shell and spears. And what had we to fight against? The darkness. Where was our enemy? Everywhere and nowhere. We were able neither to see him, nor to know his whereabouts, nor to guess his designs, nor to take the offensive ourselves, ignorant as we were of where our blows might fall. There remained for us only to be on guard, to shut ourselves in, to watch and to wait.

M. Arthur Rance assured Rouletabille that he could answer for his gardener, Mattoni, and our young man proceeded to explain to us in a general fashion the situation. He lit his pipe, took three or four puffs, and said:

"Well, here we are. Can we hope that Larsan, after having so insolently flaunted himself before us, at our very doors, in order to defy us, will confine himself to such a platonic manifestation? Will he consider that he has accomplished enough in bringing trouble, terror and consternation among the members of the besieged party in the garrison? And content with what he has done, will he go away? I hardly think so. First, because such a thing would be foreign to his character— for he loves a fight, and is never satisfied with a partial success; and, secondly, because no one of us has the power to drive him off. Consider that he can do anything that he will to injure us, but that we can make no move against him save to defend ourselves if he strikes, provided we are able when it may suit him to do so. We have, of course, no hope of any help from outside. And he knows it well; that is what makes him so bold and audacious. Whom can we call to our aid?"

"The authorities," suggested Arthur Rance. He spoke with some hesitation, for he felt that if this plan had not been entertained by Rouletabille, there must be some reason for it.

The young reporter looked at his host with an air of pity, which was not entirely free from reproach. And he said in a chilly tone, which showed plainly to Arthur Rance how little value there was in his proposition:

"You ought to understand, Monsieur, that I did not save Larsan from French justice at Versailles to deliver him over to Italian justice at Rochers Rouges."

M. Arthur Rance, who was, as I have said, ignorant of the first marriage of Professor Stangerson's daughter, could not understand, as did the rest of us, the impossibility of revealing the existence of Larsan without stirring up (especially after the ceremony at St. Nicolas du Chardonnet) the worst of scandals and the most dreadful of catastrophes: but certain inexplicable incidents of the trial at Versailles had impressed him sufficiently to make him realize that we dreaded above all things to bring again to the public mind what someone had called "The Mystery of Mlle. Stangerson."

He comprehended this on the evening of which I speak better than he had ever done before, and knew that Larsan must hold one of those terrible secrets on which life and honour depend, and with which the magistrates of the world can have no concern.

M. Rance bowed to M. Robert Darzac without uttering a word: but the salute signified the declaration that M. Arthur Rance was ready to combat for the cause of Mathilde, whatever it might be, as a noble chevalier, who does not bother himself about the reason of the battle in the moment when he dies for his lady. At least, I thus interpreted his gesture, and I felt certain that, in spite of his recent marriage, the American had by no means forgotten his old love.

M. Darzac said:

"This man must disappear, but in silence, whether we move him by our entreaties, or bribe him or kill him. But the first condition of his disappearance is to keep the fact that he has reappeared at all a secret. Above all—and I am speaking of the heartfelt wish of Mme. Darzac as well as my own—M. Stangerson must never know that we are menaced by the blows of this monster."

"Mme. Darzac's wishes are commands," replied Rouletabille. "M. Stangerson shall know nothing."

We went on to discuss the situation in regard to the servants and to what one might expect from them. Happily, Pere Jacques and the Berniers were already partly in the secret and would be astonished at nothing. Mattoni was devoted enough to render unquestioning obedience to Mme. Edith. The others did not count. Later there would be Walter, the servant of Old Bob, but he had accompanied his master to Paris, and would not return until he did.

Rouletabille arose, exchanged through the window a signal with Bernier, who was standing erect upon the threshold of the Square Tower. Then he came back to us and sat down again.

"Larsan probably is not far off," he said. "During dinner I made a tour of observation around the place. We possess at the North gate a natural means of defence which is really marvellous, and which completely replaces the old fortifications of the château. We have there fifty paces away, at the western shore, the two frontier posts of the French and Italian revenue officers, whose untiring vigilance may be of the greatest assistance to us. Pere Bernier is on the most friendly terms with these worthy people, and I am going with him to talk to them. The Italian customs officer speaks only Italian, but the French officer speaks both languages, as well as the patois of the country, and it is this man, whom Bernier tells me is called Michael, to whom I look to be of the greatest use to us. Through his means we have already learned that the two revenue posts are much interested in the strange manoeuvres of the little boat, which belongs to Tullio, the fisherman, whom they call 'the hangman of the sea.' Old Tullio is one of the former acquaintances of the customs men. He is the most skillful smuggler on the coast. He had with him this evening in his boat an individual whom the revenue officers had never seen. The boat, Tullio and the passenger, all disappeared at the Pointe de Garibaldi. I have been there with Pere Bernier, and we found nothing, any more than M. Darzac, who visited the spot before us. However, Larsan must have landed.

I have a presentiment of the fact. In any case, I am sure that Tullio's little boat is anchored near the Pointe de Garabaldi."

"You are sure of that?" cried M. Darzac.

"What reason have you for thinking so?" I demanded.

"Bah!" exclaimed Rouletabille. "It left the marks of the keel in the sand on the bank, and when they anchored, they let fall a little lantern, which I picked up and which the revenue officers recognised as the one used by Tullio when he fishes in the waters on calm nights."

"Larsan certainly landed!" repeated M. Darzac. "He is at Rochers Rouges."

"In any case, if the boat has been left at Rochers Rouges, he has not come back here," exclaimed Rouletabille. "The two revenue posts are situated upon the narrow road which leads from Rochers Rouges to France, and are placed in such a manner that no one can pass by whether by day or by night without being seen. You know besides that the Red Rocks from which the village takes its name from a cul de sac, and that a sentinel is on guard in front of these rocks every hundred meters around the frontier. The sentinel passes between the rocks and the sea. The rocks are steep and form a terrace sixty meters high."

"That is true," said Arthur Rance, who had not recently spoken, and who seemed greatly interested. "It is not easy to scale the rocks."

"He will have hidden himself in the grottoes," said Darzac. "There are some deep pockets in the terrace."

"I thought of that," said Rouletabille. "And I went back alone to Rochers Rouges, after I left Pere Bernier."

"That was very imprudent!" I said.

"It was very prudent," corrected Rouletabille. "I had some things to say to Larsan which I did not wish a third party to hear. Well, I went back to Rochers Rouges and called Larsan's name through all the caves."

"You called him?" cried Arthur Rance.

"Yes, I shouted into the gathering night; I waved my handkerchief as the soldiers wave their flag of truce. But whether it was that he heard me and saw my white flag or not, he did not answer."

"Perhaps he was not there," I suggested.

"Perhaps not: I don't know. I heard a noise in the grotto."

"And you did not enter?" demanded Arthur Rance.

"No," replied Rouletabille, quietly. "But you do not think that it was because I was afraid of him, do you?"

"Let us run!" we all cried in one breath, rising at the same moment. "Let us go and finish up the business immediately."

"I don't think that we shall ever have a better chance of meeting Larsan," said Arthur Rance. "We can do what we like with him at the bottom of Rochers Rouges."

Darzac and Arthur Rance were already starting off; I waited to see what Rouletabille would say. He calmed the two men with a gesture, and begged them to be seated again.

"It is necessary to remember," he said, "that Larsan would have acted exactly as he has done if he had wished to lure us tonight to the grotto of Rochers Rouges. He has shown himself to us; he has landed almost under our eyes at the Point of Garabaldi; he might as well have shouted under our windows, "You know I am at Rochers Rouges. I'll wait for you there." He would have been neither more explicit or more eloquent."

"You went to Rochers Rouges," resumed Arthur Rance, who I saw was deeply impressed with the arguments of Rouletabille—"and he did not show himself. He hid himself, meditating on some horrible crime to be committed tonight. We must have him out of that grotto."

"Doubtless," replied Rouletabille, "my promenade to Rochers Rouges produced no result because I was all alone—but if we all go, I can assure you that we shall find some results on our return."

"On our return?" echoed Darzac who did not understand.

"Yes," explained Rouletabille: "on our return to the château, where we have left Mne. Darzac all alone—and where, perhaps, we may not find her. Oh, of course," he added, as a general silence fell upon his companions, "it is only a hypothesis. But at this time we have no other means of reasoning than by hypothesis."

We looked at each other and this hypothesis over whelmed us. Evidently, without Rouletabille, we should have committed a terrible blunder and perhaps have been responsible for a terrible disaster.

Rouletabille arose and continued, thoughtfully:

"You see, tonight there is nothing that we can do except to barricade ourselves. It is only a temporary barricade, for I want the place put in an absolutely unassailable state tomorrow. I have had the iron doors closed and Pere Jacques is guarding them. I have stationed Mattoni as sentinel at the chapel. I have established a barrier under the postern, the only vulnerable point of the inner court, and I will guard that myself. Pere Bernier will watch all night at the door of the Square

Tower, and Mere Bernier, who has a good pair of eyes, and to whom I have given a spyglass, will remain until morning on the platform of the tower. Sainclair will station himself in the little palm leaf pavilion upon the terrace of the Round Tower. From the height of this terrace he will watch as I do all the inner court and the boulevards and parapets. M. Rance and M. Darzac will go into the garden and walk until daylight, the one toward the boulevard on the west, the other toward the boulevard on the east—the two boulevards which are at the edge of the outer court near the sea. The vigil will be hard tonight, because we are not yet organised. Tomorrow we shall draw up a set of rules for our little garrison, and a list of the trustworthy domestics upon whom we may depend with security.

"If there is one on the place who could come under the slightest suspicion, he must be dismissed at once. You will bring here to this cell all the arms which you can gather—rifles and revolvers. We will divide them among those who do guard duty. The sentinel is to draw upon every person who does not reply to 'Who goes there?' and who is not recognised. There is no need of a password, it would be useless. Let the countersign be to utter one's name and to show one's face. Besides, it is only ourselves who have the right to pass. Beginning tomorrow morning I will have raised at the inner entrance of the North gate the grating which until today formed its exterior entrance—the entrance which is closed, henceforth, by the iron doors; and in the daytime the commissaires can come as far as this grating with their provisions. They will place their wares in the little lodge in the tower where I have stationed Pere Jacques. At seven o'clock every night, the iron doors will be closed. Tomorrow morning M. Arthur Rance will send for builders, masons and carpenters. Every person on the place will be counted, and no one allowed, under any pretext, to pass the door of the second court. Before seven o'clock in the evening every one will be counted again, and the workpeople will be allowed to go out. In this one day the men must completely finish their work, which will consist of making a door for my postern, repairing a small breach in the wall which joins the New Castle to the Tower of Charles the Bold and another little break near the Round Tower (B in the plan), which defends the northeast corner of the outer court. After that, I shall be tranquil, and Mme. Darzac, who is forbidden to leave the château under the new order, having been placed in security, I may attempt a sortie and enter seriously into the search for the camp of Larsan. Come, M. Rance, to arms' Bring me some weapons to pass around this evening. I have loaned my own revolver to Pere Bernier, who is keeping guard before the door of Mme. Darzac's apartments."

Anyone not knowing of the events at the Glandier who had heard the words spoken by Rouletabille would have considered both him who spoke and us who listened to be beside ourselves. But, I repeat, if anyone had lived, like myself, through that terrible and mysterious time, he would have done what I did—loaded his revolver and waited for dawn without uttering a word.

VIII

Which Contains Some Pages From the History of Jean Roussel-Larsan Ballmeyer

An hour later, we were all at our posts, passing along the parapets in the moonlight, keeping close watch upon the land, the sky and the water, and listening anxiously to the slightest sounds of the night—the sighing of the sea and the voices of the birds which began to sing at about three o'clock in the morning. Mme. Edith, who said that she could not sleep, came out and talked to Rouletabille at his postern. The lad called me, placed me in charge of his postern and of Mrs. Rance, and made his rounds. The fair Edith was in the most charming humour. She looked as fresh as a rose washed in dew, and she seemed to be greatly amused at the wan countenance of her husband, to whom she had brought out a glass of whisky.

"It's the funniest thing I ever heard of," she exclaimed, clapping her tiny hands. "All of you keeping watch out here like this! How I wish I knew your Larsan I'm sure I should adore him!"

I shuddered involuntarily at the words she uttered so lightly. Beyond a doubt there do exist romantic little creatures who fear nothing, and who in their carelessness jest at fate. Ah! if the unhappy girl had only realised what was to come!

I spent two delightful hours with Mme. Edith, during the greater part of which I related to her some facts regarding the history of Ballmeyer. And since this occasion presents itself, I will at this time relate to the reader, in historical order—if I may use an expression which perfectly interprets my meaning—the characteristics and circumstances in the career of Larsan-Ballmeyer, some of which had been sufficient to make it doubtful whether he still lived at the time that he appeared to play so unexpected a part in "The Mystery of the Yellow Room." As this man's powers will be seen to extend in "The Perfume of the Lady in Black" to heights which some may believe inaccessible, I judge it to be my duty to prepare the mind of the reader to admit in the end that I am only the transcriber of an affair the like of which never has been known before, and that I have invented nothing. And, moreover, Rouletabille, in the event that I might have the hardihood to add to such a wonderful and veracious history any rhetorical ornaments or exaggerations, would certainly contradict me and riddle my story as with bullets. The great interests at stake are such that the slightest exaggeration would assuredly entail the most terrible consequences, so that I shall keep strictly to the exact details of my narrative, even at the risk of making it seem a little dry and methodical. I will refer those who believe in actual records to the stenographic reports of the trial at Versailles. M. Andre-Hesse and M. Henri Robert, who appeared for M. Robert Darzac, made admirable addresses, to which the public may easily obtain access. And it must not be forgotten that before destiny had brought Larsan-Ballmeyer and Joseph Rouletabille into contact, the elegantly mannered bandit had given considerable trouble to the authorities. We have only to open the files of the *Gazette les Tribuneaux* and to read the account of the day when Larsan was condemned by the Court of Assizes to ten years at hard labour, to be assured on this score. Then, one will understand that there is no need of inventing anything about a man concerning whom one can with truth relate such a history: and thus the reader, knowing the sort of man that he is—that is to say, his manner of working and his incredible audacity—will refrain from smiling because Joseph Rouletabille placed a drawbridge between Larsan-Ballmeyer and Mathilde Darzac.

M. Albert Bataille of *le Figaro*, who has published an admirable work on "Criminal and Civil Causes," has devoted some interesting pages to Ballmeyer.

Ballmeyer had a happy childhood and youth. He did not become a criminal as so many others have done because driven to evil doing by the hard blows of poverty and misery. The son of a rich broker in the Rue Molay, he might have chosen any vocation that he desired, but his preferred calling was to lay hands upon the money of other people. At an early age, he decided to become a swindler, just as another lad might have decided to become an engineer. His debut was a stroke of genius, and the history of it is almost incredible. Ballmeyer stole a letter addressed to his father containing a considerable sum of money. Then he took the train for Lyons and from there wrote his parent as follows:

"Monsieur, I am an old soldier, retired and with a medal of honour to show that I have served my country. My son, a post office clerk, has stolen in the mails a letter addressed to you and containing money, to pay a gambling debt. I have called the members of the family together. In a few days we shall be able to raise the sum necessary to repay you. You are a father. Have pity upon a father. Do not bring me down in sorrow and shame to my grave."

M. Ballmeyer willingly granted the petition. He is still waiting for his first remittance—or, rather, he has ceased to expect it, for the law apprised him ten years ago of the identity of the culprit.

Ballmeyer, relates M. Albert Bataille, seems to have received from nature all the gifts which go to make the successful swindler: a wonderful diversity, the talent of persuading new acquaintances to believe in him, the careful attention to the smallest details, the genius for completely disguising himself (he even took the precaution along this line of having his linen marked with different initials every time that he judged it expedient to change his name). But his strongest characteristic of all was his astonishing aptitude for evasion—for coquetting with fraud, for mocking at and defying justice. This was evinced in the malignant pleasure which he took in speaking of himself at Parquet as among those who might have been guilty, knowing how little importance would be attached by the magistrate by the clues which he gave.

This delight in jesting at the judges was apparent in every act of his life.

While he was doing military duty, Ballmeyer stole his companion's box and accused the captain.

He committed a theft of forty thousand francs from the Maison

Furet, and immediately afterward denounced M. Furet as having stolen it himself.

THE FURET AFFAIR REMAINED FOR a long time celebrated among judicial records under the appellation of "the coup of the telephone." Science, applied as an aid to knavery, has never given anything better.

Ballmeyer appropriated a draft for six thousand livres sterling from the messenger of Messrs. Furet, brothers, who were note brokers in the Rue Poissoniere, and who allowed him desk room in their offices.

He went to the Rue Poissoniere, into the house of M. Furet, and, imitating the voice of M. Edouard Furet, asked over the telephone of M. Cohen, a banker, whether he would be willing to discount the draft. M. Cohen replied in the affirmative, and ten minutes later, Ballmeyer, after having cut the telephone wire to prevent further communication and possible explanations, sent for the money by a companion named Rigaud, whom he had known not long before in the African battalion, where their common interests had made them useful to each other.

Ballmeyer kept the lion's share for himself: then he rushed to the court to denounce Rigaud, and, as I have said, M. Furet himself.

A dramatic scene took place when accuser and accused were confronted with each other in the cabinet of M. Espierre, the judge of instruction who had charge of the affair.

"You know, my dear Furet," said Ballmeyer to the amased broker, "I am heart-broken at being obliged to expose you, but you must tell the Justice the truth. It is not an affair from which you need fear serious consequences. Why don't you confess? You needed forty thousand francs to pay a little debt incurred at the race track and you intended to pay back the sum. It was you who telephoned?"

"I! I!" stammered M. Edouard Furet, almost breathless with rage and astonishment.

"You may as well confess," said Ballmeyer. "No one could mistake your voice."

The bold thief was detected within eight days and was caught; and the police furnished such a report upon him that M. Cruppi, then attorney general, now Minister of Commerce, presented to M. Furet the most humble excuses of the Department of Justice. Rigaud was also tried and condemned to twenty years at hard labour.

One might go on relating this kind of stories about Ballmeyer indefinitely. At that time, before he had entered upon the darker and more horrible pages of his career, he played a comedy—and what a comedy! It may be as well to give in detail the history of one of his escapes. Nothing could be more immensely comical than the adventure of the prisoner composing a long memorial during his trial for the sole purpose of hanging over the table of the judge, M. Villars, and of turning over the papers in order to obtain a glimpse of the formula of orders of discharge.

When he was sent back to jail at Mazas, the fellow wrote a letter signed "Villars," in which, according to the prescribed formula, M. Villars requested the superintendent of the prison to set the prisoner, Ballmeyer, at liberty without delay. But he had no paper of the kind used by the Judge for such matters.

However, so small a thing as that scarcely embarrassed Ballmeyer. He went back to the courthouse in the morning, hiding the letter in his sleeve, protested his innocence and feigning great indignation and anger. He picked up the seal that lay on the table and gesticulated with it in expressing his wrath, and he knocked the inkstand over on the blue trousers of his guard. While the poor fellow, surrounded by the inmates of the court-room, who condoled with him on his ill luck, was sadly sponging off his "Number One," Ballmeyer profited by the general diversion to apply a strong pressure of the stamp upon the order of discharge, and then began loudly excusing himself to the soldier.

The trick succeeded. The thief made his way out amid the confusion, and, negligently tossing the signed and sealed paper to the guards, remarked carelessly:

"What is M. Villars thinking of to order me to carry his papers? Does he take me for his servant?"

Then he went back to his seat. The guards picked up the paper, and one of them carried it to the warden at Mazas, to whom it was addressed. It was the order to set Ballmeyer at liberty without delay. The same night, Ballmeyer was free.

This was his second escape. Arrested for the Furet affair, he had gotten away once by throwing pepper in the eyes of the guard who was taking him to the station, and that same evening he was present in evening dress at a first night at the Comedie Francaise. Prior to this, at the time when he had been sentenced by court martial to five years' imprisonment because he had robbed his companion, he had made his way out of the Cherche Midi by having one of his comrades forge an order of release for him. A variation of the same plan had served him well once more.

But one would never finish if one tried to relate all the amazing adventures of Ballmeyer.

Known at various times as the Count de Maupas, Vicomte Drouet d'erion, Comte de Motteville, Comte de Bonneville, and under many other aliases, as an elegant man about town, setting the fashion, he frequented the summer resorts and watering places—Biarritz, Aix les Bains, Luchon, losing in play at the club as much as ten thousand francs in one evening, surrounded by pretty women, who envied each other his attentions—for this fellow was extremely popular with the fair sex. In his regiment, he had made a con quest—happily platonic—of the Colonel's daughter. Do you know the type now?

Well, it was with this man that Joseph Rouletabille was going to fight.

I thought that morning that I had sufficiently informed Mme. Edith in regard to the personality of the bandit. She listened so silently that my attention was finally drawn to the fact that she had not uttered a remark in some time, and, bending down, I saw that she was fast asleep. This circumstance should not have given me a very good opinion of the little creature. But, as I watched her sleeping face at my leisure, I felt springing up in my soul feelings which I later endeavoured in vain to chase away from my mind.

The night passed without any event. When the day dawned, I saluted it with a deep sigh of relief. Nevertheless, Rouletabille did not permit me to retire until eight o'clock in the morning, after he had settled on how matters should go on through the day. He was already in the midst of the workmen whom he had summoned, and who were labouring actively in repairing the breaches of the tower B. The work was done so expeditiously and so promptly that the strong château of Hercules was soon sealed as hermetically close as it was possible for a building to be. Seated on a big boulder in the bright sunlight, Rouletabille began to draw upon his note book the plan which I have submitted to the reader, and he said to me while I, worn out with my vigil, was making absurd efforts to keep my eyes open:

"You see, Sainclair, these people believe that I am fortifying the place to defend myself. Well, that is merely a small part of the truth, for I am fortifying the place because reason bids me do so. And, if I close up the breaches, it is less in order that Larsan cannot get in than for the sake of depriving my reason of any chance of accusing me of carelessness. For instance, I can never reason in a forest. How will you reason in a forest?

There, reason flies away on every side. But in a closed up château! My friend, it is like a sealed casket. If you are inside and are not insane, your reasoning powers must come back to you."

"Yes, yes," I murmured sleepily, nodding.

"That's it—your reason will come back to you—"

"Well, well, never mind!" answered Rouletabille. "Go to bed, old fellow. You are walking in your sleep now."

IX

IN WHICH "OLD BOB" UNEXPECTEDLY
ARRIVES

When I heard a knock at my door about eleven o'clock in the morning and the voice of Mere Bernier told me that Rouletabille wanted me to get up, I threw my window wide open and looked out in delight. The bay was of an incomparable beauty, and the sea was so transparent that the rays of the sun pierced through it as they would have done through a mirror without quicksilver, so that one could perceive the rocks, the anemones and the moss in the sea bottom just as if the waters had ceased to cover them and left them bared to the eye. The harmonious curve of the bank on the Mentone side enclosed the sea like a flowery frame. The villas of Garavan, white and rose, looked like fresh flowers which had blossomed over night. The peninsula of Hercules was a bouquet which floated upon the waters and perfumed the old stones of the château.

Never had nature appeared to me more sweet, more delightful, more exquisite, nor, above all, more worthy of being loved. The serene air, the beautiful shore, the balmy sea, the purple mountains, all this picture to which my Northern senses were so little accustomed, evoked in my mind the thought of some tender, caressing human being. As these thoughts passed through my mind, I noticed a man who was lashing the sea. Oh! he gave it a box on the ear! I could have wept if I had been a poet! The miserable wretch appeared to be furiously angry. I could not understand what had excited his wrath in this tranquil spot, but he evidently felt that he had some serious cause for vexation, for he never ceased his blows. He was armed with an enormous cudgel, and, standing erect in a tiny boat, into which a timid child might have feared to entrust its weight, he administered to the sea, with the fiercest splashings, such a castigation as provoked the mute indignation of some strangers who were standing on the shore. But as everyone under all circumstances dreads to mix himself in what is none of his affairs, these persons made no protest. What was it that could have so deeply excited the savage? Perhaps it might have been the very calm of the sea which, after having been for a moment disturbed by the insult of the madman, resumed its peaceful tranquillity.

At this point, I was interrupted by the voice of Rouletabille, who told me that breakfast was nearly ready. Rouletabille appeared in the garb of a plasterer, his clothing showing plainly that he had been working in the fresh mortar. In one hand he held a foot rule and in the other a file. I asked him whether he had seen the man who was beating the water, and he told me that it was Tullio who was frightening the fishes to drive them into his nets. It was for this reason, I realised, that Tullio had obtained the nickname of the "hangman of the sea."

Rouletabille went on to tell me that he had asked Tullio that morning about the stranger whom he had rowed about in his boat the night before, and whom he had taken all around the peninsula of Hercules. Tullio had replied that he had no knowledge whatever of whom the man might be; that he was a crazy sort of fellow whom he had taken in as a passenger at Men tone, and who had given him five francs to land him at the point of Rochers Rouges.

I dressed myself quickly and joined Rouletabille, who told me that we were to have a new guest at luncheon, in the person of "Old Bob." We waited for a few moments for him to come to the table, and then, as he did not appear, we began our repast without him in the flowery frame of the round terrace of Charles the Bold.

There was served to us a delicious bouillabaisse, smoking hot, which seemed to have drawn the best of their flavors from fishes of all species, and was tinted by a little *vino del Paese*, and which, in the light and brightness of the daytime, contributed as much as all the precaution of Rouletabille toward making us feel serene and secure. In truth, we felt not the slightest fear of the dreaded Larsan under the beautiful sunshine of the brilliant heavens, whatever we may have felt in the pale gleam of the moon and stars. Ah, how forgetful and easily impressed human nature is 'I am ashamed to say it, but we were feeling rather proud (I speak for Arthur Rance and myself, and also for Edith, whose romantic and languid nature was superficial, as such are likely to be) of the fact that we could smile and speak with scorn of our nocturnal vigils and of our armed guard upon the boulevards of the citadel—when Old Bob made his appearance. And—let me say it: let me say it here—it was not this apparition which could have turned our thoughts toward anything dark or gloomy. I have rarely seen anything more droll than Old Bob walking in the blinding sun of the springtime in the Midi, with a tall hat of black beaver; his black trousers, his black spectacles, his white hair and his rosy cheeks. Yes, yes, we sat there and laughed in the tower of Charles the Bold. And Old Bob laughed with us. For Old Bob was as gay as a child.

W hat was this old savant doing at the Château of Hercules? Perhaps this is as good a time as any to explain. How could he have made up his mind to quit his collections in America and his work and his drawings and his museum in Philadelphia? For these reasons: The reader will not have forgotten that M. Arthur Rance was already looked upon in his own country as the anthropologist of the future at the time when his un happy infatuation for Mlle. Stangerson had weaned him away from his studies and made them almost distasteful to him. After his marriage to Miss Prescott, who was deeply interested in such matters, he felt that he could resume with pleasure his researches in the science of Gall and Lavater. But at the self-same time that they visited the azure shores in the autumn which preceded the events of this history, there was much discussion in regard to the new discoveries which M. Abbo had just made at Rochers Rouges. M.M. Julien, Riviere, Girardin, Delesot had come to the spot to work, and had succeeded in interesting the Institute and the Minister of Public Instruction in their discoveries. These discoveries soon created a profound sensation, for they proved beyond the shadow of a doubt that primeval man had lived in this spot before the glacial epoch. Without doubt, the proof of the existence of the man of the quarternary epoch had been found long before; but this epoch, extending certainly two hundred thousand years into the past, was interesting in that it fixed the quarternary epoch in the proper period. Learned men were always digging at Rochers Rouges, and they came upon surprise after surprise. However, the most beautiful of the grottoes—the Barma Grande, as they called it in the country side—had remained intact, for it was the private property of M. Abbo, who kept the "Restaurant of the Grotto" not far away on the sea shore. M. Abbo was determined to dig in his own grotto himself. But now, public report (for the event had passed the bounds of the scientific world and interested people generally) said that in the Barma Grande there had been found extraordinary human bones, skeletons remarkably preserved by the ferruginous earth, contemporaneous with the mammoths of the beginning of the quarternary epoch, or even of the end of the tertiary epoch.

Arthur Rance and his wife hastened to Mentone, and while the husband passed his days in antiquarian researches, going back two hundred thousand years, digging up with his own hands the humerus of the Barma Grande and measuring the skulls of his ancestors, his young wife seemed to experience an ever renewed pleasure in rambling over the mediaeval ruins of an old fortress which reared its massive silhouette above a little peninsula, united to Rochers Rouges by a few crumbling stones. The most romantic legends were attached to this relic of the old Genoese wars; and it seemed to Edith, pensively leaning from the highest terrace, in the most beautiful scene in the world, that she was one of those noble demoiselles of ancient times, whose romantic adventures she had so dearly loved to read in the pages of her favourite romances. The castle was for sale and the price was very reasonable. Arthur Rance purchased it, and by doing so made his wife the happiest of women. She sent for masons and furnishers, and within three months she had succeeded in transforming the old fortress into an exquisite nest of love—an ideal abode for a young person who revelled in "The Lady of the Lake," or "The Bride of Lammermoor."

When Arthur Rance had found himself standing beside the last skeleton discovered in the Barma Grande, and knew that the *elephus antiquus* had come out of the same bed of earth, he was beside himself with enthusiasm, and his first impulse had been to telegraph to Old Bob and tell him that it might be that someone had discovered, a few kilometers from Monte Carlo, the relics which the old savant had been seeking for so many years in the mountains of Patagonia. But the telegram never reached its destination, for Old Bob, who had previously promised to join his nephew and niece after they had been married for awhile, had already taken the steamer for Europe. Evidently report had already brought to him the story of the treasures of the Rochers Rouges. A few days after the cable had been dispatched, he landed at Marseilles and arrived at Mentone, where he became the companion of Arthur Rance and his wife in the Château of Hercules, which his very presence seemed to fill with life and gayety.

The gayety of Old Bob appeared to us a little theatrical, but that feeling arose without doubt from the effects of our apprehensions of the evening before. The Old Bob had the soul of a child; he was as much of a coquette as an old woman (that is to say, that his coquetries frequently changed their object), and, having once for all adopted a garb of the most severe—black coat, black waistcoat, black trousers, white hair and rosy cheeks—there was constantly attached to him the idea of complete harmony. It was in this professional uniform that Old Bob had chased the tigers in the pampas and this he wore at the present time while he dug in the grottoes of Rochers Rouges in his search for the missing bone of the *elephus antiquus*.

Mrs. Rance presented him to us, and he uttered a few polite phrases, after which he opened his wide mouth in a great hearty laugh. He was jubilant, and we were soon to learn the reason why. He had brought back from his visit to the Museum of Paris the certainty that the skeleton of the Barma Grande was no more ancient than the one which he had discovered in his last expedition to Terra del Fuego. All the Institute was of this opinion, and took for the basis of its reasonings the fact that the bone of the spine of the *elephus* which Old Bob had carried to Paris, and which the owner of the Barma Grande had loaned him after having declared to him that he had found it in the same bed of earth as the famous skeleton—that this spinal bone belonged, let us say, to an *elephus* of the middle of the quarternary period. Ah, it would have done your heart good to hear the joyous contempt with which Old Bob spoke of the middle of the quarternary period. At the very thought of a spinal bone of the middle of the quarternary period, he laughed as heartily as though some one had told him the finest joke in the world. Could it be that in this day and age, a savant, worthy of being dignified by the name, could find anything to interest him in a skeleton of the middle of the quarternary period! His own skeleton (or, to be more exact, that which he had brought from Terra del Fuego) dated from the commencement of this period, and, in consequence, was older by two thousand years—you hear? *two thousand years*—! And he was sure, because of this shoulder blade having belonged to the cave bear, the shoulder blade which he had found, he, Old Bob, between the arms of his own skeleton. (He said "my own skeleton" in his enthusiasm, making no distinction between the living skeleton which he was carrying about under his black coat, his black trousers, his white hair and his rosy cheeks, and the prehistoric skeleton of Terra del Fuego.)

"Therefore, my skeleton dates from the cave. But that of Baousse-Raousse! Oh, no, no, my children! at furthest from the epoch of the mammoth, and yet—no—no—from the rhinoceros with the cloven nostrils. Therefore—One has nothing left to discover, ladies and gentlemen, in the period of the rhinoceros with the cleft nostrils.—I swear it, upon the honour of Old Bob. My skeleton comes from the chelleenne epoch, as you say in France. Well, what are you laughing at? I am not even sure that the *elephus* of Rochers Rouges dates from the Mousterian epoch. And why not from the Silurian epoch—or yet—or yet—from the Magdalenian epoch? No, no—that's too much. An *elephus antiquus* from the Magdalenian epoch would be an impossibility. That *elephus* will drive me mad! Ah, I shall die of joy. Poor Baousse-Raousse!"

Mme. Edith had the unkindness to interrupt the jubilations of her uncle by announcing to him that Prince Galitch, who had purchased the Grotto of Romeo and Juliet at Rochers Rouges, must have made some sensational discovery, for she had seen him, the very morning of Old Bob's departure for Paris, passing by the Fort of Hercules, carrying under his arm a little box which he had touched as he went by, calling out to her, "See, Mrs. Rance! I have found a treasure!" She said that she had asked him what the treasure was, but he had walked on laughing, with the remark that he would have a surprise for Old Bob on his return. And later, she had heard that Prince Galitch had declared that he had discovered "the oldest skull in the history of the human race."

Mrs. Rance had scarcely pronounced these last words when every vestige of gayety fled from Old Bob's face and manner. His eyes shot fire and his voice was husky with passion as he exclaimed:

"That is a lie—an infernal lie! The oldest skull in the history of the human race is Old Bob's skull—do you understand me?—it is Old Bob's skull."

And he shouted out:

"Mattoni! Mattoni! Bring my trunk here at once!"

Almost as soon as the words were spoken, we saw Mattoni crossing the Court of Charles the Bold with Old Bob's trunk on his shoulder. He obeyed the professor to the letter, and carried the trunk through the room and up to his master. Old Bob took his bunch of keys, got down on his knees and opened the box. From this receptacle, which contained his clothing and piles of clean linen, neatly folded, he took a hat box, and from the hat box he drew out a skull, which he placed in the middle of the table among our coffee cups.

"The oldest skull in the history of humanity!" he echoed. "Here it is! It is Old Bob's skull! Look at it! Oh, I can tell you, Old Bob never goes anywhere without his skull!"

And he took up the frightful object and began to caress it, his eyes sparkling and his thick lips parting once more in a broad smile. If you will represent to yourself that Old Bob knew French only imperfectly and pronounced it like English or Spanish (he spoke Spanish like a native), you will see and hear the scene. Rouletabille and I were unable longer to control ourselves, and nearly split our sides with laughter—all the more, because Old Bob every few moments would interrupt himself in the midst of a peal of merriment to demand of us what was the object of our mirth. His wrath was almost as funny as his mirth, and even

Mme. Darzac could not refrain from laughter, for, in truth, Old Bob, with his "oldest skull of the human race," was a droll sight to see. I must acknowledge, too, that a skull two hundred thousand years old is not such an unpleasant sight as one might expect it to be, especially when, like this one, it has all its teeth.

Suddenly Old Bob grew serious. He lifted the skull in his right hand and placed the forefinger of the left hand upon the forehead of his ancestor.

"When one looks at the skull from above, one notices very clearly a pentagonal formation which is due to the notable development of the parietal bumps and the jutting out of the shell of the occipitals. The great breadth of the face comes from the exaggerated development of the zygomatic proportions. While in the head of the troglodytes of the Baousse-Raousse, what do we find?"

I shall never know what it was that Old Bob found in the head of the troglodytes, for I did not listen to him, *but I looked at him*. And I had no further inclination for laughter. Old Bob seemed to me terrifying, horrible, as false as the Father of Lies, with his counterfeit gayety and his scientific jargon. My eyes remained fixed upon him as if they were fascinated. It seemed to me that I could see his hair move, just as a wig might do. One thought—the thought of Larsan, which never left me completely, seemed to expand until it filled my entire brain. I felt as if I must speak it out, when all at once, I felt an arm locked in mine, and I saw Rouletabille looking at me with an expression which I did not know how to read.

"What is the matter, Sainclair?" whispered the lad, anxiously.

"My friend," I returned in a tone as low as his own. "I dare not tell you; you would make sport of me."

He drew me away from the table and we walked toward the west boulevard. After he had looked closely on every side and made sure that no one was near us, he said:

"No, Sainclair, no: I won't make sport of you, for you are in the right in seeing *him* everywhere around us. If he were not there a little while ago, he is perhaps there now. Ah, he is stronger than the stones! He is stronger than anything else in the world. I fear him less within than without. And I should be very glad if the stones which I have called to my aid in hindering his entrance shall aid me to hold him inside. For, Sainclair, *I feel that he is here!*"

I pressed Rouletabille's hand, for, strange as it may seem, I shared the same impression—I felt that the eyes of Larsan were upon me—I could hear him breathe. When and how this sensation had first come over me, I was unable to say. But it seemed to me that it had come with the appearance of Old Bob.

I said to Rouletabille, scarcely daring to put into words what was in my mind:

"Old Bob?"

He did not answer. At the end of a few moments, he said:

"Hold your left hand in your right for five minutes and then ask yourself: *'Is it you, Larsan?' And when you have replied to yourself, do not feel too sure, for he may, perhaps, have lied to you, and he may be in your own skin without your knowing it.*"

With these words, Rouletabille left me alone in the west boulevard. It was there that Pere Jacques came to look for me. He brought me a telegram. Before reading it, I congratulated him on his appearance, for he showed no trace of the fact that, like all the rest of us, he had passed a sleepless night; but he informed me that the pleasure he experienced in seeing his "dear Mlle. Mathilde" happy had made him ten years younger. Then he tried to obtain from me some information in regard to the motives for the strange vigil of the night before, and the reason for the events which had occurred at the château since Rouletabille's arrival and for the exceptional precautions which had been taken to prevent the entrance of any stranger. He added that if "that monster, Larsan," were not dead, it would seem as if we dreaded his return. I told him that this was not the moment for explanations and reasoning, and that, as he was a worthy man, he ought, like all other soldiers, to observe the rules without seeking to understand them or to discuss them. He saluted me with a military gesture and started off, shaking his head. The old man was evidently puzzled, and it did not displease me at all that, since he had the watch of the North Gate, he had thought of Larsan. He also had narrowly escaped being one of Larsan's victims; he had not forgotten the fact. It would make him a better sentinel.

I was not in much of a hurry to open the dispatch which Pere Jacques had brought me, and in this I was wrong, for as soon as I cast my eyes over the words which it contained, I realised that it was of the deepest importance. My friend at Paris, whom I had requested to keep an eye upon Brignolles, sent me word that the said Brignolles had left Paris the evening before for the Midi. He had taken the 10:35 train. My friend informed me that he had reason to believe that Brignolles had taken a ticket for Nice.

What should Brignolles be doing in Nice? That was the question which I propounded to myself, and which I have since so often regretted that a foolish impulse of self-esteem kept me from putting to Rouletabille. The young reporter had made so much fun of me when I showed him the first dispatch, which stated that Brignolles had not quitted Paris, that I resolved to tell him nothing about the one which announced his departure. Since Brignolles amounted to so little, in his opinion, I would not bother him with Brignolles. And I kept Brignolles to myself, all alone and so well, that when, assuming my most indifferent air, I rejoined Rouletabille in the Court of Charles the Bold, I never mentioned the subject.

Rouletabille was ready to fasten down with bars of iron the heavy circularly cut oak board which closed the opening to the "oubliette," and he showed me that even if the shaft communicated with the sea, it would be impossible for anyone to succeed in an attempt to introduce himself into the château by this means, for the reason that he could not raise the board and would be driven to give up his plan. His brow was dripping with perspiration, his arms were bared, his collar thrown off, a heavy hammer was in his hand. It seemed to me that he was devoting considerable time and energy to a comparatively simple task, and, like a fool who does not see beyond the end of his own nose, I could not refrain from telling him so. How could I have helped guessing that the boy was voluntarily exerting himself beyond necessity, and that he was delivering himself up to all sorts of physical fatigue in order to efface the memory of the grief which filled his poor heart? But no! I was only able to understand that, half an hour later, when I came upon him lying beside the ruins of the chapel, murmuring in his dreams the one word which betrayed the sorrow of his heart—"Mother." Rouletabille was dreaming of the Lady in Black! He dreamed, perhaps, that her arms were around him as in days gone by, when he was a little fellow and came into the school parlour, flushed and breathless with running. I waited beside him for a moment, asking myself nervously if I ought to leave him in there, or whether there was any danger of anyone's else passing by and discovering his secret. But, after having relieved his overcharged heart with that one word, the lad left nothing more to be heard except his heavy breathing. He was completely exhausted. I believe that it was the first time that the boy had really slept since we had come from Paris.

I profited by his slumbers to leave the château with out informing anyone of my intention, and soon, my dispatch in my pocket, I took the train for Nice. On the way, I chanced to read this item on the first page of the *Petit Nicois*: "Professor Stangerson has arrived at Garavan, where he will spend a few weeks with M. Arthur Rance, the recent purchaser of the Fort of Hercules, who, aided by the beautiful Mme. Arthur Rance, will dispense the most gracious hospitality to his friends in this fine old medieval stronghold. As we go to press, we learn that Professor Stangerson's daughter, whose marriage to M. Robert Darzac has just taken place in Paris, has also arrived at the Fort of Hercules with her husband, the brilliant young professor of la Sorbonne. These new guests descend upon us from the North at the time when strangers usually leave us. How wise they are! There is no more beautiful springtime in the world than that of the 'azure shore.'"

At Nice, hidden behind the blinds of a buffet, I awaited the arrival of the train from Paris, by which Brignolles was due to arrive. And the next moment I saw him alighting from a car. Ah, how my heart beat, for I knew that there must be some strange reason for this journey of which he had not informed M. Darzac beforehand. And I knew that the trip was a secret one, when I saw that Brignolles was trying to avoid observation, was bending his hand as he hurried along, gliding rapidly as a pickpocket among the passengers, so that he was soon lost to sight. But I was behind him. He jumped into a closed hack and I hastily got into another closed just as tightly. At the Place Massena he left his carriage and turned toward the Jetee Promenade, where he took another cab. I still followed him. These maneuvers seemed to me more and more ambiguous. Finally, Brignolles' carriage came out upon the road de la Corniche, and I directed my coachman to take the same way. The numerous windings of this road, its accentuated curves, permitted me to see without being seen. I had promised my coachman a large tip if he helped me to keep in sight of my quarry, and he did his very best. Finally, we reached the Beaulieu railway station, where I was astonished to see Brignolles' carriage stop and the man himself get out, pay the driver and enter the waiting room. He was going to take the train. For what purpose? If I should attempt to get into the same car as he, would he not be certain to see me in this little station or on the almost deserted platform? But I decided to try it anyway. If he were to see me, I could get out of the difficulty by feigning surprise at his presence, and by sticking to him until I was sure of what he was going to do in this part of the world. But luck was with me and Brignolles did not see me. He got into a passenger coach which was bound for the Italian frontier.

I realised that all his movements were bringing him nearer to the Fort of Hercules. I got in the car behind his and watched from my window all the travellers who got out at every station.

Brignolles did not get off until we reached Mentone. He certainly had some reason for reaching there by a different train than the one from Paris, and at an hour when there was little chance of his seeing any acquaintances at the station. I saw him alight: he had turned up the collar of his overcoat and pulled his hat down over his eyes. He cast a stealthy glance around the quay, and then, as if reassured, mingled with the other passengers. Once outside the train shed, he got into a shabby old stage coach which was standing by the sidewalk. I watched him from the corner of the waiting room. What was he doing here? And where was he going in that rackety old vehicle? I inquired of an employé, who told me that that carriage was the stage to Sospel.

Sospel is a picturesque little city lost between the last counterfores of the Alps, two hours and a half from Mentone by coach. No railroad passes through there. It is one of the most retired and quietest corners of France, the most dreaded by revenue officers and by the Alpine hunters. But the road which leads to it is one of the most beautiful in the world, for, in order to reach Sospel, it is necessary to wind through I do not know how many mountain passes, to climb countless precipices, and to follow, until one reaches Castillon, the deep and narrow valley of Carei, as wild as a field in Judaea, but covered with luxuriant herbage, bright with beautiful flowers, fertile and beautiful with the shimmering gold of its forests of olive trees, which descend from the heights to the clear bed of the stream by the terraces of a giant staircase formed by nature. I had been at Sospel a few years previously with a party of English tourists in an immense carriage, drawn by eight horses, and I had brought from the trip a remembrance of vertigo which came over my mind in the future every time the name was mentioned. Why was Brignolles going to Sospel? I must find out. The diligence was crowded and had already started on its way with a loud noise of creaking springs and of shaking window panes. I hired a carriage from the station and in a few moments I, too, was climbing over the rocks to the valley of Carei. How I regretted not having spoken of my telegram to Rouletabille! The strange behaviour of Brignolles would have given him ideas, useful and reasonable, while, for my part, I had not the slightest idea of how to reason. I only knew how to follow this Brignolles as a dog follows his master or a policeman follows his quarry by the clues which he finds. And yet, had I followed them well, these clues? It was at the moment that I felt certain that nothing in the world in regard to this man's movements could be small enough to escape me that I made a formidable discovery. I had let the diligence keep a little way in advance, a precaution which I deemed necessary, and I reached Castillon ten minutes later than Brignolles. Castillon is at the highest point of the road between Mentone and Sospel. My driver asked my permission to let his horse rest for a moment, and while he watered the beast, I descended from the carriage, and, at the entrance of a tunnel through which it was necessary to pass to reach the opposite turn of the mountain, I beheld Brignolles and Frederic Larsan!

I stood staring at them, my feet as helpless as though they had taken root in the soil. I could not utter a sound nor make a gesture. Upon my honour, I was completely stupefied by the revelation. Then I recovered my wits, and at the same time felt myself overwhelmed by a feeling of horror for Brignolles, and by a feeling of admiration for my own intuition in regard to him. Ah, I had known from the start! I had been the only one to guess that the companionship of this devil of a Brignolles had been of the gravest danger to Robert Darzac. If they would have listened to me, the Professor of la Sarbonne would have gotten rid of the creature's presence long ago. Brignolles, the tool of Larsan—the accomplice of Larsan—what a discovery! Why, I had known all along that those accidents in the laboratory had not happened by chance! They would believe me now! I had seen with my own eyes Larsan and Brignolles, talking and consulting together at the entrance of the Castillon tunnel. I *had* seen them—but where were they gone now? For I saw them no longer. They must be in the tunnel. I hastened my steps, leaving my coachman behind me, and reached the tunnel in a few moments, drawing my revolver from my pocket. My state of mind was beyond description. What would Rouletabille say when I told him all about my adventure? It was I—I—who had discovered Brignolles and Larsan.

But where were they? I walked through the dark tunnel—no Larsan, no Brignolles! I looked down the road which descends toward Sospel. Not a living creature! But upon my left, toward ancient Castillon, it seemed to me that I could perceive two forms that hastened. They disappeared. I ran after them. I arrived at the ruins. I stopped. Who could say that those two figures were not lying in wait for me behind a wall?

The old Castillon was no longer inhabited, and for a good reason. It had been entirely ruined—destroyed by the earthquake of 1887. Nothing of it remained but a few piles of stone and a few mural windows, gently covered with dust by time; some headless statues, a few isolated pillars which remained standing upright, spired by the shock, and leaning sorrowfully toward the earth, melancholy at having nothing to support. What a silence there was all around me! With a thousand precautions I searched through the ruins, contemplating with horror the depth of the crevices which the earthquake of 1887 had opened in the rocks. One of these in particular seemed to be a shaft without a bottom, and as I leaned above it, hanging on to an olive tree to keep from falling in, I was almost swept into the abyss by a gust of wind. I felt the draught on my face and recoiled with a cry. An eagle darted out of the abyss, quick as a flash. He rose straight to the sun, and then I saw him descend toward me, and describe some menacing circles above my head, uttering savage shrieks, as though he reproached me for having come to trouble him in his realm of solitude and of death which the elements had given him.

Had I been the victim of an illusion? I could no longer see my two shadows. Was I also the plaything of my imagination, when I stooped and picked up from the road a bit of letter paper which looked to me singularly like that which M. Robert Darzac used at la Sarbonne?

Upon this bit of paper I deciphered two syllables which I believed Brignolles had written. These syllables seemed to be the end of a word the beginning of which was missing. All that it was possible to make out was "bonnet."

Two hours later I reëntered the Fort of Hercules and told my story to Rouletabille, who placed the bit of paper in his portfolio and entreated me to be as silent as the grave in regard to my expedition.

Astonished at having produced so different an effect from the one which I had anticipated at a discovery which I believed so important, I stared at Rouletabille. He turned his head away, but not quickly enough to hide from me that his eyes were filled with tears.

"Rouletabille!" I exclaimed.

But again, he motioned me not to speak.

"Silence, Sainclair!"

I took his hand; it was burning with fever. And I thought that this agitation could not come entirely from his apprehensions in regard to Larsan. I reproached him with concealing from me what had passed between him and the Lady in Black, but, as often happened, he made me no answer, and turned away, heaving a deep sigh.

They had waited dinner for me. It was late. The dinner was a dismal affair, in spite of the gayety of Old Bob. We scarcely attempted to hide the deep anxiety which froze our hearts. One would have said that each one of us was resigned to the blow which was threatening and that we had lost hope that it might be averted. M. and Mme. Darzac ate nothing. Mme. Edith kept looking at me with a strange expression. At ten o'clock I went to take up my station at the tower of the gardener, almost with relief. While I was in the little room where we had consulted together the night before, the Lady in Black and Rouletabille passed beneath the arch. The glimmer of the lantern fell on their faces. Mme. Darzac appeared to me to be in a state of the greatest excitement. She was urging Rouletabille to something which I could not hear. The conversation between them looked like an argument and I caught only one word of Rouletabille, "Thief!" The two entered the Court of the Bold. The Lady in Black stretched her arm toward the young man, but he did not see it, for he left her immediately and went toward his own room. She remained standing alone for a moment in the court, leaning against the trunk of the eucalyptus tree in an attitude of unutterable sadness, then, with slow steps, she entered the Square Tower.

It was now the tenth of April. The attack of the Square Tower occurred on the night between the eleventh and twelfth.

X

The Events of The Twelfth of April

This attack took place under circumstances so mysterious and so inexplicable, to all appearances, under any reasonable hypothesis, that the reader will permit me, in order to make him comprehend the issue more fully, to dwell upon certain details in regard to the manner in which we spent our time on the eleventh day of April, 1895.

(1) *The Morning*.

The day, almost from the rising of the sun, was intolerably hot and the hours on guard were almost overpowering. The sun was as torrid as in the heart of Africa and it would have blinded us to keep watch over the waters which burned like a sheet of steel, brought to a white heat, if we had not been furnished with eyeglasses of crooked glass, without which it is difficult to pass the—a son of departing winter in this part of the country.

At nine o'clock, I came down from my room and went to the postern and entered the room which we had styled "the hall of counsel" to relieve Rouletabille of his guard. I had no time to say a single word to him before M. Darzac appeared, following almost upon my heels, and announcing that he had something very important to communicate to us. We inquired anxiously the cause of his agitation and he replied that he intended to quit the Fort of Hercules at once, taking his wife with him. This declaration left Rouletabille and myself dumb with surprise. I was the first to speak and endeavoured to dissuade M. Darzac from even thinking of such an imprudence. Rouletabille frigidly inquired the reason for our friend's sudden resolution and the latter replied by informing us of a scene which had occurred during the previous evening at the château and which revealed to us in how difficult a position the Darzacs were placed by remaining at the Fort of Hercules. The story may be summed up in a few words: Mme. Edith had had a nervous attack. We understood the reason at once for there was no doubt in the mind of either Rouletabille or myself that Mrs. Rance's jealousy of Mme. Darzac was increasing every hour and that each act of courtesy performed by the husband toward the former object of his admiration was positively insupportable to his wife. The sounds of the fit of hysterics to which she had treated M. Rance and the words which she had spoken the night before had penetrated even through the heavy walls of "la Louve," and M. Darzac, who was doing sentinel duty in the outer court, had been unable to help hearing some of the echoes of the young woman's anger.

Rouletabille implored M. Darzac to endure the situation with fortitude, unpleasant as were the circumstances. He assured him that he agreed with his feeling that the stay of himself and Mme. Darzac at the Fort of Hercules must be made as brief as possible: but he also assured him that the security of both de pended in great measure on their remaining in their present quarters for the time being. A new struggle had been begun between them on the one side and Larsan on the other. If they were to go away Larsan would know on the moment how to overtake them and in a time and place that they expected him the least. Here, they were forewarned, they were upon their guard, for they *knew*. Elsewhere, they would be at the mercy of everything and every person that surrounded them, for they would not have the ramparts of the Fort of Hercules to defend them. Certainly, this situation could not endure very long, but Rouletabille asked M. Darzac to wait eight days longer— not a single one more. "Eight days," said Columbus long ago, "and I will give you a new world." "Give me eight days and I will deliver Larsan into your hands," was not what Rouletabille said, but it was what we knew that he was thinking.

M. Darzac left us, shaking his head, doubtfully. He was angrier than we had ever seen him. Rouletabille remarked:

"Mme. Darzac will not leave us and M. Darzac will stay if she does."

And he started off on his rounds.

A few moments later, I caught sight of Mme. Edith. She was charmingly dressed, with a simplicity which suited her marvellously. She smiled at me coquettishly, but her gayety seemed a little forced as she jested at my "new trade." I answered her, perhaps a little too quickly, that she was uncharitable in her jests, because she knew quite well that all the trouble which we were taking and the careful watch which we were maintaining might be the means, at any moment, of saving the sweetest of women from untold misery and danger.

She looked at me mockingly and cried with a sharp little laugh:

"Oh, surely. "The Lady in Black!" She has you all under her spell."

What a ringing laugh she had! At another time, rest assured, I would not have allowed anyone to speak so lightly of "the Lady in Black," but this morning I had not the strength of mind to assert myself. On the contrary, I laughed, too.

"Perhaps, there is a little truth in that speech," I returned.

"My husband is crazy about her! I never would have believed that he could be so romantic. But, then," she went on, with a droll little sigh, "I am romantic, too!"

And she turned upon me that same curious look which had disturbed me before.

"Ah?" That was all that I could find to answer.

"And, therefore," she continued, "I take very great pleasure in the conversation of Prince Galitch, who is more romantic than all the rest of you put together."

Whereupon I asked her who was this Prince Galitch of whom I had heard so much but had not yet seen. She told me that he was coming to luncheon—that she had invited him on our accounts; and she gave me a few particulars in regard to him from which I learned that Prince Galitch was one of the richest landholders in his own part of Russia—that portion called the "Black Lands," fertile above all others, and situated between the forests of the North and the steppes of the Midi.

Fallen heir, at the age of twenty, to one of the greatest of Muscovite estates, he had increased his patrimony by economical and intelligent management of which no one would have believed a man so young to be capable—especially one who had heretofore had his hounds and his books as his principal objects in life. He was called a hermit, a miser and a poet. He had inherited from his father a high position at court. He was a chamberlain to His Majesty and, on account of the immense services rendered by the parent, the Emperor was supposed to regard the son with a great deal of affection. He was at once as gentle as a woman and as strong as a Turk—in brief, a thorough Russian gentleman.

I cannot tell why, but I felt a singular antipathy for the Prince without ever having set eyes on him.

His relations with the Rances were those of friendly neighbourliness. Having purchased two years before the magnificent property whose hanging gardens, flowery terraces, and beautiful balconies had made it known at Garavan as "the Garden of Babylon," he had had the opportunity to be of assistance to Edith when she had begun to make the outer court of the Château of Hercules into an exotic garden. He had presented her with certain plants which had revived, in some corners of the Fort of Hercules, a tropical vegetation hitherto scarcely known except on the banks of the Tigris and the Euphrates. M. Rance sometimes invited the Prince to dinner, and always after one of these functions the Prince would send to his hostess a wonderful palm tree from Nineveh or a cactus, fabled to have belonged to Semiramis. He declared that they cost him nothing. He had too many; he was tired of them and he did not want them among his roses. Edith said that she was interested in the young Russian because he dedicated such beautiful verses to her. After he had repeated them in Russian, he would translate them into English and he had even composed them in English for her and for her alone. Verses—the verses of a real poet, dedicated to Mme. Edith! This had so flattered her that she had requested the poet to compose English verses for her and translate them into Russian. This "literary game" greatly amused Mme. Edith, but Arthur Rance cared for it not at all. The young anthropologist did not attempt to conceal that his feelings toward Prince Galitch were not of the most friendly, and I felt assured that the traits which the husband disliked most heartily were those which the wife found most attractive in the Russian, for M. Rance had no use for "verse writing fellows," nor did he care for those who were quite so prudent in their expenditures. He could not understand how a poet could be something very like a miser. The Prince kept no carriage nor motor car. He used the street cars and often did his own marketing, attended by his servant, Ivan, who carried a basket for the provisions. And—so said Mrs. Edith, who had heard these details from the cook— he haggled over prices with the fishwife when there was only two sous between what she asked and what he offered. Strangely enough, this avariciousness did not seem in the least dis tasteful to Mme. Edith, who appeared to consider it a mark of originality. And, she finished by saying, "No one has ever set foot within his doors. He has never even invited us to come and see his gardens."

"Isn't it beautifully fascinating?" demanded the young woman when she had completed her description.

"Too beautifully fascinating!" I replied. "You will see!"

I do not know why this answer should have displeased my hostess, but I could see that it did so. Mme. Edith turned away and left me and I finished my guard duty which was an hour and a half long.

The first stroke of the luncheon bell sounded: I hurried to my room to bathe my hands and face and make a hasty toilet and I mounted the steps of "la Louve" rapidly fearing that I should be late; but I paused in the vestibule, amased to hear the sound of music. Who, under the present circumstances, cared or dared to play a piano in the Fort of Hercules? And, hark someone was singing. It was a voice at once soft and sonorous singing a strange song which sounded now plaintive, now threatening! I know the song now by heart; I have often heard it since. Ah, reader, you, too, know it well, perhaps, if you have ever passed the frontiers of chill Lithuania, if you have ever entered the vast empires of the North. It is the song of the virgins who surround the traveller as he sails and destroy him without pity; it is the song that Sienkiewicz, one immortal day, made for Michel Vereszezaka. Listen.

"If you approach the Swiss lakes at the hour of night fall, the face turned toward the lake, the stars above Ayour head, the stars beneath your feet, and two moons shining before your eyes—you shall see this plant that caresses the bank—the wives and daughters of the Swiss whom God has changed into flowers. They balance their forms above the abyss, their heads white like the moths; their leaves are green as the needle of the maize tipped with gold.

"Images of innocence during life, they have kept their virginal robe after death; they live in the shadow and no blemish comes near them; mortal hands dare not touch them,

"The Tsar and his guard one day made the attempt when, after having gathered the beautiful flowers, they wished to wreath their brows and adorn their swords with them.

"All those who had gathered the blossoms were smitten with great ill or struck with sudden death.

"When time would have effaced these things from the memory of the people, the memory of the punishment is preserved, and in perpetuating it, the flowers are still called the doom of the Tsars.

"Thus saying the lady of the lake departed slowly; the lake opened for her the most profound of its depths; but the eye seeks in vain for the fair unknown whose face was born out of the mist and whose voice the traveller never heard again."

These were the words, translated into our language, of the song which was sung by the soft yet resonant voice while the piano played a weird accompaniment. I opened the door and found myself face to face with a young man who was standing. I heard the footsteps of

Mme. Rance behind me and the next moment she was introducing me to Prince Galitch.

The Prince was of the type that one reads of in romances, "handsome, pensive young man"; his clear cut and rather stern profile might have given a somewhat severe expression to his face if his eyes, as mild and clear as those of a child, and with an expression of perfect candour, had not told an altogether different story. They were framed in long black lashes so black that they almost looked as though they had been touched with a pencil; and when one had noticed this peculiarity, one realised why it was that his countenance looked so strange. His skin was fresh and rosy, almost like that of a young girl. Such was my first impression of him but I felt the prejudice which I had experienced before I saw him rise up in my heart again. But it seemed to me, in spite of this, that he was too young to be of any special importance.

I could find nothing to say to this beautiful youth who chanted foreign poems. Mme. Edith smiled at my embarassment, took my arm (which gave me great satisfaction) and led me away to walk in the perfumed gardens of the outer court while we waited for the second bell for luncheon which was to be served to us in the cabin of palm trees on the platform of the Tower of the Bold.

(2) *The Luncheon and What Followed—A Contagious Terror Spreads Through Our Midst.*

At noon we seated ourselves at the table on the terrace of Charles the Bold, the view from which was incomparable. The palm leaves covered us with their grateful shade, for the heat of the earth and the heavens was so intense that our eyes would not have been able to endure the glare if we had not taken the precaution to put on the smoked spectacles of which I have spoken before.

Those of us at the table were M. Stangerson, Mathilde, Old Bob, M. Darzac, M. Arthur Rance, Edith, Rouletabille, Prince Galitch and myself. Rouletabille, turning his back to the sea, concerned himself very little with his companions and had placed himself in such a position that he could observe everything which transpired along the entire length of the fort. The servants were at their posts. Pere Jacques was at the entrance gate, Mattoni at the postern of the gardener, and the Berniers in the Square Tower before the door of the apartments occupied by M. and Mme. Darzac.

The first part of the meal was rather silent. I looked at the others. We were rather a solemn sight to contemplate around a table spread for good cheer—mute, and turning upon each other our dark smoked glasses behind which it was as impossible to see our eyes as to read our thoughts.

Prince Galitch was the first to make a remark. He spoke politely to Rouletabille mentioning the fame which the young reporter had won. This appeared to embarrass the lad a little and he made a confused and rather ungracious reply. The Prince did not seem to feel rebuffed, but went on to explain that he was particularly interested in the exploits of my friend for the reason that, as a subject of the Tsar, he knew that Rouletabille would shortly be sent to Russia. But the reporter replied that nothing had yet been decided and that he would prefer to say nothing on the subject until he had received his directions from his paper; whereupon, the Prince astonished us by drawing a newspaper from his pocket. It was a journal of his own country from which he translated to us a few lines announcing the fact that Rouletabille was soon to be in St. Petersburg. There was occurring in that city, the Prince went on to read to us, a series of events so strange and inexplicable in high governmental circles that, upon the advice of the Chief of the Secret Service at Paris, the Superintendent of Police had decided to ask the Epoch to lend him the young reporter. Prince Galitch had presented the affair so vividly that Rouletabille blushed to the roots of his hair as he replied dryly that he had never in the course of his short life done detective work and that the Chief of the Secret Service at Paris and the Superintendent of Police at St. Petersburg were two idiots. The Prince showed his fine teeth in a hearty laugh and it seemed to me that his laughter was not pleasant but cruel and savage. He seemed to be of Rouletabille's opinion in regard to the Government officers, and, as if to prove the fact, he added:

"It sounds good to hear anyone talk like that, for now one expects tasks of journalists which have nothing in the world to do with their profession."

Rouletabille made no reply and the subject was abandoned.

Mme. Edith arose from her chair, speaking ecstatically of the beauty of nature. But, in her opinion, she declared, there was nothing more beautiful anywhere near than the "Gardens of Babylon." She added, mischievously: "They seem so much more beautiful, because one may only see them from a distance!"

The attack was so direct that it seemed as though the Prince must reply to it by an invitation. But he said nothing. Mme. Edith looked vexed and a moment later, said suddenly:

"I'm not going to deceive you any longer, Prince. I have seen your gardens."

"Indeed! And how was that?" inquired Galitch, not losing his presence of mind for an instant.

"Yes, I have been there, and I'll tell you all about it."

And she related while the Prince listened with an air of cold imperturbability the story of her visit to the "Gardens of Babylon."

She had come upon them, inadvertently, from the rear, in climbing over a hillock which separated the gardens from the mountains. She had wandered from enchantment to enchantment, but without being in the least astonished. When she had walked upon the seashore, she had seen enough of the "Gardens of Babylon." to prepare her for the marvels, the secrets of which she had so audaciously stolen. She had finally reached the edge of a little pond, black as ink, upon the bank of which she saw a great water lily and a little old woman with a long, peaked chin. When they saw her the water lily and the little old woman had fled away, the latter so light on her feet in running that she fairly skimmed over the ground. Mme. Edith had laughed and had called after her:

"Madame! Madame!"

But the little old woman had seemed only more terrified and had disappeared with her lily behind the barberry hedge. Mme. Edith had continued her stroll but not quite so carelessly. Suddenly she had heard a rustle in the bushes and the strange cry which is made by wild birds when, surprised by the hunter, they escape from the prison of verdure in which they have hidden themselves. It was another little old woman, still more shrivelled and wrinkled than the first, but heavier of build and who carried her cane like a battle axe. She vanished—that is to say, Edith lost sight of her in a turn of the path. And a third little old woman, leaning on two canes appeared a little further on in the mysterious garden: she escaped behind the trunk of a giant eucalyptus tree and she went so much the faster than she had done before, by running on her hands and knees so rapidly that it was amazing that she did not get all tangled up. Mme. Edith still went on. And at last she came to the marble steps of the villa with their climbing roses over head, but the three little old women were standing guard on the highest step like three rooks on a branch and they opened their threatening beaks from which escaped threatening sounds. It was then Mme. Edith's turn to flee.

The little woman had related her adventure in a manner so charming and with such grace, borrowed as it was from the fairy tales of childhood, that I was enraptured and began to comprehend how certain women who have nothing natural about them can supplant in the heart of men those whose gifts are only those of nature.

The Prince did not seem in the least embarrassed by the little history. He said without a smile:

"Those are my three fairy godmothers. They have never left me since the hour of my birth. I can neither work nor live without them, I can only leave them when they permit it and they watch over my verse making with a fierce jealousy."

The Prince had scarcely ceased giving us this fantastic explanation of the presence of the three old women in the "Gardens of Babylon" when Walter, Old Bob's man servant, brought a dispatch to Rouletabille. The latter asked permission to open it and read aloud:

"Return as soon as possible. We are waiting for you very anxiously. A magnificent assignment at St. Petersburg."

This dispatch was signed by the Editor in chief of the Epoch.

"Well, what do you say to that, M. Rouletabille?" demanded the Prince. "Will you admit now that I was pretty well informed?"

The Lady in Black could not repress a sigh. "I shall not go to St. Petersburg!" declared Rouletabille.

"They will regret your decision at the Court," said the Prince. "I am certain of that, and, allow me to say, young man, that you are missing a wonderful opportunity."

The term "young man" seemed extremely displeasing to Rouletabille, who opened his lips as though to answer the Prince, but closed them again, to my great surprise, without uttering a word. Galitch went on:

"You would have found an adventure worthy of your skill. One may hope for everything when one has been strong enough to unmask a Larsan!"

The word fell into the midst of us like a bombshell and, as if by a common impulse, we took refuge behind our smoked glasses. The silence which followed was horrible. We sat as motionless as statues. *Larsan!* Why should this name which we ourselves had so often pronounced within the last forty-eight hours and which represented a danger with which we were commencing to almost feel familiar—why, I say, should that name, spoken at that precise moment, have produced an effect upon us, which, speaking for myself, was like nothing ever felt before? It seemed to me as though I had been struck by a thunderbolt. An indefinable terror glided through my body. I longed to flee but it seemed to me that if I were to stand up my limbs would not be able to support me. The unbroken silence on every hand contributed to increase this indescribable state of hypnosis. Why did no one speak? Where had old Bob's gayety vanished? He had scarcely uttered a word during the meal. And why did all the others sit so silent and so motionless behind their dark glasses? All at once, I turned my head and looked behind me. Then I understood, more by instinct than anything else, that I was the object of a common psychical attraction. Someone was looking at me. Two eyes were fixed upon me—*weighing* upon me. I could not see the eyes and I did not know from where the glance fixed upon me came, but it was there. I knew it—and it was *his* glance. But there was no one behind me, nor at the right, nor the left, nor in front, except the people who were seated at the table, motionless, behind their dark glasses. And then—then I knew that Larsan's eyes were glaring at me from behind a pair of those glasses—ah! the dark glasses— the dark glasses behind which were hidden Larsan's eyes.

And then, all at once, the sensation passed. The eyes, doubtless, were turned away from me. I drew a long breath. Another sigh echoed my own. Was it from the breast of Rouletabille—was it the Lady in Black, who perhaps, had at the same time as myself endured the weight of those piercing eyes?

Old Bob spoke:

"Prince, I do not believe that your last spinal bone goes any further back than the middle of the quaternary period."

And all the black spectacles turned in his direction. Rouletabille arose and made a sign to me. I hastened to the council room where he was waiting for me. As soon as I appeared, he closed the door and whispered:

"Well, did you fuel it, too?"

I felt smothered. I could scarcely articulate.

"He was there—at that table—unless we are going mad."

There was a pause and then I resumed, more calmly:

"You know, Rouletabille, that it is quite possible that we are going mad. This phantasm of Larsan will land us all in a madhouse yet! We have been shut up here only two days and see the state we are in!"

Rouletabille interrupted me.

"No, no; I felt him. He is there. I could have touched him! But where—but when? Since I came into that room, I have known that it was not necessary for me to go further. I will not fall into his trap. I will not go and look for him outside the castle even though I have seen him outside with my own eyes—even though you saw him with yours."

All in a moment he seemed to grow perfectly calm, passed his hand across his eyebrows, lighted his pipe and said, as he had so often said before, in happier hours when his reasoning powers, which were yet ignorant of the ties which united him to the Lady in Black, were not disturbed by the tumult of his heart:

"Let us reason it out!"

And he returned on the instant to that argument which had already served us and which he repeated again and again to himself (in order that, he said, he should not be lured away by the outer appearance of things): "Do not look for Larsan in that place where he reveals himself; seek for him everywhere else where he hides himself."

This he followed up with the supplementary argument:

"He never shows himself where he seems to be except to prevent us from seeing him where he really is."

And he resumed:

"Ah! the outer appearance of things! Look here, Sainclair! There are moments when, for the sake of reasoning clearly, I want to get rid of my eyes! Let us get rid of our eyes, Sainclair, for five minutes—just five minutes, and, perhaps, we shall see more clearly."

He seated himself, placed his pipe on the table, buried his face in his hands and said:

"Now, I have no eyes. Tell me, Sainclair—*who is within these walls?*"

"What do I see within these walls?" I echoed stupidly.

"No, no! You have no eyes at all; you see nothing. Enumerate them without seeing. Count them ALL."

"There is, first of all, you and I," I said, understanding, at last, what he wished to reach.

"Very well."

"Neither you nor I," I continued, "is Larsan."

"Why?"

"Why?" I echoed.

"Yes, why. Tell me. You must give a reason why you believe so. I acknowledge that I am not Larsan; I am sure of that, for I am

Rouletabille; but, face to face with Rouletabille, tell me why you cannot be Larsan?"

"Because you saw him—"

"Idiot!" exclaimed Rouletabille closing his eyes in with his clasped hands more firmly than before. "I have no eyes. I can't see anything! If Jerry, the croupier at Monte Carlo, had not seen the Comte de Maupas sit down at his table, he would have sworn that the man who picked up the cards was Ballmeyer! If Noblet at the garrison had not found himself face to face one evening at the Troyons, with a man whom he recognised as the Vicomte Drouet d'Eslon, he would have sworn that the man whom he came to arrest and whom he did not arrest because he had *seen* him, was Ballmeyer. If Inspector Giraud, who knew the Comte de Motteville as well as you know me, had not *seen* him one afternoon at the race course at Longchamps, chatting with two of his friends—had not *seen*, I say, the Comte de Motteville, he would have arrested Ballmeyer. Ah, you see, Sainclair!" exclaimed the lad in a voice shaken with sobs, "my father was born before I was! One will have to be very strong and very shrewd to capture my father!"

The words were uttered so despairingly that the little force of reasoning I possessed vanished completely. I threw out my hands before me, a gesture which Rouletabille did not see, for he saw nothing.

"No—no! It isn't necessary to *see* any of them" he repeated. "Neither you, nor M. Stangerson, nor M. Darzac, nor Arthur Rance, nor Old Bob, nor Prince Galitch. But we must know some good reason why each of these cannot be Larsan. Only when that is accomplished shall I be able to breathe freely behind these stone walls!"

There was no freedom in my breathing. We could hear, under the arch of the postern, the regular steps of Mattoni as he kept guard.

"Well, how about the servants?" I asked, with an effort. "Mattoni and the others?"

"I am absolutely certain that none of them was absent from the Fort of Hercules when Larsan appeared to Mme. Darzac and to M. Darzac at the railway station at Bourg." "Own up, Rouletabille!" I cried. "That you don't trouble yourself about them because none of their eyes were behind the black spectacles."

Rouletabille tapped the ground impatiently with his foot and said:

"Be quiet, please, Sainclair. You make me more nervous than my mother."

This phrase, uttered in vexation, struck me strangely.

I would have questioned Rouletabille in regard to the state of mind of the Lady in Black, but he resumed, meditatively:

"First, Sainclair is not Larsan, because Sainclair was at Trepot with me while Larsan was at Bourg."

"Second: Professor Stangerson is not Larsan because he was on his way from Dijon to Lyons while Larsan was at Bourg. As a fact, reaching Lyons one minute before him, M. and Mme. Darzac saw him alight from the train."

"But all the others, if it is necessary to prove that they were not at Bourg at that moment, might be Larsan, for all of them might have been at Bourg."

"First M. Darzac was there. Arthur Rance was away from home during the two days which preceded the arrival of the Professor and of M. Darzac. He arrived at Mentone just in time to receive them (Mme. Edith herself informed me in reply to a few careless questions of mine that her husband had been absent those two days on business). Old Bob made his journey to Paris. Prince Galitch was not seen at the grottoes nor outside the Gardens of Babylon.

"First, let us take M. Darzac."

"Rouletabille!" I cried. "That is a sacrilege."

"I know it."

"And it is a piece of the grossest stupidity."

"I know that, too. But why?"

"Because," I exclaimed, almost beside myself, "Larsan is a genius, we are aware; he might be able to deceive a detective, a journalist, a reporter, and even a Rouletabille—he might even deceive a friend, under some circumstances, I admit. But he could never deceive a daughter so far that she would take him for her father. That ought to reassure you as to M. Stangerson. Nor would he deceive a woman to the point of taking him for her betrothed. And, my friend, Mathilde Stangerson knew M. Darzac and threw herself into his arms at the railway station."

"And she knew Larsan, too!" added Rouletabille coldly. "Well, my dear fellow, your reasons are powerful but as I do not know at present what form the genius of my father has assumed as a disguise, I prefer rather to bestow, for the sake of supposition, a personality on M. Robert Darzac which I have never expected to fasten upon him, in order to base my argument against the possibility a little more solidly: If Robert Darzac were Larsan, Larsan would not have appeared on several occasions to Mathilde Stangerson, for it is the apparition of Larsan that has created a gulf between Mathilde Stangerson and Robert Darzac."

"Pshaw!" I cried. "Of what use are such vain reasonings when one has only to open his eyes—open them, Rouletabille!"

He opened them.

"Upon whom?" he asked with a trace of bitterness in his voice. "Upon Prince Galitch?"

"Why not? Do you like him, this prince from the Black Lands who sings Lithuanian folk songs?"

"No," replied Rouletabille. "But he entertains Mme. Edith."

And he smiled. I pressed his hand. He acted as though he had not felt the touch, but I knew that he did.

"Prince Galitch is a Nihilist and I am not troubled over him in the least degree," he said, tranquilly. "Are you sure of it? Who told you?"

"Bernier's wife, who knows one of the three old women whom Mrs. Edith told about at luncheon. I have made an investigation. She is the mother of one of the three men hanged at Kazan for the attempted assassination of the Emperor. I have seen the photograph of the poor wretches. The other two old women are the other two mothers. There's nothing interesting about that!"

I could not refrain from a gesture of admiration.

"Ah, you haven't lost any time."

"Neither has *he*!" he muttered.

I folded my arms.

"And Old Bob?" I asked.

"No, dear boy, no!" scoffed Roultubille, almost angrily. "Not he, either. You have noticed that he wears a wig, I suppose. Well, I assure you that when my father wears a wig, it will fit him."

He spoke so mechanically that I rose to leave him, thinking he had no more to say to me. He stopped me:

"Wait a minute. We have said nothing of Arthur Rance."

"Oh, he has not changed at all since we were at Glandier," I exclaimed. "That is out of the question." "Always the eyes! Take care of your eyes, Sainclair!"

And he put his hand on my shoulder for a moment as I turned away. Through my clothing I felt that his flesh was burning. He left the room and I remained for a moment where I stood, lost in thought. In thought of what? Of the fact that I had been wrong in saying that Arthur Rance had not changed at all. For one thing, now, he wore a slight moustache, something very rarely seen in an American of his type; next, his hair had grown longer with a lock falling over the forehead. And again, I had not seen him in two years—and everyone changes in two years—and again, Arthur Rance, who had used to drink heavily, now tasted only water. But then, there was Edith—what about Edith? Ah! was I going insane, I, too? Why do I say, "I, too," like—like the Lady in Black; like—like Rouletabille. Did I believe that Rouletabille's brain was becoming slightly turned? Ah, the Lady in Black had us all under her spell. Because the Lady in Black lived in the perpetual fear of her memories, here were we all trembling with the same horror as she. Fear is as contagious as the cholera.

(3) How I Spent My Afternoon up to Five O'clock.

I profited by the fact that I was not on guard to go to my room for a little rest; but I slept badly and dreamed that Old Bob, M. Rance and Mme. Edith had formed themselves into a band of brigands who had sworn death to Rouletabille and myself. And when I awakened under this pleasant impression and saw the old towers and the old château with their menacing walls rising before me, I came near thinking that my nightmare was real and I said to myself half aloud: "It's a fine place in which we have taken refuge!" I put my head out of the window. Mrs. Edith was walking in the Court of the Bold, chatting carelessly with Rouletabille and twisting the stem of a beautiful rose between her pretty fingers. I went down immediately. But when I reached the court, I found no one there. I followed Rouletabille whom I saw on his way to make his inspection of the Square Tower.

I found him quite calm and entirely master of him self—and also, entirely the master of his eyes, which were not closed now but open wide and keenly on the watch for anything that might turn up. Ah, it was worth while to see the manner in which he looked at everything around him! Nothing escaped him. And the Square Tower, the abode of the Lady in Black, was the object of his constant surveillance.

And at this point, it seems to me opportune, a few hours before the moment at which that most mysterious attack occurred, to present to the reader the interior plan of the inhabited story of the Square Tower the story which was on a level with the Court of Charles the Bold.

When one entered the Square Tower by the only door (K) one found himself in a large corridor which had previously formed a part of the guard room. The guard room had formerly taken up all the space at O, O, O" and O" and was shut in by walls of stone which still existed with their doors opening upon the other rooms of the Old Castle. It was Mrs. Arthur Rance who in this guard room had had wooden partitions raised to make quite a large room which she wished to use for a bathroom. This room, also, was now surrounded by the two passages at right angles to each other. The door of the room which served as the lodge of the Berniers was situated at S. It was necessary to pass in front of this door to reach R, where was the only door affording admission to the apartment of the Darzacs. One or other of the Berniers was always in the lodge. And no one save themselves had a right to enter it. From this lodge one could easily see from a little window at Y, the door V which opened off the suite of Old Bob. When M. and Mme. Darzac were not in their apartment, the only key which opened the door R was in the keeping of the Berniers; and it was a special kind of key made purposely for the room within the last twenty-four hours in a place which no one but Rouletabille knew. The young reporter had let no one into the secret.

Rouletabille would have wished that the watch which he had had placed upon the rooms of the Darzacs might have been kept also upon those of Old Bob, but the latter had opposed such an idea with an earnestness so comical that it was necessary to abandon it. Old Bob swore that he would not be treated like a prisoner and he said that on no account would he give up the privilege of going and coming to his own rooms when he saw fit without asking the keys from the lodge-keepers. His door must remain unlocked so that he might go as many times as he liked to his rooms, whether it might be to his bed chamber or to his sitting room in the Tower of Charles the Bold, without disturbing or worrying himself or anyone else. On account of his insistence, it was necessary to leave the door at K open. He demanded it and Mme. Edith upheld her uncle in so intense a manner and spoke so pertly to Rouletabille that he knew she was seeking to convey the idea that she believed that Rouletabille was treating Old Bob with discourtesy at the instigation of Professor Stangerson's daughter. So he had not insisted on what he believed to be best. Mme. Edith had said with her lips pressed together in a narrow little line: "But, M. Rouletabille, my uncle doesn't think that anyone is coming to carry *him* away!" And Rouletabille had realised that there was nothing for him to do save to laugh with the Old Bob over this absurd idea that one could be trying to steal as they would a pretty woman, the man who had the oldest skull in the world. And so he had laughed—had laughed even louder than Old Bob, but had imposed the condition that the door at K should be locked with a key after 10 o'clock at night and that the key should be left in the keeping of the Berniers, who would come and open it whenever anyone desired. Even this was against the inclination of Old Bob, who sometimes worked very late in the Tower of Charles the Bold. But, nevertheless, he declared, he would submit to it for he did not wish to have the appearance of opposing the worthy M. Rouletabille, who had told him that he was afraid of robbers. For, be it said in exculpation of Old Bob, that, if he lent himself so ungraciously to the defensive plans of our young friend it was because it had not been judged expedient to inform him in regard to the resurrection of Larsan. He had, of course, heard of the extraordinary series of fatalities which had formerly occurred in the history of poor Mlle. Stangerson; but he was a thousand miles from doubting that all her troubles had ceased long before she had become Mme. Darzac. And then, too, Old Bob was an egoist, like nearly all savants. Happy because he possessed the oldest skull in the history of the human race, he could not conceive that the whole world did not revolve around his treasure.

Rouletabille, after having politely inquired after the health of Mere Bernier, who was gathering up potatoes and putting them in a bag at her side, requested Pere Bernier to open the door of the Darzacs' room for us.

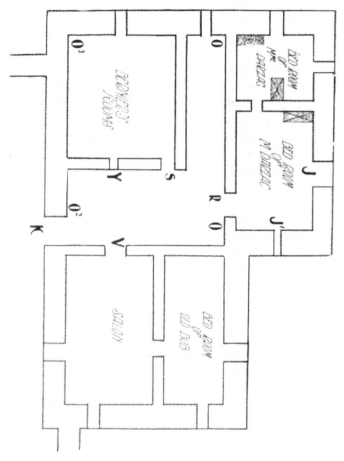

The Plan of the Inhabitied | Loot of the Square Tower

This was the first time that I had entered the apartment. The atmosphere was almost freezing, and the whole place seemed to me cold and sombre. The room, very large, was furnished with extreme simplicity, containing an oak bed, and a toilet table which was placed at one of the two openings in the wall around which there had formerly been loopholes. So thick was the wall and so large the opening that this embrasure (J) formed a kind of little room beside the big one and of this M. Darzac had made his dressing closet. The second window (J') was smaller. The two windows were fitted with bars of iron between which one could scarcely pass one's arm. The high bedstead had its back to the outer wall and had been drawn up against the partition of stone which separated M. Darzac's apartment from that of his wife. Opposite in the angle of the tower was a panel. In the centre of the room was a reading table on which were some scientific books and writing materials. And there was an easy chair and three straight-backed chairs. That was all. It would have been absolutely impossible for anyone to hide in this chamber, unless, of course, behind the panel. And then, too, Pere and Mere Bernier had received orders to look every time they visited the room both behind the panel and in the closet where M. Darzac hung his clothes, and Rouletabille himself, who, during the absence of the Darzacs often came to cast his eye around this room, never neglected to search it thoroughly.

He did so now, as I stood there. When we at length passed into the sleeping room of Mme. Darzac, we were absolutely certain that we had left nothing behind us of which we did not know. As soon as we entered the room, Bernier, who had followed us, had taken care, as he always did, to draw the bolt which closed from the inside the only door by which the apartment communicated with the corridor.

Mme. Darzac's room was smaller than that of her husband. But it was bright and well lighted from the way that the windows were placed. As soon as we set foot over the threshold, I saw Rouletabille turn pale and he turned to me and said:

"Sainclair, do you perceive the perfume of the Lady in Black?"

I did not. I perceived nothing at all. The window, barred, like all the others which looked out on the sea, was wide open and a light breeze rustled the hangings which had been drawn in front of a set of hooks for gowns which had been placed in one corner. The other corner was occupied by the bed. The hooks were placed so high that the gowns and peignoir which they held were covered by the hangings in front scarcely more than half way down, so that it would have been entirely out of the question for any person to conceal himself there without leaving his legs exposed to view from the knees to the feet. Nor would anyone have been able to hide in the corner where the portmanteaux and trunks were placed, although, nevertheless, Rouletabille examined it with the greatest care. There was no panel in this room. Toilet table, bureau, an easy chair, two other chairs, and the four walls between which there was no one but ourselves, as we could have sworn by all that we held most sacred.

Rouletabille, after having looked under the bed, gave the signal for departure and motioned us from the room. He lingered for a moment, but no longer. Bernier locked the door with the tiny key which he put in his inside pocket and tightly buttoned his coat over it. We made the tour of the corridors and also that of Old Bob's apartment which consisted of a bedroom and sitting room as easy to examine and as incapable of hiding anyone as those of the Darzacs. No one was in the suite, which was furnished rather carelessly, the chief article noticeable being an almost empty bookcase with the doors standing open. When we left the room Mere Bernier brought up her chair and placed it on the threshold where she could see clearly and still go on with her work, which seemed to be always that of paring potatoes.

We entered the rooms occupied by the Berniers and found them like all the others. The other stories were inhabited and communicated with the ground floor by a little inner stairway which began at the angle O' and ascended to the summit of the tower. A trap door in the ceiling of the Berniers' room closed this stairway. Rouletabille asked for a hammer and nails and nailed up the trap door, thus making the stairway unusable.

One might say, in short and in fact, that nothing escaped Rouletabille and that when we had made the rounds of the Square Tower we had left no one behind us save M. and Mme. Bernier. One would have said, too, that there could have been no human being in the apartment of the Darzacs before Bernier, a few minutes later, opened the door to M. Darzac himself as I am now about to relate.

It was about five minutes before five o'clock when, leaving Bernier in his corridor in front of the door of the Darzacs' room, Rouletabille and myself found ourselves again in the Court of the Bold.

At that moment we climbed to the platform of the ancient tower at B". We seated ourselves upon the parapet, our eyes looking down to the ground, attracted by the echoes of the Rochers Rouges. At that moment, we noticed upon the edge of the Barma Grande which opened its mysterious mouth in the flaming face of Baousse Raousse, the disturbed and wrathful countenance of Old Bob. His shadow was the only dark thing about. The red cliff's rose from the waters with such a vivid radiance that one might have readily believed that they were still glowing with the same fires which are found in the interior of the earth. By what a prodigious anachronism it was that this modern scholar with his coat and hat in the height of fashion should be moving about, grotesque and ghoulish, in front of this cavern three hundred thousand years old formed by the ardent lava to serve as the first roof for the first family in the first days of the world! Why this sinister gravedigger in this beautiful corner of the earth? We could see him brandishing his skull as he had done at the table and we could hear him laugh—laugh—laugh! Ah, his laughter made us ill even to think of it! It tore our ears and our hearts.

From Old Bob our attention was drawn to M. Darzac, who was coming through the postern of the gardener and crossing the Court of the Bold. He did not see us. Ah, he was not laughing! Rouletabille felt the deepest pity for him for he saw that he was at the end of his endurance. In the afternoon he had said to my friend, who now repeated the words to me: "Eight days is too much! I do not believe that I can bear this torment for eight days!"

"And where would you go?" Rouletabille had asked him.

"To Rome," he had replied. Evidently Professor Stangerson's daughter would accompany him nowhere else and Rouletabille believed that it was the idea that the Pope could arrange the affair which was driving him wild with grief that had put the journey to Rome into the mind of poor M. Darzac. Poor, poor M. Darzac! No, in truth, his face wore no smile.

We followed him with our eyes to the door of the Square Tower. We could see from his looks that he could endure no more. His head was moodily bent toward the ground; his hands were in his pockets. He had the air of a man fatigued and disgusted with the whole world. Yes, with his hands buried in his pockets, he looked out of humour with everything.

But, patience! he will take his hands out of his pockets and one will not smile at him always. I confess that I smiled. Well, M. Darzac a little after this gave me cause to experience the most frightful thrill of terror which could freeze human bones! And I did not smile then.

M. Darzac went straight to the Square Tower, where, of course, he found Bernier, who opened the door for him. As Bernier had been keeping constant guard before the door of the room, as he had kept the key in his pocket and as we had proven by our investigation that the place was empty when we had left it, we had established the fact that *when M. Darzac entered his room, there could be no one else there*. And this is the truth.

Everything that I have said could have been sworn to "after" by each one of us. If I tell it to you "before," it is that I am haunted by the mystery which lurks in the shadow and makes ready to reveal itself.

At the moment that we saw M. Darzac go to his room, we heard a clock strike five.

(4) *What Happened from Five O'clock that Night Until the Moment When the Attack on the Square Tower Began.*

Rouletabille and I remained chatting, or, rather, trying to reason things out, upon the platform of the Tower B for another hour. Suddenly, my friend struck me a little tap on the shoulder and exclaimed, "For my part, I think—" and then, without completing the sentence, he started for the Square Tower. I followed him.

I was a thousand miles from guessing what he thought. He thought of Mere Bernier's bag of potatoes which he emptied out on the white floor of the room to the great amazement of the good woman: then, satisfied with this act which evidently corresponded to the state of his mind, he returned with me to the Court of the Bold, while, behind us, we could hear Pere Bernier laughing as he picked up the potatoes.

As we reached the court we saw the face of Mme. Darzac appearing for a moment at the window of the room occupied by her father on the first story of "la Louve."

The heat had become insupportable. We were threatened with a violent storm and we believed that it would begin to lighten immediately.

Ah, how much the storm would relieve us, we thought. The sea had a thick and heavy quietude as though it had been saturated with oil. The sea was heavy and the air was heavy and our hearts were heavy. No one or nothing on the earth or in the heavens was lighter than Old Bob, whose form had appeared again at the edge of the Barma Grande and who was still moving around agitatedly. One would have said that he was dancing. No, he was making a speech To whom? We leaned over the railing to see. There was apparently someone upon the strand to whom Old Bob was addressing some long-winded scientific discourse. But the palm leaves hid his auditor from us. Finally, the listener moved and advanced, and approached the "black professor," as Rouletabille called him. And we saw that Old Bob's congregation was composed of two persons. One was Mme. Edith—we could easily recognize her with her languishing graces, clinging like a vine to her husband's arm. To her husband's arm! But this was not her husband? Who, then, was the young man upon whom Mme. Edith was playing off so many pretty airs?

Rouletabille turned around, looking for someone of whom to make inquiries—either Mattoni or Bernier.

We saw Bernier upon the threshold of the door of the Square Tower and Rouletabille beckoned him. Bernier approached and his eye followed the direction indicated by Rouletabille's finger.

"Who is that with Mme. Rance?" asked the young reporter.

"The young man?" responded Bernier without hesitation. "That is Prince Galitch."

Rouletabille and I looked at each other. It is true that we had never seen Prince Galitch walking at a distance, but I would not have imagined that his manner of walking would be like this, and he had not seemed to me to be so tell. Rouletabille understood my thoughts, I knew. He shrugged his shoulders.

"All right," he said to Bernier. "Thanks."

And we continued to gaze at Mme. Edith and her Prince.

"I can only say one thing," said Bernier as he turned to leave us. "And that is that I don't care for this prince at all. He is too soft spoken and too blonde and his eyes are too blue. They say that he is a Russian. That may be, but there are some who leave the country because they have to. But he comes and goes in a strange fashion and takes no leave beforehand. The time before the last that he was invited here to luncheon Madame and Monsieur waited and waited for him and dared not begin without him. Well, after an hour or two they received a wire, begging them to excuse him because he had missed the train. The dispatch was sent from Moscow."

And Bernier, chuckling, returned to his vantage post.

Our eyes remained fived upon the beach. Mme. Edith and her prince continued their stroll toward the grotto of Romeo and Juliet; Old Bob suddenly ceased to gesticulate, descended from the Barma Grande and came toward the château, entered the gate, crossed the outer court, and we saw, even from the height of the plat form of the tower, that he had ceased to smile. Old Bob's face had become sadness itself. He was silent. He passed beneath the arch of the postern. We called him, he did not seem to hear us. He carried before him in the crook of his arm his "oldest skull in the world," and all at once we saw him fly into the fiercest of passions. He addressed the worst of insults to the skull. He descended into the Round Tower and we heard the mutterings of his wrath for moments after he was out of sight. Then heavy blows resounded. One would have said that he was hurling himself against the wall.

At this moment six strokes resounded from the old clock of the New Castle. And at almost the same instant a clap of thunder echoed over the sea. And the line of the horizon grew black.

Then a groom of the stables, Walter, a brave, stupid fellow who was incapable of a single idea, but who had shown for years past the blind devotion of a brute toward his master, Old Bob, passed under the postern of the gardener, entered into the Court of Charles the Bold, and came to us. He held in his hand a letter which he gave to Rouletabille. He handed me another and continued on his way toward the Square Tower.

Rouletabille, calling after him, inquired what errand was taking him to the Square Tower. He answered that he was taking the mail for M. and Mme. Darzac to Pere Bernier. He spoke in English for Walter understood no other language; but we spoke it well enough to understand him and make him understand. Walter was charged with distributing the mail because Pere Jacques had no right to leave his lodge on any account. Rouletabille took the letters from the man's hands and said to him that he would take it in himself.

A few drops of water had begun to fall.

We turned to the door of M. Darzac's room. Bernier was smoking his pipe in the corridor, sitting astride a chair.

"Is M. Darzac still there?" asked Rouletabille.

"He hasn't stirred since he went in," Bernier replied.

We knocked. We heard the heavy bolt drawn from the inside. (These bolts can only be used by the person within the room.)

M. Darzac was writing letters when we entered. He had been seated beside the little reading table facing the door R. Now mark well all our movements. Rouletabille complained that the letter which he held in his hand confirmed the telegram which he had received in the morning and pressed him to return to Paris. His paper insisted upon his proceeding at once to Russia.

M. Darzac read indifferently the two or three letters which we had brought him and put them in his pocket. I held out to Rouletabille the letter which I had received. It was from my friend in Paris who, after having given me some important details regarding the departure of Brignolles, informed me that the laboratory assistant had left his address for mail to be forwarded to Sospel, the Hotel des Alps. This was extremely interesting and M. Darzac and Rouletabille were greatly excited over it. We decided to go to Sospel as soon as it could be arranged and, after talking of the matter for a few minutes, we went out of the room. The door of Mme. Darzac's sleeping room was not closed. Here is what we noticed as we passed out:

I have mentioned that Mme. Darzac was not in her own room. As soon as we made our exit, Pere Bernier immediately—immediately, I say, for I saw him—turned the key in the lock and then took it out and put it in his pocket—in the little inside pocket of his waistcoat. Ah, I can still see him putting the key into his inside pocket—I swear it!—and he buttoned his coat over it!

Then the three of us went out of the Square Tower, leaving Pere Bernier in his corridor like the good watch dog that he never ceased to be until the last day of his life. One may be a poacher and a good watch dog into the bargain, you know. Even watch dogs poach sometimes. And I bear witness here and now, among all the events which followed, Pere Bernier always did his duty and never told lies. And his wife, Mere Bernier, was an excellent servant, faithful, intelligent and not too talkative. Since she has been a widow, I have had her in my service. She will be glad to read here the tribute which I pay to her and to her husband. They both deserved it.

It was about half past six o'clock when, in emerging from the Square Tower, we went to pay a visit to Old Bob in the Round Tower, Rouletabille, M. Darzac and I. As soon as we entered the low basement M. Darzac uttered an exclamation of surprise and indignation at seeing the destruction which had been wrought upon a wash drawing upon which he had been working ever since the evening before in the endeavour to distract his mind, and which represented the plan for a great scaling ladder for the Fort of Hercules of the kind which had existed in the Fifteenth Century and of which Arthur Rance had shown us the pictures. This drawing had been gashed with a knife and paint had been smeared over it. He endeavoured in vain to obtain some explanation from Old Bob, who was kneeling beside a box containing a skeleton and was so wrapped up in a shoulder blade that he did not even answer us.

I desire here, by way of parenthesis, to ask the pardon of the reader for the mathematical precision with which for the last few pages, I have enumerated our every act and movement, but I will assure him, once and for all, that even the smallest circumstances have in reality a considerable importance, for everything which we did at this time was done, though alas, we did not guess it, on the brink of a precipice.

As Old Bob seemed to be in a churlish humour, we left him—that is, Rouletabille and myself did. M. Darzac remained gazing at his spoiled drawing, but thinking, doubtless, of altogether different things.

As we went out of the Round Tower, Rouletabille and I raised our eyes to the sky which was rapidly becoming covered with great, black clouds. The tempest was near at hand. In the meantime, the air seemed to grow more and more stifling.

"I am going to lie down in my room," I said. "I can't stand any more of this. Perhaps it may be cooler there with all the windows open."

Rouletabille followed me into the New Castle. Suddenly, as we reached the first landing of our winding staircase, he stopped me:

"Ah," he said in a low voice; "*she* is there!"

"Who?"

"The Lady in Black. Can't you smell the perfume?"

And he hid himself behind a door, motioning me to continue without waiting for him. I obeyed.

What was my amazement in opening the door of my room to find myself face to face with Mathilde!

She uttered a low cry and disappeared in the shadow, gliding away like a surprised bird. I rushed to the staircase and leaned over the balustrade. She swept down the steps like a ghost. She soon gained the ground floor and I saw below me the face of Rouletabille, who, leaning over the rail of the first landing, looked at her, too.

He mounted the steps to my side.

"Oh, my God!" he cried. "What did I tell you! Poor, poor soul!"

He seemed to be in the greatest agitation.

"I asked M. Darzac for eight days!" he went on.

"But this thing must be ended in twenty-four hours or I shall no longer have strength to act."

He entered my room and threw himself into a chair as if exhausted. "I am smothering!" he moaned. "I can't breathe!" He tore his collar away from his throat. "Water!" he entreated. "Water!"

I started to fetch some, but he stopped me.

"No—I want the water from the heavens! I must have it!" and he waved his hands toward the dark skies from which huge drops were slowly beginning to fall.

For ten minutes he remained stretched out in the chair, thinking. What surprised me was that he asked no question or uttered no conjecture as to what the Lady in Black had been seeking in my room. I would not have known how to answer, if he had done so. At length, he rose.

"Where are you going?" I asked.

"To take the guard at the postern."

He would not even come in to dinner and sent word to have some soup brought out to him as though he were a soldier. The dinner was served in la Louve at half past eight. Darzac, who came to the table from Old Bob's workroom, said that the latter refused to dine also. Mme. Edith, fearing that her uncle might be ill, went immediately to the Round Tower. She would not even allow her husband to accompany her—indeed, she seemed to be much out of humour with him.

The Lady in Black came in on the arm of her father. She cast on me a look of sorrowful reproach which disturbed me greatly. Her eyes seemed never to wander from me.

It was a gloomy meal enough. No one ate much. Arthur Rance looked every moment in the direction of the Lady in Black. All the windows were open. The atmosphere was suffocating. A flash of lightning and a heavy clap of thunder came in rapid succession—and then, the deluge! A sigh of relief issued from our over charged breasts. Mme. Faith reappeared just in time to escape being drenched by the furious rain which beat down like cannon balls upon the peninsula.

The young woman told us in excited tones and with her hands clasped, how she had found Old Bob bending over his desk with his head buried in his hands. He had refused to have anything to say to her. She had spoken to him affectionately and he had treated her like a bear. Then, as he had obstinately held his hands to his ears, she had pricked one of his fingers with a little pin set with rubies which she used to fasten the lace scarf which she wore in the evening over her shoulders. Her uncle, she said, had turned upon her like a mad man, had snatched the little pin from her and thrown it upon the desk. And then he had spoken to her—"brutally, rudely as he had never done before in his life!" she exclaimed. "Get out of here and leave me alone!" was what he had said to her. Mme. Edith had been so much pained that she went out without saying a word, promising herself, however, that she would not soon set foot again in the Round Tower. But she had turned her head for a last look at her old uncle and had been almost struck dumb by what she saw.

The "oldest skull in the history of the human race" was upon the desk, and Old Bob, a handkerchief stained with blood in his hand, was spitting in the skull. He had always treated it with the most severe respect and had insisted that others should do the same. Edith had hurried away, almost frightened.

Robert Darzac reassured her by telling her that what she had taken for blood was only paint and that Old Bob's skull had been spattered by the paints which had been used in the wash drawing.

I left the table to hurry out to Rouletabille and also to escape from Mathilde's glances. What had the Lady in Black been doing in my bedroom? I was not to wait long to know!

When I started out the thunder was pealing loudly and the rain falling with redoubled force. It took me only one bound to reach the postern. No Rouletabille was there! I found him on the terrace B", watching the entrance to the Square Tower and receiving the full strength of the storm at his back.

I entreated him to take shelter under the arch.

"Leave me alone!" he said impatiently. "Leave me alone. This is the deluge. Ah, how good it is! how good—all this anger of the heavens! Have you ever had a desire to roar with the thunder? I have—and I am roaring now. Listen, while I cry out—alas! alas! alas! My voice is stronger than the thunder!"

And he plunged into the darkness making the shadows resound with his savage clamours. I believed this time that he had surely gone mad! But in my heart I knew that the unhappy lad was breathing forth in these indistinct articulations of frightful anguish the misery that burned him, and which he was constantly trying to hinder from burning up the heart and the soul in his body—the misery of being the son of Larsan.

I turned helplessly and as I did so, I felt a hand seize my wrist and a dark form cried out to me above the tempest:

"Where is he?"

It was Mme. Darzac who was also seeking Rouletabille. A new peal of thunder burst and we heard the boy in his mad delirium hurling wild shouts of defiance to the heavens. She heard him. She saw him. We were drenched with water from the rain and the breaking of the sea on the terrace. Mme. Darzac's clothing clung around her like a rag and her skirt dripped as she walked. I took the wretched woman's arm and held her up, for I saw that she was about to fall, and at that moment, in the midst of that terrible unchaining of the elements, in that mad tempest, under this terrible downpour on the breast of the raging sea, I all at once breathed the perfume—the odour so sweet and penetrating and haunting that its fragrance has remained with me ever since—the Perfume of the Lady in Black. Ah, I understood now how Rouletabille had remembered it all these years.

Yes, it was a fragrance full of sadness—something like the perfume of an isolated flower which has been condemned to be seen by no one but to blossom for itself all alone. It was a fragrance which set such ideas as these running through my brain, although I did not analyse them at the time—a sweet, soft and yet insistent perfume which seemed to steal away my senses in the midst of this battle of the elements, as soon as I perceived it. A strange perfume! Surely it was that, for I had seen the Lady in Black hundreds of times without noticing it, and now that I had done so, it was everywhere and above all things and I knew that the memory of it would abide with me while life should last. I understood how when one had—I will not say smelled but seised (for I do not think that everyone would have been able to catch the subtle fragrance of the perfume of the Lady in Black, any more than I myself had done before this night in which my senses seemed to have become sharpened to the keenest point)—yes, when one had seised this adorable and captivating odour, it was for life. And the heart would be perfumed by it, whether it was the heart of a son, like Rouletabille: or the heart of a lover, like M. Darzac.; or the heart of a villain, like Larsan. No, no—the knowledge of it could never pass. And now, by some sudden insight, I seemed to understand Rouletabille and Darzac and Larsan and all the misfortunes which had attended the daughter of Professor Stangerson.

There in the night and the tempest, the Lady in Black called aloud to Rouletabille and he fled from us and rushed further into the night, shrieking aloud, "The perfume of the Lady in Black! The perfume of the Lady in Black!"

The unhappy woman sobbed. She drew me toward the tower. She struck with desperate hands at the door which Bernier opened to us and her weeping would have melted the heart of a stone.

I could only utter the veriest commonplaces, begging her to calm herself, although I would have given everything I had in the world to find words which, without betraying anyone, might perhaps have made her understand my own part in the sorrowful drama which was being played out between the mother and the child.

Suddenly she seemed to recover herself in some degree and she motioned me to enter the little parlour at the right which was just outside the bed chamber of Old Bob. The door stood open but there we were as much alone as we could have been in her own room, for we knew that Old Bob worked late in the Tower of Charles the Bold.

I can assure you that in my memories of that horrible night the thought of the moments which I spent in the company of the Lady in Black are not the least sorrowful. I was put to a proof which I had not expected, and it was like a blow full in the face when, without even taking time to speak of the way in which we had been treated by the elements, Mme. Darzac looked me full in the eyes and demanded: "How long is it, M. Sainclair, that you were at Trepot?"

I was struck dumb—overpowered more completely than I had been by the fury of the storm. And I felt that, at the moment when nature, wearied out, was beginning to grow more quiet, I was to suffer a more dangerous assault than that of thunderbolts or lightning flashes. I must, by my expression, have betrayed the agitation which was aroused in my mind by this unexpected remark, for I could see by her eyes as she looked at me that she was aware how deeply I was moved. At first I made no answer: then I stammered out some disconnected words of which I remember nothing, save that they were ridiculous. It is years now since that night, but as I write I am living over the scene as if I were a spectator instead of the actor which I actually was, and as if it were even now going on in front of my eyes.

There are people who may be drenched to the skin and yet not look in the least ridiculous. The Lady in Black was one of them. Although, like myself, she had experienced the full fury of the storm, she was majestic and beautiful with her dishevelled locks, her bare neck and magnificent shoulders which, through the thin silk which clothed them seemed to have merely a light veil thrown across the flesh. She seemed to be a sublime statue, carved by Phidias from the immortal clay to which his chisel has given form and beauty. I am well aware that, even after all the years which have elapsed, my description sounds too glowing and I will not linger on the subject. But those who have known Professor Stangerson's daughter will understand me, I think, and I desire, here, with Rouletabille near me, to affirm the sentiments of respectful admiration which filled my heart at the sight of this mother, so divinely beautiful, who, in the state of disorder to which the fearful tempest had brought her, and with her whole heart filled with agony, was endeavouring to make me break the oath that I had sworn to the lad who was my friend.

She took both my hands in hers and said in a voice which I shall never forget:

"You are his friend. Tell him, then, that he is not the only one who has suffered." And she added with a sob which shook her whole frame:

"Why will he insist on not telling me the truth!"

I had not a word to say. What could I have answered? This woman had always seemed so cold and formal to the world in general and (as I had thought) to me in particular that it was as if I had not existed for her, and now she was laying bare her heart before me as though I were an old friend. And I had breathed the perfume of the Lady in Black.

Yes, she treated me as an old friend. She told me everything that I already knew in a few sentences as piteous and as simple as a mother's love itself—and she told me other things which Rouletabille had kept a secret from me. Evidently the game of hide and seek could not have lasted long. The relationship between them had been guessed by the one as surely as by the other. Led by a sure instinct Mme. Darzac had resolved to take means to learn who was this Rouletabille who had saved her from death and who was of the age of her own son—and who resembled the lad whom she had mourned as dead. And since her arrival at Mentone, a letter had reached her containing the proof that Rouletabille had lied to her in regard to his early life and had never set foot in any school at Bordeaux. Immediately, she had sought the youth and had asked for an explanation, but he had hurried away without replying. But he had seemed disturbed when she spoke to him of Trepot and of the school at Eu, and the trip which we had made there before coming to Mentone.

"How did you know?" I exclaimed, betraying my secret without realizing that I was doing so. She showed no sign of triumph at my involuntary confession, and in a few words went on to reveal to me her stratagem. That evening when I had taken her by surprise, it was not the first time that she had been in my room. My luggage bore the labels of the hotels at which we had stopped on our recent journey.

"Why did he not throw himself into my arms when I opened them to him?" she moaned. "Ah, my God! If he refuses to be Larsan's son, will he never consent to be mine!"

As she told me her story, it seemed to me that Rouletabille had conducted himself in an atrocious fashion toward this poor woman who had believed him dead, who had mourned for him in despair, and who, in the midst of her terrible dread and mortal anguish, experienced a thrill of the keenest joy in realizing that her son was still alive. Ah, the poor mother! The evening before, he had mocked at her when she had cried out to him with all her soul that she had a son and that that son was he! He had mocked her, even while the tears had streamed down his cheeks. I could never have believed that Rouletabille could have been so cruel or so heartless—or, even, so ill-bred!

Certainly he behaved in an abominable fashion! He had told her with a sardonic smile that "he was nobody's son—not even the son of a thief." It was these words that had sent her flying to her room in the Square Tower and had made her long to die. But she had not found her son only to give him up so easily and she would—she must have him acknowledge her!

I was almost beside myself. I kissed her hands and entreated pardon for Rouletabille. Here was the result of my friend's schemes to save her pain. Under the pretext of saving her from Larsan, he had plunged a knife into her heart. I felt as though I had no wish to know any more of the story. I knew too much already and I longed to run away. I hastened out of the room and called Bernier, who opened the door for me. I went out of the Square Tower, cursing Rouletabille roundly. I went to the Court of the Bold to look for him, but found it deserted.

At the postern gate Mattoni had come to take the ten o'clock watch. I saw a light in Rouletabille's room and I hastened up the rickety stairway of the New Castle and quickly found myself outside his door. I opened it without knocking. Rouletabille looked up.

"What do you want, Sainclair?"

I told him all that I had heard and my opinion of him for his actions which had so deeply wounded Mme. Darzac.

"She didn't tell you everything, my friend," he replied, coldly. "She did not tell you that she forbade me to touch that man."

"That is true!" I cried. "I heard her."

"Well, what have you come here to tell me then?" he went on, roughly. "Do you know what she said to me yesterday? She ordered me to go away. She would rather die than see me take issue *against my father*."

And he laughed—laughed. Such laughter, I hope not to hear again.

"Against my father! She thinks, I suppose, that he is stronger than I!"

His face was not a pleasant sight to see as he uttered the words.

But suddenly it seemed to be transformed and to glow with unearthly beauty.

"She is afraid for me!" he said, softly. "And I—I am afraid for her—only for her. And I do not know my father. And, God help me! I do not know my mother!"

At that moment the sound of a shot rang out on the night, followed by a cry of mortal agony! Ah, it was again the cry that I had heard two years ago in the "inexplicable gallery." My hair rose on my scalp and Rouletabille tottered as though the bullet had struck himself.

And then he bounded toward the open window, filling the fortress with a despairing burst of anguish:

"Mother! Mother! Mother!"

XI

The Attack of the Square Tower

I leaped after him and threw my arms around his body, dreading what he might attempt. There was in that cry, "Mother! Mother! Mother!" such a madness of despair, a call, or rather, an assurance of coming aid so beyond the realization of human strength, that I was obliged to fear that the young fellow had forgot ten that he was only a man and had not the power to fly straight out of the window of the tower and to traverse, like a bird or a flash of lightning, the black space which separated him from the crime which had been committed and which he filled with his frightful cries. Quickly, he turned on me, threw me off, and precipitated himself wildly, through corridors, apartments, stairways and courts toward the accursed tower from which had come that same death cry that we both had heard—a moment ago, and also two years before when it had resounded through the "inexplicable gallery."

As for me, I had thus far only had the time to gaze out of the window, rooted to my place by the horror of that cry. I was still there when the door of the Square Tower opened, and in its frame of light, there appeared the form of the Lady in Black. She was standing upright, living and unharmed, in spite of that cry of death, but her pale and ghastly visage reflected a terror like that of death itself. She stretched out her arms toward the night and the darkness cast Rouletabille into them, and the arms of the Lady in Black closed around him and I heard no more only sobs and moans and again the two syllables which the night repeated over and over, "Mother! Mother!"

I descended from my tower into the court, my temples throbbing, my heart beating so fast that it almost stifled me. What I had seen on the threshold of the Square Tower had not by any means assured me that nothing terrible had taken place. It was in vain that I attempted to reason with myself and to say: "Nonsense! At the very moment when we believed that all was lost, is not, on the contrary, everything found? Are not the mother and son united?"

But why, then, this cry of death when she was alive and well? Why that scream of agony before she had appeared standing on the threshold of the tower?

Strange to say, I found no one in the Court of the Bold when I crossed it. No one then had heard the pistol shot! No one had heard the cries! Where was M. Darzac? Where was Old Bob? Was he still working in the lower basement of the Round Tower? I might have believed so, for I perceived a light in the window of the tower. But Mattoni—Mattoni—had he heard nothing, either?—Mattoni, who kept watch at the postern of the gardener? And the Berniers? I saw neither of them. And the door of the Square Tower still stood open. Ah, the soft murmur, "Mother! Mother! Mother!" And I heard her voice answer back, tenderly, though choked with sobs, "My boy! My little one!" They had not even taken the precaution to close the door of Old Bob's parlour. It was into that room where I had talked with her a little while before that she had led her child.

And they were there alone, clasped in each other's arms, repeating over and over again, "Mother!" and "My little one!" And then they murmured broken sentences, phrases without end—with the divine foolishness of a mother and her child. "Then, you were not dead!" That was sufficient to make them both fall to sobbing. And then, how they embraced each other, as though to make up for all the years they had lost. I heard him murmur, "You know, mamma, it was not true that I stole!" And one would have thought from the sound of his voice that he was still the little lad of nine years—my poor Rouletabille. "No, my darling—you never stole! My little boy! my little boy!" Ah, it was not my fault that I heard—but my heart was torn in two as I listened.

B ut where was Bernier? I entered the lodge from the left, for I wished to know the meaning of the cry and of the shot which I had heard.

Mere Bernier was at the back of the room which was lighted only by a tiny taper. She was like a black bundle on a sofa. She must have been in bed when the shot was heard and she had hastily donned some clothing. I picked up the taper and brought it near. Her features were distorted with fear.

"Where is Bernier?" I asked.

"He is there," she replied, trembling.

"There. Where is that?"

But she made no answer.

I took a few steps toward the interior of the lodge and I stumbled. I bent down to know what I had stepped upon and found out that it was Mere Bernier's potatoes. I lowered the light and looked at the floor; it was strewn with potatoes; they had rolled everywhere. Could it be that Mme. Bernier had not gathered them up after Rouletabille had emptied out the bag?

I arose and turned to Mere Bernier.

"Someone fired off a pistol!" I said. "What has happened?"

"I do not know," she responded.

And, at that moment, I heard someone open the door of the tower and Pere Bernier stood on the threshold.

"Ah! it is you, M. Sainclair?"

"Bernier! What has happened?"

"Oh, nothing very serious, M. Sainclair, I am glad to say." (But his voice was too palpably endeavouring to sound strong and brave for me to feel as reassured as he was trying to make me!) "An accident without any importance whatever. M. Darzac, while placing his revolver on the stand beside his bed, accidentally fired it off. Madame, naturally, was frightened, and screamed; and, as the window of their room was open, she thought that you and M. Rouletabille might have heard something and started out to tell you that it was nothing." "M. Darsac has come in, then?"

"He got here almost as soon as you had left the tower, M. Sainclair. And the shot was fired almost immediately after he entered his bedroom. You can guess that I had a pretty fright! I rushed to the door! M. Darzac opened it, himself. Happily, no one was injured!"

"Did Mme. Darzac go to her own room as soon as I left the tower?"

"At once. She heard M. Darzac when he came in and followed him directly to their apartments. They went in almost at the same moment."

"And M. Darzac? Is he still in his room?"

"Here he is now."

"I turned and saw Robert Darzac; despite the gloom of the place, I saw that his face was ghastly pale. He made me a sign and then said very calmly and quietly:

"Listen, Sinclair! Bernier told you about their little accident. It is not worth mentioning to anyone, unless someone should speak of it to you. The others, perhaps, have not heard the shot. It would be useless to frighten all these good people; don't you think so? Now I have a little favour to ask of you."

"Speak, my friend," I bade him. "Whatever it is, I will do it: you know that without my saying so. Make any use of me that you like."

"Thanks; but it is only to persuade Rouletabille to go to bed: when he is gone, my wife will calm herself and will try to get the rest that she needs. Every one of use has need of rest and calmness, Sainclair. We all need calm and silence."

"Surely, my friend: you may count upon me."

I pressed his hand with a force which attested my sentiments towards him. I was persuaded that both he and Bernier were concealing something from us—something very grave!

Darzac reached his room and I went to find Rouletabille in the sitting room of Old Bob.

But upon the threshold of the apartment, I jostled against the Lady in Black and her son who were passing out. They were both so silent and wore an expression unexpected to me who had overheard their exclamations of love and joy only a few moments before that I stood before them without saying a word or making a movement. The extremity which induced Mme. Darzac to leave Rouletabille so soon under such extraordinary circumstances as those which had attended their reunion, puzzled me so greatly that I could not find words to say what I thought and the submission of Rouletabille in taking leave of her so quickly amased me. Mathilde pressed a kiss upon the lad's forehead and murmured: "Good-night, my darling," in a voice so soft, so sweet and at the same time so solemn that it seemed to me that it must resemble the leave-taking of one who was about to die. Rouletabille, without answering his mother, took my arm and led me out of the tower. He was trembling like a leaf.

It was the Lady in Black herself who closed the door of the Square Tower. I was sure that something strange was passing within those walls. The account of the pistol shot which had been given me satisfied me not at all: and it is not to be doubted that Rouletabille would have agreed with me if his reasoning powers and his heart had not been giddy from the scene which had taken place between the Lady in Black and himself. And then, after all, how did I know that Rouletabille did not agree with me? We had scarcely gotten outside the Square Tower before I demanded of Rouletabille the meaning of his strange manner. I drew him into that corner of the parapet which joins the Square Tower to the Round Tower in the angle formed by the jutting out of the Square Tower upon the court.

The reporter, who had allowed me as docilely as a little child to lead him wherever I would, spoke to me in a low tone:

"Sainclair, I have sworn to my mother that I will see nothing or hear nothing of that which may pass this night in the Square Tower. It is the first promise that I have made to my mother, Sainclair; but I will break it for her sake just as I would give up my hope of heaven for her. I must see and I must hear!"

We were at that moment not far from a window in which a light was still burning and which opened upon the sitting room of Old Bob and sloped out upon the sea. This window was not closed, and it was this, doubtless, which had permitted us to hear so distinctly in spite of the thickness of the walls of the tower, the pistol shot and the cry of agony that had followed it. From the spot where we were now stationed, we could see nothing through this window, but was it not something to be able to hear? The storm was past, but the waters were not yet appeased and the waves broke on the rocks of the peninsula with a violence that would have rendered the approach of any vessel impossible. The thought of a vessel crossed my mind because I believed for an instant that I could see the shadow of a vessel of some sort appearing or disappearing in the gloom. But what could it be? Evidently a delusion of my mind which beheld hostile shades everywhere—an illusion of a mind which was assuredly more agitated than the waters themselves.

We stood there, motionless, for more than five minutes, before we heard a sigh—ah, how long it was, that mournful sound!—a groan, deep as an expiration, like a moan of agony, a heavy sob, like the last breath of a departing soul—which reached our ears from that window, and brought the sweat of terror to our brows. And then, nothing more—nothing except the intermit tent sobbings of the sea.

And suddenly the light in the window went out. The outline of the Square Tower blended with the blackness of the night.

My friend and I grasped each other's hand as if instinctively, commanding each other, by this mute communication, to remain motionless and silent. *Someone was dying, there, in that tower!* Someone whom they had hidden. Why? And who? Someone who was neither M. Darzac nor Mme. Darzac, nor Pere Bernier, nor Mere Bernier, nor—almost beyond the shadow of a doubt, Old Bob; *someone who could not have been in the tower.*

Leaning against the parapet to support ourselves, our necks stretched toward that window through which there had come to us that sigh of agony, we listened. A quarter of an hour passed thus—it might have been a century! Rouletabille pointed out to me the window of his own room in the New Castle which was still illuminated. I understood: it was necessary to extinguish this light and return. I took a thousand precautions. Five minutes later, I was back again with Rouletabille. There was now no other light in the Court of the Bold than the feeble ray which told of the late vigil of Old Bob in the lower basement of the Round Tower and the light at the gardener's postern where Mattoni was standing sentinel. In truth, considering the positions which they occupied, one might easily understand how it was that neither Old Bob nor Mattoni had heard anything that had passed in the Square Tower, nor even, in the heart of the storm, could the clamours of Rouletabille have reached their ears. The walls of the postern were heavy and Old Bob was entombed in a veritable subterranean cavern.

I had scarcely time to steal back to Rouletabille in the corner of the parapet, the post of observation which he had not quitted, before we distinctly heard the door of the Square Tower moving softly upon its hinges. As I attempted to lean further out of my corner, and see further down into the court, Rouletabille pushed me back and allowed only his own head to look over the wall; but as he was leaning far over, I allowed myself to violate his command and looked over his head; and this is was I saw.

First, Pere Bernier, perfectly recognizable, in spite of the darkness, who came out of the tower and directed his steps noiselessly to the gardener's postern. In the middle of the court, he paused, looked up at the side where our windows were, and then returned to the side of the court and made a signal which we interpreted as a sign that all was well. To whom was this signal addressed? Rouletabille leaned further over; but he quickly retreated, pushing me back with him.

When we hared to look out in the court again, no one was there. But in a few moments, we again beheld Pere Bernier (or, rather, we heard him first, for there ensued between him and Mattoni a brief conversation the echoes of which were carried to us.) And then we heard something which climbed under the arch of the gardener's postern and Pere Bernier reappeared with the black and softly rolling form of a carriage beside him. We could see that it was the little English cart drawn by Toby, Arthur Rance's pony. The Court of the Bold was of beaten earth and the little equipage made no more sound than as if it were gliding over a carpet. Toby was so intelligent and so quiet that one would have said that he had received his instructions from Pere Bernier. The latter, reaching, at length, the "oubliette," raised again his face toward our windows, and then, still holding Toby by the bridle, came to the door of the Square Tower. Leaving the little equipage before the door, he entered the tower. A few moments passed by which seemed to us like hours, particularly to Rouletabille, who was seised with a fit of trembling which shook his frame like an aspen leaf. Pere Bernier reappeared. He crossed the court alone and returned to the postern. It was then that we were obliged to lean further out and, certainly, the persons who were now upon the threshold of the Square Tower might have perceived us, if they had looked up at our side, but they were not thinking of us. The night had become clear and a beautiful moon had arisen which threw its rays over the sea and stretched its radiance across the Court of the Bold. The two persons who came out of the tower and approached the carriage appeared so surprised that they almost recoiled at what they saw. But we could hear the Lady in Black repeating again and again in low, firm tones: "Courage, Robert, courage! You must be brave now!"

And Robert Darzac replied in a voice which froze my blood: "It is not courage which I lack!" He was bending over something which he dragged before him and then raised in his arms as though it were a heavy burden and tried to slip under the long seat of the English cart. Rouletabille had taken off his cap. His teeth were chattering. As well as we could distinguish, the thing was in a sack. To move this sack M. Darzac was making the greatest efforts and we heard him breathe a sigh of exhaustion. Leaning against the wall of the tower, the Lady in Black watched him without offering any assistance. And, suddenly, at the moment that M. Darzac had succeeded in loading the sack into the cart, Mathilde pronounced these words in a voice shaken with horror:

"It is *moving*."

"It is the end!" said M. Darzac, wiping his forehead with his pocket handkerchief. Then he took Toby by the bridle and started off, making a sign to the Lady in Black, but she, still leaning against the wall, as though she had been placed there for some punishment, made no signal in reply. M. Darzac seemed to us to be quite calm. His figure straightened up: his step grew firm—one might almost say that his manner was that of an honest man who has done his duty. Still with the greatest precaution, he disappeared with his carriage beneath the postern of the gardener and the Lady in Black went back into the Square Tower.

After this, I wished to emerge from our corner, but Rouletabille restrained me. It was well that he did so, for Bernier came up to the postern and crossed the court, directing his way again toward the Square Tower. When he was not more than two meters from the door, which was closed, Rouletabille glided softly from the corner of the parapet, stepped between the door and the figure of Bernier, who was struck with terror. He put his hands upon the shoulders of the concierge.

"Come with me!" he commanded.

Bernier seemed absolutely powerless. I, too, came out of my hiding place. The old man looked at us both standing there in the moonlight: his face was sorrowful and he murmured sadly:

"This is a great misfortune!"

XII

The Impossible Body

"It will be a great misfortune if you don't tell the truth," muttered Rouletabille, in smothered tones. "But if you conceal nothing, the trouble may not be so great. Come this way."

And he drew him, clasping him by the fist, toward the New Château, I following. I saw that a great change had come over Rouletabille. He was completely his old self again. Now that he was so happily relieved of the sorrow of separation from his mother which had pressed on his mind ever since his early childhood, now that he had again found the perfume of the Lady in Black, he seemed to have reconquered all the forces of his spirit and was ready to enter eagerly into the strife against the mysteries which surrounded us. And, until the day when all was ended—until the last supreme moment—the most dramatic that I have ever lived through in the whole course of my existence—*the moment in which life and death spoke out and were explained by his lips*—he never again made a sign of hesitation in the forward march: he never spoke another word which could have been taken as an attempt to warn us against the dreadful situation which arose from the siege of the Square Tower by the attack of that night between the twelfth and thirteenth of April.

Bernier resisted him no further. When others tried to do so, he held them in his grasp until they cried for mercy.

Bernier walked in front of us, his head bent, looking like an accused man who is being led on his way to trial. And when we reached Rouletabille's room, the young reporter bade Bernier sit down facing us. I lighted the lamp. Rouletabille sat silent for a moment, looking at Bernier, lighting his pipe the while, and evidently seeking to read in the face of the concierge all the honesty which he could find. Soon his knitted brows relaxed, his eye grew clearer and, after he had blown a few rings of smoke toward the ceiling, he said:

"Well, Bernier, how did they kill him?"

Bernier shook his shaggy head.

"I have sworn to say nothing and I will say nothing, monsieur. And, upon my word of honour, I know nothing."

"All right," went on Rouletabille, unconcernedly. "Tell me what you don't know. For if you do not tell me what you don't know, Bernier, I will be responsible for nothing, no matter what happens."

"And for what could you be responsible in any case, monsieur?"

"For one thing, I won't answer for your safety, Bernier."

"For my safety? I have done nothing."

"For the safety of all of us, then for our lives, even!" replied Rouletabille, arising from his chair and pacing restlessly across the room, in order, doubtless, to give himself an opportunity to perform some necessary mental algebraic operation. Then he paused and went on, "Where was he? In the Square Tower?"

Bernier did not speak but he nodded assent.

"Where? In Old Bob's bedroom?"

"No," Bernier shook his head. "Hidden in your rooms?"

Bernier shook his head vehemently.

"Well, where was he then? He could certainly not have been in the apartments of M. and Mme. Darzac!"

Bernier bowed his head.

"Miserable hound!" cried Rouletabille and he leaped at Bernier's throat. I rushed to the rescue of the concierge and snatched him from the young man's clutches. As soon as he could breathe, the old servant looked up, piteously.

"Why did you try to strangle me, M. Rouletabille?" he asked.

"How dare you ask, Bernier? How dare you? And you acknowledge that *he* was in the apartment of M. and Mme. Darzac! Who, then, gained him entrance to that apartment? No one but yourself. You, the only person who had the key when the Darzacs were not there!"

Bernier arose to his feet. He was as pale as a ghost, but his look and attitude were full of dignity.

"M. Rouletabille, do you accuse me of being an accomplice of Larsan?"

"I forbid you to pronounce that name!" shouted the reporter. "You know very well that Larsan is dead—and has been dead for months!"

"For months!" echoed Bernier, ironically. "Yes, that is true—I was wrong to forget it. When one devotes oneself to his masters and permits himself to be beaten and abused for them, it is necessary to ignore everything, no matter what they may do to you. I beg your pardon, sir."

"Listen to me, Bernier. I know that you are a brave man and I respect you. It is not your good faith that I am questioning, but I am censuring your negligence."

"My negligence!" Bernier, as pale as his face had been, flushed crimson. "My negligence! I have not budged from my lodge—not even from the corridor. I have always worn the key in my breast pocket and I swear to you that no one entered that room—no one at all—after you were there at five o'clock, except M. and Mme. Darzac, themselves. I do not count, of course, the few moments that you and M. Sainclair were there at about six o'clock."

"What!" exclaimed Rouletabille. "Do you want me to believe that this individual—you have forgotten his name, I think, Bernier—let us call him 'the Man'—that the man was killed in M. Darzac's rooms if he was not there?"

"I do not. And, furthermore, I can swear to you that he *was* there."

"Yes, but how could he have been?" That is what I ask you, Bernier. And you are the only one who can answer because you alone had the key in the absence of M. and Mme. Darzac. And M. Darzac never took the key with him when he left the room and no one could have gotten into the room to hide while he was there."

"That is the mystery, monsieur. That is what puzzles M. Darzac more than all the rest. But I have only been able to answer him as I have answered you. There is the mystery."

"When you left the room with M. Darzac, M. Sainclair and myself at about a quarter after six, did you lock the door immediately?"

"Yes, monsieur."

"When did you open it after that?"

"Not at all."

"And where were you in the meantime?"

"In front of the door of my lodge, watching the door of the apartment. My wife and I took our dinner in that same spot at about half after six, on a little table in the corridor, because, on account of the door of the tower being open, it was quite light and was pleasanter. After dinner, I sat in the doorway of the lodge, smoking a cigarette and chatting with my wife. We were so seated that, even if we had wished to do so, we would not have been able to withdraw our eyes from M. Darzac's rooms. It is a mystery!—a mystery more extraordinary than the mystery of the Yellow Room. For, in the former case, we did not know of what had passed *before*. But now, monsieur, one knows all that happened beforehand since you yourself visited the apartment at 5 o'clock and saw that no person was there: one knows all that passed during the interim, for either I had the key in my pocket, or M. Darzac was in his room and must have seen the man who opened his door and entered the room for the purpose of assassinating him. And while I was sitting in the corridor before the door, I must have seen the man pass! And we know what took place *after*. After, there was the death of the man and that proved that the man was there. Ah, it is a mystery!"

"And from five o'clock until the moment of the tragedy, you declare that you never quitted the corridor?"

"I swear it."

"You are absolutely certain?" persisted Rouletabille.

"Ah, pardon, monsieur—there was one moment—the moment that you called me."

"That is good, Bernier. I wanted to see if you remembered that."

"But I was not away from my post more than an instant or two, and M. Darzac was in his room then. He did not leave it while I was gone. Ah! what a mystery!"

"How do you know that M. Darzac didn't go out during those moments?"

"Why, because if he had done so, my wife, who was in the lodge, must have seen him! And then all would be explained and we would not be so puzzled, nor Madame either. Ah! must I say it to you over again? No one has entered that room except M. Darzac at five o'clock and you two at six, and no person got in between the time that M. Darzac went out and the time when he came in at night with Mme. Darzac. He was like you—he didn't want to believe me. I swore it to him upon the corpse that lay before us!"

"Where was the corpse?"

"In M. Darzac's bedroom."

"It was really a dead body?"

"Oh, he was breathing still—I heard him."

"Then it was not a corpse, Pere Bernier."

"Oh, M. Rouletabille, where was the difference? He had a bullet in his heart."

At last, Pere Bernier was going to tell us of the body. Had he seen it? Who was it? One would have said that this seemed of secondary importance in the eyes of Rouletabille. The reporter seemed engrossed only with the problem of finding how the body had come to be there. How had that man happened to be killed? But, indeed, Pere Bernier knew only very little. The whole thing had been as sudden as a rifle shot—so it seemed to him—and he was behind the door. He told us that he was going to his lodge and felt so drowsy that he had intended to throw himself down on the bed for a few moments, when he and Mere Bernier heard such a commotion issue from the apartment of M. Darzac that they were seised with terror. It was as if the furniture were being thrown about and blows were rained upon the walls.

"What is the matter?" cried Mere Bernier, and the same instant they heard the voice of Mme. Darzac, shouting, "Help! help!" This was the cry that we, too, had heard in the New Château. Pere Bernier, leaving his wife almost fainting from horror, rushed to the door of M. Darzac's room and beat against it, crying aloud to him to open, but obtaining no reply. The struggle within was still going on. Bernier heard the laboured breathing of two men and he recognised the voice of Larsan when he heard the words: "With this blow, I shall have your life!" Then he heard M. Darzac, who called his wife to his aid in a voice almost stifled, as though he were gagged, "Mathilde! Mathilde!" Evidently he and Larsan must have been engaged in a life and death struggle when, suddenly, the pistol shot had saved him. This pistol shot had frightened Pere Bernier less than the cry which had followed it. One would have thought that Mme. Darzac, who had uttered the cry, had been mortally wounded. Bernier was unable to understand Mme. Darzac's attitude in the matter. Why did she not open the door and admit him to help her husband? Why did she not draw the shades? Finally, almost immediately after the pistol shot, the door, upon which Pere Bernier had not stopped knocking all the time, was opened. The room was wrapped in darkness, which did not surprise the concierge, for the light of the chandelier which he had perceived under the door during the fight had been suddenly extinguished and at the same moment he had heard the chandelier itself fall heavily to the floor. It was Mme. Darzac who had opened the door and Bernier could distinguish through the gloom the form of M. Darzac leaning over something which the concierge knew was a dying man. Bernier had called to his wife to bring a light, but Mme. Darzac had cried: "No, no! No light! no light! And, above all, be sure that *he* knows nothing." And immediately she had rushed to the door of the tower, calling out, "He is coming! he is coming! I hear him Open the door, Pere Bernier' I must go and meet him!" And Pere Bernier had opened the door, the while she kept on moaning, "Hide yourselves! Go in Don't let him know anything!"

Pere Bernier went on:

"You came like a waterspout, M. Rouletabille. And she drew you into Old Bob's sitting room. You saw nothing. I stayed with M. Darzac. The rattle in the throat of the man on the floor had ceased. M. Darzac still bending over him said to me: "Get a sack, Bernier, a sack and a stone, and we will throw him into the sea and no one will ever hear his voice again!"

"Then," Bernier went on, "I thought of my sack of potatoes; my wife had gathered them up and put them back in the sack after you had emptied them out; I emptied the bag again and brought it to him. We made as little noise as possible. During this time, Madame was, I suppose, telling you the story in Old Bob's sitting room and we heard M. Sainclair questioning my wife in the lodge. Moving very quietly, we had slipped the body, which M. Darzac had tied up, into the sack. But I said to M. Darzac: 'Let me beg of you not to throw it into the water. It is not deep enough to hide it. There are days when the sea is so clear that one may look down to the bottom.' 'What shall we do, then?' whispered M. Darzac. I answered: 'Heaven help us, I don't know, monsieur! All that I could do for you and for Madame and for humanity against a villain like Frederic Larsan, I have done and willingly. But don't ask any more of me and may God protect you!' And I went out of the room and found you in the lodge, M. Sainclair. And then you went for M. Rouletabille at the request of M. Darzac, who had come out of his own apartment. As for my wife, she was almost swooning with terror when she suddenly saw that both M. Darzac and myself were covered with blood. See, messieurs, my hands are red Pray Heaven, it doesn't bring us misfortune! But we have done our duty. Oh, he was a miserable wretch!—But do you want me to tell you?—well, one could never keep such a history secret—and, in my opinion, it would be better to go immediately with it to the justice. I have promised to keep silence and I did keep silence so long as I was able, but I'm glad enough to relieve myself of such a burden before you gentlemen who are the friends of Monsieur and Madame—and who may, perhaps, be able to make them listen to reason. Why should they hide the facts? Isn't it an honour to have killed Larsan!—Pardon me for having spoken his name—I know well, it was not right—but is it not an honour to have saved the whole world from a scoundrel in saving oneself? Ah! hold! a fortune! Mme. Darzac promised me a fortune, if I would keep silence. What do I care for that? Could one have a better fortune than to be of service to the poor lady who has had so many troubles? Never in the world' But, how she looked! Why should she have feared? I asked her when we thought that you had gone to bed and that we three were all alone in the Square Tower with our corpse. I said to her, 'Tell everyone that you have killed him All the world will praise you!' She answered: 'There has been too much scandal already, Bernier: and as much as it depends on me to do, and as much as is possible, I will hide this new horror forever! It would kill my father!' I had nothing to say to that, but I wanted to speak. It was upon the tip of my tongue to say, 'If the business comes out later, one will believe that you did something wrong and monsieur, your father, will die just as surely.' But it was her idea. She wished that all should be concealed! Well, I promised her. That's all!"

Bernier turned toward the door, showing us his hands.

"I must rid myself of the blood of the accursed pig!" he said, dryly.

Rouletabille stopped him.

"And what was M. Darzac saying all this time? What was his opinion?"

"He repeated: 'What Mme. Darzac says is right. She must be obeyed implicitly.' His shirt was torn and he had a slight wound in his throat, but it did not seem to bother him at all, and, indeed, there was only one thing in which he seemed interested, and that was as to how the miserable wretch had gotten into his rooms. I told him what I have told you—that he could not have entered without my seeing him, and I told him just how I had passed every moment of my time. His first words on the subject had been: 'But when I came in a little while ago, there was no one in my room and I shut and bolted the door.'"

"Where did this conversation take place?"

"In the lodge, in the presence of my wife, who was nearly frightened to death, poor thing!"

"And the body? Where was that?"

"It lay in the sleeping room of M. Darzac."

"And how was it decided that it should be disposed of?"

"I can't say as to that for certain, but their resolution was taken, for Mme. Darzac said to me: 'Bernier, I am going to ask of you one last service: go and bring the English cart from the stable and harness Toby to it. Don't waken Walter, if you can help it. If you wake him and he asks for any explanations, say this to him and also to Mattoni, who has the watch at the postern: "It is for M. Darzac, who must be at Castelar at four o'clock in the morning to see the tournament in the Alps."' Mme. Darzac said also: 'If you meet M. Sainclair, bring him to me, but if you meet M. Rouletabille, say nothing to him and do nothing that may attract his attention.' Ah, Monsieur! Madame did not let me go out until the window of your room was closed and your light extinguished! And, then, we were not entirely certain in regard to the body which we believed to be dead, before it sighed once more—and, my God! what a sigh! The rest, Monsieur, you saw for yourself and now you know as much as I. God help us!"

When Bernier had finished relating this incredible story, Rouletabille put his hand on his arm, thanking him most earnestly for his great devotion to his master and mistress, and begged him to use the utmost discretion. The young reporter entreated the old servant to pardon his roughness and ordered him to say nothing to Mme. Darzac of anything that had passed between them. Bernier extended his hand in token of fidelity, but Rouletabille drew back:

"No—I can't, Bernier! You are covered with blood."

Bernier left us to look for the Lady in Black.

"Well!" I said when we were alone. "Larsan is dead!"

"Yes," answered Rouletabille. "I fear so!"

"You fear so why, in Heaven's name?"

"Because," he answered in a strange tone, which I could scarcely recognize as his. "Because the death of Larsan, who is carried out dead from a place which he never entered dead or alive, terrifies me more than his life itself!"

XIII

In Which the Fears of Rouletabille Assume Alarming Proportions

It was literally true that he was frightened. And I was more terrified myself than words could express. I had never seen him in such a state of mental inquietude. He walked up and down the room nervously, occasionally stopping in front of the mirror and passing his hand over his forehead, as if he were asking his own image, "Can it be you, Rouletabille, who have such thoughts? How dare you harbour them?" What thoughts? He seemed rather to be upon the point of thinking than to be actually doing so, and to be using every means of driving thought away. He shook his head savagely and started for the window as though he meant to leap out, leaning forth into the night, listening for the slightest noise on the distant bank of the sea, expecting, perhaps, to hear the wheels of the little carriage and the echo of Toby's shoes. One might have thought him a beast at bay. The surf was quiet; the waves had grown entirely appeased. A white ray appeared suddenly shining over the black waters. It was the dawn. And in a moment the old château seemed to rise out of the night, pale and livid with the same pallor as our own—the pallor of one who has not slept. "Rouletabille," I asked, trembling as I spoke, for I felt that I was intruding upon ground where my feet had no right to tread; "your interview with your mother was very brief and you separated in silence. I want to ask you, my boy, whether she told you the story of the accident with the revolver on the night stand that Bernier told me?"

"No," he answered without turning his face toward me.

"She told you nothing of that kind?"

"No."

"And you did not ask her for any explanation of the pistol shot nor of the death cry—the cry that was the echo of the one which we heard two years ago from her lips in the 'inexplicable gallery'?"

"Sainclair, you are too curious—you are more curious than I. I asked her nothing."

"And you swore to see nothing and to hear nothing without her saying anything to you about the pistol shot and the cry?"

"Truly, Sainclair, it was necessary for me to believe—for my part, I respected the secrets of the Lady in Black. I had nothing to ask of her when she said to me, 'We must leave each other now, my child, but nothing can ever separate us again!"

"Ah, she said that to you—'Nothing can ever separate us again'?"

"Yes, my friend—and there was blood upon her hands."

We looked at each other in silence. I was now at the window and beside the reporter. Suddenly his hand touched mine. Then he pointed to the little taper which was burning at the entrance to the subterranean door which led to Old Bob's study in the Tower of the Bold.

"It is dawn," said Rouletabille. "And Old Bob is still at work. This old fellow is certainly industrious and we will go and have a peep at him at his labours. That will change our current of thought and I shall be able to get away from these horrors that are smothering me and driving me half wild."

And he heaved a long sigh.

"Will Darzac never return!" he murmured, more as though he were speaking to himself than to me.

A few moments later we had crossed the court and had descended into the octagon room of the Tower of Charles the Bold. It was empty. The lamp was burning on the work table, but there was no sign of Old Bob.

"Oh!" cried Rouletabille. He picked up the lamp and carried it from place to place examining everything around him. He tried in turn the lock of every little window which opened from the walls of the basement. Nothing had changed its place, and all was arranged in order and scientific etiquette. While we were looking around at the bones and shells and horns of the prehistoric ages, the "hanging crystals," the rings made out of bone, the buckles formed from teeth, and the other treasures of the savant, we came to the little desk table. There we found the "oldest skull in the history of humanity"; and it was true that it had been spattered with the red paint of the wash drawing which M. Darzac had set to dry upon that part of the desk which faced the window and was exposed to the sun. I went from one window to the other and shook the iron bars in order to assure myself that they had not been touched nor tampered with in any way. Rouletabille saw what I was doing and said:

"What are you about? Before thinking about how he could have gotten out at the windows, wouldn't it be better to find out whether he went by the door?"

He set the lamp upon the parapet and looked for traces of footprints. Then Rouletabille said:

"Go and knock at the door of the Square Tower and ask Bernier whether Old Bob has come in. Ask Mattoni at the postern and Pere Jacques at the iron gate. Go, Sainclair—quick!"

Five minutes after I went out I was back with the information. No one had seen Old Bob in any part of the fortress. He had not passed by anywhere. Rouletabille had his face close to the parapet. He said:

"He left this lamp burning in order to make people believe that he was at work." And then he added, softly: "There is no sign of a struggle of any sort and in the sand I find the traces of the footprints of only M. Arthur Rance and M. Robert Darzac, who came to this room during the storm last night and have brought on their feet a little earth from the court of the Bold and also of the claylike soil of the outer court. There is no footprint which could be Old Bob's. Old Bob reached here before and, perhaps, went out while the tempest was raging, but, in any case, he has not come in since." Rouletabille stood erect. He replaced upon the desk the lamp the rays of which fell directly upon the skull which had been splashed by the red paint in a frightful fashion. Around us there were dozens of skeletons but certainly their presence was less alarming to me than the absence of Old Bob.

Rouletabille stood for a moment staring at the crimson skull, then he took it in his hands and held his eyes close to its empty orbits. Then he raised the skull higher and held it at arms' length, gazing at it with an almost breathless interest; he looked at the profile. Then he placed the hideous object in my hands and told me to raise it to the level of my head, as carefully as thought it were the most precious of burdens while Rouletabille brought the lamp very close to it.

Like a flash an idea pierced through my brain. I let the skull fall on the desk and rushed through the court till I came to the oubliette. I discovered that the iron bars which closed it were still fast. If anyone had fled by that way or had fallen into the shaft or had thrown himself down, the bars would have been opened. I hurried back, more anxious than ever.

"Rouletabille! Rouletabille! There is no way that Old Bob could have gotten out except in the sack!"

I repeated the sentence, but my friend was not listening and I was surprised to see him deeply engrossed in a task of which I found it impossible to guess the meaning. How, at a time as tragic as the present, while we were awaiting only the return of M. Darzac to complete the circle in which the impossible body was found—while in the Square Tower, the Lady in Black, like Lady MacBeth, must be occupied in effacing from her hands the stains of the strangest of crimes, Rouletabille seemed to be amusing himself by making drawings with a foot rule, a square, a measure and a compass. There he was, seated in the old geologist's easy chair with Robert Darzac's drawing board before him and he also was making a plan—quiet and imperturbable as an architect's clerk.

He had pricked the paper with one of the points of his compass while the other point traced the circle which might represent the Tower of the Bold as we could see it in the design of M. Darzac. Then, dipping his brush into a tiny dish half full of the red pain which M. Darzac had been using he carefully spread the paint over the entire space occupied by the circle. In doing this, he was extremely particular, giving the greatest attention to seeing that the paint was of the same thickness at every point, just as a student might have done in preparing a lesson. He bent his head first to the right and then to the left as though to see the effect, moistening his lips with his tongue as though he were meditating earnestly. In a moment he gave a little start and then sat motionless. His eyes were fixed on the drawing as thought they had been glued to it. They did not even move in their sockets. The stillness was horrible, but it was not much better when his lips opened to utter an exclamation of breathless horror. His face looked like that of a maniac. And he turned toward me so quickly that he upset the great easy chair in which he had been seated.

"Sainclair! Sainclair! Look at the red paint! Look at the red paint!"

I leaned over the drawing breathless terrified of the savage exultation of his tone. But I could see a little drawing carefully done. "The red paint! The red paint!" he kept groaning, his eyes staring in his head as though he were witnessing some frightful spectacle.

"But what—what is it?" I stammered.

"'*What is it*?' My god, man, can't you see? Don't you know that that is *blood*?"

No, I did not know it indeed. I was quite sure that it wasn't blood. It was merely red paint. But I took care not to contradict Rouletabille. I feigned to be interested in this idea of blood.

"Whose blood?" I inquired. "Do you think that it can be Larsan's?"

"Oh! oh! oh! Larsan's blood? Who knows anything about Larsan's blood? Who has ever seen the colour of it? To see that, it would be necessary to open my own veins, Sainclair. That's the only way!"

I was completely overwhelmed and astonished. "My father would not let his blood be spilled like that!"

He was speaking again with that strange, desperate pride of his father.

"When my father wears a wig, it will fit! My father would not let his blood be spilled like that!"

"Bernier's hands were covered with it and you yourself saw it upon the hand of the Lady in Black."

"Yes, yes! That is true—that is true! But they could never kill my father like that!"

He seemed to grow more excited every moment and he never ceased gazing on the little wash drawing. At last he spoke, his breast shaken with a great sob.

"O, God! O God! O God, have pity on us! That would be too frightful!"

He ceased for a moment and then spoke again:

"My poor mother did not deserve this I did not deserve it—nor any one in the world!" A tear ran down his cheek and fell into the little dish of paint.

"Ah!" he cried. "It isn't necessary to fill it any fuller." And he picked up the tiny cup with infinite care and carried it to the cabinet.

Then he took me by the hand and bade me look at him carefully—carefully—and tell him whether he had not really gone suddenly insane.

"Let us go! let us go!" he said, drearily, at last. "The time is come, Sainclair. No matter what happens, we can never turn back now! The Lady in Black must tell us everything—*everything about the man who is in that sack*! Ah, if M. Darzac were to return immediately—immediately—it might be less painful—but I dare wait no longer!"

Wait for what? Wait for whom? And why should he be so terrified now? What fear had made his eyes so wild? Why did his teeth chatter?

I could not restrain myself from asking him again: "What are you afraid of: Do you think that Lar san is not dead?"

And he answered, gripping my hand as though he would never release it :"I tell you I fear his death more than I fear his life!"

And he knocked at the door of the Square Tower before which we were standing as he spoke. I asked him whether he did not wish me to leave him alone with his mother. But, to my great surprise, he begged me not to abandon him "for anything in the world—so that the circle should not be closed." And he added mournfully. "Perhaps it may never be!"

The door of the Tower remained closed. He knocked again; then it was opened and we saw Bernier's face appear. He seemed embarrassed at the sight of us. "What do you want? What are you doing here again?" he demanded. "Speak low. Madame is in Old Bob's sitting room. And the old man has not come in yet."

"Let us enter, Bernier" said Rouletabille. And he pushed the door further open.

"But whatever you do, don't let Madame suspect—"

"No, no!" replied Rouletabille, impatiently.

We were in the vestibule of the Tower. The darkness was almost impenetrable.

"What is Madame doing in Old Bob's sitting room?" asked the reporter in a low voice.

"She is waiting—waiting for the return of M. Darzac. She dare not reënter *the room* until he comes—nor I, either!"

"Well, go back into your lodge, Bernier!" ordered Rouletabille. "And wait until I call you."

The young reporter opened the door of Old Bob's salon, and we saw the form of the Lady in Black, or, rather, her shadow, for the apartment was very dark and the first faint rays of the sun had scarcely penetrated it. The tall, sombre silhouette of Mathilde was standing but it leaned against the corner of the window which looked out upon the court of Charles the Bold. She never moved at our entrance, but her lips opened and a voice that I should never have recognised as hers, murmured:

"Why are you come? I saw you crossing the court. You have been there all night. You know all. What do you want now?"

And she added in a tone of unutterable misery:

"You swore to me that you would seek to know nothing."

Rouletabille went to her side and took her hand reverently.

"Come, Mother, dearest!" he said and the simple words upon his lips sounded like a prayer, tender and imploring. "Come—come!"

And he drew her away. She did not resist in the least. It was as though as soon as he touched her hand, he could bend her to his will. But when he led her to the door of the fatal chamber, her whole frame seemed to recoil. "Not there!" she moaned.

And she reeled against the wall to keep herself from falling. Rouletabille tried the door. It was locked. He called Bernier, who opened the door and then hurried away as though he were bent on escaping from some deadly peril.

Once the door was opened, we looked into the room. What a spectacle we beheld! The chamber was in the most frightful disorder. And the crimson dawn which entered through the vast embrasures rendered the disorder still more sinister. What an illumination for a chamber of horrors! Blood was upon the walls and upon the floor and upon the furniture! The blood of the rising sun and the blood of him whom Toby had carried off in the sack, no one knew whither—in the potato bag! The tables, the chairs, the sofas were all overturned. The curtains of the bed to which the man in his death agony had tried desperately to cling were half torn down and one could distinguish upon one of them the mark of a bloody hand.

It was into this scene that we entered, supporting the Lady in Black, who seemed ready to swoon, while Rouletabille kept murmuring to her in his gentle and pleading tones: "It has to be done, Mother! It has to be done!" And as soon as he had placed her upon a couch which I had turned right side up, he began to question her. She answered in monosyllables, by signs of the head or movements of the hands. And I saw that the further the examination progressed, the more troubled and restless Rouletabille became. He was visibly affected. He endeavoured to regain his composure and to help his mother maintain hers but it was difficult for him to succeed in either effort. He spoke to the unhappy woman as though he were still her little child. He called her "mamma" and tried in every way to show his reverence and love for her. But she had utterly lost courage. He held out his arms and she threw herself into them; the son and mother embraced and that seemed to give her a little more strength and she burst into a fit of weeping which seemed to relieve a little the terrible weight upon her breast. I made a movement as if to retire, but both sought to detain me and I saw that they did not wish to be left alone in this room red with blood.

Mme. Darzac, after her sobs had ceased, murmured:

"We are delivered!"

Rouletabille had fallen upon his knees at her side and, as she uttered the words, he said entreatingly: "Mother, dearest, in order that we may be sure of that—quite sure—you must tell me all that happened—everything that you saw."

Then she told us the story. She looked at the closed door; she looked with what seemed to be new horror at the overturned furniture and the blood-spattered walls and floor and she narrated the details of the frightful scene through which she had passed in a voice so low as to be almost inaudible, and I was obliged to bring my ear close to her to hear at all. In short, halting phrases, she told us that as soon as M. Darzac had entered his room, he had drawn the bolt and had walked straight to the little table which was placed in the centre of the room. The Lady in Black was standing a little nearer the left, ready to pass into her own sleeping room. The apartment was lighted only by a wax candle placed on the night commode, at the left, near Mathilde's door. And this is what happened:

The silence of the room was suddenly broken by a loud crash, like that of a piece of furniture falling to the ground, which made both M. and Mme. Darzac quickly raise their heads while their hearts were struck at the same moment by the same thrill of terror. The crash came from the little panel. And then all was silent. The pair looked at each other without daring to utter a word, perhaps without being able to do so. Darzac made a movement toward the panel which was situated at the back of the room on the right hand side. He was nailed to the spot where he stood by a second crash, louder than the first, and this time it seemed to Mathilde that she could see the panel move. The Lady in Black asked herself whether she were the victim of a hallucination, or if she had really seen the panel move. But Darzac had seen the same thing, for he made a hasty step in that direction. But at that very moment, the panel swung open before them. Pushed by an invisible hand it turned on its hinges. The Lady in Black tried to cry out, but her tongue clove to the roots of her mouth. But she made a gesture of terror and bewilderment which threw the wax candle to the ground at the very moment when a shadowy form issued from the panel. Uttering a cry of rage, Robert Darzac rushed upon the figure.

"And that shadow—that shadow had a face that you could see?" interrupted Rouletabille. "Mamma, why did you not see the face? You have killed the shadow, but how do we know that it was Larsan, if you did not see his face? Perhaps you have not even killed Larsan's shadow."

"Oh, yes," she replied, almost listlessly. "He is dead." And then for a moment, she said no more.

And I looked at Rouletabille, asking myself: Who could have been killed if it were not Larsan? If Mathilde had not seen his face, she had certainly heard his voice. She shuddered yet at the recollection— she heard it yet. And Bernier, too, had heard the voice and recognised it—that terrible voice of Larsan's—the voice of Ballmeyer, who in that fearful conflict in the middle of the night, had promised death to

Robert Darzac. "This blow will end your life!" while Darzac could only groan in the tones of a dying man, "Mathilde! Mathilde!" Ah, how he had cried to her!—how he had called with the rattle in his throat, as he lay already vanquished and in the shadow of death! And she—she had only to throw her own shadow, swooning with terror, into the midst of those two other shadows, while the man she loved called upon her for the aid she could not give and which could not come from elsewhere. And then, suddenly, there had come the pistol shot and she had uttered that terrible shriek—as though she had been wounded, herself. "Who was dead? Who was living? Who was speaking? Whose voice would she hear?"

And then it was Robert who spoke.

Rouletabille took the Lady in Black into his arms once more, lifted her up and carried her tenderly to the door of her own room. And there, he said to her: "Mamma, you must leave me now. I have work to do—for you, for M. Darzac and for myself."

"Don't leave me! I beg of you not to leave me until Robert comes back!" she cried in terror. Rouletabille begged her to try and take some rest and promised to remain near her if she would close her door, when someone knocked at the door of the corridor. Rouletabille asked who was there and the voice of Darzac answered.

"At last!" cried Rouletabille, and he threw the door open.

The man who entered looked like a corpse. Never was human face so pallid, so bloodless, so devoid of all semblance of life. So many emotions had ravaged his visage that it expressed not a single one.

"Ah! you were there!" he said. "Well, it is over." And he fell into the chair from which Rouletabille had just raised the Lady in Black. He looked up at her.

"Your wish is realised," he said. "It is where you wished it to be."

"Did you see his face?" questioned Rouletabille excitedly.

"No," answered Darzac, wearily. "I have not seen it. Did you think that I was going to open the sack?"

I thought that Rouletabille would have shown discomfiture at this answer but, on the contrary, he turned to M. Darzac and said:

"Ah, you did not see his face. That's very good, indeed." And he pressed his hand affectionately.

"The important thing now," he went on, "is not that, at all. It is necessary that we should close the circle. And you will help us do that, M. Darzac. Wait a moment."

And almost joyously, he threw himself down on all fours and crawled around among the furniture and under the bed as I had seen him do in the Yellow Room. And from time to time, he raised his head to say:

"Ah, I shall find something—something that will save us."

I answered, looking at M. Darzac: "Aren't we saved already?"

"Which will save our brains," Rouletabille went on.

"The boy is right!" exclaimed M. Darzac. "It is absolutely necessary for us to know how that man got into the room."

Suddenly Rouletabille rose to his feet, holding in his hand a revolver which he had found under the panel.

"Ah! you have found his revolver!" cried M. Darzac.

"Fortunately, he did not have time to use it." As he spoke M. Darzac took from his pocket his own revolver—the revolver which had saved his life—and held it out to the young man.

"This is a good weapon!" he said.

Rouletabille examined it closely and looked into the empty barrel out of which had sped the ball which had dealt death; then he compared the pistol with that which he had found under the panel and which had fallen from the hand of the assassin. The latter was a "bull dog" and bore the mark of a London gunsmith; it seemed to be quite new, every barrel was filled and Rouletabille declared that it had never been fired.

"Larsan only avails himself of firearms in the last extremity," said the young man. "He hates noise of any kind. You may be sure that he intended merely to frighten you with his revolver, otherwise he would have fired it immediately."

And Rouletabille returned M. Darzac's revolver and put Larsan's in his pocket.

"Of what use is it to be armed now?" cried M. Darzac, shaking his head. "I assure you it is quite futile."

"You believe so?" demanded Rouletabille.

"I am certain of it."

Rouletabille made a few steps through the room and said:

"With Larsan, one can never be sure of anything. Where is the body?"

M. Darzac replied.

"Ask my wife. I want to forget all about it. I know nothing more about this horrible thing. When the remembrance of that dreadful journey shall return to me, I shall try to make myself believe that it was a nightmare. And I will drive it away. Never speak to me of it again. No one save Mme. Darzac knows where the body is. She may tell you, if she likes."

"I have forgotten, too!" said Mathilde. "I was obliged to do so."

"Nevertheless," insisted Rouletabille, shaking his head, "you must tell me. You said that he was in his agony. Are you sure that he is dead now?"

"I am perfectly sure," replied M. Darzac, simply.

"Oh, it is finished. Is it not entirely ended?" pleaded Mathilde. She arose and walked to the window. "See! there is the sun! This horrible night is dead—dead, forever! Everything is over!"

Poor Lady in Black! The yearnings of her soul revealed themselves in her words. "It is finished!" And the fact, as she believed it, made her forget all the horror of the scene which had passed in this room. Larsan no more! Larsan buried! Buried in the potato sack!

And we all started up in affright, when the Lady in Black began to laugh—the frantic laugh of a mad woman! She ceased as suddenly as she had begun and a horrible stillness followed. We dared look neither at her nor at each other she was the first to speak.

"It is all over!" she said. "Forgive me: I won't laugh again."

And then Rouletabille said, speaking in a very low tone:

"It will be over when we know how he got in."

"What good would it do?" replied the Lady in Black.

"It is a question to which he alone knows the answer. He is the only one who could tell us and he is dead."

"He will not be truly dead for us until we know that," responded Rouletabille.

"Evidently," said M. Darzac, "so long as we do not know that, we shall be uneasy and he will be there in our minds. He must be driven away! he must be!"

"Let us try to drive him away then," said Rouletabille.

And he went to the Lady in Black and gently took her hand in his and attempted to draw her into the next room, begging her to lie down and rest. But Mathilde declared that she would not go. She said: "What! you would drive Larsan away and I not here!" And her voice sounded as though she were about to laugh again. I made a sign to Rouletabille not to insist upon her absence.

Rouletabille opened the door leading into the corridor and called Bernier and his wife. They did not wish to enter, but we insisted on their doing so, and a general consultation took place from which we deduced the following facts:

(1) Rouletabille had visited the apartment at five o'clock and searched behind the panel and at that time there was no one in the room.

(2) After five o'clock, the door of the apartment had been twice opened by Pere Bernier, who alone had the right to open it in the absence of M. and Mme. Darzac. The first time was at five o'clock to permit M. Darzac to enter; the next at eleven o'clock to admit M. and Mme. Darzac.

(3) Bernier had locked the door of the apartment when M. Darzac went out with us between a quarter past and half past six.

(4) The door of the apartment had been locked and bolted by M. Darzac as soon as he entered his room, both in the afternoon and in the evening.

(5) Bernier had stood guard before the door of the apartment from five o'clock till eleven o'clock with a brief interruption of not more than two minutes at six o'clock.

When we had discussed and fully established these facts, Rouletabille, who was sitting at M. Darzac's desk taking notes, arose and said:

"So far, it is very simple. We have only one hope. It is in the few moments that Bernier was off guard about six o'clock. At least, at that time, no one was in front of the door. But there was someone behind it. It was you, M. Darzac. Can you reiterate, after having thoroughly searched your memory, that when you went into your room, you instantly closed the door and drew the bolt?"

"I can!" replied M. Darzac, solemnly; and he added:

"And I opened that door only when you and Sainclair knocked upon it. I swear it."

And in saying this, as later events proved, the man spoke the truth.

Rouletabille thanked the Berniers and dismissed them to get some rest. Then, his voice trembling, the lad said:

"It is well, M. Darzac, you have closed the circle. The apartment in the Square Tower is now closed as firmly as was the Yellow Room which was like a strong box, or as the 'inexplicable gallery.'"

"One would guess immediately that Larsan was mixed up in the affair!" I exclaimed. "It is the same mode of procedure!" "Yes," observed Mme. Darzac. "Yes, M. Sainclair, it is the same mode of procedure."

And she unfastened her husband's collar to show the wounds hidden beneath it.

"See!" she said. "They are the same nail prints. I know them well."

There was a sorrowful silence.

M. Darsac, caring only to solve this strange problem, reviewed the crime of the Glandier. And he repeated what he had said in the Yellow Room:

"There must be a passage in the floor, in the ceiling or in the walls."

"There is not," replied Rouletabille.

"Then he must have found some way to make one," persisted M. Darzac.

"Why?" asked Rouletabille. "Did he do anything of the sort in the Yellow Room?"

"Oh, this isn't the same thing at all!" I exclaimed. "This apartment is more firmly closed than the Yellow Room since no one could have gotten into it before nor after."

"No, it is not the same thing," pronounced Rouletabille. "It is just the opposite. In the Yellow Room, there was a body missing: in the room in the Round Tower, there is a body too many."

And he tottered out, leaning on my arm so as not to fall. The Lady in Black rushed toward him. He had strength enough left to stop her with a gesture.

"Oh—this is nothing!" he said. "I'm a little tired, that's all!"

XIV

The Sack of Potatoes

While M. Darzac, with the assistance of Bernier, busied himself, as Rouletabille advised, with obliterating all signs of the tragedy, the Lady in Black, who had hastily changed her dress, hurried to her father's rooms in order not to run the risk of encountering any of the other members of the party. Her last word was to counsel us to prudence and silence. Rouletabille also took leave of us.

It was now about seven o'clock in the morning and things began to stir in and about the château. We could hear the fishermen singing in their boats. I threw myself upon my bed, and in a few moments I was sleeping profoundly, vanquished by the physical weariness which was stronger than my powers of resistance. When I awakened, I lay for a few moments on my couch in a pleasant bewilderment, but as the events of the night dawned on my remembrance, I started up in terror.

"Ah!" I cried out, "A body too many! No, no! It can't be! It's impossible!"

It was this which surged across the dark gulf of my thoughts, above the abyss of my memory; this impossibility of "a body too many." And the horror which I found in my heart at my awakening was not confined to myself—far from it! All those who had mingled, near or far, in this strange drama of the Square Tower, shared it; and even though the horror of the event itself were appeased—the horror of the body in its last throes of agony thrown into a sack which a man carried off at night to cast it into who knows what far off and profound and mysterious tomb where it might gasp out its last breath of life—even if, I say, this horror should be forgotten and blotted out of the mind, and effaced from the vision, yet still the impossibility of this "body too many" grew and increased and rose up before us higher and higher and more threatening and more dreadful. Certain persons there are—like Mme. Edith, for example—who deny almost from habit, anything which they cannot understand—who deny the presentation of the problem which destiny holds for us (such as we have established in the preceding chapter) even while every event and every circumstance among those which had the Fort of Hercules for their theatre rendered proof of the exactitude of the presentation.

First of all, the attack! How had the attack been made? At what moment? By what means of approach? What mines, trenches, covered paths, breaches—in the domains of the mental fortifications—have served the assailant and delivered the château over into his hands? Yes, under the existing conditions, where was the attack? The answer is—silence. And yet, the facts must be brought to light. Rouletabille has said so: he ought to know. In a siege as mysterious as this, the attack may be in everything or in nothing. The assailant is as still as the grave itself and the assault is made without clamour and the enemy approaches the walls walking in his stocking feet. The *attack*? It is, perhaps, in the very stillness itself, but again, it may, perhaps, be in the spoken word. It is in a tone, in a sigh, in a breath. It is in a gesture, but if perhaps it may be in all which is hidden, it may be, also, in all that is revealed—in *everything which one sees and which one does not see.*

Eleven o'clock! Where was Rouletabille? His bed had not been disturbed. I dressed myself hurriedly and went to look for my friend, whom I found in the outer court. He took me by the arm and led me into the vast drawing room of "la Louve." There, I was surprised to find, although it was not yet time for luncheon, everybody assembled. M. and Mme. Darzac were there. It seemed to me that M. Rance's manner was rather frigid. When he shook my hand in wishing me good morning, he barely touched my fingers. As soon as we entered the room Mme. Edith, from the dark corner where she was reclining carelessly on a sofa, saluted us with the words:

"Ah, here is M. Rouletabille with his friend, Sainclair. Now we shall know why we have all been summoned here!"

To this remark, Rouletabille responded by first excusing himself for having requested us all to gather at so early an hour; but he had, he went on to say, such a serious and important communication to make to us that he had not wished to delay it one moment longer than was absolutely necessary. His tone was so grave that Edith pretended to shiver and counterfeited an infantile terror. But Rouletabille, without noticing her, continued: "Before you shiver, Madame, wait until you know what you have to be afraid of. I have some news for you which is very far from pleasant."

We all looked at him, and then at each other! What was he about to say? I endeavoured to read in the faces of M. and Mme. Darzac what they thought of the matter. Both showed remarkably little evidence of last night's horrors! But what was it that Rouletabille had to say to us?

He entreated those who were standing to be seated and then he began to speak. He addressed himself to Mme. Rance.

"First of all, Madame, permit me to inform you that I have decided to suppress the 'guard' which surrounded the Château of Hercules, like an inner wall, and which I judged necessary for the protection of M. and Mme. Darzac which you kindly allowed me to establish, although it vexed you, showing the most charming of good humour and accommodating spirit."

This direct allusion to the mocking remarks and innuendos of Mme. Edith at the time when we mounted guard made Mr. Rance and his wife both smile. But no smile arose to the lips of M. or Mme. Darzac nor myself, for we had begun to ask ourselves anxiously what the boy was preparing to say.

"Ah, really, are you going to withdraw the guard for the château, M. Rouletabille? Well, I am very glad to hear it, although I assure you that it did not vex me in the least!" exclaimed Mme. Edith with an affectation of gayety. "On the contrary, it had interested me very much, because, you know, I am of a very romantic nature, and if I rejoice at the change, it is because the fact proves to me that M. and Mme. Darzac are no longer in any danger."

"This is true, Madame," replied Rouletabille, "since last night."

Mme. Darzac could not refrain from a hasty movement which no one save myself perceived.

"So much the better!" cried Mme. Edith. "May Heaven be praised! But how is it that my husband and I are the last to hear the news? Interesting things must have been happening last night! The nocturnal trip of M. Darzac to Castelar was one of them, without doubt!" As she spoke, I could see the embarrassment of M. and Mme. Darzac. The former, after a glance at his wife, started to speak, but Rouletabille would not permit him to do so.

"Madame, I do not know where M. Darzac went last night, but it is necessary that you should know one thing: and that is the reason why M. and Mme. Darzac have ceased to run any danger. Your husband, Madame, has told you of the frightful tragedy of the Glandier two years ago and of the villainous part played in it by—"

"Frederic Larsan—yes, monsieur, I know all that."

"You know also, of course, that the reason why we have placed such a strong guard here around M. Darzac and his wife was because we had seen this man again?"

"I do."

"Well, M. and Mme. Darzac are no longer in danger because this man cannot appear again ever."

"What has become of him?"

"He is dead."

"When did he die?"

"Last night."

"And how did he die last night?"

"He was killed, madame."

"And where was he killed?"

"In the Square Tower."

We all sprang to our feet at this declaration in the greatest agitation. M. and Mme. Rance seemed completely stupefied by the words which they had heard and M. and Mme. Darzac and myself were plunged into the most profound agitation by the fact that Rouletabille had not hesitated to reveal the secret.

"In the Square Tower?" cried Mme. Edith. "And who, then, has killed him?"

"M. Robert Darzac," replied Rouletabille. "And he entreats everyone to sit down."

It was astonishing how we seated ourselves with one accord, as though, at such a moment, we had nothing to do except to obey this youngster. But almost immediately Mme. Edith arose and seizing M. Darzac by the hand, she exclaimed with an emphasis which made me decide that I had judged her wrongly when I called her affected:

"Bravo, Monsieur Robert! All right! You are a gentleman!" Then she paid some exaggerated compliments—for after all, it was her nature to exaggerate things—to Mme. Darzac. She swore eternal friendship for her; she declared that she and her husband were ready, under all circumstances, to stand by the Darzacs and that the latter might count upon their zeal and their devotion and that they would swear whatever one liked before all the judges in the tribunal.

"Gently, dear Madame," interrupted Rouletabille. "There is no question of judges and we hope that there may not be. There's no need of it. Larsan was a dead man in the eyes of the whole world long before he was killed last night—he will continue to be dead, that is all! We have decided that it would be useless to reopen a scandal of which M. and Mme. Darzac have already been made the innocent victims and we have counted upon your assistance. The affair has happened in so mysterious a fashion that even you, if we had not informed you in regard to it, would never have suspected. But M. and Mme. Darzac are endowed with sentiments too noble to permit them to forget what they owe to their hosts. The most simple rules of hospitality ordered them to tell you that they killed a man in your house last night. How foolish it would be to lay bare this unfortunate story to some Italian police officer and subject you to the inconvenience of having your names coupled with the miserable business, and, it might easily be, to have a search made of your house and hired servants of the law under your roof! M. and Mme. Darzac, for your sakes alone, are anxious that you should not run the risk of being the object of idle gossip, or, perhaps, of having the police descend upon your home."

M. Arthur Rance, who up to this time had remained speechless, arose and said, his face as pallid as though he had seen a ghost:

"Frederic Larsan is dead. Well, so far so good, and no one is more rejoiced than myself to know it. And if he has received the punishment due to his crimes from the hand of M. Darsac, no one is more to be congratulated than M. Darzac. But I consider that it would be wrong for M. Darzac to make any attempt to conceal an act which is an honour to himself. It would be better to inform the authorities and without delay. If they should come to learn of this affair from others, rather than by our means, think of what the situation would be! If we give out the information ourselves, we shall show that an act of justice has been committed. If we conceal anything, we shall place ourselves in the category of malefactors. People might even suppose—"

To listen to M. Rance's stammering speech and to observe his demeanour, one might almost have imagined that he was the slayer of Frederic Larsan—he who was in danger of being accused of murder and dragged to prison.

"It is necessary to think of everything, gentlemen," he concluded. And Edith added: "I believe that my husband is right. But before we come to a decision, we ought to know just what has happened."

And she addressed herself directly to M. and Mme. Darzac. But both of the latter were still under the spell of surprise which Rouletabille had caused them by his remarks—Rouletabille who that very morning, in my presence, had promised to be silent and had sworn us all to silence. Neither the one nor the other had a word to say. M. Rance repeated, nervously: "Why should we conceal anything? Why should we? We must tell everything."

All at once, the reporter seemed to take a sudden resolution. I understood by the expressions which chased themselves over his face in rapid succession that something of considerable moment was passing through his mind. He leaned toward Arthur Rance, whose right hand was resting on a cane, the head of which was carved in ivory, beautifully cut by a famous carver at Dieppe. Rouletabille took the cane in his hand.

"May I look at it?" he asked. "I am an amateur ivory carver myself and my friend, Sainclair, here, has told me about this beautiful cane. I had not noticed it before. It is really very beautiful. It is a figure by Lambesse and there is no better workman on the Norman shore."

The young man seemed to be entirely engrossed in studying the cane. As he touched the carving, the stick fell from his hand and rolled toward M. Darzac. I picked it up and returned it immediately to M. Rance. Rouletabille cast a withering look at me, and I read in that glance that, somehow or other, I had shown myself an idiot.

Mme. Edith rose to her feet, tapping her little foot impatiently and seemingly very nervous at the tension of the situation—by the carelessness of Rouletabille and the silence of M. and Mme. Darzac.

"Dearest," she said to Mme. Darzac, in the sweetest tones. "You are completely tired out. The experiences of this horrible night have overpowered you. Let me take you into my own room so that you may rest a little."

"Pardon me for asking you to wait a few moments, Madame," interrupted Rouletabille. "What I have yet to say may be of special interest to you."

"Very well, monsieur, but speak out, please. Don't drag the recital along so."

She was perfectly justified in her remarks. Did Rouletabille realize it? At all events, he certainly made up for his previous deliberation by the rapidity and clearness with which he retraced the events of the night. In no other words could the problem of the "body too many" have been presented before us with such mysterious horror. Mme. Edith shivered—and if her shudder was counterfeit, I never saw a real one! As for Arthur Rance, he sat with his chin resting on the head of his cane, murmuring with a truly American coolness, but in accents of the strongest conviction: "What a devilish history! The story of the body which could not have gotten into the room is a page from the notebook of Satan himself!"

While he was speaking, he was gazing at the tip of Mme. Darzac's shoe which peeped out from the hem of her gown. In the moment which followed the closing of Rouletabille's narration, conversation became a little more general; but it was less a conversation than such a confused mixture of exclamations and interruptions, of interjections and indignation and demands for explanations on one point or another that the confusion seemed more increased than ever before. They spoke also of the horrible departure of "the body too many" in the potato sack, and at this point, Mme. Edith took occasion to once more express her admiration for M. Robert Darzac as a hero and a gentleman. Rouletabille never opened his lips during this torrent of words. It was plain to be seen that he despised this verbal manifestation of perturbation of spirits, but he endured it with the air of a professor who permits a few moments relaxation to pupils who have been well behaved in school. This was a mannerism of his which often vexed me and with which I sometimes reproached him, but without having any effect on him, for Rouletabille was likely to give himself whatever airs he chose.

At length—probably when it appeared to him that the recreation had lasted long enough, he asked abruptly of Mrs. Rance:

"Well, Madame, do you think we ought to inform the authorities?"

"I think so more than ever," she replied. "That which we are powerless to discover, they would certainly find out." (This allusion to the intellectual incapacity of my friend left him profoundly indifferent). "And I warn you of one thing, M. Rouletabille, and that is that we may already be too late in seeking out the officers of justice. If we had told them of our fears at the very beginning, you would have been spared some long hours of watching and sleepless nights which have profited you nothing, since, as now appears, they did not prevent what you dreaded from coming to pass."

Rouletabille seated himself, evidently conquering some strong emotion which made him tremble as though he were chilled to the bone. Then with a wave of the hand which he strove to render careless, he motioned Mme. Edith to a chair and again picked up the cane which M. Rance had laid down upon a sofa. I said to myself: "What is he trying to do with that stick? This time, I won't touch it, I'm certain. I must keep a lookout."

Playing with the cane, Rouletabille replied to Mme. Edith with an attack almost as sharp as her own.

"Madame, you are wrong in asserting that all the precautions which I had taken for the safety of M. and Mme. Darzac have been useless. If

I am obliged to acknowledge the unexplainable presence of one body too many, I am also compelled to refer to the absence—perhaps less inexplicable—of one member of our own party."

We stared at each other, some of us seeking to understand, the others dreading to do so.

"What is that?" inquired Mme. Edith, with a mocking little smile. "In such a case, I fail to see how you find any mystery at all." And she added with a flippant imitation of the reporter's words and manner: "A body too many on the one side; an unexplained absence on the other! Everything is for the best."

"Perhaps," rejoined Rouletabille. "But the most frightful thing of all is that the unexplained disappearance comes just at the right time to make known to us, apparently, the identity of the 'body too many.' Madame, I deeply regret to tell you that the person for whose whereabouts we are unable to account, is none other than your uncle, Monsieur Bob."

"Old Bob!" screamed the young woman. "Old Bob has disappeared!"

And we all cried out with her:

"Old Bob has disappeared?"

"Unfortunately, it is true!" said Rouletabille.

And he let the cane drop to the ground.

But the news of the sudden disappearance of Old Bob had so seised the Rances and the Darzacs that no one paid any attention to the cane as it fell.

"My dear Sainclair, will you be kind enough to pick up that cane?" asked Rouletabille.

I did as I was ordered and quickly, too, but Rouletabille did not even deign to thank me. Mme. Edith turned like a lioness upon Robert Darzac, who recoiled from her almost in fear as she shrieked:

"You have killed my uncle!"

Her husband and myself, with difficulty, prevented her from flying at him. We entreated her to be calm and to remember that because her uncle had absented himself from the peninsula did not necessarily mean that he had disappeared in the potato sack and we reproached Rouletabille with his brutality in blurting out an idea which could only be, at the present time, at all events, an hypothesis of his uneasy mind. And we added, imploring Mme. Edith to listen to us, that this hypothesis could under no circumstances be looked upon by her either as an injury or an insult, even admitting that it might be the true one, as it would only show the superhuman cunning of Larsan, who must, in that case, have taken the place of her respected uncle. But the young woman ordered her husband to be quiet, and said, turning scornfully to me:

"M. Sainclair, I sincerely hope that my uncle's absence from here will only be of short duration; for if it should turn out otherwise, I should accuse you of being an accomplice in the most cowardly of murders. As to you, monsieur," and she turned to Rouletabille, "the mere idea that you have ever dared to compare a man like Larsan with my uncle, the gentlest, kindliest soul and the greatest scholar of his time, forbids me to ever again consider you in the light of a friend, and I hope that you will have the courtesy to relieve me of your presence as soon as possible."

"Madame," replied Rouletabille, bowing very low, "I was just about to ask your permission to take leave of you. I have a short journey of twenty-four hours to take. At the expiration of that time, I shall return, ready to be of any possible assistance to you in whatever difficulties may arise in accounting for the disappearance of your uncle."

"If my uncle has not returned within twenty-four hours, I shall lodge a complaint in the hands of the police, monsieur."

"It is a good plan, Madame; but before having recourse to it, I advise you to question all the servants in whom you have confidence—particularly Mattoni. You trust Mattoni, do you not?"

"Yes, monsieur, I trust Mattoni."

"Well, then, Madame, question him—question him. Ah—before I take my departure, allow me to leave with you this excellent and historical book." And Rouletabille drew a small volume from his pocket.

"What foolery is this?" demanded Mme. Edith, superbly disdainful.

"This, Madame, is a work of M. Albert Bataille, a copy of his 'Civil and Criminal Cases,' in which I advise you to read the adventures, disguises, travesties and deceptions wrought by an illustrious swindler whose true name was Ballmeyer."

Rouletabille entirely ignored the fact that he had only the day before spent two hours in recounting to Mme. Edith the exploits of Ballmeyer.

"After having read this," he went on, "ask yourself carefully whether the cleverness of such an individual would have found very great difficulty in presenting himself before your eyes under the guise of an uncle whom you had not seen in four years—for it was four years, Madame, since you had seen Old Bob, until that time that you started out to the heart of the Pampas to look for him. As to the memory of M. Arthur Rance, who started out with you on that journey, it would be even less distinct than your own and he would be more capable of being deceived than yourself with your intuition of kinship added to your recollections of your relative. I implore you on my knees, Madame, do not lose patience with us. The situation, Heaven knows, is grave enough for each and every one of us. Let us remain united. You tell me to rid you of my presence. I am going but I shall return; for if it is necessary, taking everything into consideration, to arrive at the intolerable conclusion that Larsan has assumed the name and likeness of Monsieur Bob, it will remain for us only to seek Monsieur Bob himself, in which case, Madame, I shall be at your disposal and your most humble and obedient servant."

Mme. Edith assumed the attitude of an outraged tragedy queen and Rouletabille, turning to Arthur Rance, continued:

"For all that has happened, M. Rance, I make you my humblest excuses and also to your wife. And I count upon you as the loyal gentleman that you are and always have been to persuade her to have patience a little longer. I realize that you feel that you have reason to reproach me with having stated my hypothesis too quickly and too abruptly, but, please remember, it is only a few moments since Madame reproached me with being too slow."

But Arthur Rance seemed to have ceased to listen. He took his wife's arm and both moved toward the door and were about to leave the room when the portals flew open and the stable boy, Walter, Old Bob's faithful servant, rushed into our midst. His clothing was torn, muddy and covered with burs and thistles. Perspiration was streaming down his forehead and cheeks, his hair was in disorder and his face wore an expression of rage mingled with terror which made us fear some new misfortune. He carried in his hand a dirty rag which he threw upon the table. This repulsive object, stained with great blotches of reddish brown was (as we divined immediately, recoiling from it in horror) nothing other than the sack which had served to carry off the mysterious body.

With a harsh voice and savage gestures, Walter howled forth a thousand incomprehensible things in his broken jumble of French and English and all of us with the exception of Arthur Rance and Mme. Edith, asked each other, "What is he saying? What is he saying?"

Arthur Rance interrupted him from time to time, while Walter shook his fists menacingly at the rest of us and cast fiery glances at Robert Darzac. Once, for a moment, it seemed as though he intended to seize Darzac by the throat, but a gesture from Mme. Edith restrained him. When he finished speaking, Arthur Rance translated his words for us.

"He says that this morning he noticed blood stains on the English cart and saw that Toby seemed very greatly fatigued. This puzzled him so much that he decided to speak of it at once to Old Bob, but he sought his master in vain. Then, seised by a dark foreboding, he followed the prints of the horse's feet and the wheels of the vehicle which he could easily do because the road was muddy and the wheels had sunk deep. Finally he reached the old Castillon and noticed that the wheels led up to a deep chasm into which he descended, believing that he should find the body of his master; but he saw merely this empty sack which may have contained the corpse of Old Bob, and now, having caught a ride in a peasant's wagon, he has returned to ask for his master, to learn whether anyone has seen him, and, if he is not found, to accuse Robert Darzac of having caused his death."

We stood confounded. But, to our great astonishment, Mme. Edith was the first to recover her self-possession. She spoke a few words to Walter which appeared to quiet him, promising him that she would soon bring him face to face with Old Bob, who was perfectly safe and well. And she said to Rouletabille:

"You have twenty-four hours, Monsieur; make the best use of it."

"Thanks, Madame," said Rouletabille. "But if your uncle should not return in that time, it will be because my idea was correct."

"But where can he be!" she cried. "I cannot tell you, Madame. He is not in the sack now, at all events."

Mme. Edith cast a withering glance at him and left the room, followed by her husband. The sight of the sack seemed to have stricken Robert Darzac speech less. He had thrown the bag into an abyss and it was brought back empty. After a moment's pause, Rouletabille spoke:

"Larsan is not dead, be sure of that! Never has the situation been so frightful as it is today and I must hurry away at once. I have not a minute to lose. Twenty-four hours—in twenty-four hours, I shall be back. But promise me—swear to me, both of you, that you will not quit the château. Swear to me, M. Darzac, that you will watch over your wife—that you will prevent her from leaving these walls, even by force, if it is necessary. Ah—and again—it is no longer necessary that you should sleep in the Square Tower. No, you ought not to do so. In the same wing where M. Stangerson is lodged, there are two empty rooms. You must occupy them. It is absolutely necessary that you should. Sainclair, you will see that this change is made. After my departure, see that neither the one nor the other of them shall set foot in the Square Tower. Adieu! Ah, wait!—let me embrace you—all three."

He pressed us to his heart: M. Darzac first, then myself, and then, falling into the arms of the Lady in Black, he burst into a passion of sobs. This show of weakness and of grief on the part of Rouletabille, in spite of the gravity of the circumstances of his departure, appeared to me very strange. Alas! how easy it was for me to understand it afterward!

XV

THE SIGHS OF THE NIGHT

Two o'clock in the morning! Every person and everything in the castle seemed wrapped in slumber. Silence brooded over the heavens and the earth. While I stood at my window, my forehead burning and my heart frozen, the sea yielded its last sigh and in a moment the moon appeared riding like a queen in the cloudless sky. Shadows no longer veiled the stars of the night. There, in that vast, motionless slumber which seemed to envelope all the world, I heard the words of the Lithuanian folk song: "But his glance seeks in vain for the beautiful unknown who has covered her head with a veil and whose voice he has never heard." The words were carried to my ear, clear and distinct, in the still air of the night. Who had pronounced them? Was the voice that of a man or a woman? or was the song only an hallucination evoked by my memories? What should the Prince from the Black lands be doing on the Azure shore with his Lithuanian melodies? And why should his image and his songs pursue me thus?

Why was Mme. Edith attracted toward him? He was ridiculous with his melancholy eyes and his long lashes and his Lithuanian songs! And I—I was ridiculous, too. Had I the heart of a college boy? I think not. I would rather believe that the emotion which was excited in me by the personality of Prince Galitch rose less from my knowledge of the interest which Mme. Edith felt in him than from the thought of *that other*. Yes, it was surely that. In my mind the thought of the Prince and that of Larsan somehow went together. And the Prince had not returned to the château since the famous luncheon at which he was presented to us—that is to say since the day before yesterday.

The afternoon following Rouletabille's departure had brought us nothing new. We received no news from him nor from Old Bob. Mme. Edith had locked herself up in her own apartments, after having questioned the domestics and visiting her uncle's rooms and the Round Tower. She made no effort to penetrate into the apartments of the Darzacs in the Square Tower. "That is an affair for the police," she had said. Arthur Rance had walked for an hour on the western boulevard, his manner restless and impatient. No one had spoken a word to me. Neither M. nor Mme. Darzac had stirred out of "la Louve." All of us had dined in our own rooms. No one had seen Professor Stangerson.

And now, so far as the eye could see, everyone in the château seemed to be lost in dreams. But a shadow appeared on the bosom of the starry night—the shadow of a canoe which slowly detached itself from the shadow of the fort and glided out upon the silvery water. Whose is this silhouette, which arises proudly in the front of the boat while another shade bends over a silent oar? It is yours, Feodor Feodorowitch! Ah, here is a mystery which might be easier to solve than that of the Square Tower, O Rouletabille! And I who believed that Mme. Edith had too good a brain and too fine a mind to lend herself to a vulgar intrigue!

What a hypocrite is the night! Everything seems to sleep and all the while slumber is far from all eyes! Who was there that might be sleeping among those in the château of Hercules? Was Mme. Edith sleeping, perhaps? Or M. or Mme. Darzac" And how could M. Stangerson, who seemed to have been slumbering all day, be dreaming away the night also?—he whose couch, ever since the revelation of the Glandier, had not ceased to be haunted by the pale ghost of insomnia? And I—could I sleep?

I left my bedchamber and went down into the court of the Bold and my feet bore me rapidly over to the boulevard of the Round Tower—so rapidly that I arrived there in time to see the bark of Prince Galitch landing on the strand in front of the "Gardens of Babylon." He leaped out of the boat and his man, having picked up the oars, followed. I recognised the master and servant. It was Feodor Feodorowitch and his serf, Jean. A few seconds later, they disappeared in the protecting shade of the century plants and the giant eucalypti.

I turned and walked around the boulevard of the court. And then my heart beating wildly, I directed my steps toward the outer court. The stone slabs of the walks resounded under my tread and I seemed to see a form arise in a listening attitude from beneath the arch of the ruined chapel. I paused in the thick darkness of the shadow cast by the gardener's tower and drew my revolver from my pocket. The form did not move. Was it really a human creature who stood there listening? I glided behind a hedge of vervain which bordered the path that led directly to "la Louve" through bushes and thickets, heavy with the perfume of the flowers of the spring. I had made no noise, and the shadow, doubtless reassured, made a slight movement. It was the Lady in Black. The moon, under the half ruined arch, showed me that she was as pale as death. And suddenly her figure vanished as if by enchantment. I approached the chapel and as I diminished the space which lay between me and the ruins, I heard a soft murmur of words mingled with such bitter sobs that my own eyes grew moist as I listened. The Lady in Black was weeping there behind that pillar. Was she alone? Had she not chosen in this night of anguish to come to this altar decked with flowers there to pour out her prayers in solitude to the balmy air?

Suddenly I perceived a shadow beside the Lady in Black and I recognised Robert Darzac. From the corner where I was I could now hear all that they were saying. I knew that my behaviour in listening was degraded and shameless, but, curiously enough, it was borne upon me that it was my duty to listen. Now I thought no longer of Edith and her Prince Galitch. I thought only of Larsan. Why? Why was it on account of Larsan that I bent my ears so anxiously to hear all that went on between those two? I learned from their words that Mathilde had descended stealthily from la Louve to be alone in the garden with her agony and that her husband had followed her. The Lady in Black was weeping. And she took Robert Darzac's hands and said to him:

"I know, dear—I know all your grief. You need not speak of it to me when I see you so changed-so wretched I accuse myself of being the cause of your sorrow. But do not tell me that I no longer love you. Oh, I will love you dearly, Robert—just as I have always done. I promise you."

And she seemed to sink into a deep fit of thought, while he, almost as though incredulous, still stood as though he were listening to her. In a moment, she looked up again and repeated in a tone of firm conviction: "Yes—I promise you."

She pressed his hand and turned away, casting upon him a smile so sweet and yet so sorrowful that I wondered how this woman could speak to a man of future happiness. She brushed past me without seeing me. She passed with her perfume and I no longer smelled the laurel bushes behind which I was hidden.

M. Darzac remained standing in the same spot, looking after her. Suddenly he said aloud with a violence which startled me:

"Yes, happiness must come! It must!"

Assuredly, he was at the end of his patience. And before withdrawing in his turn, he made a gesture of protest—against fate, it seemed to me—a gesture of defiance to destiny—a gesture which snatched the Lady in Black through the space which divided them and caught her to his breast and held her there.

He had scarcely made this gesture when my thought took form— my thought which had been wandering about Larsan stopped at

Darzac. Oh, how well I remember that instant! The fancy was gone in a moment, but as I beheld gesture of defiance and rapture, I dared to say to myself, "If HE should be Larsan!"

And in looking back to the depths of my memory, I realize now that my thought was even stronger than that. To the gesture of this man, my mind answered with the cry, "This is Larsan!"

I was white with terror and when I saw Robert Darzac coming in my direction, I could not refrain from a movement which revealed my presence while I was trying to conceal it. He saw me and recognised me, and, grasping me by the arm, he exclaimed:

"You were there, Sainclair: you were watching. We are all watching, my friend. And you heard what she said. Sainclair, her grief is too great. I can bear no more. We would have been so happy. She began to believe that misfortune had forgotten her when that man reappeared. Then all was finished; she had no longer strength to desire love or to feel it. She is bowed down by destiny. She imagines that she is to be pursued by eternal punishment. It was necessary for the frightful tragedy of last night to prove to me that this woman did love me—once. Yes, for one moment, all her fears were for me—and I, alas, have blood on my hands only because of her. Now she has returned to her old indifference. She cares no longer—her only desire is that the old man shall be kept in ignorance."

He sighed so sorrowfully and so sincerely that the abominable idea which it had harboured fled from my mind. I thought only of what he was saying to me—of the sorrow of this man who seemed to have lost completely the woman whom he loved in the moment when the woman had found a son of whose existence the husband continued to be ignorant. In fact, he had in no way been able to understand the attitude of the Lady in Black as regards the facility with which she had detached herself from him—and he found no explanation for this cruel metamorphosis other than the love heightened by remorse of Professor Stangerson's daughter for her father.

"What good did it do me to kill him?" groaned M. Darzac. "Why did I fire the shot? Why did she impose upon me such a criminal, horrible silence if she did not intend to recompense me for it by her love? Did she fear arrest for me? Ah, no! Not even that, Sainclair, not even that! She fears only the agony of her father and the danger that he will succumb entirely under this new disgrace. Her father! Always her father! I do not exist for her. I have loved her for twenty years and when I believe at last that I have won her, the thought of her father takes my place."

And I said to myself: "The thought of her father—and of her child."

He seated himself on an old moss grown boulder by the chapel and said again, as if speaking to himself: "But I will snatch her away from this place—I cannot see her roaming about on the arm of her father—as if I were not in the world."

And, while he said this, I looked up and I fancied that I beheld the shadow of the father and the daughter passing and repassing in the dawn, beneath the sombre height of the Tower of the North, and I likened them in my mind to the old Oedipus and his daughter, Antigone, walking under the walls of Colone, dragging with them the weight of a grief beyond human endurance.

And then suddenly, without my being able to recall myself to reason, perhaps because Darzac made again the gesture which had startled me before, the same frightful fancy assailed me, and I demanded:

"How did it happen that the sack was empty?"

He was not in the least confused or taken aback.

He replied simply:

"Rouletabille must tell us that." Then he pressed my hand and wandered away through the undergrowth of the garden. I looked after him and said to myself:

"I have gone mad!"

XVI

Discovery of "Australia"

The moon was shining full on his face. He believed himself to be alone in the night and certainly it was one of the moments in which he would cast aside the mask of the day. First the black glasses had ceased to shade his eyes. And if his figure, during the hours of disguise, was more bent than nature had made it, if his shoulders were rounded by pretence instead of study, this was the moment when the magnificent body of Larsan, away from all observers, must relax itself. Would it relax now? I hid in the ditch behind the barberry hedge. Not one of his movements escaped me.

Now he was standing erect upon the western boulevard which looked like a pedestal beneath his feet; the rays of the moon enveloped him with a cold and mournful light. Is it you, Darzac? or your spectre? or the ghost of Larsan, come back from the house of the dead?

I felt that I had gone mad. What a piteous state was ours—all of us madmen! We saw Larsan everywhere, and, perhaps, Darzac himself might more than once have gased at me, Sainclair, saying to himself: "Suppose that he were Larsan!" More than—once! I speak as though it were years since we had been locked up in the château and it was now just four days. We came here on the eighth of April in the evening.

It is true that my heart had never beaten so wildly when I had asked myself the same terrible question about the others; perhaps, because it was less terrible when there was question of any of the others. And then, how strange that such a thought should have come to me! Instead of my spirit recoiling in affright before the black abyss of such an incredible hypothesis, it was, on the contrary, attracted, enchained, horribly bewitched by it. It was as though struck with vertigo which it could do nothing to evade. It glued my eyes to that figure standing upon the western boulevard, making me find the attitudes, the gestures, a strong resemblance from the rear—and then, the profile—and even the face. Yes, all—all. He did look like Larsan. Yes, but just as strongly did the face and figure resemble Darzac.

How was it that this idea had come to me that night for the first time? Now that I thought of it—it should have been our first hypothesis of all. Was it not true that, at the time of "The Mystery of the Yellow Room," the silhouette of Larsan had been confounded at the moment of the crime with that of Darzac" Was it not true that the man who was believed to be Darzac, who had come to inquire for Mlle. Stangerson's answer at Post Office Box No. 40, had really been Larsan himself? Was it not true that this emperor of disguises had already undertaken with success to appear to be Darzac?—and to such good purpose that Mlle. Stangerson's fiancé had been accused of being the perpetrator of the crimes committed by the other?

It was true—all true—and yet when I ordered my restless heart to be quiet and listen to reason, I knew that my hypothesis was absurd. Absurd? Why? Look at him there, the ghost of Larsan which strides session. She spoke a few words to Walter which appeared to quiet him, promising him that she would soon bring him face to face with Old Bob, who was perfectly safe and well. And she said to Rouletabille:

"You have twenty-four hours, Monsieur; make the best use of it."

"Thanks, Madame," said Rouletabille. "But if your uncle should not return in that time, it will be because my idea was correct."

"But where can he be!" she cried. "I cannot tell you, Madame. He is not in the sack now, at all events."

Mme. Edith cast a withering glance at him and left the room, followed by her husband. The sight of the sack seemed to have stricken Robert Darzac speech less. He had thrown the bag into an abyss and it was brought back empty. After a moment's pause, Rouletabille spoke:

"Larsan is not dead, be sure of that! Never has the situation been so frightful as it is today and I must hurry away at once. I have not a minute to lose. Twenty-four hours—in twenty-four hours, I shall be back. But promise me—swear to me, both of you, that you will not quit the château. Swear to me, M. Darzac, that you will watch over your wife—that you will prevent her from leaving these walls, even by force, if it is necessary. Ah—and again—it is no longer necessary that you should sleep in the Square Tower. No, you ought not to do so. In the same wing where M. Stangerson is lodged, there are two empty rooms. You must occupy them. It is absolutely necessary that you should. Sainclair, you will see that this change is made. After my departure, see that neither the one nor the other of them shall set foot in the Square Tower. Adieu! Ah, wait!—let me embrace you—all three."

He pressed us to his heart: M. Darzac first, then myself, and then, falling into the arms of the Lady in Black, he burst into a passion of sobs.

This show of weakness and of grief on the part of Rouletabille, in spite of the gravity of the circumstances of his departure, appeared to me very strange. Alas! how easy it was for me to understand it afterward!

Those shoulders are those of Darzac.

I must admit that my suspicions are absurd. I say absurd because anyone who was not Darzac might have passed for him in the shade and the mystery that surrounded the drama of the Glandier. But here we have lived with the man. We have talked with him—touched him.

We have lived with him? No!

To begin with, he was rarely there among us. Always locked in his own room or bending over that useless work in the Tower of the Bold. A fine pretext, that of drawing, to prevent anyone's seeing your face and to make it appear natural to answer questions without turning the head!

But he was not drawing all the time! Yes, but at other times, always, except tonight, he wore his dark glasses. Ah! that accident in the laboratory had been well contrived. That little lamp which exploded knew—I have always thought so, it seems to me—the service which it was going to do for Larsan when Larsan should have taken the place of Darzac. It permitted him to evade always and everywhere the full light of day—because of the weakness of his eyes. How then! Was it not always Mlle. Stangerson or Rouletabille who had managed to find dark corners where M. Darzac's eyes could not be exposed to the sun? But, lately, he himself, more than anyone else now that I reflected upon it, had been careful to keep in the shadow—we have seen him seldom and always in the shadow. That little "hall of counsel" was very dark, "la Louve" was dark, and he had chosen the two rooms in the Square Tower which are plunged in semi-darkness.

But still—still—Rouletabille could not be deceived like that—even for three days. But, as the lad himself said, Larsan was born before Rouletabille and was his father.

And suddenly there recurred to my mind the first act of Darzac when he came to meet us at Cannes and entered our compartment with us. He drew the curtain. The shadow—always the shadow!

The figure on the western boulevard is still standing there. I can look him full in the face. No spectacles now! He was not moving. He stood as if he were posing for a photograph. Do not stir There! that is he! Yes, it is Robert Darzac—only Robert Darzac!

He began to walk again—I was certain no longer. There is something in his walk which is not Darzac's—something in which I seem to recognize Larsan—but what?

Yes, Rouletabille must have seen! And yet—Rouletabille reasons more often than he looks! And has he ever had a chance to look at him like this?

No! We must not forget that Darzac went to spend three months in the Midi—That is true! Ah, what might not have happened in that time! Three months during which none of us saw him. He went away ill; he returned almost well. There could be nothing astonishing in the fact that a man's appearance should be changed when he went away with the look of a dead man and returned with the look of one living and strong!

And the wedding had taken place immediately after that. How little any of us had seen of him before the ceremony! And, besides, a week had not yet elapsed since the marriage. A Larsan could easily wear his mask for so short a time.

The man—was it Darzac or was it Larsan?—descended from his pedestal and came straight toward me. Had he seen me? I crouched down behind my barberries.

(Three months of absence during which Larsan might have had a chance to study every gesture, every mannerism of Darzac! And then—how easy to put Darzac out of the way and to take his place and his bride! Not a difficult trick—for a Larsan!)

The voice? What more easy than to imitate the voice of a native of the Midi? One has a little more or a little less of accent than the other, that is all. Occasionally I have fancied that *his* accent was a little stronger than before the wedding.

He was almost upon me. He passed by. He had not Seen me.

"It is Larsan! I could swear that it was Larsan!" But he paused for a second and gased sorrowfully upon all nature slumbering around him—him whose suffering was in loneliness and solitude, and a groan escaped his lips, unhappy soul that he was!

"It is Darzac!"

And then he was gone—and I remained there behind my hedge overwhelmed with the horror of the thought which I had dared to harbour.

How long did I remain thus, lying on the ground? One hour? Two? When I arose, I was so stiff that I could scarcely stir and my mind was as worn out as my body—worn out and distracted. In the course of my unthinkable hypotheses, I had even gone so far as to ask myself whether, by chance (by chance!) the Larsan who had been in the potato sack had not succeeded in substituting himself for Darzac who had carried him off in the little English cart with Toby drawing it, meaning to throw him into the gulf of Castillon. I could picture the body of the victim rising up suddenly and ordering M. Darzac to take its place. So far from all reason had my wild supposition driven me, that in order to drive away from my mind this ridiculous idea, I was compelled to recall word by word a private conversation that had occurred between M. Darzac and myself that morning when we went out from the terrible session in the Square Tower at which had been so clearly presented the problem of the "body too many." In this conversation, I had received an absolute proof of the impossibility of my supposition. I had, while we talked, proposed to M. Darzac a few questions in relation to Prince Galitch, whose image would not cease to pursue me, and my friend had answered by making allusion to another conversation, involving certain scientific facts, which had taken place between us the night previous, and which could not possibly have been heard by any other person than our two selves and which had also concerned Prince Galitch. On this account, there could be no real doubt in my mind that the Darzac whom I had talked with in the garden was none other than the same man I had seen the evening before.

As senseless as was the idea of this substitution, it was, nevertheless, in a certain degree, pardonable. Rouletabille was a little to blame for it by his fashion of talking of Larsan as a very god of metamorphosis. And after casting it aside, I returned to the sole possible idea under which Larsan could have taken the place of Darzac—the idea of a substitution before the marriage ceremony at the time when Mlle. Stangerson's fiancé returned to Paris after three months absence in the Midi.

The despairing plaint which Robert Darzac, believing himself alone, had allowed to escape his lips only a little while before, in my hearing, could not entirely banish this supposition from my head. I saw him again entering the church of St. Nicolas du Chardonnet, in which parish he had requested that the wedding should take place—perhaps, thought I, because there is no darker nor more gloomy church in all Paris.

Ah, one's fancy plays strange tricks on a moon light night, when one is lurking behind a barberry hedge, with a mind and brain filled with Larsan!

"I am a veritable imbecile!" I told myself, beginning to wish that I were in the quiet little room in the New Castle, where my undisturbed bed awaited me. "For if Larsan had been masquerading as Darzac, he would have been satisfied with carrying off Mathilde and he would not have reappeared in his own likeness to frighten her and he would not have brought her to the Château of Hercules and he would not have com mitted the foolhardy act of showing himself again in the bark of Tullio. For at that moment, Mathilde belonged to him and it was from that moment that she had cast him off. The reappearance of Larsan had divided the Lady in Black from Darzac, and, therefore, Darzac could not be Larsan."

Dear Heaven, how my head ached! It was the moon light above which must have turned my brain—I was moonstruck.

And then, too, had not *he* appeared to Arthur Rance himself in the gardens at Mentone after he had accompanied Darzac to the train which had taken him to Cannes, where he met us. If Arthur Rance had spoken the truth, I might go to my couch in tranquility. And why should he have lied?—Arthur Rance who had been in love with the Lady in Black and who had not ceased to love her. Mme. Edith was not a fool—she knew that Mme. Darzac still held the heart of the young American. Well, it was time for me to go to bed!

I was still beneath the arch of the gardener's postern and I was just about to enter the Court of the Bold when it seemed to me that I heard something moving—it sounded as though a door might have been closed. Then there was a sound as of wood striking on iron. I thrust my head out from under the arch and I believed that I could see the shadow of a person near the door of the New Castle—a shadow which somehow seemed to mingle with that of the castle itself. I snatched my revolver from my pocket and with three steps was at the place where I believed I had seen the shape. But it was there no longer. I could see nothing but darkness. The door of the castle was closed and I was certain that I had left it open. I was disturbed and anxious. I felt that I was not alone—who, then, could be near me? Evidently if that shadow had existed elsewhere than in my imagination, it could have vanished only within the New Castle or must still be in the court.

And the court was deserted.

I listened attentively for more than five minutes without making the slightest sound. Nothing! I must have been mistaken. But, nevertheless, I did not even strike a match, and as silently as I could, I ascended the staircase which led to my chamber. When I reached it, I locked myself in and only then began to breathe freely.

This vision or whatever it had been continued to disturb me more than I was willing to confess to myself, and even after I had gotten into bed I could not sleep. Without my being able to account for it at all this vision and the thought of Darzac-Larsan began to mingle strangely in my restless spirit.

The effect on my mind was so strong that, at last, I said to myself: "I shall never know peace again until I am certain that M. Darzac is not Larsan. And I shall take means to make myself certain, one way or the other, on the first occasion." Yes, but how? Pull his beard off? If my suspicion was baseless, he would take me for a madman, or else he would guess what I was thinking of and such a knowledge would add yet another to the load of misfortunes, already too heavy for him to bear. Only this misery was lacking to him still—to know that he was suspected of being Larsan.

Suddenly I threw off the bedclothes, jumped up and cried almost aloud:

"Australia!"

An episode had returned to my mind of which I have spoken at the beginning of this story. The reader may remember that, at the time of the accident in the laboratory, I had accompanied M. Robert Darzac to a druggist. While his injuries were being attended to, he had been obliged to remove his study coat, and the sleeve of his shirt had fallen back, leaving his arm bare through the entire session with the druggist, and placing in full view just above the right elbow, a large birth mark, the shape of which resembled that of Australia as it appears on the maps in the geographies. Mentally, while the chemist was at work, I had amused myself by trying to locate upon the arm in the positions which they occupied on an actual map, the cities of Melbourne, Sydney, Adelaide, etc.; and directly beneath this large mark, there was another smaller one which was situated like the country known as Tasmania.

And when, by any chance, the thought of that accident had happened to recur to my mind, I had always thought of the half hour at the chemist's and the birth mark shaped like the outlines of Australia.

And in this sleepless night, it was the thought of Australia that came to me.

Seated on the edge of my bed, I had scarcely had time to congratulate myself upon having found a means to prove decisively the identity of Robert Darzac and to try to devise some way of bringing it to an immediate test, when a singular sound made me prick up my ears. The sound was repeated—one would have said that gravel was cracking beneath slow and cautious footsteps.

Breathless, I hurried to my door and, with my ear at the keyhole, I listened. Silence for a moment and then once more the same sound—footsteps, beyond a doubt. Someone was now ascending the staircase—and someone who desired his presence to be unknown. I thought of the shadow which I had believed I saw as I was entering the Court of the Bold—whose could this shadow be and what was it doing on the staircase? Was it coming up or going down?

Silence again! I profited by it to hastily don my trousers and, armed with my revolver, I succeeded in opening my door without letting it creak on its hinges. Holding my breath, I advanced to the head of the stairs and waited. I have told of the state of dilapidation of the New Castle. The pale rays of the moon light entered obliquely through the high windows which opened at each landing, cutting with exact squares of soft light the black darkness of the stairway which was very wide and high. The ruined condition of the château, thus lighted up in spots, only appeared more complete. The broken balustrade and railings of the staircase, the walls overrun with lizards over which here and there hung floating rags of once priceless tapestry—all these things which I had scarcely noticed in the daylight, struck me strangely in this lonely night and my whirling brain felt quite prepared to find in this gloomy scene the fit setting for the appearance of a phantom. Indeed and in truth, I was afraid. The shadow which I had seen a little while ago had practically slipped between my fingers—for I had been near enough to have touched it. But, surely a phantom might walk in an empty house without making any sound. Though the footsteps were silent now!

All at once, as I was leaning on the broken balustrade, I saw the shadow again—it was lighted up by the moonbeams as though it were a flambeau. And I recognised Robert Darzac.

He had reached the ground floor, and, crossing the vestibule, raised his head and looked in my direction as though he felt the weight of my eyes upon him. Instinctively, I drew back. And then I returned to my post of observation just in time to see him disappear into a corridor which led to another staircase winding up to the battlements. What could this mean? Was Robert Darzac spending the night in the New Castle? Why did he take such precautions not to be seen? A thousand suspicions crossed my mind—or rather all the terrible thoughts that had come to haunt me since we had been in the Fort of Hercules seised me again in their grasp and I felt that I must set my spirit at rest, immediately. I must follow Robert Darzac and discover "Australia."

I had reached the corridor almost as soon as he quitted it and I saw him beginning to climb very quietly the moth-eaten wood of the stairway. I saw him pause at the first landing and push open a door. Then I saw nothing more. He had been swallowed up by the darkness— and, perhaps, by the room of which he had opened the door. I reached this door and finding it locked, I gave three little taps, certain that he was inside. And I waited. My heart was beating wildly. All these rooms were uninhabited—abandoned. What should M. Darzac be doing in one of these haunted chambers!

I waited for a few moments which seemed to me like hours and as no one answered and the door did not open, I knocked again and waited again. Then the door was opened and I heard Darzac's voice saying:

"Is it you, Sainclair? What is it, my friend?"

"I wanted to know what you could be doing here at such an hour?" I replied, and it seem d to me that my voice was that of another man, so great was my terror.

Tranquilly, he struck a match and said:

"You see. I am preparing for bed."

And he lit a candle which was placed on a chair, for there was no night stand in this dilapidated apartment. A bed in one corner—an iron bed which must have been brought there during the day, and a single chair, comprised all the furnishings.

"I thought that you were going to sleep near Mme. Darzac and the Professor on the first floor of 'la Louve'?"

"The rooms are too small. I was afraid of inconveniencing Mme. Darzac," answered the unhappy man, bitterly. "I asked Bernier to fetch me a bed here. And then what difference does it make where I am, since I do not sleep?"

We were both silent for a moment. I was ashamed of myself and of my wretched suspicions. And, frankly, my remorse was so great that I could not refrain from giving it expression. I confessed everything to him; my infamous ideas and how I had even believed when I saw him wandering so mysteriously over the New Castle that it was upon some evil errand; and so had decided to go and look for the "Australia" birthmark. For I did not conceal from him that for a moment, I had placed all my hopes upon the Australia.

He listened to me with such an expression of reproachful sorrow that it wrung my heart; then he quietly rolled up his shirt sleeve and bringing his bare arm close to the light, he showed me the birthmark, which made a sane man of me once more. I did not wish to look at it, but he even insisted upon my touching it and I knew beyond a doubt that it was a natural scar upon which one might place little dots with the names of the cities, "Sydney," "Melbourne," "Adelaide." And beneath it there was another little blotch shaped like Tasmania.

"You may rub it as much as you choose," said Darzac, gently, "It will not come off."

I begged his pardon a thousand times over, with tears in my eyes, but he would not forgive me until he had made me pull at his beard which remained firmly attached to his chin, instead of coming off in my hand.

Then, only, he allowed me to go back to my room, which I did, cursing myself for an idiot.

XVII

OLD BOB'S TERRIBLE ADVENTURE

W hen I awakened my thoughts were still dwelling on Larsan. And, in truth, I did not know what to think either of myself or any other person—of Larsan's death or of his life. Had he been wounded less seriously than we had believed? Or shall I say, "Was he *less dead* than we had thought?" Had he been able to extricate himself from the sack which Darzac had cast in the gulf of Castillon? After all, the thing was not impossible, or, rather, the possibility was not altogether without the bounds of what might be looked for from the superhuman cunning and prowess of a Larsan—particularly since Walter had explained that he had found the sack three meters from the mouth of the abyss upon a natural landing place the existence of which M. Darzac assuredly did not suspect when he believed that he was throwing Larsan's body into the orifice.

My second thoughts turned to Rouletabille. What was he doing now? Why had he gone away? Never had his presence at the Fort of Hercules been so necessary as now. If he delayed his return, this day could scarcely pass without bringing the unfriendly feeling between the Rances and the Darzacs to an open issue.

As I lay there puzzling my brain over the outcome of the affair, I heard someone knocking at my door. It was Pere Bernier, who brought me a brief note from my friend which had been handed to Pere Jacques by a little lad from the village. Rouletabille wrote: "I shall return early in the morning. Get up as soon as this reaches you and be good enough to go fishing for my breakfast and catch some of the fine trout which are so plentiful among the rocks near the Point of Garibaldi. Do not lose an instant. Thanks and remembrances.—ROULETABILLE."

This communication gave me more food for thought, for I knew by experience that whenever Rouletabille seemed most occupied with trivial matters, his activity was really most thoroughly engaged with important subjects.

I dressed myself in haste, provided myself with some old tackle which was furnished me by Bernier, and set out to obey the request of my young friend. As I went out of the North gate, having encountered nobody at that early hour of the morning (it was about seven o'clock), I was joined by Mme. Edith, to whom I showed what Rouletabille had written. The young woman was greatly dejected over the unexplained absence of her uncle, remarked that the letter was "so queer that it made her nervous," and she informed me that she intended to follow me to the trout streams. On the way, she confided to me the fact that her uncle had not an enemy in the world, so far as she knew, and she said that she had been hoping against hope that he would yet return and that everything would be satisfactorily explained, but now the idea had entered her brain that by some frightful mistake, Old Bob had fallen a victim to the vengeance of Darzac and she was nearly wild with apprehension.

And she added, between her pretty teeth, a few words of contempt and wrath for the Lady in Black. "My patience can hold out until noon, I hope!" she said, and then was silent.

We started to fish for Rouletabille's trout. Mrs. Rance and I both removed our shoes and stockings, but I concerned myself more about the dainty bare feet of my pretty hostess than about my own. The fact is, that Edith's feet, as I discovered in the Bay of Hercules, were as beautifully shaped and pink as flowers and they made me forget the trout of my poor Rouletabille to such an extent that he must certainly have gone without his breakfast if Edith had not shown more energy than I. She clambered into the pools and crept among the rocks with a grace which enchanted me more than I dared express. Suddenly we both desisted from our task and pricked up our ears at the same moment. We heard cries from the shore where the grottoes are. Upon the very threshold of the Grotto of Romeo and Juliet we distinguished a little group, the persons in which were making gestures of appeal. Urged on by the same presentiment, we hastily rushed to the beach and in a few seconds we learned that, attracted by moans, two fishermen had just discovered in a cave in the Grotto of Romeo and Juliet an unfortunate human being who had fallen into the chasm and who must have been there helpless for several hours.

The quick conjecture which rushed into both our minds at once proved to be the right one. It was Old Bob who had been fished out of the cave. When he had been drawn up on the beach in the full light of day, he certainly presented a pitiable spectacle. His beautiful black coat was torn and covered with mud and his white shirt was as black as tar. Mme. Edith burst into tears and nearly went into hysterics when she found that the old man had a torn collarbone and a sprained foot, and was so pale that he looked as if he were about to die.

Happily, the old man's injuries were far less serious than it at first had seemed. He was, according to his own account, on his bed in his room in the Square Tower. Would anyone believe that he absolutely refused to become undressed, even so far as to have his coat on before the arrival of the doctors? And Mrs. Rance, increasingly nervous, installed herself next to his bedside until the physicians came, and Old Bob instructed her not only to leave his room but to go outside of the Square Tower altogether. And he insisted that the door should be locked after her.

The precaution was a great surprise to us all. We stood assembled in the Court of the Bold, M. and Mme. Darzac, M. Arthur Rance and myself, as well as Bernier who haunted my footsteps, waiting the news. When Mme. Edith quitted the tower after the dismissal of the medical men, she came to us and said:

"Let us hope that his injuries won't be serious. Old Bob is solid as a rock. What did I tell you about him? I made him confess, the old sinner! He was trying to steal Prince Galitch's skull which he believe to be more ancient than his own. Just the jealousy of one savant toward another. We shall all laugh at him when he is cured!"

At that moment the door of the Square Tower opened and Walter, Old Bob's faithful servant, appeared. His face was pale and he seemed very nervous.

"Oh, Miss Edith!" he cried out. "He is covered with blood! He doesn't want anything to be said about it, but he must be saved—"

Edith had already rushed into the Square Tower. As to us we dared not utter a word. Soon the young woman returned.

"Oh!" she sobbed. "It is frightful. His whole breast is torn open!" I started to offer her the support of my arm, for, strangely enough M. Arthur Rance had withdrawn to some distance and was walking upon the boulevard, whistling and with his hands behind his back. I tried to comfort and to soothe Mme. Edith, but neither M. nor Mme. Darzac uttered a word.

Rouletabille reached the castle about an hour after these events. I watched for his return from the highest part of the western boulevard and as soon as I saw his form appearing in the distance I hurried to meet him. He cut short my demands for an explanation and asked me immediately if I had made a good catch, but I was not at all deceived by the expression of his countenance, and wishing to reply to him in his own style of banter, I replied:

"Oh, yes: a very good catch. I fished up Old Bob."

He started violently. I shrugged my shoulders, for I believed that he was counterfeiting surprise, and I went on :

"Oh, go on! You knew very well what kind of fish I should find when you sent your message!"

He fixed an astonished glance on me.

"You certainly must be unaware of the purport of your words, my dear Sainclair, or else you would have spared me the trouble of protesting against such an accusation."

"What accusation?" I cried.

"That of having left Old Bob in the Grotto of Romeo and Juliet, knowing that he might be dying there."

"Oh, nonsense!" I cried. "Old Bob is far from dying. He has a sprained foot and a broken collar bone, and his story of his misfortune is perfectly plain and straightforward. He declares that he was trying to steal Prince Galitch's skull."

"What a funny idea!" exclaimed Rouletabille, bursting out laughing. He leaned toward me and looked full into my eyes.

"Do you believe that story? And—and that is all? No other injuries?"

"Yes," I replied. "There is another injury, but the doctors declare that it is not at all serious. He has a wound in the breast."

"A wound in the breast!" repeated Rouletabille, touching my hand, nervously. "And how was this wound made?"

"We do not know. None of us have seen it. Old Bob is strangely modest. He would not even permit his coat to be taken off in our presence; and the coat hid the wound so well that we should never have suspected it was there if Walter had not come to tell us, frightened at the sight of the blood."

As soon as we came to the château, we encountered Mme. Edith, who appeared to have been watching for us.

"My uncle won't have me near him," she said, regarding Rouletabille with an air of anxiety different from anything I had ever noticed in her before. "It's in comprehensible!"

"Ah, Madame," replied the reporter, making a low bow to his hostess. "I assure you that nothing in the world is incomprehensible, when one is willing to take a little trouble to understand it." And he offered her his congratulations upon having had her uncle restored to her at the moment when she was ready to despair of ever seeing him again.

Mme. Edith seemed about to inquire into the purport of the enigmatical words at the beginning of my friend's remarks when we were joined by Prince Galitch. He had come to ask for news of his old friend, Bob, of whose misfortune he had learned. Mme. Edith reassured him as to her uncle's condition and entreated the Prince to pardon her relative for his too excessive devotion to the "oldest skulls in the history of humanity." The Prince smiled graciously and with the utmost kindliness when he was told that Old Bob had been attempting to steal his skull.

"You will find your skull," Mrs. Rance told him, "in the bottom of the cave in the grotto where it rolled down with him. Your collection will be unimpaired, Prince."

The Prince asked for the details. He seemed very curious about the affair. And Mme. Edith told how her uncle had acknowledged to her that he had quitted the Fort of Hercules by way of the air shaft which communicated with the sea. As soon as she said this, I recalled the experience of Rouletabille with the flask of water and also the close iron bars, and the falsehoods which Old Bob had uttered assumed gigantic proportions in my mind, and I was sure that the rest of the party must hold the same opinion as myself. Mme. Edith told us that Tullio had been waiting with his boat at the opening of the gallery abutting on the shaft, to row the old savant to the bank in front of the Grotto of Romeo and Juliet.

"Why so many twists and turnings when it was so simple to go out by the gate?" I could not restrain myself from exclaiming.

Mme. Edith looked at me reproachfully and I regretted having even seemed to have taken part against her in any way.

"And this is stranger yet!" said the Prince. "Day before yesterday, the 'hangman of the sea' came to bid me adieu, saying that he was going to leave the country, and I am sure that he took the train for Venice, his native city, at five o'clock in the afternoon. How then could he have conveyed your uncle in his boat late that night? In the first place, he was not in this part of the world; in the second, he had sold his boat. He told me so, adding that he would never return to this country."

There was a dead silence and Prince Galitch continued:

"All this is of little importance—provided that your uncle, Madame, recovers speedily from his injuries and, again," he added with another smile, more charming than those which had preceded it—"if you will aid me in regaining a poor piece of flint which has disappeared from the grotto and of which I will give you the description. It is a sharp piece of flint, twenty-five centimeters long and shaped at one end to the form of a dagger—in brief, the oldest dagger of the human race. I value it greatly and, perhaps you may be able to learn, Madame, through your uncle, Bob, what has become of it."

Mme. Edith at once gave her promise to the Prince, with a certain air of haughtiness which pleased me greatly, that she would do everything possible to obtain for him news of so precious an object. The Prince bowed low and left us. When we had finished returning his parting salutes, we saw M. Arthur Rance before us. He must have heard the conversation for he seemed very thoughtful. He had his ivory-headed cane in his hand, and was whistling, according to his habit. And he looked at Mme. Edith with an expression so strange that she appeared somewhat exasperated.

"I know exactly what you are thinking, sir!" she said. "It does not astonish me in the least. And you may keep on thinking so, if it amuses you, for aught I care.

"And she stepped nearer Rouletabille, smiling nervously.

"At all events," she exclaimed. "You can never explain to me how, when *he* was outside the Square Tower, *he* could have hidden behind that panel."

"Madame," said Rouletabille, slowly and impressively, looking at the young woman as though he were trying to hypnotize her, "have patience and have courage. If God is with me, before night I shall explain to you all that you wish to know."

XVIII

How Death Stalked Abroad at Noon Day

A little later, I found myself in the lower parlour of "la Louve," tete-a-tete with Mme. Edith. I attempted to reassure her, seeing how restless and nervous she was; but she buried her pale face in her hands and her trembling lips allowed the confession of her fears to escape them.

"I am frightened" she murmured. I asked her what frightened her and she looked at me wildly and said, "And aren't you afraid, too?" I kept silence, for I was afraid, myself. She said again. "You know something of what is going on—here or there or all around us! Ah, I am all alone! all alone! And I am so frightened."

She turned toward the door.

"Where are you going?" I asked.

"I am going to look for someone. I won't stay here alone."

"For whom are you going to look?"

"For Prince Galitch."

"Your 'Feodor Feodorowitch,'" I cried. "What do you want with him? Am I not here?"

Her nervousness, unfortunately, seemed to increase in proportion to my efforts to drive it away and I began to realize that a fearful doubt as to the personality of her uncle, Old Bob, had entered her mind.

"Let us go out into the air!" she said, impatiently. "I can't breathe in this place." We left "la Louve" and entered the garden. It was approaching the hour of noontide and the court was a dream of perfumed beauty. As we had not donned our smoked spectacles, we were obliged to put our hands before our eyes in order to shield them from the glaring rays of the sun and the too glowing hues of the flowers. The giant geraniums struck on our eyeballs like bleeding wounds. When we had grown a little more used to the dazzling sight, we advanced over the shining sands, Edith clinging to my hand like a little child. Her hand burned hotter than the sun and seemed like a veritable flame. We looked down at our feet in order to prevent our eyes from falling on the blinding expanse of the waters and also, it may be, in order not to glance toward the buildings in which so many strange things had taken place—perhaps, were taking place even now.

"I am afraid!" murmured Edith once more. And I, too, was afraid—overwhelmed after the mysteries of the night by the vast, desolate silence of the noon.

The broad glare of daylight in which one knows that something strange and terrible is going on is more awful than the deepest and darkest night. Everything sleeps and yet everything wakes. Everything is dead and everything is living. Everything is wrapped in silence and still there are sounds everywhere. Listen to your own ear. It sounds as loud as a conch shell filled with the most mysterious sounds of the sea. Close your lids and look into your own eyes; you will find there a throng of crowding visions more mysterious than the phantoms of the night.

I looked at Mme. Edith. Beads of perspiration stood out on her forehead and her face was pale as death. I was trembling and chilled, for, alas! I could do nothing to help her and destiny was weaving its inexorable web all around us and that nothing which we could say or do would hinder in the slightest degree its slow, undeviating march. Edith led the way toward the postern gate which opens upon the Court of the Bold. The vault of this postern formed a black arch in the light and at the extremity of this tunnel, we perceived, facing us, Rouletabille and M. Darzac, who were standing at the edge of the inner court, like two white statues. Rouletabille was holding in his hand Arthur Rance's ivory-headed cane. Why this latter fact should have disturbed me, I do not know, but so it was. Motioning with the cane, he showed Robert Darzac something on the summit of the vault which we could not see and then he pointed us out in the same way. We could not hear what he said. The two talked together for a few moments with their lips scarcely moving, like two accomplices in some dark secret. Mme. Edith paused, but Rouletabille beckoned to her, repeating the signal with his cane.

"Oh, what does he want with me now?" she cried like a frightened child. "Oh, M. Sainclair, I am so miserable. I am going to tell my uncle everything and we shall see what will happen them."

We went on until we reached the vault and the others watched us without making a movement to meet us. They stood like two statues, and I said aloud in a voice which sounded strangely in my own ears:

"What are you two doing here?"

We had come up close to them by this time, upon the threshold of the Court of the Bold, and they bade us turn around with our backs toward the court so that we could see what they were looking at. There was on top of the arch, an escutcheon, the shield of the Mortola, barred with the mark of the cadet branch. This escutcheon had been carved in a stone now loose, which seemed in imminent danger of falling and crushing the heads of the passersby. Rouletabille had without doubt noticed this danger, and he asked Mme. Edith if she had any objections to its being pulled down until it could be replaced more solidly.

"I am sure that it will fall before long and it might do serious damage," he said, touching it with the end of his cane, and then passing the stick to Mme. Edith.

"You are taller than I," he went on. "See if you can reach it."

But both she and I tried in vain to touch the stone; it was too high for us and I was about to inquire what was the meaning of this singular exercise when all at once, behind my back, *I heard the cry of a dying man in his last agony*.

We turned with one impulse, uttering an exclamation of horror. Ah, that cry of mortal agony which rang out on the air of the noonday just as it had through the night! Would we never be free from murder? When would that fearful sound which I had heard for the first time that night at the Glandier, never be done with announcing to us that a new victim had been struck down among us? that one of our own number had fallen beneath some fatal blow, as suddenly as though by some frightful pestilence? Surely, the mark of the epidemic itself is less invisible and terrible than that of the hand which kills.

We all stood there, shivering, our eyes wide with horror, questioning the deeps of the sky still vibrating from that cry of death. Who was dead? Who was dying? What expiring breath had emitted that terrible sound? One might have thought that it was the clearness of the day itself which cried out in suffering.

Rouletabille was the most terrified of us all. I have seen him, under the most untoward circumstances, maintain a composure which seemed greater than any human creature could hold; I have seen him, at a like horrible cry of death, rush into the danger of the darkness and cast himself like a heroic rescuer into the sea of shadows. Why should he tremble so today in the full splendour of the noon? He remained fixed to the spot, as weak as a baby, he, who a little while ago, declared that he would prove himself the master of the hour. He had not foreseen this moment then? this moment in which a human life had been snatched away under the noonday sun!

Mattoni, who was passing through the garden, and who had also heard the cry, rushed up. At a gesture from Rouletabille he stood rooted to the spot an immovable sentinel; and now the young man had gained sufficient power to advance toward the cry—or, at least, toward the centre of the cry, for it seemed still to echo everywhere around us and to circle about in the all embracing space. And we hurried behind him, our breath coming fast, our arms stretched out, as one holds them when one is groping in the dark and fears to stumble against something which one does not see.

We approached the place from which the shriek had come and when we had passed the shade of the eucalyptus we found the cause. The cry had come, indeed, from a soul passing into the unknown. It was Bernier—Bernier in whose throat sounded the death rattle, who was trying in vain to rise and who was at the last gasp of his life. It was Bernier from whose breast flowed a stream of blood—Bernier over whom we leaned, and who, with one last, fearful struggle, summoned strength enough to utter the two words: "Frederic Larsan!"

Then his head fell back and he was dead. Frederic Larsan! Frederic Larsan! He who was everywhere and nowhere! He always and forever. Here, yet again, was his mark. A dead body—and no one anywhere near who could have committed the murder, by any possibility of human reason. For the only means of egress from the spot on which the crime had occurred was by this postern where we four had been standing. And we had turned, with one impulse and one movement, at the very instant that the cry rang out—so quickly that we had almost seen the stroke of death given. And when we looked, there had not even been a shadow before our eyes—nothing but the light! We rushed, moved by the same sentiment, it seemed to me, into the Square Tower, the door of which still stood open; we entered in a body the bedroom of Old Bob, passing through the empty sitting room. The injured man was lying quietly on his bed within, and near him a woman was watching—Mere Bernier. Both were as calm and still as the day itself. But when the wife of the dead concierge saw our faces she uttered a cry of affright, as though smitten by the knowledge of some calamity. She had heard nothing. She knew nothing. But she rushed into the air like a streak of lightning and went straight, as though impelled by some hidden force, directly to the place where the body was lying.

And now it was her groans that sounded on the air, under the terrible sun of the Midi, over the bleeding corpse. We tore the shirt from the dead man's breast and found a gaping wound just above the heart. Rouletabille looked up with the same expression which I had seen at the Glandier when he came to examine the wound of the "inexplicable body."

"One would say that it was the same stroke of the knife!" he said. "It is the same measurement. But where is the knife?"

We looked for the weapon everywhere without finding it. The man who had struck the blow had carried the knife away. Where was the man? Who was he? What we did not know, Bernier had known before he died and it was, perhaps, because of that knowledge that his life had been forfeited. "Frederic Larsan!" We repeated the last words of the dying man in fear and trembling.

Suddenly on the threshold of the postern, we saw the Prince Galitch, a newspaper in his hand. He was reading as he came toward us. His air was jovial and his face wore a smile. But Mme. Edith rushed up to him, snatched the paper from his hands, pointed to the corpse and cried out:

"A man has been murdered! Send for the police!"

The Prince stared at the body and then at us without uttering a word and then turned hastily away, saying that he would send for the authorities immediately, Mere Bernier kept up her wild lamentations. Rouletabille seated himself on the edge of the shaft. He seemed to have lost all his strength. He spoke to Mme. Edith in a low tone:

"Let the police come then, Madame, but remember, it is you who have insisted upon it!"

Mrs. Rance gave him a withering glance from her black eyes. And I knew what her thoughts were as well as though she had spoken them out. She felt that she hated Rouletabille, who had for a single moment been able to make her suspect Old Bob. While Bernier had been assassinated, had not Old Bob been quietly in his chamber, watched over by Mere Bernier herself?

Rouletabille was examining the iron bars and heavy lid which closed the shaft, but his manner was distrait and discouraged. After he had finished what seemed to be a very careless inspection he stretched himself out on the ground as if it were a couch in which he was trying to get some rest. Turning once more to his hostess, he said in the same low voice:

"And what will you tell the police when they get here?"

"Everything!"

Mrs. Rance fairly snapped out the word between her teeth, her eyes flashing fire. Rouletabille shook his head sorrowfully and closed his eyes. He seemed utterly exhausted and vanquished. Robert Darzac touched him on his shoulder. M. Darzac wanted to search through the Square Tower, the Tower of the Bold, the New Castle—all the dependencies of the fort from which no one could have made his escape, and where, therefore, the assassin must still be concealed. The reporter shook his head drearily, and said that it would be of no use. Rouletabille and I knew only too well that any search would be in vain. Had we not made a search at the Glandier after the phenomenon of the dissolution of matter, for the man who had disappeared in the inexplicable gallery? No, no! I had learned that there was no use in looking for Larsan with one's eyes.

A man had been murdered just behind our backs. We had heard him cry out when the blow struck him down. We had turned around and had seen nothing except the daylight. To see clearly, it was better to close the eyes as Rouletabille was doing at this moment.

And when he opened them, he was another man! A new energy animated his features. He stood erect as though he had thrown off a weight. He clenched his fist and raised it toward the heavens.

"That is not possible!" he cried. "Or there is no more good in reasoning."

And he threw himself on the ground, creeping on his hands and knees, his nose to the earth, like a hound following the scent, going round the body of poor Bernier and around Mere Bernier, who had blankly refused to leave her husband—around the shaft—around each of us. He moved about like a pig, nosing its nourishment out of the mire, and we all stood still, looking at him curiously and half in alarm. Suddenly he started to his feet, almost white with dust and uttered a shout of triumph as though he had found Larsan himself in the gravel. What new victory did the boy feel that he had achieved over the mystery? What had given this new firmness to his step and steadiness to his glance? What had given back to him the strength of his voice? For when he addressed M. Robert Darzac his tones were full of vigour and resolution.

"It's all right, Monsieur! *Nothing is changed!*"

And, turning to Mme. Edith—

"There is nothing more to do, Madame, except to wait for the police. I hope that they will not be long."

The unhappy woman shuddered. I knew that she was again struck with mortal fear.

"Yes, let them come!" she cried, taking my arm. "And let them attend to everything! Let them think for us! Whatever may happen, let it come as soon as it will."

Attracted by the sound of voices we looked around and saw Pere Jacques approaching, followed by two gendarmes. It was the brigadier of la Mortola, who, summoned by Prince Galitch, had hurried to the scene of the crime.

"The gendarmes! the gendarmes! They say that murder has been done!" exclaimed Pere Jacques, who as yet knew nothing of what had happened.

"Be calm, Pere Jacques!" exhorted Rouletabille, and when the old man, panting and breathless, drew near to the reporter, the latter said to him in low tones:

"*Nothing is changed*, Pere Jacques!"

But Pere Jacques was gazing at Bernier's body.

"Only one more dead man!" he sighed. "This is Larsan's work again!"

"It is the work of destiny!" answered Rouletabille. Larsan and destiny—both were as one. But what did Rouletabille mean by his "Nothing is changed," if not that, despite the incidental murder of Bernier, everything which we dreaded, which made us shudder and which we had no understanding of, continued just as before?

The gendarmes were busy examining the body and chattering over it in their uncomprehensible jargon. The brigadier informed us that they had telephoned to the Garibaldi Tavern, a few steps away, where at this moment the delegato, or special commissioner, stationed at Vintimille, was even now breakfasting. The delegato would have power to begin the investigation, which would be continued when the examining magistrate had been notified.

The delegato arrived. It was easily to be seen that he was enchanted, even though he had not had the time to finish his repast. A crime! actually a crime! And in the Château of Hercules. He was fairly radiant; his eyes shone. He was full of business, full of importance. He ordered the brigadier to station one of his men at the gate of the château with directions to permit no person to pass in or out. Then he knelt down beside the body while a gendarme, despite her protestations and tears, led Mere Bernier away to the Square Tower, where her groans sounded louder than ever. The delegato examined the wound and said in very good French:

"That was a magnificent stroke!"

The man was enchanted. If he had had the assassin under arrest, he would assuredly have paid him his compliments. He looked at us. Then he looked at us again. Perhaps he was seeking among us for the criminal to tell him of his admiration. At last he rose from his knees.

"And now how did all this happen?" he asked encouragingly, smacking his lips as though in the anticipation of hearing a story of thrilling interest. "It is terrible!" he added—"terrible! In the five years that I have been delegato, we have never had a murder, Monsieur the examining magistrate—." Here he checked himself but we knew well what he had been on the point of saying: "Monsieur the examining magistrate will be very much pleased." He brushed away the white dust which covered his knees, wiped the perspiration from his forehead and repeated "It is terrible!" his Southern accent seeming to grow stronger. And at that moment, he noticed in a new arrival who entered the court, a doctor from Mentone who had come to continue his treatment of Old Bob.

"Ah, doctor, I am glad that you are here! Just look at this wound and tell me what you think of such a knife stroke. But be as careful as possible about changing the position of the corpse before the arrival of the examining magistrate."

The doctor sounded the depth of the wound and gave us all the technical details which we could desire. There was no doubt about it at all. It was a truly magnificent stroke of the knife which had penetrated from high to low in the cardiac region and the point of the knife had certainly opened a ventricle. During the colloquy between the delegato and the doctor, Rouletabille never took his eyes off Mme. Edith, who was still clinging to my arm as though she knew that I was her only refuge. Her eyes fell before the eyes of Rouletabille which seemed to hypnotize her and to command her to be silent. But I knew that she was trembling with the desire to speak.

At the request of the delegato, we all entered the Square Tower. We took our places in Old Bob's sitting room, where the inquest was to be held and where each of us in turn recounted what we had seen and heard. Mere Bernier was first questioned, but little or nothing could be gained from her testimony. She declared that she knew nothing about anything. She had been in Old Bob's bedroom, attending to the needs of the injured man, when we had rushed madly into the room. She had been with Old Bob for an hour, having left her husband in the lodge of the Square Tower, ready to work at making a rope.

It was a curious fact, but I was less interested at that moment in what was going on under my eyes than in what I could not see and yet knew *that I expected*.

Would Edith speak? She was looking out of the open window, her lips compressed, her brows drawn. A gendarme was standing near the corpse over the face of which a handkerchief had been laid. Edith, like myself, was paying very little heed to what was going on inside the room. Her eyes were fixed upon Bernier's body.

An exclamation from the delegato struck upon our cars. The further the evidence of the witnesses progressed, the greater became the amazement of the Commissioner, and the more and more inexplicable he found the crime. He was on the point of finding it impossible that it should have been committed at all, when it came Mme. Edith's turn to be interrogated.

They questioned her. Her lips were already opened to answer the first question when Rouletabille's quiet voice was heard:

"Look at the end of the shadow of the eucalyptus." "What is there at the end of the shadow of the eucalyptus?" demanded the delegato. "The weapon with which the crime was committed," replied the reporter.

He jumped out of the window to the court and picked up from the bloody stones a sharp, shining piece of flint. He brandished it in our eyes. We all recognised it. It was "the oldest dagger of the human race."

XIX

In Which Rouletabille Orders the Iron Doors to Be Closed

The weapon belonged to Prince Galitch, but there was no doubt in the mind of any one of us that it had been stolen by Old Bob, and we could not forget that with his latest breath Bernier had accused Larsan of being his assassin. Never had the image of Old Bob and that of Larsan been so inextricably confounded in our restless spirits as since Rouletabille had found "the oldest dagger known to the human race" dripping with the blood of Bernier. Mme. Edith had at once realised that henceforth the fate of Old Bob lay in the hands of Rouletabille. The latter had only to say a few words to the delegato relative to the singular incidents which had accompanied the fall of Old Bob into the cave in the "Grotto of Romeo and Juliet, enumerating the reasons which had given occasion for fear that Old Bob and Larsan were one and the same, and, finally, repeating the accusation made by the last victim of Larsan, in order to fix the suspicions of the delegato firmly upon the wigged head of the professor of geology. And, therefore, Mme. Edith, who in her filial affection had not ceased to believe that the man who lay on his bed in the Square Tower was really her uncle, had begun to imagine, thanks to the bloody weapon, that the invisible Larsan had woven so strong a web of circumstantial evidence around old Bob that it could scarcely be broken, with the design, doubtless, of making the old man suffer the punishment for the wretch's own crimes and also the dangerous weight of his personality. Mme. Edith trembled for Old Bob and for herself. She trembled with fear, like an insect in the centre of the web in which it has lost itself—this mysterious web woven by Larsan, attached by invisible threads to the old walls of the Château of Hercules. She felt as though if she were to make a sudden movement—to say anything even—both she and her uncle would be lost, and that some horrible beast of prey awaited only this signal to spring upon and devour her. So she who had been so anxious to speak out stood silent and when Rouletabille was called upon, it was her turn to fear. She told me afterward of her state of mind at this time and she acknowledged to me that her terror of Larsan had reached such a pitch as even we, who had known so much of his evil power already, had never experienced. This were wolf whose name she had so often heard spoken in accents of horror which had made her smile, had begun to interest her, when she learned of the events of the Yellow Room, because of the impossibility of the police discovering the manner of his exit. Her interest had increased when she had heard the story of the attack of the Square Tower because of the impossibility of anyone's explaining how Larsan could have entered; but, now—now, in the full glare of the noonday sun, Larsan had killed a man almost under her own eyes, and within a radius in which there was at the time only herself, Robert Darzac, Rouletabille, myself, Old Bob and Mere Bernier, each and every one of them far enough away from the body so that not one could have struck Bernier down. And Bernier had accused Larsan! Where was Larsan? *In whose body?*—according to the reasoning which I had set forth to her myself in telling her the story of the "inexplicable gallery"? She had been under the arch with Darzac and myself, standing between us, with Rouletabille in front of us, when the death cry had resounded at the end of the shadow of the eucalyptus tree—that is to say, at least, seven meters away. As to Old Bob and Mere Bernier, they had not been separated; the one had watched over the other. If she placed them outside the realms of possibility, there was no one left to kill Bernier. Not alone this time was everyone ignorant how *he* had departed but also of *how he had been present*. Ah, she understood now that when one thought of Larsan there were moments in which one shivered to the marrow of one's bones! Nothing! Nothing anywhere around the corpse but the stone knife which Old Bob had stolen! It was frightful—it was reason enough for us to think of everything—to imagine everything!

She read the certainty of this conviction in the eyes and in the manner of Rouletabille and of Robert Darzac. But she understood as soon as the young man began speaking that he seemed to have no other end in view than to save Old Bob from the suspicions of the authorities.

Rouletabille was given a seat between the delegato and the examining magistrate who had arrived while Mme. Edith had been testifying, and he gave his evidence (or rather, reasoned the matter out) holding the "oldest knife known to the human race" in his hand. It seemed definitely established that the guilty person could have been no other than one of the living men and women who were near the dead man and whom I have enumerated above, when Rouletabille proved with a logical accuracy that overwhelmed the examining magistrate and plunged the delegato into despair that the deed could only have been committed by the dead man himself. The four persons at the postern gate and the two persons in Old Bob's room had each been looking at the others and had not lost sight of each other while *someone* was killing Bernier a few steps away, so it was impossible to believe that the killing could have been done by any other than the victim.

To this the examining magistrate, greatly interested, replied by inquiring whether any of us had reason to suspect any motive for suicide on the part of Bernier, to which Rouletabille answered that the supposition of suicide might easily be laid aside and that of accident substituted for it. "The weapon of the crime," as he called ironically the "oldest knife known to the human race," testified to the truth of this theory by its presence. Rouletabille declared that there would be no chance of an assassin meditating the commission of a murder with an old piece of stone as an instrument. And still less could one believe that Bernier, if he had resolved upon suicide, would not have found another means toward his end than the one which had been used. But if, on the contrary, that stone, which might have attracted his attention by its strange form, had been picked up by Pere Bernier, and if he had happened to slip and fall while holding it in his hand, everything would be explained and very simply. Pere Bernier, undoubtedly, must have thus unfortunately fallen upon this triangular flint which had pierced his heart.

After Rouletabille had stated this hypothesis, the physician was recalled, the wound examined once more and confronted with the fatal object from which the scientific conclusion was reached that the wound was made by the object. From this to the theory of accident, as stated by Rouletabille, there was only a step. The judges spent six hours in clearing up the matter—six hours during which they questioned us without weariness but without result.

As to Mme. Edith and your humble servant, after some futile and useless questions, asked while the doctors were at the bedside of Old Bob, we were allowed to leave the room and we went to sit in the little parlour just outside the bedroom and were there when the magistrates were ready to depart. The door of this parlour which opened upon the corridor of the Square Tower had not been closed. We could hear the sobs and groans of Mere Bernier, who was watching beside the body of her husband which had been carried into the lodge. Between this body and the wounded man, the injury to one as inexplicable as the death of the other, the situation of both Mrs. Rance and myself had become extremely painful, in spite of Rouletabille's efforts, and all the terrors which we had experienced before grew pale and simple before the thought of what might be yet to come. Edith suddenly seised me by the hand and cried out:

"Do not leave me! I beg of you, don't leave me! I have only you left. I do not know where Prince Galitch is—I do not know anything about my husband. That is what makes this so horrible. Arthur sent me a message, saying that he was going in search of Tullio. He does not know even yet that Bernier has been murdered. Has he found the 'hangman of the sea'? It is from this man—from Tullio now that I expect the truth! And not a word has come! It is horrible!"

As she took my hand so confidingly and held it for a moment in her own, I felt that I was for Mme. Edith with all my heart and soul and I assured her that she might rely upon my devotion. We murmured a few words of trust and eternal fidelity to each other in low voices while there in the corridor we could see, passing back and forth, the dark forms of the emissaries of justice, now preceded, now followed by Rouletabille and M. Darzac. Rouletabille never failed to cast a glance in our direction every time he had the opportunity. The window remained open.

"Ah, he is watching us!" exclaimed Mme. Edith.

"Why is that, I wonder? Probably we are in his way and M. Darzac's when we remain here. But, whatever may happen, we shall not stir, shall we, M. Sainclair?"

"You ought to be grateful to Rouletabille," I ventured to remind her; "for his intervention and his silence relative to the 'oldest knife known to the human race.' If the officers had learned that this stone dagger belonged to your uncle, Bob, what could have hindered them from placing him under arrest? Or if they knew that Bernier in dying had accused Larsan of his murder, the story of the accident would have found very little credence."

I placed an emphasis upon these last words.

"Oh!" she cried, bitterly. "Your friend has as many good reasons to keep silence as I have! And I dread only one thing, M. Sainclair—I dread only one thing!"

"And what is that?"

She arose, her eyes shining with fever.

"I fear lest he has saved my uncle from the authorities only to ruin him more completely."

"How can you think such a thing for a moment?" I asked her, convinced that her fears were robbing her of her senses.

"I am sure that I could read some such plan in the eyes of your friend a little while ago. If I were sure that I were right, I would rather hand my uncle over to the mercies of the authorities."

I managed to quiet her a little and to make her cast aside such an impossible supposition, and, at length, she said:

"At all events, it is necessary to be ready for anything, and I know how to defend him so long as I draw breath."

And she showed me a tiny revolver which was hidden in her gown.

"Ah!" she cried again. "Why is Prince Galitch not here?"

"Again?" I exclaimed, angrily.

"Is it actual truth that you are ready to defend me?" she demanded, turning her beautiful eyes full upon my own."

"I am ready."

"Against the whole world?"

I hesitated. She repeated the words again:

"Against the whole world?"

"Yes."

"Against your friend even?"

"If it should be necessary," I answered with a sigh, passing my hand across my forehead.

"Very well: I believe you!" she answered. "In that case. I will leave you here for a few minutes. You will guard this door for *me*!"

And she pointed to the door behind which Old Bob was resting. Then she ran out of the room. Where was she going? She confessed to me later. She was going to look for the Prince Galitch! Oh, woman, woman!

She had scarcely disappeared under the arch when Rouletabille and M. Darzac entered the room. They had heard all that had passed. Rouletabille advanced to my side and told me quietly that he was aware that I had betrayed him.

"You are using a large word, Rouletabille!" I exclaimed. "You know that I am not in the habit of betraying anyone! Mme. Edith is really very much to be pitied and you do not pity her enough, my friend."

"Ah, well! you pity her too much!"

I blushed to the roots of my hair. I started to make some reply but Rouletabille cut short my words with a dry gesture.

"I ask you only one thing—only one, you understand. It is that, no matter what may happen—*no matter what may happen*—you shall not address one word to either M. Darzac or to myself."

"That will be a very easy thing to promise!" I replied, foolishly irritated, and I turned my back upon him. It seemed to me that it was with difficulty that he refrained from uttering some angry speech.

But at the same moment, the officers, coming out of the New Castle, called to us. The inquest was at an end. There was no doubt, in their eyes, after the declaration of the doctors, that the affair had been an accident and that was the verdict which they felt obliged to render. M. Darzac and Rouletabille accompanied them to the outer gate. And as I stood leaning on my elbows, at the window which opens upon the Court of the Bold, assailed by a thousand sinister presentiments and awaiting with an increasing anxiety for the return of Mme. Edith, while a few steps away in the lodge, where the candles had been lighted around Bernier's bier, Mere Bernier kept on sobbing and praying beside the corpse of her husband, I suddenly heard a sound which fell upon the evening air like the blow of an immense gong; and I knew that it was Rouletabille who had ordered the iron gates to be closed.

Not a single minute passed after that when I saw Mme. Edith rush into the room and hurry to me as though I were her only refuge.

Then I saw M. Darzac appear—

Then Rouletabille, and leaning on his arm was the Lady in Black.

XX

In Which Rouletabille Gives a Corporeal Demonstration of the Possibility of "The Body of Too Many"

Through the window I could see Rouletabille and the Lady in Black entering the Square Tower. Never had the young reporter walked with such solemn stateliness. His demeanour might have made one smile, if instead, at this tragic moment, it had not added to our apprehensions. Never had magistrate or counsellor, wearing the purple or the ermine, entered the court room where the accused waited him with more of threatening yet tranquil majesty. But I fancy, too, that never had a judge looked so pale.

As to the Lady in Black, it could easily be seen that she was making a powerful effort to hide the sentiments of horror which, in spite of all, pierced through her troubled glance, and to hide from us the emotion which made her cling feverishly to the arm of her young companion. Robert Darzac, too, had the sombre and resolute mien of a judge. But that which most of all added to our surprise and affright was the entrance of Pere Jacques, Walter and Mattoni into the Square Tower. All three were armed with muskets, and placed themselves in silence before the door, where they stood with military precision while they received from the lips of Rouletabille the order to let no person *go out* from the Old château. Edith was overwhelmed with terror, and demanded of Mattoni and Walter, both of whom were greatly attached to her, what their presence signified and what their weapons threatened; but, to my great astonishment, they returned no answer. Then the little woman rushed to the door which gave access to Old Bob's room, and, extending her two arms across the threshold, as if to bar the passage, she cried:

"What are you going to do? You do not mean to kill *him*?"

"No, Madame," replied Rouletabille, gravely. "We are going to judge him. And in order to be sure that the judges shall not be executioners we are all going to swear upon the body of Pere Bernier, after having laid down our arms, that each of us will keep guard over himself."

And he led us into the chamber where Mere Bernier continued to groan beside the bier of her spouse whom "the oldest knife known to the human race" had smitten. There we laid aside our revolvers and took the oath which Rouletabille exacted. Mrs. Rance alone made some difficulties about giving up the weapon which Rouletabille was well aware that she had concealed in her clothing. But upon the urging of the reporter who made her understand that the general disarming ought to reassure her, she finally consented.

The oath having been taken, Rouletabille, with the Lady in Black still on his arm, went from the funereal chamber into the corridor; but instead of directing our steps toward the apartment of Old Bob as we expected him to do, he went straight to the door which afforded entrance to the chamber of "the body too many." And, drawing from his pocket the little special key of which I have spoken, he opened the door.

We were all astonished in entering the rooms which had been occupied by M. and Mme. Darzac to see upon M. Darzac's desk the drawing board, the wash drawing upon which our friend had worked at the side of Old Bob in the latter's workshop in the Court of the Bold, and also the little dish full of red paint and the tiny brush drenched with the paint. And, lastly, in the middle of the desk, there was placed, appearing very much at its ease, upon its bloody jaws, "the oldest skull of humanity."

Rouletabille locked and bolted the door and said to us, himself greatly affected, while we listened with stupe faction:

"Sit down, if you please, ladies and gentlemen."

Some chairs were arranged around the table and in these we seated ourselves, a prey to the most disquieting fancies—I might almost say to an agony of suspense. A secret presentiment warned us that all the familiar appurtenances of drawing which were displayed before us might hide, under their apparent common place tranquility, the terrible causes which helped to bring about this most fearful of dramas. And as we looked upon it, the skull seemed to smile like Old Bob.

"You will acknowledge," began Rouletabille, "that there is here, around this table one chair too many, and, in consequence, one person too few—to particularize, M. Arthur Rance, for whom we cannot wait much longer."

"Perhaps at this very moment my husband possesses the proofs of Old Bob's innocence!" observed Mme. Edith, whom all these preparations had disturbed more than anyone else. "I entreat Mme. Darzac to join me in imploring these gentlemen to do nothing until Arthur's return."

The Lady in Black had no opportunity to intervene, for before Mme. Edith finished speaking, we heard a loud noise outside the door of the corridor. A knock came at the door and we heard the voice of Arthur Rance begging us to open immediately.

He cried:

"*I have brought the pin with the ruby head!*"

Rouletabille opened the door.

"Arthur Rance, you are come then at last!" he exclaimed.

Edith's husband seemed plunged in the deepest melancholy.

"What have you to tell me? What has happened? Some new misfortune? Ah, I feared so—feared that I had arrived too late when I saw the iron gate closed and heard the prayers for the dead chanted in the tower. Yes—I knew that you had *executed* Old Bob!"

Rouletabille, who had closed and bolted the door behind Arthur Rance turned to the American and said:

"Old Bob is alive and Pere Bernier is dead. Be seated, Monsieur."

Arthur Rance stared at the speaker in amazement; then looked in consternation at the drawing board, the dish of paint and the bloody skull and demanded:

"Who killed him?"

Then, condescending to notice that his wife was there, he pressed her hand, but his eyes were fixed upon the Lady in Black.

"Before his death, Bernier accused Frederic Larsan," answered M. Darzac.

"Do you mean to say by that that he accused Old Bob?" interrupted M. Rance indignantly, "I will not suffer that. I, too, had some doubts in regard to the personality of our beloved uncle, but I tell you that I have the ruby-headed pin!"

What was he talking about with his "little ruby headed pin"? I remembered that Mme. Edith had told us that Old Bob had snatched one from her hand when she had playfully pricked him with it on the night of the drama of the Square Tower. But what relation could there be between this pin and the adventure of Old Bob Arthur Rance did not wait for us to ask him, but hurried on to tell us that this little pin had disappeared at the same time as Old Bob and that he had found it in the possession of "the Hangman of the Sea," fastening a sheaf of bank notes which the old uncle had paid him on that fated night for his complicity and his silence in having brought him in the fisher boat to the grotto of Romeo and Juliet. And M. Rance told us moreover that

Tullio had withdrawn from the spot at dawn, greatly disquieted at the non appearance of his passenger. Rance concluded, triumphantly:

"A man who gives a ruby pin to another man in a boat cannot be at the same moment tied up in a potato sack in the Square Tower."

Upon which Mrs. Rance inquired:

"What gave you the idea of going to San Remo: Did you know that Tullio was to be found there?"

"I received an anonymous letter informing me of his whereabouts."

"It was I who sent it to you," said Rouletabille, tranquilly. And, then, turning to the rest of us, he said in frigid tones:

"Ladies and gentlemen, I congratulate myself upon the prompt return of M. Arthur Rance. At the present moment there are reunited around this table all the members of the house party of the Château of Hercules for whom my corporeal demonstration of the possibility of the 'body too many' may have some interest. I entreat you to give me your undivided attention."

But Arthur Rance halted him with a quick movement.

"What do you mean by the expression: 'There are united around this table all the members of the party for whom the corporeal demonstration of the possibility of the body too many can have any interest'?"

"I mean," declared Rouletabille, "all those among whom we may hope to find Larsan."

The Lady in Black, who had up to this time not uttered a word, arose trembling to her feet.

"Do you mean," she breathed, her eyes filled with agonised apprehension, "that Larsan is now among us?"

"I am sure of it," Rouletabille replied, gravely.

There was an awful silence during which none of us dared look at each other.

The reporter continued, still in the same frigid tone:

"I am sure of it—and there is no reason why the idea should surprise you, Madame, since it has not for a moment left your own mind. As to the rest of us, is it not true, gentlemen, that the idea has occurred to each one of us at the same moment on the day when we took luncheon on the terrace of the Bold when all our eyes were hidden by the black glasses? If I except Mrs. Rance, who is there among us that did not feel the presence of Larsan at that time?"

"That is a question which ought to be propounded to Professor Stangerson as well as to the rest of us," interposed Arthur Rance, instantly. "For from the moment when we begin any course of reasoning along these lines, I can see no object in not having the Professor, who was at the table at luncheon with us on that day, here at this time also."

"Mr. Rance!" cried the Lady in Black.

"Yes, I must repeat it, if you will pardon me," replied Edith's husband, haughtily. "Monsieur Rouletabille was wrong to generalize when he said, 'All the members of the house party—'"

"Professor Stangerson is so far from us in spirit that I have no need of his presence here," pronounced Rouletabille in a tone so stern and solemn that it fell impressively on the ears of each and every one among us. "Although Professor Stangerson had lived with us in the Château of Hercules, he was not one of us in regard to feeling the presence of Larsan on that day. And Larsan is here among us."

This time we stole stealthy glances at each other as though we suspected each other of stealing, and the idea that Larsan might really be among us appeared to me so mad that I exclaimed, forgetting that I had promised not to address Rouletabille:

"But at that luncheon on the terrace, there was still another person whom I do not see here."

Rouletabille cast an angry look at me as he answered: "Still Prince Galitch! I have already told you, Sainclair, with what task the Prince is occupying himself on this frontier and I swear to you that it is not the trouble of Professor Stangerson's daughter which concerns him. Leave Prince Galitch to his humanitarian labours!"

"All that is not reasonable," I remarked almost mechanically.

"To tell the truth, Sainclair, your nonsense prevents me from reasoning."

But I had launched out, and, forgetting that I had promised Mme. Edith to defend Old Bob, started in to attack him for the pleasure of proving Rouletabille in the wrong—and, besides, I felt, Edith would not bear to rancor against me for very long.

"Old Bob," I began, in the clearest and most assured tones I could command, "was also at the luncheon on the terrace and you take him entirely out of your calculations on account of this little ruby pin. But of what use is this little pin to prove to us that Old Bob was rowed away by Tullio, who waited for him at the orifice of a gallery leading from the shaft to the sea, if we cannot discover how Old Bob could, as he said, have gone by way of the shaft which we found closed from above and on the outside?"

"Which *you* found closed, you mean," returned Rouletabille, fixing his eyes upon me with a strange expression which somehow embarrassed me. "I, on the contrary, found the shaft open. I had sent you after Mattoni and Pere Jacques. When you came back, you found me in the same place in the Court of the Bold, but I had time to run to the shaft and find out that it had been opened."

"And to lose it again!" I cried. "And why did you close it? Whom did you wish to deceive?"

"*You, monsieur!*"

He pronounced these two words with a contempt so crushing that the blood rushed to my face. I arose. Every eye was turned upon me and as I remembered the rudeness with which Rouletabille had treated me a little while before M. Darzac, I had trouble feeling that every eye was suspecting me—accusing me! *Yes! I felt myself entirely wrapped around by the atrocious fancy in the mind of each and all that I might be Larsan*!

I! Larsan!

I looked at each one in turn. Rouletabille did not lower his eyes while my own were seeking to make him feel the fierce protestation of my whole being and my indignation against such a monstrous supposition. Anger ran through my veins like a flame. "Now, it is high time to end this farce!" I cried. "If Old Bob is removed from consideration and Professor Stangerson and Prince Galitch, there remain only ourselves— we who are locked up in this room—and if Larsan is among us, show us to him, Rouletabille!"

I repeated the words furiously, for the eyes of the boy, although they were piercing through me, seemed to be fixed upon something outside of and apart from me.

"Show him to us! Name him! You are as slow here as you were at the Court of Assizes."

"Had I not good reason at the Court of Assizes for being as slow as I was?" he replied, without betraying any emotion.

"You want him to escape this time, too, then?"

"No! I swear to *you* that this time he shall *not* escape."

Why did his voice continue to be so threatening when he addressed me? Could it be really—*really* that he suspected me of being Larsan? My eyes wandered to those of the Lady in Black. She was gazing on me in terror.

"Rouletabille!" I cried madly, feeling my voice almost smothered in my throat. "You do not—you cannot suspect!"

At this moment, a pistol shot sounded outside, very near to the Square Tower. We all leaped to our feet, remembering the order given by the reporter to the three servants to fire upon anyone who should attempt to go out of the Square Tower. Edith uttered a cry and tried to run out of the room, but Rouletabille, who had not made so much as a gesture, calmed her with a word.

"If anyone had drawn upon *him*," he said, "the three men would have fired together. That pistol shot was merely a signal—a direction for me to begin."

Turning to me, he continued:

"M. Sainclair, you ought to know that I never suspect any person or anything without previously having satisfied myself upon the 'ground of pure reason.' That is a solid staff which has never yet failed me on the road and on which I invite you all to lean with me. Larsan is here among us, and the power of pure reason is going to show him to you; so be seated again, if you please, and do not take your eyes from me, for I am going to begin on this paper the corporeal demonstration of the possibility of 'the body too many'!"

First of all, he investigated to make sure that the bolts of the door behind him were closely drawn; then, returning to the table, he took up a compass.

"I have the intention of making my demonstration," he said, "along the same lines on which the "body too many has produced itself. It will be, thereby, only the more irrefutable."

And, with his compass, he took, upon M. Darzac's drawing, the measure of the radius of the circle which represented the space occupied by the Tower of the Bold, so that he was immediately afterward able to trace the same circle upon an immaculate piece of white paper which he had fastened with copper-headed nails to another drawing board.

When the circle was traced, Rouletabille, putting down his compass, picked up the tiny dish of red paint and asked M. Darzac whether he recognised it as the colouring matter he had used. M. Darzac, who, from all appearances, understood the significance of the young man's words and actions no better than the rest of us, replied that, to the best of his belief, it was the same paint which he had mixed for his wash drawing.

A good half of the paint had dried up in the bottom of the dish, but, according to the opinion expressed by M. Darzac, the part which remained would, upon paper, give nearly the same tint with which he had "washed" the drawing of the peninsula of Hercules.

"No one has touched it," said Rouletabille very gravely, "and nothing has been added to it, save a single tear. Besides, you will see that a tear more or less in the paint cup would detract nothing from the value of my demonstration."

Thus saying, he dipped the brush in the paint and began carefully to "wash" all the space occupied by the circle which he had previously traced. He did this with the care and exactitude which had already astonished me in the Tower of the Bold when I had been nearly stupefied in seeing him absorbed in a drawing when we knew that someone had been assassinated.

When he had finished he looked at his immense silver watch and said:

"You may see, ladies and gentlemen, that the coating of paint which covers my circle is neither more nor less thick than that which covers the circle of M. Darzac. It is almost the same thing—the same tint."

"Undoubtedly," rejoined M. Darzac. "But what does all this signify?"

"Wait!" replied the reporter. "It is understood, then, that it is you who have made this plan and this painting?"

"I was certainly in enough of an ill humour when I found the state it was in that time I went with you into Old Bob's cabinet when we came out of the Square Tower. Old Bob had ruined my drawing by letting his skull roll over it."

"We are there!" spoke up Rouletabille, quick as a flash. And he lifted from the bureau the "oldest skull of the human race." He turned it over and showed the crimsoned jaws to M. Darzac. Then he inquired:

"Is it your opinion that the red which we see upon that under jaw is no different from the red which would be taken off by any object coming in contact with your plan?"

"I don't see how there could be any doubt of it! The skull was upside down on my drawing when we entered the workshop."

"Let us continue then to remain of the same opinion!" said the reporter.

Then he arose, holding the skull in the crook of his arm, and went into the alcove in the wall, lighted by a large window and crossed by bars, which had been a loophole for cannon in the ancient times, and which M. Darzac had used as a dressing room. There he struck a match and lighted a lamp filled with spirits of wine which stood upon a little table. Upon this lamp he set a little pot which he had previously filled with water. The skull still lay in the crook of his arm.

During this weird cookery, we never took our eyes off him. Never had Rouletabille's behaviour appeared to us so incomprehensible nor so mysterious nor so disturbing. The more he explained matters to us and the more he did, the less we understood. And we were afraid because we felt that someone—*someone among us*—*one of ourselves*—had reason for fear. Who was this one? Perhaps the most calm of us all!

But the calmest of all was Rouletabille between his skull and his casserole.

But what? Why did we all suddenly recoil with a single movement? Why were the eyes of M. Darzac wide with a new terror—why did the Lady in Black—Arthur Rance—I, myself—utter the same syllable—a name which expired on our lips: "*Larsan!*"?

Where had we seen him? Where had we discovered him this time, we who were gazing at Rouletabille? Ah, that profile, in the red shadow of the approaching twilight, that brow in the background of the alcove upon which the sunset rays stream as did the dawn on the morning of the crime! Oh, that stern jaw, bespeaking an iron will, which appeared before us, not, as in the light of day, gentle though a little bitter, but evil and threatening. How like Rouletabille was to Larsan! How in that moment the son resembled his father! It was Larsan's very self!

Another transformation. At a moan from his mother Rouletabille came out of his funereal frame and appeared before us as a bandit, and as he hurried toward us, he was Rouletabille once more. Mme. Edith, who had never seen Larsan, could not understand. She whispered to me, "What is going on?"

Rouletabille was there before us with his hot water in the casserole, a napkin and his skull. And he washed the skull.

It was soon done. The paint disappeared. He made us bear witness to the fact. Then, placing himself in front of the bureau, he stood in mute contemplation before his own drawing. This lasted for ten minutes, during which he had, by a sign, ordered us to keep silence—ten minutes which seemed as long as the same number of hours. What was he waiting for? What did he expect? Suddenly, he seised the skull in his right hand, and with the gesture familiar to those who play at bowling, he tossed it about so that it rolled hither and yon over the drawing; then he showed us the skull and bade us notice that it bore no trace of red paint. Rouletabille drew out his watch again.

"The paint has dried upon the plan," he said. "It has taken a quarter of an hour to dry. Upon the 11th of April we saw at five o'clock in the afternoon, M. Darzac entering the Square Tower and coming from out of doors. But M. Darzac, after having entered the Square Tower, and after having fastened behind him the bolts of his door, as he tells us, has not gone out again until we came to fetch him after six o'clock. As to Old Bob, we had seen him enter the Square Tower at six o'clock and there was no paint on this skull then!"

"How was this paint which has taken only a quarter of an hour to dry upon this plan, fresh enough still—more than an hour after M. Darzac had left it—to stain Old Bob's skull when the savant, with a movement of anger, threw it down on the plan as he entered the Round Tower? There is only one explanation of this, and I defy you to find another—and that is that the Robert Darzac who entered the Square Tower at five o'clock and whom no one has seen going out again, was not the same as the one who came to paint in the Round Tower before the arrival of Old Bob at sir o'clock and whom we found in the room in the Square Tower without having seen him enter there and with whom we went out. In one word—he was not the same man as the M. Darzac here present before us. The testimony of pure reason shows that there are two personalities appearing in the guise of Robert Darzac!"

And Rouletabille turned his eyes full upon the man whose name he had uttered.

Darzac, like all the rest of us, was under the spell of the luminous demonstration of the young reporter. We were all divided between a new horror and a bound less admiration. How clear was every word that Rouletabille had uttered! How clear—and how terrible! Here again we found the mark of his prodigious and logical mathematical intelligence!

M. Darzac cried out:

"It was thus, then, that *he* was able to enter the Square Tower under a disguise which made him, without doubt, my very image! It was thus that he was able to hide behind the panel in such a way that I did not see him myself when I came here to write my letters after quitting the Tower of the Bold, where I left my drawing. But how could Pere Bernier have opened to him?"

"Doubtless," replied Rouletabille, who had taken the hand of the Lady in Black in both his own as though he wished to give her courage, "he must have believed that it was yourself."

"That then explains the fact that when I reached my door I had only to push it open. Pere Bernier believed that I was within." "Exactly: that is good reasoning!" declared Rouletabille. "And Pere Bernier, who had opened to Darzac No. 1, had not troubled himself about No. 2, since he did not see him any more than yourself. You certainly reached the Square Tower at the moment that Sainclair and myself called Bernier 'to the parapet to see whether he could help us in understanding the strange gesticulations of Old Bob, talking at the threshold of the Barma Grande to Mrs. Rance and Prince Galitch."

"But More Bernier" cried M. Darzac. "She had gone into her lodge. Was she not astonished to see M. Darzac come in a second time when she had not seen him go out?"

"Let us suppose," replied the young reporter with a sad smile; "let us suppose, M. Darzac, that Mere Bernier at that moment—the moment when you passed into your apartments—that is to say, when the second apparition of Darzac passed in—was occupied in picking up the potatoes and putting them back into the sack which I had emptied upon her floor—and we shall suppose the truth."

"Well, then, I can congratulate myself on the fact that I am still upon earth!"

"Congratulate yourself, M. Darzac? congratulate yourself!"

"When I remember that as soon as I entered my room, I drew the bolts as I have told you that I did, that I began to work and that this wretch was hidden behind my back. Why, he might have killed me without hindrance!"

Rouletabille stepped close to M. Darzac and fixed his eyes upon him with a look that seemed to read his soul.

"Why did he not kill you then?" he asked.

"You know very well that he was waiting for someone else," replied M. Darzac, turning his face sorrow fully toward the Lady in Black.

Rouletabille was now so close to M. Darzac that their shadows on the floor looked like that of one strangely formed being. The lad put his two hands on the older man's shoulders.

"M. Darzac," he said, his voice again clear and strong, "I have a confession to make to you. When I began to understand how the 'body too many' had effected an entrance and when I had discovered that you did nothing to undeceive us in regard to the hour of five o'clock at which we had believed—at which everyone, rather, except myself, believed—that you had entered the Square Tower, I felt that I had the right to suspect that the murderer was not the man who at five o'clock entered the Square Tower under the form of Darzac. I thought, on the contrary, that that Darzac might be the true Darzac and you might be the false one. Ah, my dear M. Darzac, how I have suspected you!"

"That was madness!" cried M. Darzac. "If I did not tell you the exact hour at which I entered the Square Tower it was because the time was somewhat vague in my own mind and I did not attach any importance to it."

"In such a manner, M. Darzac," continued Rouletabille, without paying any attention to the interruptions of his interlocutor, the emotion of the Lady in Black and our attitude, more than over filled with terror. "In such a manner as that you could have stolen away the true Darzac when he came from outside and, by your own carefulness and the too faithful help of the Lady in Black, could have taken his place and have been perfectly able to defy detection of your audacious enterprise. This was my imagination—only my imagination, M. Darzac; don't let it disturb you. But in such a manner as this, I had thought that, you being Larsan, the man who was put in the sack was Darzac. Ah! the fancies that I have had! and the useless suspicions!"

"Bah!" responded Mathilde's husband, gloomily. "We are all suspicious here!"

Rouletabille turned his back upon M. Darzac, put his hands in his pocket and said, addressing himself to Mathilde, who seemed ready to swoon before the horror of Rouletabille's imaginings:

"Courage for a little while longer, Madame!"

And he began speaking again, in his "teacher's" voice which I knew so well, and with the air of a professor of mathematics propounding or resolving a theorem:

"You see, M. Darzac, there are two manifestations of Robert Darzac. To know which was the true one and which was the one which formed a disguise for Larsan—my duty, M. Darzac—that which the power of pure reason showed me—was to examine, without fear or reproach, both of these manifestations—*in all impartiality*. Thus, I begin with you—M. Darzac."

M. Darzac replied: "It does not matter since you suspect me no longer. But you must tell me immediately who is Larsan. I insist upon it—I demand it!"

"We all demand it—and at once!" we all cried, turning upon both of them. Mathilde rushed up to her child and placed herself in front of him, as if to protect him. We felt the pathos of her attitude but the scene had endured too long and we were beyond the limits of patience.

"If he knows who is Larsan let him speak out and make an end of this!" exclaimed Arthur Rance.

And suddenly, just as the thought crossed my mind that I had heard the same cries of anger and impatience two years before at the Court of Assizes, another pistol shot sounded outside the door of the Square Tower, and we were all so seised with consternation that our anger fell away in a moment and we found ourselves not threatening Rouletabille but entreating him to put an end as soon as possible to this intolerable situation. At this moment, it actually seemed as though we were each imploring him to speak out, as though we calculated that by doing so, we would prove, not only to the others but to ourselves, that we were not Larsan.

As soon as the second shot was heard, the countenance of Rouletabille changed completely. His face seemed transformed and his whole being appeared to vibrate with a savage energy. Laying aside the half bantering manner which he had used toward M. Darzac and which we had all found extremely disagreeable, he gently released himself from the clasp of the Lady in Black, who still clung to him, walked toward the door, folded his arms and said:

"You see, my friends, in an affair like this, it does not do to neglect any point. There were two manifestations of Robert Darzac which entered the Square Tower. There were two manifestations which came out— and one of these was in the sack! That is where one loses oneself. And *even now*, I do not wish to make any mistakes! Will M. Darzac, here present, permit me to say that I had a hundred excuses for suspecting him?"

Then I thought to myself: "How unlucky that he did not mention his suspicions to me! I would have told him about the map of Australia!"

M. Darzac strode across the room and planted himself in front of the young reporter and said in a tone nearly inaudible from anger:

"What excuses? I ask you, what excuses?"

"You will soon understand, my friend," said the reporter with the utmost calmness. "The first thing that I said to myself while I was examining the conditions surrounding *your* manifestation of Larsan, was this: 'Nonsense! if he were Larsan, would not Professor Stangerson's daughter have perceived it?' That is self evident—the common sense of that thought—is it not? But when I tried to look into the mind of the lady who has become Mme. Darzac, I discovered beyond a doubt, Monsieur, that all the while she could not free herself from just this fear—the fear that you might be Larsan!"

Mathilde, who had fallen half fainting into a chair, gathered strength enough to start up and to protest against the words with a frightened, despairing gesture.

As for M. Darzac, his face was a picture of hopeless anguish. He sank upon a couch and said in a voice so low that it was scarcely audible and so full of wretchedness that it pierced our hearts:

"And could you have thought that, Mathilde?"

His wife dropped her eyes and spoke not a word. Rouletabille, still merciless, continued:

"When I recall all the acts of Mme. Darzac after your return from San Remo, I can see now in each one of them an expression of the terror which she experienced from her fear that she should allow the secret of her suspicion and her constant agony to escape her. Ah, let me speak, M. Darzac! Everything must be said—everything must be explained here and now if there is to be peace in the future! We are about to clear up the situation. To go on then, there was nothing natural or happy in Mlle. Stangerson's behaviour. The very eagerness with which she assented to your desire to hasten the marriage ceremony proved the longing which she felt to definitely banish the torment of her soul. Her eyes—I remember it now!—used to say at that time—how often and how clearly 'Is it possible that I continue to see Larsan everywhere, even in the face of the man who is at my side, who is going to lead me to the altar and to take me away with him?'"

"From the moment of your return from the South until the apparition at the railroad station, monsieur, she lived in the most utter misery. She was already crying for help-for help against herself—against her thoughts—and, perhaps, even against *you*! But she dared not reveal her thought to any person because she dreaded that any confidant might say to her—"

And Rouletabille leaned over and said in M. Darzac's ear, not so low that I could not hear, but so softly that the words did not reach Mathilde: "Are you going mad again?"

Then, lifting his head again, he continued:

"You ought to understand everything better now, my dear M. Darzac—both the strange coldness with which you were treated occasionally and also the fits of remorseful tenderness which, in the doubt which filled her brain, would impel Mme. Darzac to surround you with every evidence of attention and affection. And, furthermore, allow me to tell you that I myself have sometimes found you so gloomy and *distrait* that I have fancied that you must have discovered that whenever Mme. Darzac looked at you, she could not, in spite of herself, chase from her mind the image of Larsan. It came upon her when she spoke to you and when she was silent—when you were beside her and when you were at a distance. And, consequently—let us understand each other completely—it was *not* the belief that Professor Stangerson's daughter would have known it' which removed my suspicions, since, in spite of herself, she entertained the fear all the while that you and Larsan were one. No! no my suspicions were removed by another cause!"

"They might have been removed," exclaimed M. Darzac, at once ironically and despairingly—"they might have been removed, it would seem, by the simple course of reasoning that if I had been Larsan, wedded to Mlle. Stangerson, having her for my wife, I would have had every cause for making her believe in Larsan's death! And I would have never resuscitated myself! Was it not upon the day that Larsan returned to earth that I lost Mathilde?"

"Pardon, monsieur, pardon" replied Rouletabille, whose face had grown as white as a sheet. "You are abandoning now, if I may say so, the directions of pure reason. The facts which you mentioned show us just the contrary of that which you believe we should see. For my part, it seems to me that when one has a wife who believes, or who comes very near to believing, that one is Larsan, one has every interest in showing her that *Larsan exists outside of oneself*!"

As Rouletabille uttered these words, the Lady in Black, supporting herself by groping with her hands against the wall as she walked, came stumblingly to the side of Rouletabille, and devoured with her eyes the face of M. Darzac which had grown frightfully harsh and strained. As to the rest of us, we were so struck by the novelty and the irrefutability of Rouletabille's reasoning, that we experienced no other emotion than an ardent desire to know what was to follow, and we took care not to interrupt, asking ourselves to what such a formidable hypothesis might not lead. The young man, imperturbably, went on:

"And, if you had an interest in showing her that Larsan existed elsewhere than in your body, there arose an exigency in which that interest was transformed into an immediate necessity. Imagine—I say *imagine*, M. Darzac, that you had really brought Larsan to life once— once only—in spite of yourself—in your own rooms—before the eyes of Professor Stangerson's daughter—and you will be, I repeat, under the necessity of bringing him to life again and yet again—outside of yourself, in order to prove to your wife that the Larsan whom she has seen returned to life is not you! Ah, calm yourself, my dear M. Darzac, I entreat you. Have I not told you that my suspicion has been banished—completely banished? But it is as well that we should divert ourselves for a few moments in reasoning the matter out a little, after these long hours of anguish when it seemed as though there would never be any place for reasoning again. See, then, where I am obliged to come in considering this hypothesis as realised (these are the procedures of mathematics which you know better than I—you who are a scholar!)—in considering, as I said, as realised the hypothesis that you are the counterfeit Darzac, the one which hides Larsan. According to my reasoning, then, you are Larsan! And I asked myself what could have happened in the railway station at Bourg to make you appear in the form of Larsan before the eyes of your wife. The fact of such an appearance is undeniable. It exists. And its occurrence at that moment cannot be explained by any desire on your part to have Larsan seen!"

He paused for a moment, but Robert Darzac did not utter a word.

"As you were saying, M. Darzac," Rouletabille went on, "it was because of this apparition of Larsan that your cup of happiness was dashed empty to the ground. Therefore, if this resurrection should not have been voluntary there is only one other way in which it could have happened—through accident. And now just let us consider how this latter supposition clears up the entire situation. Oh, I have spent a lot of thought upon the incident at Bourg—you see, I am still reasoning out the problem! You (the you who is Larsan, be it understood) are at Bourg in the buffet. You believe that your wife is waiting for you somewhere in the station as she told you she would do. After having finished your letters, you wish to go to your compartment in the car in order to attend to some detail of your toilet—or, shall we say to cast a critical eye over your disguise to see if in any point it might be lacking? You think to yourself: 'A few more hours of this comedy and we shall have passed the frontier, she will be all my own—entirely alone with me, and I will throw aside this mask'—for the mask wearies you a little, we may imagine—so much so, indeed, that, once arrived in your compartment, you grant yourself the grace of a few moments of repose. You cast away your assumed character and your disguise. You relieve yourself of the false beard and the spectacles—and at that very moment the door of the section opens. Your wife, thrown into a spasm of terror at the sight of Larsan's smooth, beardless face in the glass, does not wait to make any further investigation and rushes out into the night, her screams drowned by the noise of another train. You comprehend the danger at once. You realize that everything is lost unless you can *immediately* arrange matters so that your wife shall see Darzac somewhere else. You quickly resume the mask; you hurry out of the compartment and reach the buffet by a shorter route than that taken by your wife, who rushes there to look for you. She finds you standing up. You have not even had time enough to seat yourself before she enters. Is everything safe now? Alas, no! Your troubles are only beginning. For the fearful thought that you may be at one and the same time both Darzac and Larsan will not leave her mind. Upon the platform of the station, while passing beneath the gas jet, she casts a frightened glance at you, lets go your hand and runs wildly into the office of the station master. You read her thought as though she had spoken it. The abominable idea must be banished without a moment's delay. You quit the office, leaving the lady in the care of the superintendent, and immediately return, closing the door quickly, seeking to give the impression that you, too, have seen Larsan. In order to ease her mind, and, also, for the purpose of deceiving us all, in case she dared reveal her suspicions to anyone, you are the first to warn me that something unforeseen has happened—to send me a dispatch. See how clear and plain as the day your every act becomes! You cannot refuse to take her to rejoin her father. She would go without you. And, since nothing is yet really lost, you have the hope that everything may be regained. In the course of the journey, your wife continues to have alternating periods of faith in you and of fear of you. She gives you her revolver, in a sort of half delirium, which might sum itself up in some such phrase as this: 'If he is Darzac, let him protect me; if he is Larsan, let him kill me! But in pity, let me know which he is.' At Rochers Rouges, you realised once more how utterly she had withdrawn herself from you and in order to reassure her as to your identity, you showed her Larsan again."

See how in accordance with reason such a proceeding would be, my dear M. Darzac! Every fact would fit perfectly into every other under the supposition which I am placing before you. There is not a single point up to your appearance as Larsan at Mentone, during your journey as Darzac to Cannes, at the time when you came to meet us, which cannot be explained in the easiest way imaginable. You had taken the train at Mentone-Garavan before the eyes of your friends, but you alighted from the train at the next station, which is Mentone, and there, after a short stay for the purpose of altering your looks, you appeared in the image of Larsan to the same friends who were promenading in the gardens at Mentone. The following train brought you to Cannes, where you met Sainclair and myself. Only, as you had on this occasion the vexation of hearing from the lips of Arthur Rance when he met us at the station at Nice, the news that Mme. Darzac had not, on this occasion, caught sight of Larsan, you were under the necessity that same evening of showing her Larsan under the very windows of the Square Tower, standing erect in the prow of Tullio's boat. So, you see, my dear M. Darzac, how even those things which appear most complicated would have become entirely simple and logically explicable, if, by chance, my suspicions should have been confirmed."

At these words, I myself, who had seen and touched "the map of Australia," was unable to repress a shudder as I looked pityingly at Robert Darzac, just as one might look at some poor man who is on the point of becoming the victim of some hideous judicial error. And all the others, seated around me, shuddered as well, whether for him or on account of him, for the arguments of Rouletabille were becoming so terribly *possible* that each of us was asking himself how, after having so completely established the possibility of guilt, the young reporter could prove Darzac's innocence. As to Robert Darzac, after having at first evinced the deepest agitation, he had grown quite tranquil and calm, as he listened attentively to every word that escaped the young man's lips. And it seemed to me that his eyes held the same expression of astonishment, amased and frightened, and yet full of breathless interest, which I had seen in the eyes of accused men at the bar of the Assizes when they had heard the Procurer General de liver one of his wonderful disquisitions which almost convinced the prisoners themselves that they were guilty of a crime which sometimes they had never committed.

"But since you no longer have these suspicions, monsieur!" he exclaimed, his intonation singularly calm, in spite of the fact that his voice was raised, "I should be glad to know, after all this exercise of your talent of reasoning, what could have driven them away?"

"In order to have them driven away, monsieur, one thing was essential—an *absolute certitude*! And I found it—a simple but conclusive proof which showed me in a manner complete and undeniable which of the two manifestations of Darzac was in reality Larsan. That proof, monsieur, was, happily, furnished me by yourself at the very moment when you *closed the circle*—the circle in which there had been found the 'body too many'!—the time when, after having sworn that which was the truth—that you had drawn the bolt of your apartment as soon as you had entered your sleeping room, *you had lied to us in concealing from us that you had entered that room at six o'clock instead of at five o'clock as Pere Bernier said and as we ourselves could have proved. You were then the only person except myself who knew that the Darzac who had entered at five o'clock and of whom we had spoken to you as yourself was in reality another man. But you said nothing. And you need not pretend that you did not attach any importance to that hour of five o'clock. What interest could the real Darzac have in hiding the fact that another Darzac, who might be Larsan, had come and hidden in the Square Tower before you came in? Larsan was the only one who could have a reason for concealing the knowledge that there was another Darzac besides himself. Of the two, false and the real Darzac, the false one was necessarily the one who lied. Thus were my suspicions dispelled by a certainty. You were Larsan, and the man in the wardrobe was Darzac!*"

"You are a liar!" howled the man as he sprang at Rouletabille.

But we got between them, and Rouletabille, who was not in the least disturbed, pointed at the cupboard and said:

"He is in there now!"

None of us will ever forget what followed. Just as on the memorable night, an invisible hand opened the door of the cupboard, and the body appeared before us again.

Exclamations of surprise, excitement and fear rang through the Square Tower. The voice of the Lady in Black rose above all the others.

"Robert! Robert! Robert!"

And it was a cry of joy! Two Darzacs before us so exactly similar that every one of us save the Lady in Black might have been deceived. But her heart told her the truth, even admitting that her reason, not withstanding the triumphant conclusion of Rouletabille, might have hesitated. Her arms outstretched, her eyes alight with love and joy, she rushed toward the second manifestation of Darzac—the one which had descended from the panel. Mathilde's face was radiant with new life; her sorrowful eyes which I had so often beheld fixed with sombre gloom upon *that other*, were shining upon this one with a joy as glorious as it was tranquil and assured. It was he! It was he whom she had believed lost—whom she had sought in vain in the visage of the other and had not found there and, therefore, had accused herself, during the weary hours of day and night, of folly which was akin to madness.

As to the man who, up to the last moment I had not believed to be guilty—as to that wretch who, un veiled and tracked to earth, found himself suddenly face to face with the living proof of his crimes, he attempted yet again, one of the daring coups which had so often saved him. Surrounded on every side, he yet endeavoured to flee. Then we understood the audacious drama which in the last few moments, he had played for our benefit. When he could no longer have any doubt as to the issue of the discussion which he was holding with Rouletabille, he had had the incredible self control to permit nothing of his emotions to appear, and had also been able to prolong the situation, permitting Rouletabille to pursue at leisure the thread of the argument at the end of which he knew that he would find his doom, but during the progress of which he might discover perchance some means of escape. And he had effected his manoeuvers so well that at the moment when we beheld the other Darzac advancing toward us, we could not hinder the imposter from disappearing at one bound within the room which had served as the bedchamber of Mme. Darzac and closing the door violently behind him with a rapidity which was nothing less than marvellous. We only knew that he had vanished when it was too late to stop his flight.

Rouletabille, during the scene which had passed had thought only of guarding the door opening into the corridor and he had not noticed that every movement of the false Darzac, as soon as he realised that he was being convicted of his imposture, had been in the direction of Mme. Darzac's room. The reporter had attached no importance to these movements, knowing as he did that this room did not offer any way by which Larsan might escape. But, however, when the scoundrel was behind the door which afforded his last refuge, our confusion increased beyond all proportions. One might have thought that we had become suddenly bereft of our senses. We knocked on the door. We cried out. We thought of all his strokes of genius—of his marvellous escapes in the past!

"He will escape us! He will get away from us again!"

Arthur Rance was the most enraged of us all. Mme. Faith, who was clinging to my arm, drove her fingernails into my hand in a paroxysm of nervous fear. None of us paid any heed to the Lady in Black and Robert Darzac who, in the midst of this tempest, seemed to have forgotten everything, even the clamour and confusion around them. Neither one had spoken a word but they were looking into each other's eyes as though they had discovered another world—the world which is love. But they had not discovered it; they had merely found it again, thanks to Rouletabille.

The latter had opened the door of the corridor and summoned the three domestics to our assistance. They entered with their rifles. But it was axes that were needed. The door was solid and barricaded with heavy bolts. Pere Jacques went out and fetched a beam which served us as a battering ram. Each of us exerted all his strength and, finally, we saw the door beginning to give way. Our anxiety was at its height. In vain, we told ourselves that we were about to enter a room in which there were only walls and barred windows. We expected anything—or, rather, we expected nothing, for in the mind of each and every one of us was the recollection of the disappearances, the flights, the actual "dissolution of matter" which Larsan had brought about in times past and which at this moment haunted us and drove us nearly mad.

When the door had commenced to yield, Rouletabille directed the servants to take up their guns, with the order, however, that the weapons were to be used only in case it should be impossible to capture Larsan living. Then the young reporter set his shoulder to the door with one last powerful effort and as the boards, wrenched from their hinges, fell to the ground, he was the first to enter the room.

We followed him. And behind him, upon the threshold, we all halted, stupefied by the sight which met our eyes. Larsan was there—plainly to be seen by everyone. And this time there was no difficulty in recognizing him. He had removed his false beard; he had put aside his "Darzac mask"; he had resumed once more the pale, clean-shaven face of that Frederic Larsan whom we had known at the Château of Glandier. And his presence seemed to fill the entire room. He was lying back comfortably in an easy chair in the centre of the room and was looking at us with his great, calm eyes. His arm was stretched along the arm of the chair. His head was resting on the cushion at the back. One would have said that he was giving us an audience and was waiting for us to make known our business. It seemed to me that I could even discern an ironical smile on his lips.

Rouletabille advanced toward him.

"Larsan," he said in a voice which was not quite steady, "Larsan, do you give yourself up?"

But Larsan did not reply.

Then Rouletabille touched the man's face and his hand and we saw that Larsan was dead.

Rouletabille pointed to a ring on the middle finger. The collet was open and showed a hollow cup which was empty. It must have contained a deadly poison.

Arthur Rance put his head against the man's chest and assured us that all was over. And Rouletabille entreated us to leave him alone in the Square Tower and to try and forget the terrible events which had passed there.

"I will charge myself with everything," he asserted gravely. "Here is the 'body too many.' No one will inquire into the disposition which may be made of it."

And he gave an order to Walter which Arthur Rance translated into English. "Walter, bring me the sack which you found at the Castillon yesterday."

Then he made a gesture to which we were all obedient—a gesture of dismissal. And we left the son face to face with the corpse of the father.

The next moment we saw that M. Darzac was swooning and we were obliged to carry him into Old Bob's sitting room. But it was only a passing faintness and soon he opened his eyes again and smiled at Mathilde when he saw her beautiful face bending over him with the look of dread in which we read the fear of losing her beloved husband at the very moment in which she had, through a chain of circumstances which still remained wrapped in mystery, found him again. He succeeded in convincing her that his life was not in any danger and he added his entreaties to those of Mme. Edith that she would go away for a little while and try to get some rest. When the two women had left us, Arthur Rance and myself turned our attention to our friend, inquiring of him, first of all, in regard to his curious state of health. For how could a man whom all of us had believed to be dead, and who had been, with the death rattle in his throat, tied up in a sack and carried away, have been able to rise again and step-down living from the fateful panel? But when we had opened his shirt and discovered the bandage which hid the wound that he bore in his breast, we recognised the fact that this injury, by a chance so rare that one would scarcely believe that it could exist, after having brought about an almost immediate state of coma, was not a very serious one. The ball which had struck Darzac in the midst of the savage fight which he had been obliged to make against Larsan, had planted itself in the sternum, causing a bad external hemorrhage and weakening the entire organism, but, fortunately, suspending none of the vital functions.

As we finished the task of dressing the wound Pere Jacques came to close the door of the parlour which had remained open and I wondered what might be the reason which had led the old man to this precaution until I heard steps in the corridor and a strange noise—the sound that one hears when a body is carried away on a stretcher. And I thought of Larsan and of the sack which was holding now for the second time "the body too many."

Leaving Arthur Rance to watch over M. Darzac I hurried to the window. I had not been mistaken. I beheld the sinister funeral cortege in the court outside.

It was nearly nightfall. A gathering gloom surrounded everything. But I could distinguish Walter, who had been stationed as a sentinel under the arch of the gardener's postern. He was looking toward the outer court, ready, evidently, to bar the passage of anyone who might desire to penetrate into the Court of the Bold.

Moving onward in the direction of the oubliette, I saw Rouletabille and Pere Jacques—two dark shadows bending over another shadow—a shadow which I recognised and which, on that other night of horror, I had believed to contain another dead body. The sack seemed heavy. The two men were scarcely able to lift it to the edge of the shaft. And I could see that the little passageway was open—yes, the heavy wooden lid which ordinarily closed it had been removed and was lying on the ground. Rouletabille leaped lightly over the edge of the oubliette and then made a step downward. He showed no hesitation; the way seemed to be familiar to him. In a few moments his figure vanished from sight. Then Pere Jacques pushed the sack into the passageway and leaned over the edge, apparently still holding on to his burden which I could no longer see. Then he stood back, closed up the opening and adjusted the iron bars and in doing so made a sound which I suddenly remembered—the sound which had puzzled me so much that evening when, before the "discovery of Australia," I had rushed in pursuit of a shadow which had suddenly disappeared and which I had searched for up to the very door of the New Castle.

I felt that I must see—up to the very last moment. I must know all! Too many strange and inexplicable things were filling my soul with anxiety already. I had learned the most important part of the truth, but I had not all of the truth—or, rather, something which would explain the truth was still lacking.

I left the Square Tower: I went to my own room in the New Castle, I stationed myself at the window and my eyes lost themselves in the depths of the shadows which covered the sea. Thick darkness: jealous shadows. Nothing more. And then I strained my ears to listen, although I knew that there was not the faintest sound of the strokes of the oar.

All at once—far–very far off—it seemed to me that all this was passing so far over the sea that it crossed the horizon—or, rather, approached the horizon—I fancied that I could see in the narrow red band which was all that remained of the setting sun something that seemed more unreal than a vision.

Into that narrow red band an object entered—something dark and very small, but to my eyes, which were fixed upon it in breathless suspense, it seemed the greatest and most formidable sight that I had ever beheld. It was the shadow of a fishing smack which glided over the waters as automatically as though it were propelled by machinery and as its movements became slower, and I saw it emerging from the gloom, I recognised the form of Rouletabille. The oars ceased to move and I saw my friend rise to his feet. I could recognize him and see everything which he did as clearly as if he had not been ten yards away from me. His gestures were out lined against the red background of the sunset with a fantastic precision.

What he had to do did not take long. He leaned over and got up again, lifting in his arms something which seemed to mix with his form and become a part of himself in the darkness. And then the burden glided down into the water and the man's figure reappeared alone, still bending, still leaning over the edge of the boat, remaining thus for an instant motionless, and then once more picking up the oars of the bark which resumed its automatic motion until it had disappeared completely from the dying glare of the ever narrowing band of red. And then the band of red, too, vanished.

Rouletabille had consigned the body of Larsan to the waves of Hercules.

EPILOGUE

Nice–Cannes–Saint-Raphael—Toulon. I saw without regret all the stages of my return trip passing before my eyes. Upon the very day which had followed all the horrible things I have related, I hastened to quit the Midi, anxious to find myself once more in Paris and to plunge into my business affairs—and anxious also to find myself alone with Rouletabille, who was now only a few feet away from me, locked up in a private compartment with the Lady in Black. Up to the very last moment—that is to say, as far as Marseilles, where they were obliged to separate, I was unwilling to interrupt their tender and sorrowful confidences, their plans for the future, their fond farewells. Despite all the prayers of Mathilde Rouletabille was determined to leave her, to return to Paris and to his paper. The son had the superb heroism of effacing himself for the sake of the husband. The Lady in Black had not been able to resist Rouletabille and the boy had dictated exactly what should be done. He had directed that *M. and Mme. Darzac* must continue their honeymoon trip as if nothing remarkable had happened at Rochers Rouges. It was one Darzac who had begun the journey; it was another Darzac who was to finish it—this trip which had become such a happy one—but in the eyes of all the world Darzac would be the same man without any suspicion that things had ever been otherwise.

M. and Mme. Darzac were married. The civil law united them. As to the religious law, as Rouletabille said, the affair might easily be laid before the Pope while the couple were in Rome and there would, without doubt, be found means of regularizing the situation, if there was found to be need of it or if the conscientious scruples of the couple desired it. And Robert Darzac and his wife were happy—completely happy. They belonged to each other.

At Rochers Rouges—at the "Louve" itself, we had said adieu to Professor Stangerson. Robert Darzac had departed immediately for Bordighera, where Mathilde was to join him. Arthur Rance and Mme. Edith accompanied us to the railroad station. My charming hostess, contrary to my hope, evinced no great amount of concern at my departure. I attributed this indifference to the fact that Prince Galitch had come to the quay to see us off. Mme. Edith was giving him the latest bulletin from Old Bob's bedside (which was excellent, by the way), and paid no further attention to me. I felt a real pang of-was it grief or wounded self love? And here and now, I have a confession to make to the reader. Never would I have allowed myself to betray the sentiments which I had entertained toward her, if, several years later, after the death of Arthur Rance, which was surrounded and followed by a most terrible tragedy of which I may relate the history one day, I had not married the dark eyed, melancholy, romantic Edith!

W e were approaching Marseilles.
        Marseilles!

The farewells were heart rending, although neither Rouletabille nor the Lady in Black uttered a word. And as the train bore us away we saw her standing on the platform in the station, without a movement or gesture, her arms hanging at her side, looking in her sombre draperies like a statue of mourning and of sorrow.

I saw in front of me Rouletabille's shoulders shaken with sobs.

L yons. We could not sleep. We alighted from the train and walked about the station. Both of us recalled the moment when we had been there before—only a few days past—when we were rushing to the rescue of the most unhappy of women. My thoughts plunged once more into the memories of the tragedy and I knew that Rouletabille's were following the same track. And now Rouletabille spoke—spoke in a voice which he tried to make sound careless and light hearted and which made me understand that he was endeavouring to efface from his mind the thought of the grief which had made him sob like a little child only a short while ago.

"Old man!" he said, with a smile, throwing his arm across my shoulder. "That Brignolles was really a beast!" and he looked at me with such an air of reproach that he almost succeeded in making me believe for a moment that I had ever taken the creature for an honest man.

And then he told me everything—all the marvellous, horrible story which I am compressing here into a few lines. Larsan had had need of some relative of Darzac in order that he might obtain the necessary signature for the incarceration of the Sorbonne professor in a madhouse. And he discovered Brignolles. He could not have fallen upon a better man for his purpose. Everyone knows how simple it is, even today, to have a human being, no matter who he may be, locked up in a cell. The desire of a relative and the signature of a medical man is sufficient in France, impossible as the thing appears, for the accomplishment of this task which may be performed with the utmost celerity. The matter of a signature never embarrassed Larsan in his life. He forged one—that of an eminent alienist—and Brignolles, richly reimbursed, charged himself with the rest. When Brignolles came to Paris, he was already a party to the combination. Larsan had formed his plan—to take Darzac's place before the wedding. The accident to the young professor's eyes had been, as I had believed from the first, the result of design. Brignolles had been directed to manage in some manner so that Darzac's eyes might be sufficiently injured that Larsan, when he took his place, might have in his trickery the important adjunct of dark spectacles, or, failing spectacles, which one cannot wear always, the right to sit in the shadow without arousing suspicion.

The departure of Darzac for the Midi must have strangely facilitated the plans of the two villains. It was not until the end of his sojourn at San Remo that Darzac had been, by the efforts of Larsan who had never ceased to spy upon him, actually dragged to the lunatic asylum.

He had been assisted materially in this affair by that "special police force" which has nothing to do with police officials and which puts itself at the disposal of families in certain disagreeable cases which demand as much discretion as rapidity in their execution.

One day M. Darzac was taking a walk in the mountains. The asylum was not far away—in fact, only a few steps from the Italian frontier—and every prep a ration for the reception of "the unfortunate man" had been made some time before hand. Brignolles, before leaving for Paris at all, had made arrangements with the proprietor and had presented to him his proofs of relationship, and his representative—Larsan himself. There are certain directors of such institutions who do not ask for explanations, provided that the provisions of the law are complied with—and that one pays well. And both these conditions were easily carried out. And such things are done everyday!

"But how did you find out all these things?" I demanded of Rouletabille.

"You remember, my friend," the reporter replied, "that little piece of paper which you brought back to the Château of Hercules on the day when, without giving me any warning, you took it upon yours. If to follow the trail of the excellent Brignolles, who had come to make a short stay in the Midi? That bit of paper, which bore the heading of the Sorbonne and the two syllables, *bonnet*, gave me the most important assistance. First of all, the circumstances under which you found it—you recollect that you picked it up after you had seen Larsan and Brignolle?—rendered it precious to me. And thin the place where it had been thrown was nearly a revelation for me when I began to take up the search for the real Darzac, after I had gained the conviction that his was 'the body too many' which had been tied up in the sack and carried out in it."

And Rouletabille went on in the simplest manner possible, taking me in his narrative over the different phases necessary for my comprehension of the mysteries which, up to that time, had remained so inexplicable to every one of us. The first step in his reasoning had come from the conclusions which he had drawn from the fact that the paint on the drawing would dry less than fifteen minutes after it had been laid on, and following that, the other formidable fact that a lie must have been told by one of the two manifestations of Darzac. Bernier, under the cross examination to which Rouletabille subjected him before the return of the man who had carried the sack, had reported the lying words of the man whom everyone had believed to be Darzac. That was what had astonished Bernier—that the man who had come in at six o'clock had not told him that the man who had entered at six o'clock *was not he*! He was trying to conceal the fact that there existed a second manifestation of Darzac and he would have had no interest in concealing it, if his own personality had been the true one. That was clear as the light of day! When the horror of the thing dawned upon Rouletabille, he nearly swooned. His limbs refused to support him: his teeth chattered; everything grew black in front of his eyes. But he was not entirely without hope, even yet. Bernier might have been mistaken. Perhaps he had not correctly understood the words which M. Darzac had spoken in his amazement and confusion' Rouletabille decided that he himself would question M. Darzac. Then he would soon see. How he longed for his return! It would be for M. Darzac himself to "close the circle." He waited impatiently—and when Darzac returned how the young reporter's feeble hopes were crushed! "Did you look at the man's face?" he had asked: and when the so-called Darzac replied, "No, I did not look at him!" Rouletabille could hardly hide his joy.

It would have been so easy for Larsan to have answered, "I saw him. The face was that of Larsan!" And the young man had not understood that this was the last piece of malice, the furthest limit of hatred in the mind of the villain, and too, one which fitted so well into his role. The real Darzac would not have acted otherwise. He would have gotten rid of his frightful booty as soon as possible without wishing to look at it. But what could all the articles of a Larsan accomplish against the reasonings of a Rouletabille? The false Darzac, under the questionings of Rouletabille had "closed the circle." He had lied. Now Rouletabille *knew*! And besides his eyes, which always looked *behind* the reason, could see now.

But what was to be done? Could he expose Larsan and in doing so, perhaps, give him a chance to escape? Could he reveal to his mother the fact that she was married to Larsan and had helped him to kill Darzac? He felt the need of reflection of combining circumstances and possibilities. He wish to strike a blow when he was ready to strike at all. He asked for twenty-four hours. He made sure of the safety of the Lady in Black by begging her to take the unoccupied room in Professor Stangerson's suite and he made her take a secret oath that she would not leave the chateu. He deceived Larsan by making him think that he was firmly convinced of the guilt of Old Bob. And when Walter rushed into the chateu with his empty sack the first gleam of hope that Darzac might still be alive dawned upon his mind. At last, he rushed off to find him, dead or living. He had in his possession the revolver belonging to the real Darzac which he had found in the Square Tower—a new revolver of which he had noticed the style in a shop at Mentone. He went to that shop; he showed the clerk the revolver; he learned that the weapon had been purchased a few days before by a man of whom he was given a description—a soft hat, a loose grey overcoat and a heavy beard. From there he lost all trace of the man, but he was not discouraged. He took up another trail, or, rather, he resumed that one which had led Walter to the gulfs of Castillon. When he arrived there, he did what Walter had not done. The latter, as soon as he had found the sack, looked for nothing more but hurried back to the Fort of Hercules. But Rouletabille, on the contrary, continued to follow the scent—and he perceived that this scent (which consisted of the exceptional clearness of the impressions left by the two wheels of the little English cart) instead of going back toward Mentone, after having stopped at the abyss of Castillon, went toward the other side, crossing by the mountain toward Sospel. Sospel! Had not Brignolles been reported as having gone to Sospel? Brignolles! Rouletabille remembered my sudden and interrupted journey. What could Brignolles be doing in these parts? His presence might be closely allied to the solution of the mystery. Certainly, the reappearance and disappearance of the true Darzac suggested the idea that he must have been kept some where in confinement. But where? Brignolles, who was undoubtedly in the confidence of Larsan, had not made the journey from Paris for nothing. Perhaps he had come at that critical moment to watch over this place of confinement.

Meditating thus and pursuing the logical tenor of his reasoning, Rouletabille had questioned the landlord of the inn near the Castillon tunnel, who had acknowledge to him that he had been very much puzzled the day before by the passage through the tunnel of a man who perfectly answered the description which had been given by the gunsmith. This man had entered the tavern to drink. His manner and appearance were so strange that the landlord had feared that he might have escaped from the sanatorium. Rouletabille felt that he was right on track and asked as indifferently as he could, "You have a sanatorium near here then?" "Oh, yes," replied the landlord; "the Mount Barbonnet sanatorium for mental diseases." It was at this point that the memory of the two syllables "bonnet" flashed in full significance upon the brain of Rouletabille. Henceforth, he had no longer any doubt that the real Darzac had been immolated by the false one as a madman in the sanatorium of Mount Barbonnet. He was resolved to know everything and to venture everything! He was certain that as a reporter of the Epoch he possessed the means of loosening the tongue of proprietors of sanatoriums of the kind which take college professors as patients and ask no questions. He hired a carriage and had himself driven to Sospel, which is at the foot of the mountains. He realised that he was running the change of encountering Brignolles. But, fortunately, nothing of the kind happened and the young man reached Mount Barbonnet and the sanatorium in safety. His mind was filled now with the thought that he was at least definitely to learn what had become of Robert Darzac! For at the moment that the sack had been found without the corpse—from the moment that the tracks of the little carriage descended toward Soepl or elsewhere and lost themselves; from the moment he had discovered that Larsan had not considered it prudent to relieve himself of Darzac by throwing him in the sack into one of the gulfs of Castillon, Rouletabille had believed that Larsan might have been found it to his interest to return the living Darzac to the madhouse at Sospel. And the reasoning powers of Rouletabille showed him that this might well be so. Darzac living might be more useful to Larsan than Darzac dead. What hostage would he have otherwise on the day when Mathilde should discover his imposture?

And Rouletabille had guessed right. At the very door of the asylum, he had encountered Brignolles. Immediately, without warning, he had seised him by the throat and threatened him with his revolver. Brignolles was a coward. He entreated Rouletabille to spare him, vowed that Darzac was living. A quarter of an hour later, Rouletabille knew the whole story. But the revolver had not sufficed, for Brignolles, who feared and hated the thought of death, loved life and everything which renders life desirable, particularly money. Rouletabille had not much trouble to convince him that he was lost if he did not betray Larsan and that he had much to gain if he helped the Darzac family to extricate itself from the present situation without scandal. At the close of the interview, both men entered the institution and were received by the director, who listened to what they had to say with an amazement which soon transformed into terror and later to the greatest affability which showed itself in immediate preparations for the release of Robert Darzac.

Darzac, by the miraculous chance which I have already explained, had sustained only a very slight injury from a wound which might easily have been mortal. Rouletabille, almost wild with joy, took him at once to Mentone. I will pass over the transports of both the rescuer and the rescued. They had disposed of Brignolles by agreeing to meet him in Paris for the settling of the accounts. On the journey, Rouletabille learned from the lips of Darzac that the Sorbonne Professor in his prison had a few days before happened to see the newspaper which spoke of the fact that M. and Mme. Darzac, whose wedding had just taken place in Paris, were guests at the Fort of Hercules. He had no further to look in order to comprehend why all his misfortunes had taken place and it was not difficult to guess who had had the fantastic audacity to take his place at the side of the unfortunate woman whose still wavering mind would have rendered so wild an enterprise not impossible. This discovery seemed to give him strength which he had not guessed that he possessed. After having stolen the overcoat of the director in order to conceal his asylum garb and having found a purse containing an hundred francs in the pocket, he had succeeded, at the risk of his life, in scaling a wall which under any other circumstances he would certainly have found insurmountable, and he had gone to Mentone. He had hastened to the Fort of Hercules. And he had seen Darzac with his own eyes! He had seen his very self. He spent a few hours in making himself so like his double in dress and appearance that the other Darzac himself might have been puzzled to find out which was which. His plan was simple. He would make his way into the Fort of Hercules in his own proper person—would enter the apartment of Mathilde and show himself to the other man in Mathilde's presence, confounding him with the truth. He had questioned the people of the coast and had learned that the Darzacs' suite was located at the back part of the Square Tower. "The Darzacs' suite"! All that he had suffered up to that time seemed like nothing in comparison with what he felt at those words. And this suffering had been without surcease until he had seen with his own eyes, at the time of the corporeal demonstration of the possibility of the "body too many," the Lady in Black. Then he had understood all. Never would she have dared to look at him like that, never would have so joyously flown to the refuge of his arms, if for a single instant, in body or in spirit, she had been the victim of the machinations of that other man and had belonged to him as his wife. Robert Darzac and Mathilde had been separated—but they had never lost each other!

Before putting his project into execution, Darzac had purchased a revolver at Mentone, had disembarrassed himself of his overcoat which he had managed to lose, believing that it would be a means of identification, had procured a suit of clothes which in colour and in cut was the counterpart of that worn by the other Darzac and had waited until five o'clock—the hour at which he had resolved to act. He had hidden himself behind the Villa Lucie, high up on the boulevard at Garavan, at the top of a little hillock from which he could see plainly all that was passing in the château. When he had passed by us and we had both seen him he had had a fierce desire to cry out and tell us who he was, but he had strength of mind enough to contain himself, desiring to be recognised first of all by the Lady in Black. This hope alone sustained his steps. This only was worth the trouble of living and an hour afterward, when he had had the life of Larsan at his disposal while the latter sat in the same room with his back turned to him, writing letters, he had not even been tempted by the idea of vengeance. After so many sorrows, there was no room in Robert Darzac's heart for hatred of Larsan; it was too full of love for the Lady in Black. Poor dear pitiful M. Darzac!

We know the rest of the adventure. That which I did not know was the way in which the true M. Darzac had penetrated a second time into the Fort of Hercules and had obtained entrance a second time into the recess hidden by the panel. And Rouletabille told me how on the same night that he had taken M. Darzac to Mentone, he had learned through the flight of Old Bob that there existed an entrance to the castle through the oubliette and so he had, by the help of a little boat, smuggled M. Darzac into the château by the way which Old Bob had taken in going out. Rouletabille wish d to be master of the hour when he came to confound Larsan and strike him down. On that night it was too late to act, but he felt that he could count upon finishing up the affair on the night following. The only thing was how to hide M. Darzac on the peninsula. And with the aid of Bernier, he had found him a quiet, deserted little corner in the New Château.

At this point of the narrative, I could not hinder myself from interrupting Roultabille with a cry which had the effect of sending him into a burst of laughter.

"It was really he then!" I exclaimed.

"It really was!" answered my friend. "That was how I was able to find the 'map of Australia'! It was the true Darzac with whom I stood face to face that night! And I who understood nothing that was going on! For it was not only the 'Australia'—it was the beard as well. And it did not come off—it was natural!" "Oh, now, I understand everything!"

"You've taken time enough about it!" replied Rouletabille, tranquilly. "That night, old fellow, you caused us a lot of trouble. When you made your appearance in the Court of the Bold, M. Darzac had come to take me back to my underground passage. I had only time enough to close the wooden lid above my head, while M. Darzac rushed back to the New Castle. But when you had retired, after your experience with the beard, he came back to me and we were bothered enough, I assure you. If, by chance, you should speak of this adventure upon the morrow to the other M. Darzac, believing that he was the same man you had seen in the New Château, there would be a catastrophe. But I dared not yield to the pleadings of M. Darzac, who begged me to go to you and tell you the whole truth. I was afraid that, knowing how matters stood, you would be unable to hide your feelings during the following day. You have a rather impulsive nature, Sainclair, and the sight of a bad man usually arouses in you a praiseworthy irritation which at such a moment might have ruined us. And then, the other Darzac was so cunning and so clever! I resolved to bring about the climax without saying anything to you! I would return to the château the next morning. And from that time on it was necessary to manage things so that you should not speak to Darzac. That was why, as soon as it was daylight, I sent you word to go fishing for brook—"

"Oh, I understand!"

"You always finish by understanding, Sainclair! I hope that you have forgiven me for that fault which gave you such a charming hour with Mme. Edith!"

"Apropos of Mme. Edith, why did you take such a mischievous pleasure in putting me into such a fit of anger?" I demanded.

"In order to have the right to abuse you and to forbid you to speak henceforward, one word to me *or to M. Darzac*! I repeat to you that, after your adventure of the night before, it would not have done to let you talk to M. Darzac. Try to understand the position, Sainclair!"

"I'll try, my friend!"

"Much obliged!"

"And still there is one thing that I don't understand!" I exclaimed. "The death of Pere Bernier. Who killed Bernier?"

"It was the cane!" said Rouletabille, gloomily. "It was that damned cane!"

"I thought that it was 'the oldest dagger known to humanity.'"

"It was both of them; the cane and the flint. But it was the cane which decided his death; the stone was only his executioner." I stared at Rouletabille, asking myself whether, this time, I had not come to the end of his intelligence.

"You never understood, Sainclair—among other things—why upon the morrow of the day on which I had come to comprehend everything, I had let fall Arthur Rance's ivory-headed cane in front of M. and Mme. Darzac. It was because I hoped that M. Darzac would pick it up. You remember, Sainclair, the ivory headed cane which Larsan used to carry and the gestures he was in the habit of making with it while we were at the Glandier? He had a fashion of holding his cane which was all his own. I wanted to see whether Darzac would hold an ivory-headed cane as Larsan had used to do. And this fixed idea pursued me until the morrow, even after my visit to the insane asylum. Even after I had seen and felt the true Darzac, I longed to see the imposter make the gestures of Larsan. Ah, to see him suddenly brandish his cane like a bandit—forget the disguise of his figure for one single moment! throw back his falsely stooped shoulders. 'Knock it, please! Knock at the shield of the Mortolas with heavy blows of the cane, dear, dear M. Darzac!' And he knocked it—and I saw his form—erect—undisguised and another man saw it and he is dead! It was poor Bernier, who was so horrified at the sight that he stumbled and fell so unfortunately on the 'oldest dagger' that the wound killed him. He is dead because he picked up the flint which, doubtless, had fallen out of Old Bob's overcoat and which Bernier had intended to take to the workshop of the Professor in the Round Tower! He is dead, because at the same moment that he picked up the flint he saw Larsan brandishing his cane—saw the scoundrel's figure and his gestures'. All battles, Sainclair, have their innocent victims!"

We were both silent for a moment. And I could not keep myself from mentioning the bitterness which I felt at the knowledge that he had had so little confidence in me. I could not pardon him for having deceived me as he had done everyone else in regard to Old Bob.

He smiled.

"That was something that didn't bother me at all. I was certain enough that he was not in the sack! However on the night before he was fished out of the grotto after I had hidden the true Darzac, under the guidance of Bernier, in the New Château, and had left the gallery of the underground passage after having left there my boat in readiness for my projects of the morrow—my boat which had belonged to Paolo, a fisherman, and a friend of 'the Hangman of the Sea,' I regained the bank by my oars. I was undressed and carried my clothing in a package on my head. As I went on, I met Paolo who was amased to see me taking a bath at such an hour and invited me to go fishing with him. I accepted. And then I learned that the bark which I had used belonged to Tullio. The 'Hangman of the Sea' had suddenly become rich and had announced to everyone that he was about to return to his native country. He said that he had sold some precious shells to the old professor for a very great deal of money and, in fact, for many days past, he had been seen a great deal in the old professor's company. Paolo knew that before going to Venice, Tullio intended to stop at San Remo. When I heard all this, I had a clear insight into Old Bob's behaviour and disappearance. He had needed a boat in quitting the château and this boat was that of the 'Hangman of the Sea.' I asked him for the address of Tullio in San Remo and sent it to Arthur Rance in an anonymous letter. Rance started for San Remo, believing that Tullio could inform him as to the fate of Old Bob. And, in fact, Old Bob had paid Tullio to take him to the grotto and then to disappear. It was out of pity for the old savant that I had decided to warn Arthur Rance; for I feared that some accident might have befallen his relative. As for myself, all that I could ask was that the old dandy would not put in an appearance before I had finished with Larsan, for I wanted the false Darzac to believe that Old Bob was occupying my mind to the exclusion of everything else. And when I learned that he really had returned, I was, at first, only half pleased, but I confess that the news of the wound in his breast (because of the wound in the breast of the man in the sack) did not cause me any pain at all. Thanks to that injury, I might hope to continue my game a few hours longer."

"And why should you not have abandoned it immediately."

"Don't you understand that it would have been impossible for me to have gotten rid of the body of Larsan in the daylight? A whole day was necessary to prepare for the disappearance by night. But what a day we had with the death of Bernier! The arrival of the gendarmes only served to simplify the affair. I waited until I knew that they were gone. The first rifle shot that you heard when we were in the Square Tower was to inform me that the last gendarme had quitted the tavern at Albo, at the Point of Garibaldi: the second told me that the customs officers had gone into their cabins and were at supper and that the *sea was free!*"

"Tell me, Rouletabille," I said, looking into his clear eyes. "When you left Tullio's boat at the end of the gallery of the passageway, for the carrying out of your plans, did you know already *what that boat would carry away on the morrow?*"

Rouletabille bowed his head.

"No," he answered, sadly and slowly. "No–do not think that, Sainclair! I did not expect that it would carry away a corpse. After all—he was my father! *I believed that the boat would carry the 'body too many' to the madhouse!* You understand, Sainclair? I would only have condemned him to prison—forever. But he killed himself. It is God who did it. May God forgive him!"

We never spoke again of that night.

At Laroche I was anxious for a hot supper, but Rouletabille refused to join me. He bought all the Paris papers and buried himself in the events of the day. The journals were filled with news from Russia. A great conspiracy against the Czar had been discovered at St. Petersburg. The facts related were so wonderful that they were almost incredible.

I unfolded the Epoch and I read in great black letters on the first column of the first page:

"Departure of Joseph Rouletabille for Russia."

And underneath:

"The Czar Implores His Aid."

I passed the paper to Rouletabille, who shrugged his shoulders and said: "That's a nice thing! Without even asking my opinion! What does that fool of an editor think that I am going to do out there? I'm not interested in the Czar. Let him and his Nihilists settle their squabbles for themselves! It is their affair, not mine! To Russia? I shall apply for a vacation—that's what I'll do! I need rest. I'll tell you, Sainclair, you and I will go somewhere together. We'll take a nice, quiet rest—"

"Not if I know it!" I cried hastily. "Thanks very much but I have had enough of your kind of 'nice, quiet rest!' I have a wild desire to work!"

"Just as you like. I won't insist."

As we drew nearer Paris, he bathed his hands and face, combed his hair and turned out his pockets. And in one of them he was surprised to find a red envelope which had come there without anyone knowing how.

"What nonsense is this?" he remarked carelessly, tearing it open.

Then he burst into a peal of laughter. I had found my gay Rouletabille again and I was anxious to know the reason for this hilarity.

"Why, I'm going, old man!" he exclaimed. "I'm going to start immediately! When things begin to come like this, it's a little different. I shall take the train tonight."

"Where to?"

"To St. Petersburg."

He handed me the letter and I read:

"We know, monsieur, that your paper has decided to send you to Russia, on account of the incidents which are at this time disturbing the court of Turkoie-Selo. *We are obliged to warn you that you will not reach St. Petersburg alive.*"

(Signed)

The Central Revolutionary Committee

I looked at Rouletabille, whose eyes were shining with delight. "Prince Galitch was at the station," I remarked. He understood me and shrugging his shoulders indifferently, he repeated:

"Ah, now, old fellow, this begins to be amusing!"

And this was all that I could get out of him, in spite of my protestations. And that night when, at the Northern station, I put my arms around him and begged him not to go, the tears in my eyes as I spoke—he laughed again and repeated:

"This is just beginning to be amusing!"

And that was his farewell.

The following day I took up the work which was waiting for me at the Palace. The first of my colleagues whom I saw were M.M. Henri Robert and Andre Hesse.

"Did you have a pleasant holiday?" they asked me.

"Delightful!" I responded.

But I made such a grimace as I spoke that they both dragged me off to take a drink with them.

THE END

A Note About the Author

Gaston Leroux (1868–1927) was a French journalist and writer of detective fiction. Born in Paris, Leroux attended school in Normandy before returning to his home city to complete a degree in law. After squandering his inheritance, he began working as a court reporter and theatre critic to avoid bankruptcy. As a journalist, Leroux earned a reputation as a leading international correspondent, particularly for his reporting on the 1905 Russian Revolution. In 1907, Leroux switched careers in order to become a professional fiction writer, focusing predominately on novels that could be turned into film scripts. With such novels as *The Mystery of the Yellow Room* (1908), Leroux established himself as a leading figure in detective fiction, eventually earning himself the title of Chevalier in the Legion of Honour, France's highest award for merit. *The Phantom of the Opera* (1910), his most famous work, has been adapted countless times for theatre, television, and film, most notably by Andrew Lloyd Webber in his 1986 musical of the same name.

A Note from the Publisher

Spanning many genres, from non-fiction essays to literature classics to children's books and lyric poetry, Mint Edition books showcase the master works of our time in a modern new package. The text is freshly typeset, is clean and easy to read, and features a new note about the author in each volume. Many books also include exclusive new introductory material. Every book boasts a striking new cover, which makes it as appropriate for collecting as it is for gift giving. Mint Edition books are only printed when a reader orders them, so natural resources are not wasted. We're proud that our books are never manufactured in excess and exist only in the exact quantity they need to be read and enjoyed.

Discover more of your favorite classics with Bookfinity™.

- Track your reading with custom book lists.
- Get great book recommendations for your personalized Reader Type.
- Add reviews for your favorite books.
- AND MUCH MORE!

Visit **bookfinity.com** and take the fun Reader Type quiz to get started.

Enjoy our classic and modern companion pairings!

Printed in the USA
CPSIA information can be obtained
at www.ICGtesting.com
JSHW022218140824
68134JS00018B/1123

9 781513 282947